What Readers
A FAR STRANGE

- Goodreads - ★★★★★

"The author is a trained artist and approaches her writing that way, using the senses to bring about character development - a rare find for me and a refreshing change."

"She [Arielle Hunter] used such beautiful words to describe the 60s. Can't wait for the second book. Please hurry I'm dying here."

"The author does not lack vocabulary and knows how to turn a sentence quite poetically . . . this story could provide the basis for an interesting movie."

- Readers' Favorite - ★★★★★

"This trip to 'A Far Strange Country' was a wild and emotional one, but totally worth the price of admission!"

"What a finish. Ms. Hunter knows how to write, that's for sure, and she knows how to draw a reader in. Excellent work, bring on book 2!"

"Beneath the backdrop of the excitement and danger of the time's social and cultural changes, we also unravel the author's amazing creative writing style. 'A Far Strange Country' is absolutely worth picking up."

- Amazon.com - ★★★★★

"I love the way the author paints such vivid word-pictures that the events come alive. I'm glad I ordered both volumes."

"Descriptions of physical scenes made it feel like I was right there, and could easily visualize them in my head. Like watching an interactive movie!"

"What a wonderful and well written book. You really feel like you've been taken to another place and time. I'd say this book has definitely been one of my favorite reads this year."

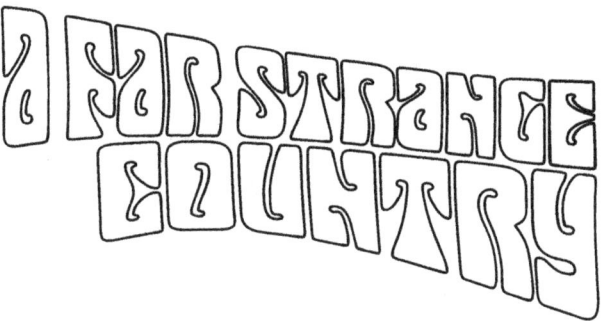

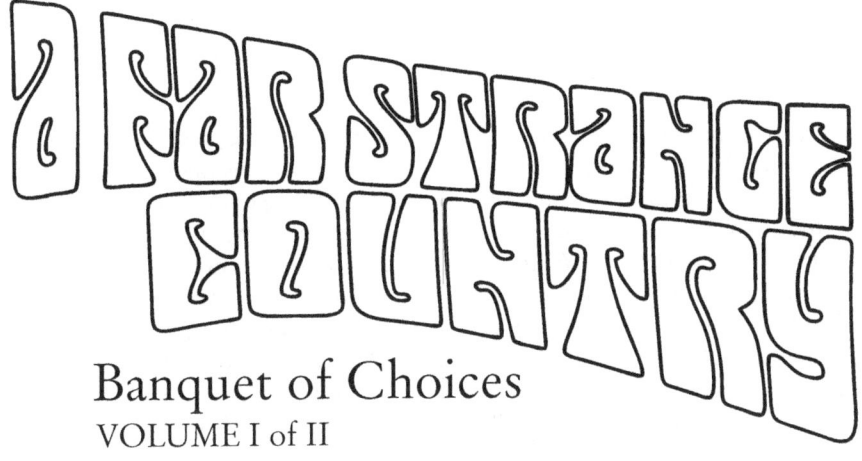

Banquet of Choices
VOLUME I of II

ARIELLE HUNTER
& Robert Windfield

RIVER3 DIGITAL PRESS

A Far Strange Country : Banquet of Choices - Vol. 1 of 2 -
By Arielle Hunter
Contributor and Editor - Robert Windfield
Copyright © MMXV Arielle Hunter/Robert Windfield

ISBN: 978-0-9834442-8-2
Published by River3 Digital Press
Registered with the US Copyright Office - No. TXu001902692
Registered with the Writers Guild of America - No. 2060484
Library of Congress No. 2014932281 (Vol. 1 and 2)

This is a work of fiction. Names, characters, and incidents are either products of the author's imagination, taken from life experiences or are used fictitiously. Any resemblance to historical events, locales or persons, living or dead, may not be one hundred percent factual or may be coincidental. We have respectfully made a diligent effort to portray fictional characters of different cultures, races and religions in a practical light without gratuitous representation. Some of the characters in this book, while being fictional, are based on real people known by or witnessed by the author and/or editor who were born and raised in California. In the context of this historical fiction there are common terms, speech, practices and lifestyles that were considered normal in the tumultuous years of 1968 through 1970 in which this book takes place.

This publication is protected under the US Copyright Act of 1976 and all other applicable international, federal, state and local laws, and all rights are reserved. No part of this publication may be copied, reproduced, stored in a retrieval system, or transmitted in any form by any means electronic, OCR, photocopy, recording, digitizing for search engines, storage or archiving without the prior written permission of the publisher, except in the case of brief quotations embodied in critical reviews.

ISBN: 978-0-9834442-6-8   (eBook/ePub)
ISBN: 978-0-9834442-3-7   (Pending - Audiobook)

All Fonts are licensed and cataloged with our account at
MyFonts.com or are free for commercial use or in public domain.

PRINTED AND DIGITIZED IN THE UNITED STATES OF AMERICA
FIRST EDITION - JANUARY 2020

❖❖❖❖❖❖❖❖❖❖❖❖❖❖❖❖❖❖❖❖❖❖❖❖❖❖❖❖❖❖

Anyone who can introduce this novel(s) to a Film or Television Producer who <u>would</u> adapt A Far Strange Country into a movie for theater or television will recieve 10% of the first initial cash advance for the project. Email: rvwindfield@gmail.com with Subject: AFSC Producer

For Robert

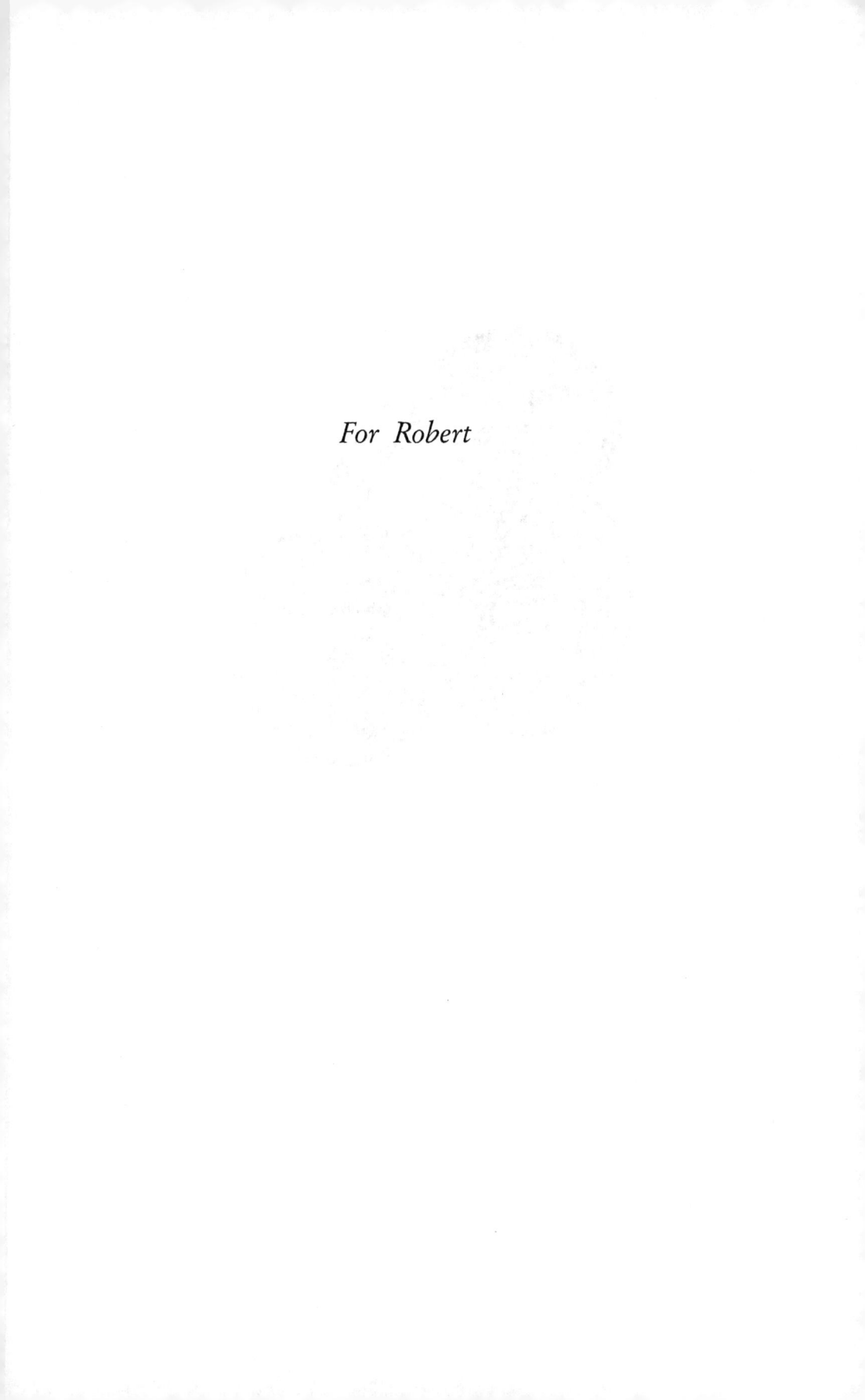

- Prologue -
Chasing the Dragon
Berkeley, California 1968

PICTURE THE TIME.
    Picture the place.
    Picture a gaunt young man sitting by a fire on a threadbare Turkish rug spread over a hardwood floor, wearing loose paisley pants in crimson and saffron, tied at the waist with a woman's scarf. Now picture a small, naked boy nearby, playing a silent game.
    Rain crawling down the windowpane melts away the ashen clouds. Cedar smolders in the fireplace and incense burns in a brass pot filling the room with the scent of woodland and spice. Peace signs and daisies balance on a mobile hanging from the ceiling. And in a photograph on the mantle, two young soldiers in jungle fatigues pose in front of a moss laden temple.
    Nouveau lithographs and psychedelic posters watch from the wall. And the room is awash in a liqueur from the spirit-world so thick it could be poured out and served to guests, but there are none. Only the young man and his child.
    A bottle of wine sparkles in the firelight. The young man empties the bottle into a glass. Swirling the blood-red liquid, he tips the glass and drinks, then picks up a pencil and paper and begins writing.

A violet sky standing in exile

Tapping the pencil on his forehead, he crosses out what he just wrote, and begins again.

~~A violet sky standing in exile~~
A violent sky stands in exile
Souls twist in time like a witness tree
Young men smoke carnelian dreams
And the old again begin to sing
Of a far strange country

 He starts a record spinning on the turntable, then sits down. A haunting guitar resonates in the room, and a lone voice follows.
 Taking a match from a brass box, he lights a candle. A wisp of sulfurous smoke trails away, replaced by a flame. The candlelight illuminates a smudged outline of black kohl surrounding his eyes; his pale skin is almost translucent in the glow. A long strand of tangled dark hair falls from a crooked part in the center of his forehead, but he takes no notice. He is slave to another master.
 He picks up a piece of aluminum foil and pinches it into a shape resembling a tiny Chinese sampan, the way he learned in a hovel on the edge of Da Nang. And into the aluminum sampan, he empties a packet of unrefined brown crystal. Heroin -- the blood of the poppy, scraped away by a knife that turns and cuts the poppy again.
 Leaning forward, he holds the little boat over the candle. As the heroin warms, it turns to a muddy liquid. Small droplets race inside the tiny craft, then vaporize into smoke. Following the swirling smoke with a straw, he inhales, rocking the boat back and forth over the candle. The hot resinous smoke burns his throat, then his lungs.
 Chasing the Dragon they call it.
 He sits motionless, waiting. Then, trapped in a momentary eternity of blinding awareness, he remembers drinking the last of the wine. He grabs the pencil.

Too late I ride the Dragon

In slow motion, his eyes roll back. He sits suspended for a moment before succumbing to gravity's relentless pull. His head drops to one side and draws him crashing to the floor.

The little boy scrambles to his father's side and shakes him. "Daddy!"

No response.

"Daddy! Wake up!"

Nothing.

The boy begins to cry. And cries, and cries, until there are no more tears. Then the exhausted child falls asleep in the hollow between his father's knees and chest.

The arm of the turntable spins into the center, filling the room with rhythmic static. Daylight wanes. The fire burns itself out. Cold creeps into the room. And the candle melts into a pool of wax, swallowing the tiny aluminum sampan and the vicious, vaporous dragon the young man unleashed.

> In those days there was no king, so every
> man did what was right in his own sight.

1

ON A CRISP Sunday morning in the Sierra Nevada foothills just before the full bloom of spring, a flock of sparrows ascended as one then fell, then ascended again at some unseen bidding that only they perceived.

Pauline Harper stood at her kitchen sink gazing out the window washing dishes. The ticking of a cuckoo clock punctuated the quiet. She took an iron skillet from the stove, and the smell of bacon wafted through the room. Sliding the pan into the soapy water, she looked up at an aging family picture on the windowsill above the sink.

Pale sunlight, filtering in through a curtain, divided the photograph into light and shadow. Her son, her only child, was lost in darkness. Steven, born late in her life, long after she had given up hope of ever having a child.

Tears pooled in her eyes. She dropped her dishrag on the tiled counter and picked up the picture. With a corner of the apron covering her flowered house-dress, she brushed away a film of dust. *I wish I could wipe away this heartache . . .*

She set the picture back on the windowsill. *Five years. Where has it gone? Five years since I looked forward to the change of seasons. Five years since I looked forward to a holiday. Five years* since Steven enlisted and went away to war. I'm trapped in time -- mother of the boy he once was.

"Steven, where are you?" She gripped the front of her dress. The pain of missing him came, piercing and desperate, stabbing like a knife.

Just then, a muffled call came from the upstairs bathroom. "Pauleeen!"

She wiped her eyes and tightened the hairpins in a French knot that, according to fashion, was a decade out of date and far too black for a woman her age. "Husbands," she said under her breath. "He should be dressed by now." *Any other morning he'd be up and dressed -- but not on Sunday.* She planted her hands on her hips and shouted, "Honestly, Buck! What?"

"Turn on the radio! There's too much static up here. Something about a rockslide on the highway . . ."

"You'd think all those rocks would have fallen by now," she muttered, switching on a radio on a shelf above the counter.

> " . . . another massive rockslide west of Pacific House on Highway Fifty between Sacramento and the summit. Traffic is at a standstill and the highway could remain closed for a week . . ."

"They said the highway could be closed for a week," Pauline shouted toward the stairs.

Turning back to the sink, she looked up to see a shadow passing by the kitchen window. Moments later the doorbell rang. A wirehair terrier bounded into the kitchen, yelping and scratching on the door. The dog's black and tan markings made it appear he was wearing a custom-made jacket.

"Tailor! Stop it!" she snapped. "Coming," she called, taking off her apron and smoothing her hair.

The bell rang again. The dog barked louder and scratched harder.

"Tailor! Get!" Scooting the dog out of the way with her foot, she opened the door.

A young Western Union courier held out a light tan envelope. "Telegram for Mr. Buck Harper."

2

THAT SAME SUNDAY morning, Donatello Dragghi paced the length of a picture window stretching from ceiling to floor in his suite at the Beverly Palms Hotel. He stared at a telephone on a nearby end table. "Why you don't ring?" he muttered with a thick Italian accent. "All morning, you are silent."

Sitting on the edge of a table, he tapped the ash off his cigarette, set it in an ashtray, and pushed a strand of dark, wavy hair off his face. Sunlight refracting through a bottle of vodka splintered into a rainbow across the table. He picked up the bottle. Resting it in the crook of his arm, he unscrewed the cap, then filled a small glass and drank the biting liquid in one long swallow. As it slid down his throat, warmth spread across his chest.

"Thank God, for good vodka," he said under his breath.

He turned and stared out the window, past gently swaying palms, to the sepia sky. The day threatened to be as unseasonably hot as the day before. *This city -- I hate. The freeway -- I hate. And the people. They all stink like the smog. But I hate most -- small people wishing to be big stars.* He thrust out his jaw. "I am Donatello Dragghi. I am not one of them."

Resting his forehead on the window, he allowed his mind to wander along a well-worn path. *Brusco. Brusco Caggiano. Of everything I hate, I hate him most of all. The Sicilian. The member of Parliament. The Deputy of Derriere Wiping. Whose mistress was so expensive.*

Donatello fumbled with the buttons on his shirt and struggled to slip it off his shoulders. He looked down at his right hand, bandaged like a mummy. Only the thumb and fingertips were exposed. *Already, it has been three months.* Stretching his fingers over the splint that immobilized his hand, he winced as a sharp ache shot up his arm. *Will it never heal?*

With his other hand, he absently twisted the chain of a gold crucifix around his finger. A wave of loneliness and regret washed over him. Regret, he dismissed, but loneliness lingered like a cloying guest.

"Meika . . . Meika . . . Meika . . ." he whispered. "Why you did this to me?" Rolling his forehead over the window, he was lost in a recollection.

> He stood on the balcony of his family home -- a marble villa overlooking the Mediterranean. The sky was cold and gray, and the sea shimmered like quicksilver in the wind.
>
> "Why can't you be good like your brother!" his father, Demetri, shouted in raspy Italian, throwing his hands into the air.
>
> "But Papa, I am 'The Bounty Killer,'" Donatello protested. "Leo, he is a priest."
>
> "Dona, you are not a bounty killer. You make up stories for a living." Demetri paced the perimeter of the balcony, then stopped again in front of Donatello. "Are there not enough women in the world for you? Why must you embarrass me with Caggiano's Austrian whore? She is old enough to be your mother!"
>
> "Mieka is not a whore, and not that old," Donatello countered. "Only seventeen years . . ."
>
> "Dona, are you lunatic? You know Caggiano.

Thanks be to God it was not his wife." Demetri looked heavenward, kissed his thumb, then made the sign of the cross over his chest and forehead.

Donatello feigned a laugh. "Oh Papa, who cares about Caggiano?"

"Dona, listen to me. The only reason you are not dead, and me too by the way, is because Caggiano was my friend. You notice I say *was*. He did me a favor not to kill you."

"Oh Papa..."

"No, Dona, you listen!" Demetri snapped, waving a stout forefinger at him. "You no, oh Papa me! Why can't you keep your pants on? You make enough trouble to put me in my grave." Demetri grabbed his hair with both hands. "You see my hair! It turns white!"

"Your hair already was white," Donatello said.

Demetri shook his head. "No! I tell you why. Because you won't be good."

"But Papa..."

"Even my friend Benito tried to reason with Caggiano. He told him he should be flattered a young man like you would want his mistress. But you know, he was not flattered." Demetri paused, staring at Donatello, then looked down at his watch. The anger in his eyes faded into agony. "Dona, I cannot stop what is to happen. There is nothing I can do." Shaking his head, he turned away.

"Papa?" Donatello called after him.

Demetri stopped outside the open door to the balcony. A balding older man and a younger man with eyes black and vacant like a shark passed him without speaking. He went inside as the men came toward Donatello.

"Caggiano?" Donatello whispered.

The younger man pushed Donatello back against the marble railing. Caggiano fumbled in his coat and pulled out a Beretta pistol. Pointing the gun in Donatello's face, he cocked it.

Donatello went limp. *God, I am a dead man.*

Caggiano grabbed Donatello's hand and held it against the rail. "Now you will learn, 'Bounty Killer,' not to take what is not yours." He swung back, then smashed the butt of the gun into Donatello's hand.

"Papa!" Donatello screamed.

Caggiano swung again. The lip on the magazine cut through Donatello's flesh.

"Papa!"

Caggiano swung again. Blood splattered his face and coat. And again. Crushing the bones in Donatello's hand.

"Papa," Donatello moaned, sinking against the rail.

Caggiano nodded, the younger man released his grip, and Donatello slumped onto the balcony. Caggiano stepped back and took a handkerchief from inside his coat. He wiped his face, then the butt of the gun as Demetri hesitantly approached.

"Get him a doctor," Caggiano said with a guttural growl. He dropped the handkerchief beside Donatello, then he and the other man left.

"Papa, my hand . . ." Donatello cried as Demetri knelt beside him.

"I know, Dona. You are lucky to be alive. Caggiano said only because you are my son, he would have mercy. But if ever, ever, he sees you again, he swore to me he will kill you."

"But . . ."

"I arranged for you to stay with Uncle Lorenzo in San Francisco. There, maybe you will be safe."

"When can I come back?"

"Dona, you cannot come back. Not ever." Demetri helped him to his feet. "We need to call a doctor."

Just then the phone rang, jolting Donatello back to the hotel room. He shuddered and grabbed the receiver. "Mark?"

"Hey, Donatello!" Mark blurted. "Sorry I didn't get back to you last night, man. I was out late, but hey, great news. I just about got the part sewn up," he continued, rapid-fire. "They want you, man, they're dead serious, and by the time they start shooting, you should have the bandage off your hand, so no problem. There's only one thing . . ." Mark paused for a breath. "Since they're making a romantic comedy, they want -- I mean they need you to do a screen test. Whadda ya say?"

"What you mean?" Donatello said in a measured tone.

"They need you to do a screen test."

"What you mean they need me do a screen test?"

"Sheesh. You sound like a broken record. The producer wants you to read because he's worried about your accent and -- "

"Accent? What you mean, accent?"

"You know, how you talk, they wanna make sure they can work around it."

"I know what you mean!" Donatello exploded. "How they dare to ask me read like I never make a movie!" He threw his bandaged hand into the air. "Like I am a no one!"

"That's nobody. Geeze, Donatello, you've got an ego the size of the Roman Coliseum. Relax. It's just a screen test. It won't kill you. And hey, it's a job."

"It is not just a screen test, it is insult. All over Europe I am a star."

"I know it's a drag being here, starting over and all. But I've been working my butt off to get you this part, and it's not like it's the easiest thing in the world to get work for an Italian actor in this town." There was a short pause. "It wouldn't be so bad if you would've done something besides sweaty spaghetti westerns. They think it's all you can do."

"Why you say this? *The Bounty Killer* is the biggest film in Europe. There I am -- "

"Yeah, yeah, I know, you're a star in Europe, but it's not like anybody in Hollywood gives a damn. As long as *The Bounty Killer* is hung up at the ratings board, believe you me, nobody cares."

"But Mark . . ."

"It doesn't matter how big you are -- or were -- in Europe, you're here now, and if you don't knock off all this prima donna crap, you're sure as hell gonna be a has-been. And as you know, you're only as good as your last movie."

"But . . ."

"Here's the deal. They want you, but they're tired of screwin' around, either you do the screen test or they offer the part to Franco Nero. Now, are you gonna do it, or not?"

Donatello exhaled a long sigh. "I . . ."

"Look, I gotta go. The producer will be at his office 'til 6:00, then he's goin' to Vegas for a couple a days. If he doesn't hear from you before he leaves, that's it. They give the part to someone else."

Icy silence.

"You got that?"

More silence.

"Well?"

"Sì. Sì. I call."

"And, uh, Donatello? Don't jerk me around. If you blow off this job, I don't care how big a star you think you are, you can find yourself another agent."

A sharp click and the phone went dead.

Donatello froze, holding the receiver in mid-air, then slammed it onto its cradle.

A noise from behind startled him.

A young woman came into the room. Tall and striking -- with long chestnut hair, dark olive skin, and haunting eyes the color of tarnished gold. She yawned and wrapped a towel with the hotel's monogram around her. "Who that wass?" she asked in English even more broken than his.

He glared at her. "Mark."

She looked incoherently at him.

"Mark. My agent."

She raised her thick, dark eyebrows. "He hass good news?" she said with a heavy Slavic accent.

"Yes . . . no . . . I don't know!" Donatello threw his hands into the air. "Get out my way. Why did I believe the fortuneteller? You bring me no luck." Pushing past her, he stomped into the bedroom and slammed the door behind him.

Late-morning glare streamed into the bedroom. Reaching up to grab the drapes, he banged his bandaged hand on the windowsill. "Damn!" He held the splinted mitt to his chest and jerked on the curtain with his other hand. The heavy brocade screeched as it came off the track.

He threw himself onto the bed. Hidden in darkness, his tears distorted the blade of light cutting across the room through the sagging drapes. His body vibrating with rage, he gripped his crucifix.

"Jesus, Mary, Mother of God," he said in one long breath. "Our Father in heaven, I am Donatello Dragghi, not a no one."

He took another breath.

The oracle said I was born under fortunate stars.

Another breath.

But here, beneath the brown California sky, the stars are falling and my fortune has abandoned me.

Then a strange, yet familiar, sensation washed over him. *The pounding, is it my head . . . or my heart.* The taste of metal flooded his mouth, and panic crashed in on him like a wave. With an intense electric shudder, his mind seized and his world faded to black.

The young woman tightened the towel and slumped onto a chair beside the picture window. Her name was Slovika -- Donatello's wife. She stared at the bedroom door. *I hate him. With everything in me, I hate him.* She slid lower in the chair. *But it is my curse, that I love him even more.*

Slovika picked up Donatello's half-finished cigarette from the ashtray and stared at the chocolate-brown paper. Putting it to her lips, she struck a match. After a deep inhale, she propped her long, olive-skinned legs on the table. As she exhaled the smell of tobacco permeated the room. *Almost noon.*

"So boring," she muttered, looking around the suite. *Nice. But like all other hotels.* "He goes to dinner. He goes to parties.

He goes to lunch. Does he take me?" *Never. I am a prisoner. Like a piece of luggage, I never leave the room. Not even to the pool. And this day will be like all the rest.*

She tapped the ash off the cigarette, then took another long drag and stared out the window at the late-morning haze. Then at the people sunbathing around the swimming pool several floors below. A young man, tall and tan with an arrogant swagger, walked across the courtyard. He stepped up onto a diving board at the end of the pool and placed his feet on the edge. With his arms overhead, he sprang into the air, then straightened and pierced the water like a dagger.

Why do men think they are gods? "Ow!" she gasped as the cigarette burned to the end. She dropped it in the ashtray and licked her fingers.

Standing and stretching, she let the towel slip to the floor. She picked up Donatello's shirt, held the slick cotton to her face, and inhaled the lingering scent of his cologne. Passion flooded her, followed by a rush of despair. She slipped the shirt over her shoulders and slid her arms into the sleeves. Smoothing the fabric over her breasts, she embraced herself. *Why doesn't he love me?*

Slovika wound her chestnut hair into a knot, held it on top of her head, then turned and stared at her reflection in a mirror above the sofa. She seductively lowered her eyes and pursed her lips. *My face is strong, but not ugly. I am beautiful. I think.* She let her hair fall. *Why did he marry me, if he doesn't find me so?* The background became a blur and the room melted away, leaving only the empty golden-brown eyes staring back at her.

"What has happened to me?" *So young. Old. Lost.*

A sound in the bedroom caught her attention. *How long have I stared into the mirror? Hours? Days? A lifetime?*

She sighed. "I don't know. It doesn't matter." *Because there is no Slovika left. Only the empty shell that answers to her name.*

3

HOURS PASSED.
   The smell of cold bacon hung in the Harper's kitchen, and evening shadows crept into the house. Buck sat across from Pauline at a chrome table. The cuckoo clock chimed six. He picked up the telegram and held it to the light.

> **MR. BUCK HARPER=**
> **YOUR SON STEVEN IS IN THE HOSPITAL=**
> **CALL 415-363-1018=**

   No matter how many times I read it the words never change. With all my heart I wish Pauline had never answered that door. He set the crumpled paper on the imitation marble tabletop, and ran his fingers over his silver crew cut. "It's past dinner time and the fire's gone out."
   "Try again," Pauline demanded.
   He took off his wire-rimmed glasses, and rubbed the bridge of his nose. "We've tried it a thousand times, but there's no answer. And we've called all the hospitals in the bay area at least twice. There's no mention of what happened, which hospital, or who sent it. Maybe it's a sick joke."

Pauline shot a resolute glare at him. "Try again -- or I will."

"Alright already." He rubbed his palms on his khaki work pants, then re-tucked his matching shirt and picked up the receiver from its cradle on the wall. Amid the buzzing dial tone, he heard a click on the other end of the line, then a TV in the background. "I'm on the phone, Alma," he grumbled, scuffing at a hairline crack in the black and white linoleum.

No response.

"I need to make a call. Will you *please* get off the line?"

"You've been on all day," a creaking female voice replied.

"Al-ma . . ."

"Fine."

Another click and the line went dead.

"Damn party line." Buck slapped the hook several times. The phone came back to life, and he dialed the number. After three rings, a vacant female voice answered. He nodded to Pauline. She jumped to her feet and put her ear to the receiver next to his. He gripped her hand.

"This is Buck Harper. I'm calling about my son, Steven," he blurted.

"Just a minute. Shara, it's for you . . ."

The voice trailed off into the background, then the echo of footsteps came toward the phone.

"Hello."

"Who is this!" Buck snapped.

No answer.

"What happened to Steven?"

"I'm Shara, his girlfriend," a hesitant, child-like voice replied.

"Girlfriend?" Buck rubbed his forehead. "What happened?"

Silence.

"Calm down. She might hang up," Pauline whispered.

He took a long breath. "Please . . . what happened?"

"Steven overdosed."

"What?" the Harpers gasped in unison.

"He overdosed . . . smoking heroin. And I don't know what to do," Shara stammered.

"Smoking heroin? I've never heard of -- " Buck began.

"Oh my God," Pauline moaned, slumping into her chair.

12

Buck gripped her shoulder. "When -- " His voice cracked. He cleared his throat. "When did this happen?"

Shara burst into tears. "Last night . . . I wasn't home when they found him. I didn't know your phone number, but there was an old letter in his duffle bag . . . it had your address on it, and my friend told me . . . told me to send a telegram," she said between sobs.

"Could -- couldn't Steven tell you the number?" Buck said.

"No. He can't talk."

"Can't talk?" His voice cracked again.

Pauline buried her face in her hands. "Oh, dear God, no."

"Where is he?" Buck said, stiffening his jaw.

"He was in Oakland, but they're transferring him to another hospital in the city."

"What hospital? What city?"

"San Francisco. I don't know what hospital. They won't tell me anything. This is totally freaking me out! I . . . I don't know what to do. Will you come and help us?"

Between her choking sobs, the hollow sound of a child crying echoed in the background.

"Okay, okay, take it easy. Of course we'll come." He paused, running his hand over his hair again. "Damn. The rockslide. Look, we're in the foothills up above Sacramento. There was a rockslide and the road's closed. But we'll catch the next flight out of Reno." He took a long breath. "Don't panic. We'll get there as soon as we can."

4

DONATELLO WOKE FROM a dreamless sleep, shaken and ashen. He pushed the sweat-soaked hair off his face, then struggled to sit up. *God . . . my head.* He dropped back on the bed. *Another seizure.*

Sunlight cutting across the room had been replaced by evening shadows.

Where am I? What day? What time?

He stared up at the ceiling. *Sunday. California.* He turned over and looked at a clock radio on the nightstand. The digital cards flipped.

6:46

The luminous numerals held no meaning. He reached for the timepiece. It was bolted to the table. The digital cards flipped again.

6:47

"Sei, quaranta, sette," he said under his breath. He looked at the clock again, rubbed his eyes, and shuddered. *The time . . .* He put his hand over his eyes. *The producer has gone to Las Vegas. Now I have no agent.*

"Why does this happen to me?"

Familiar voices replied.

> *You brought this upon yourself...*
> *It is nothing more than you deserve...*
> *Your father will never take pride in you...*
> *You can never go home...*
> *If only you had been like your brother...*

Donatello sat up. Catching his reflection in the mirrored closet door, he wiped the perspiration off his forehead and squared his shoulders, then turned on the radio. Bouncy bossa nova flared from the speakers.

"Quel che sarà sarà," he said, staring at his reflection. "I am Donatello Dragghi, and I will conquer this."

Slovika looked up as Donatello came into the suite's living room. He leaned against the doorjamb in a pale silk shirt open almost to his waist, skin-tight velvet pants, and snakeskin boots with Cuban heels.

She sank back on the sofa. *He ignores me all day long, and now he's going out again.*

"I look good, no?" he asked with a flourish of his splinted hand.

"As always," she said.

"Then, come. We will go out together. To the ristorante of my friend Vincente on the Sunset Strip."

Slovika stared blankly at him.

"You want go or not?" he said, winding the chain of his crucifix around his finger.

She managed a feeble nod. "There will be dancing?"

He shrugged. "We will see. But you no can wear mia camicia... uh, wear my shirt. Hurry. Go and dress, I'll not wait all night."

Slovika sprang off the couch and skipped past him into the bathroom. Smiling into the mirror above the sink, she giggled and hugged herself. *I cannot believe he takes me too! I must make myself beautiful.*

She splashed water on her face and dried it with a thick hotel towel. Then colored her full lips dark red and lined her golden-brown eyes with a black kohl pencil. She slipped large hoops with tiny bells into the holes in her ears, wound her hair into a knot, and secured it with a tortoiseshell comb.

Throwing off Donatello's shirt, she rushed into the bedroom and opened the closet. *What will he like?* Rifling through her clothes, she stopped and took out a flowing paisley skirt, a peasant blouse, and laced sandals. "Maybe this." She stepped into the skirt and slipped on the blouse. Sitting on the bed, she tied the laces around her ankles. She stood and slid the mirrored closet door closed, then stepped back to study her reflection.

Straightening the blouse hanging below her olive shoulders, she smiled. "Yes. I am beautiful."

5

THE NEXT FLIGHT out of Reno turned out to be the final flight of the day, and the Harpers were the last passengers to get off the plane in San Francisco late that evening. Most of the business travelers, weekend gamblers, and other passengers had already gone when they entered the terminal.

"Baggage claim and rent-a-cars are downstairs," Buck said, pointing toward the escalator.

"But it's Sunday night. The car rentals are probably closed," Pauline moaned.

"Then we'll get a cab."

A blonde PSA flight attendant in a red and orange mini-dress, red knee-high boots, and a fishbowl-shaped cap came from behind. "Evening," she said. Her voice and footsteps echoed through the sterile quiet of the terminal as she passed them and stepped onto the escalator.

Pauline followed her, then Buck got on.

Pulling off his glasses, he closed his eyes and the sinking sensation swallowed him. *God, I feel like . . . it's all too much . . .* Glancing down, he stepped off just before the stairs slipped away. He put on his glasses again, tugged on the lapels of his tweed jacket, and took Pauline's arm. "Baggage is this way."

As the Harpers entered the baggage area, the lonely sound of grinding metal reverberated through the space. The single remaining bag, a suitcase the size of a folding card table, disappeared through a split curtain as the luggage carousel turned. "Have to wait 'til it comes around again," Buck said with a weak smile.

Standing like ancient statues in a deserted city, they watched the machine slowly rotating. Pauline gripped the collar of her camelhair coat. "It's been all day . . ." Her voice cracked, and her eyes filled with tears. "First we couldn't get tickets. Then that stupid man on the plane blocked the aisle, and now -- "

Buck caught her hand. "Pauline, don't. We can't fall apart. We'll get there."

Biting her lip, she nodded, then glanced at a newspaper hanging in a nearby rack. "It seems like there's nothing but trouble . . . trouble everywhere."

"What do you mean?"

"March on Memphis Turns Violent," she read, pointing to the headline. "What's happened to everyone? This morning everything was fine." Tears spilled down her cheeks. "Then Steven . . . and now . . . it's like we're in another country and the whole world is going crazy!" she cried, throwing her hands into the air.

He put his arm around her. "Pauline, please. Don't. We can't. Not yet."

She took a long breath, then wiped her eyes. "You're right."

"There it is," Buck said as their suitcase came around again. He yanked it off the carousel and nodded toward a revolving door in a glass wall at the far end of the baggage claim. "That way."

They hurried to the door, then slipped into the vacuous space between the walls of turning glass. After half a rotation, it spit them out on the street. Dark, low-hanging clouds and damp air carrying a hint of the ocean met them on the other side. An odd muffled clattering punctuated the urban noise.

A battery of gritty panhandlers flanked either side of the door -- some intent on their purpose, others sitting dejectedly on the sidewalk. A wraith-like woman holding an illegible cardboard sign stared vacantly into an alternate universe. A few steps away, a grizzled man wrapped in a sleeping bag waved at the Harpers.

"Hey, how 'bout it? Spare change?" he called.

As the man started toward them, Buck took Pauline's arm. "Watch your purse," he said. "Taxis are over there."

Turning a corner, they came upon the source of the clattering. A barefoot, saffron-robed gathering beating drums, tambourines, and finger cymbals danced and chanted with ecstatic abandon.

> Hare Krishna, Hare Krishna . . .
> Krishna, Krishna
> Hare, Hare . . .
> Hare Rama, Hare Rama . . .
> Rama, Rama Hare, Hare . . .

A tall man wrapped in an orange sheet stepped away from the group. He thrust a basket across Buck's path. Pulling out a flower, the man waved it sinuously through the air. "Krishna, Krishna," he sang. "An offering for Krishna?"

"No," Buck said over the jangling noise. "Now, if you'll excuse us . . ."

The man held out the basket. "Hare, Hare . . ."

"I *said* no, thank you!" Buck snapped, then pushed the man out of the way, spilling coins, finger cymbals, and flowers onto the sidewalk.

"That was totally un-cool," the man muttered.

Buck grabbed Pauline's hand. "Come on," he said, stepping over the artifacts of bliss scattered on the walkway.

The suitcase banged against his thigh as they hurried to the taxi stand. "Damn, it's heavy," he muttered, dropping the bag near the curb. "And those people are pushy." He looked back at the chanting crowd. "Everybody wants something. And who the hell is Harry Christian, anyway? I wish he'd keep his people off the sidewalk."

A few minutes later, an old black cab pulled up. Buck leaned in the window. "Immaculate Heart Hospital."

The driver nodded, then jumped out and hoisted their suitcase into the trunk. The Harpers slid into the back seat, which smelled of stale cigarettes. After a quick glance over his shoulder, the cabbie drove away.

Bedraggled transients walked along the road, heading toward the highway. Hitchhikers stood shoulder to shoulder, waiting at the on-ramp. All the human detritus disappeared into the rearview mirror as the driver accelerated onto the freeway.

   Buck ran his hand over the black vinyl seats, cracked with wear, then looked up at the frayed gray fabric lining the roof. *I feel old as this cab.* He glanced at Pauline; she stared out the window while fidgeting relentlessly with the strap of her purse. "It's good Steven's at Immaculate Heart," he said.

   She looked up at him. The desperation in her eyes left him crestfallen. He turned back to the window.

   Stony silence descended in the taxi as evening settled over the bay. They passed mile after mile of bleak, featureless, shoebox buildings overhung by sagging power lines on treeless streets. A never-ending landscape of stucco, concrete, and asphalt. Small lackluster cities strung together by a thread of freeway that seemed to stretch past infinity. The relentless monotony seemed to heighten their sense of urgency.

   At Army Street, like the turn of a page, the backdrop changed. Wind-bent cypress stood like sentries watching over the luxuriant tapestry of San Francisco, spreading over the edge of the bay. Many threads of highway ran together, and the traffic slowed to a crawl.

   Rain began to fall. They stopped at an intersection. Lights blurred and slid down the taxi window, as if the city itself was crying. The rain on the roof and the soft, rhythmic splashing of the wipers weakened Buck's composure. His lips began to tremble. He closed his eyes. *One tear falls and the dam will break. Got to stay strong for Pauline. For Steven.*

   The buoyant lilt of the driver's voice rescued Buck from the impending flood. "If you ask me, we're in for a real gully-washer tonight," the cabbie announced with a broad grin, glancing in the rearview mirror. "Hey, you don't look so good. Are you okay?"

   Buck stiffened. "Our son's at Immaculate Heart."

   The driver looked over his shoulder. "Oh. Is it serious?"

   "Don't know yet."

The driver nodded, then turned back as light changed.

Buck grasped Pauline's hand. "Another block. Almost there."

Pulling into the hospital's circular driveway, the driver stopped at a covered loading zone. In a flash, Pauline was out of the cab and hurrying toward the entrance. Buck waited as the driver got their suitcase from the trunk and took it to the curb. He handed the cabbie a roll of bills. "Keep the change."

"Gee, thanks," the driver said, greedily flipping through the roll. "Hope everything comes out all right . . . for your son, I mean." He slammed the trunk shut, then jumped in the cab, closed the door, and sped away.

6

THE NIGHT WAS hot for early spring. A reddish glow canopied the sky. The smell of cigarettes, marijuana, and stale beer hung in the air along the Sunset Strip. Music pulsed from bustling clubs and restaurants. Lights dashed to and fro, blurring into a rainbow of neon. Swirling with rhythm and blues, surf riffs, surreal psychedelic, and soul, the night took on an infectious, driving beat of its own.

People on the sidewalk turned and stared as Donatello's long, low sports car rolled by, rumbling with the tightly geared hum of surplus horsepower. Swinging the car around in the middle of the street, he pulled alongside the curb and stopped at a valet station.

The valet jumped up and went around to open the door for Slovika. "Evening miss," he said, extending his hand. He helped her out, went to the other side, and opened the door for Donatello.

"Don'a park on street." Donatello got out and threw the keys at him.

"Sure bet," the valet replied in a tone suggesting he had no intention of complying.

Donatello's nostrils flared. "I mean it."

The valet half-smiled and handed him a numbered ticket. "Like I said, sure bet."

Donatello grabbed Slovika's arm and stomped away. "You see? I tell you, the city full of imbecilli. Always rude. They are, how you say? Lunatic. If ever you wonder, this is why I no bring you," he snapped, almost dragging her along.

Walking on Sunset Boulevard was like looking through the window of a costume shop. Two young men wearing musketeer hats and tight pants with Errol Flynn haircuts. Three black-robed nuns strolling arm-in-arm. Inebriated sailors weaving on and off the sidewalk. Girls in bright mini-dresses and go-go boots. Laughing boys in prep-school outfits with longish hair combed over their ears. Drunken men sleeping in a doorway. Pimps and prostitutes making their rounds. Barefoot young women panhandling in dirty, bedraggled clothes beside a van painted flaming red, electric green, and magenta day-glo. Across the street fashionably clean-cut hipsters, smoking pot and cigarettes, while waiting in a long line at a restaurant.

"Many strange people here," Slovika said breathless and flushed with excitement. The gilt in her eyes sparkled in the flashing neon. And the light danced on the chestnut tendrils falling around her face.

He put his arm around her with a crooked smile. "Is okay. 'The Bounty Killer' will protect you." A warm gust blew his silk shirt open and her skirt fluttered in the breeze. The heels of his boots clacked on the pavement as his steps fell in line with hers, and he slid into a comfortable swagger.

Slovika looked up at him. "Where we go?"

He nodded in the direction they were walking. "Villa Nova. My friend Vincente Minnelli, he own it. I meet him in Cannes at the preview of his movie *Blow-Up* and he tell me, if ever I am in LA to go his ristorante."

Just then, a man dragging a large wooden cross with a wheel on the bottom, came around a corner, followed by a small entourage. He stopped, blocking the sidewalk as Donatello and Slovika approached. "The hour is late, time to come to Jesus, man," he said with an impassioned smile.

Frowning, Donatello held up his crucifix. "That, I do since I am bambino," he said, motioning with his splinted hand for the entourage to move out of the way. Trying to pass, he bumped into the cross, knocking it off the man's shoulder. It tumbled to the sidewalk with a dull thud. Pedestrians stopped. As if the Sunset Strip had been drawn into a vortex, the music, cars and people all seemed suspended in time.

"Consider the path your feet are walking, my friend," the man said as one of his followers picked up the cross. Staring at Donatello, his eyes glistened with tears. "One false step, and then the fall . . . broad is the way that leads to destruction."

Donatello shrugged his shirt back in place and glared at him. He grabbed Slovika's arm and stomped down the block. "You see? I tell you -- imbecilli everywhere."

As they came to the corner, the traffic light turned red. They stopped and Donatello looked back. The man with the cross stood, watching him. "Why he say that to me?"

Slovika looked up. "What?"

"Niente," he muttered, shaking his head.

The light turned green, he took her arm and they hurried across the street. On the next block, they came to a line of people spilling from the entrance of a restaurant built like a large A-frame cabin with an add-on upstairs nightclub.

Donatello pushed through the crowd and went to the head of the line. Taking Slovika's hand, he went around a sign reading:

Please wait here.
The host will seat you.

"Hey, whadda ya think you're doin'?" a man near the front of the line grumbled.

"Yeah. Who do you think you are?" another complained.

"Donatello Dragghi," he replied with a nonchalant wave.

He stopped at a tall reservation desk just inside the door. Behind the desk, a young man in the last stages of puberty waged a valiant battle against the crowd. Donatello placed a fifty-dollar bill on the desk, then cleared his throat. "You have table for me?"

The young Maître d' looked up from a list of reservations and frowned. "Are you blind?" he said with an accent fresh from New Jersey. "Can't you see the line? It's at least a forty-five minute wait."

"Vincente is here?"

"No."

Donatello whisked the bill off the desk. "Then, get Alphonse. Tell him Donatello Dragghi want table."

The host rolled his eyes. "Who doesn't? You're just another rich jerk with a lousy accent."

"Get Alphonse!" Donatello shouted, slapping the desk hard enough that Slovika, and several people at the front of the line jumped.

The Maître d' shook his head, then lumbered to a narrow doorway behind the desk. After knocking, he disappeared through the door.

Slovika tugged on Donatello's sleeve. "Maybe we should go in the line."

He shrugged off her hand. "No. You know nothing of these things," he said, waving as if to erase the thought. "My friend, Alphonse, he seat the customer by how rich or importante. This the politica the ristorante. No matter the crowd, I get table. You see."

The young host reappeared with a short, balding man. Impeccably dressed, the man straightened his bowtie and pasted on a broad smile. "Donatello, my ex-pat friend!" he gushed with open arms. "Good to see you. How goes the movie business? And your hand? Healing, I hope."

Donatello shrugged and nodded. "Alphonse," he said with a slight pout. "We are hungry. I had no time to make reservation..."

Alphonse glanced at the line of customers, then back at Donatello. He manufactured another smile. "Of course, my friend. I'll see what I can do."

"But what about the other people?" the young Maître d' said, waving in the direction of the line. "Why are you kissing his -- "

With a look, Alphonse cut the question short. "And you, since you're such a smart-mouth, go help Miguel with the dishes."

The young host glared at Alphonse, then at Donatello. Shaking his head, he sauntered toward the kitchen.

"Your host, he is molto rude," Donatello said with a frown.

"Don't mind him. He's my sister's kid from Jersey. She sent him out here to keep him out of troub -- "

"Good table," Donatello interrupted. "Not by door, or kitchen."

Alphonse sighed. "Of course. Just a moment." He snapped his fingers at a passing waiter. "Lucca! Table sixteen for Mr. Dragghi."

7

BUCK LOOKED UP at a crucifix high atop the roof of Immaculate Heart Hospital. Juxtaposed against the cold, sterile outline of the modern physicians building, the hospital's graceful Gothic lines seemed, somehow, comforting. He bent to pick up the suitcase, then stopped, staring at his hands. *What has become of this world? What has become of me?*

After a moment he came to himself and grabbed the suitcase. He followed Pauline through the hospital's wide automatic doors, into the warm, antiseptic air of the hospital. He found her waiting at the circular information desk. Resembling a military command post, the desk was staffed by a stern-looking, black-robed nun.

Pauline looked up at him with a despondent stare. "Buck, she said it's too late."

The color drained from his face. He set the suitcase down and steadied himself against the desk. "What?"

"Visiting hours are over, sir. You'll have to wait until tomorrow," the nun said with a thin, officious smile.

"Oh, thank God. I thought he was . . . *gone*."

She smiled and shook her head. "No, sir."

"But we can see him . . ."

"I'm sorry, sir, but as I told your wife, visiting hours are over."

"You don't understand," he said, drumming his fingers on the desk. "We were stuck at the Reno airport all day."

"I'm very sorry to hear that, but as I said, visiting hours are over."

He glared at her. "Now, listen. We spent all day trying to get here. And damn it, we're going to see him. Tonight. Not tomorrow. Tonight!"

The nun took a long breath. "You'll need permission. The name of your son's doctor?"

Buck looked at Pauline, then back at the nun. "I . . . I don't know."

"Your son's name then."

"We already told you. Steven Harper."

"I'll see what I can do." Turning to a wide ledger, the nun began flipping through the pages. "It'll be just a minute." She got up and exited through a door behind the desk.

"Buck . . ." Pauline moaned. "What if they won't let us see him?"

"We'll pull strings if we have to."

He went to a row of aged, hand-tinted photographs to one side of the information desk. A portrait of his parents hung above a plaque honoring them for their contributions to the hospital.

Mother's thin-lipped smile. Father . . . the mischievous look in your eye. He touched the glass over the picture. *What would you think of all this? Of your grandson? Of me?*

"Sir?"

Buck jumped.

"Found it," the nun announced. "Your son's doctor is Dr. Buehler. But let me warn you, getting him to agree to anything will take an act of congress."

"Well, fortunately, I'm a senator's son. And that'll be close enough. I'll resurrect the memory of dear old dad if I have to," he said, tapping the glass over the photograph.

The nun smiled. "I'll call his office for you." After dialing the number she gave the phone to Buck.

"Dr. Buehler's office," an irritable sounding receptionist announced.

"I'm Buck Harper. My son, Steven, is one of his patients over here at Immaculate Heart. They told me I need permission to see him."

"Visiting hours are over."

Buck rolled his eyes. "I know that. But my wife and I just flew in from Reno, and we want to see him."

"One minute."

An interlude of insipid music.

"Name of the patient?" the receptionist asked when she came back on the line.

"Steven Harper. Now look, you tell Dr. Buehler that my father, Senator Harper, was one of the major donors for the new wing of the hospital and the building you're sitting in. You tell him I want to see my son, and I want to see him, tonight."

Another musical interlude.

"Dr. Buehler wants to talk to you."

"Why?"

"I don't know. I'm just repeating his instructions. He said he'll wait half an hour." The receptionist hung up.

Buck frowned and handed the receiver back to the nun, then turned to Pauline. "The doctor wants to see us."

"What? Why?"

"Hell, I don't know."

Pauline's face fell. "Oh, Buck, what now? I don't want to talk to the doctor. I want to see Steven."

"I know." He put his arm around her. "Don't worry. We're going to see him. Tonight."

"That corridor will take you to the Physician's Building," the nun said, pointing to a long hallway. "You can leave your luggage here, behind the desk if you like. Dr. Buehler's office is on the tenth floor. Ten fifty-two, I think."

Buck set the suitcase behind the desk. He took Pauline's hand. "Come on. We'll just see about Dr. Buehler."

Cold, sterile air met the Harpers as they hurried down the long, curved corridor. The hall was deserted, except for a young black man in a dark suit, crisp white shirt and a bow tie talking and laughing with one of the doctors.

"Evening," Buck said.

"How do ya do?" the man replied. The doctor smiled and nodded and they went back to their conversation.

After walking by, Buck paused and his thoughts drifted, staring down the hallway as if in a dream. He shook his head. *Does he think like the protesters in Memphis? Why is there such injustice. Things are changing so fast right under our noses. Where is the time going -- and what's happened to me through these years?*

When he snapped back, Pauline was several paces ahead. He hurried and caught up with her.

The corridor opened into a wide lobby with banks of elevators on either side. On a narrow slice of wall between the elevators, they found a directory. Buck traced his finger over the names.

"Buehler . . . Buehler . . . there it is. The nun was right. Ten fifty-two."

8

THE LONELY ECHO of the Harpers' footsteps followed them into Dr. Buehler's office. The stuffy, overheated air was thick with the unsettling odor of disinfectant.

A middle-aged receptionist glared at them from behind a glass partition. "Mr. and Mrs. Harper?"

"Yes. We're here to see Dr. Buehler," Buck replied.

"Of course." The receptionist picked up her purse, coat and umbrella. "The Harpers are here," she said into an intercom. "May I please leave now?"

A muffled response.

"You can go in. It's down the hall, second door on the right," she said, then quickly left the office.

Buck looked over at Pauline. "I already don't like that Buehler character."

The Harpers found Dr. Buehler sitting at an immense desk, occupied by the contents of a file. A dark panorama of city lights dissolved into rivulets of rain on a window behind him. Buck yanked on his tie to loosen his collar, then cleared his throat.

Though Dr. Buehler's stare remained fixed on the file, he stood to greet them. After a moment he set the file down and looked up. "You must be Steven's grandparents," he said with a nasal drone, squinting through thick, tri-focal glasses.

"We're his parents," Buck replied.

"Parents?"

"We want to see our son," Pauline blurted.

"Oh, uh, yes." The doctor frowned, then took another file off one of the stacks on his desk and pointed the corner at Buck. "You know, up until a few years ago, we rarely had drug cases at this hospital. But ever since the hippies took over the city, it seems that's all we see in the emergency room anymore. Not to mention the overflowing maternity ward. As our illustrious governor put it, 'They dress like Tarzan, have hair like Jane, and they smell like -- '"

"Wait a minute. We don't care about all that. We just want to see him," Buck snapped.

Dr. Buehler's face reddened. He waved the file across the darkened cityscape behind him. "In the last few years they've turned the city upside down. It's literally crawling with them. They all expect service, but don't pay for it. Do you know how much it costs this hospital? And the taxpayers of this city?"

"Uh . . . no," Buck stammered.

"Plenty. It costs the taxpayers plenty. Filthy, ungrateful, drug using derelicts." Dr. Buehler slammed his fist on the desk.

"How dare you!" Pauline shrieked. Her lips quivering, she stared at the doctor a moment, then burst into tears.

With a sigh that sounded like air escaping a punctured tire, he pushed a box of tissue across the desk with the file.

Buck yanked one out and gave it to her. "Our son is not an ungrateful derelict, if that's what you're saying. We'll see to it that his bills are paid."

Dr. Buehler cocked his head back and looked at Buck through the bottom of his glasses.

"I *said*, his bills will be paid," Buck repeated. He pulled another tissue from the box and wiped the perspiration off his forehead. *What I'd like to do is punch the good doctor right in the chops. Then elbow him in the stomach just for the hell of it. And while he's doubled over -- a swift hook to the jaw . . .*

The monotone droning of Dr. Buehler's voice brought Buck back from his imaginary prizefight.

" . . . as I was saying, it doesn't appear that Steven is addicted, per se. More along the lines of psychologically addicted."

Pauline blew her nose, then wiped it with the tissue. "What on earth does that mean?"

"Psychologically addicted? Um, in other words, I don't think he'll go through withdrawal like a true addict does. He doesn't have a physical need for it -- yet. Actually, in the long run, it may be best that it happened this way."

"How dare you say such a thing!" she wailed, accompanied by another flood of tears.

"What I mean is," the doctor said with another sigh. "Assuming he recovers, this may scare him enough to keep him from developing a true physical addiction. And believe me, that can be far worse than what he's facing now. Addiction can lure a person into a living hell."

Buck struggled to swallow the lump that had formed in his throat. "Just exactly what is he facing? Give it to us straight."

"Alright." Dr. Buehler crossed his arms. "Your son was transferred here because I'm the leading specialist in the area for brain trauma, nerve damage, spinal cord injuries, and neurological disorders. Steven is partially paralyzed from a transient ischemia caused by a drug overdose. In short, the overdose resulted in a stroke."

He paused a moment, tapping the edge of the file on his desk, then continued.

"Your son made the all-too-common mistake of drinking alcohol while using heroin. Alcohol and opiates make very bad bedfellows. As I understand it, he was unconscious for approximately seven hours. At some point during that time there was a lack of blood flow to his brain. He's lucky the ischemia resolved itself. If it had gone on longer, he most likely wouldn't be here. He is hemiplegic, meaning he has no feeling on one side of his body. His left arm, leg, and that side of his face are paralyzed."

The Harpers stared as if the doctor's words had no meaning.

"Perhaps you should sit down," he said.

They robotically complied.

"But if all goes well -- and that's a big if, Steven has a reasonable chance of recovery."

Buck rubbed his forehead. "A chance? You said you're top in your field. Can't you be more specific?"

"No, I can't. There is no way to predict how well Steven's body will repair or compensate for the damage." The doctor pushed up his glasses. "But in his favor, he's young and in relatively good health. He's in a neck brace, but he has the use of his right arm. He can't speak, but he can communicate by writing, although it's laborious for him. When you talk to him, use simple words and short sentences to make it as easy as possible for him to reply. But above all, it's imperative that you don't upset him. Emotional outbursts could be devastating at this stage of his recovery. Do you understand?"

The Harpers nodded.

"Uh, also, he had several wounds that required stitches -- shards of glass embedded in the side of his head and face. Apparently, he fell on a wine glass. His hair was so long and matted the emergency room in Oakland elected to shave his head."

Dr. Buehler's expression softened.

"I'm not entirely the callous, heartless person you might think I am. More than one misguided parent has thought that. I have children of my own, and I *do* understand. But in the last few years, I've seen situations like this more often than you can imagine. The pity of it is, the suffering is self-inflicted and completely unnecessary." The doctor paused, staring at the Harpers. "You seem like decent people. I'm sorry we had to have this conversation."

A stringent, antiseptic smell permeated the air of the intensive care unit. Bathed in sterile silence and a pale unnatural glow, the intermittent beeping of machines and hushed footfalls of the personnel punctuated the quiet.

A nurse with an authoritarian expression met Buck and Pauline at the door to a small glass-walled room draped with a heavy curtain. "You're the Harpers?" she whispered.

They nodded.

"Your son is sleeping. Dr. Buehler doesn't want him disturbed. Do you understand?" she asked with a look that demanded a reply.

Buck put his arm around Pauline. "We understand."

The nurse slowly opened the door and pulled back the curtain. Buck caught his breath. *My God, Steven, what have you done?*

9

A BOTTLE OF wine and two menus waited on table sixteen for Donatello and Slovika. He paused as she slid into the booth, then set his gold cigarette case and matching lighter on the white linen cloth and sat down beside her. The smell of garlic, tobacco, and men's cologne hung in the air, making the large, crowded room feel claustrophobic and small.

A passing waiter stopped at the table. He picked up the bottle and cut off the leaded foil. "Compliments of Alphonse," he announced. After pulling the cork, he poured a small amount into a goblet and passed it to Donatello.

Donatello forced a smile. *Cheap house wine, but I will appear grateful.* He swirled the crimson liquid, inhaled the bouquet, then took a sip. His eyes widened. Rolling his tongue over his palette, he motioned to the waiter.

The waiter held up the bottle.

Donatello examined the label. *A fine Valpolicella.* "Alphonse has been generous."

"In honor of the beautiful lady," the waiter replied, smiling at Slovika. "Is it to your liking?"

"Sì. Thank Alphonse," Donatello said with a shallow nod.

"Certainly, Mr. Dragghi." The waiter filled their glasses. "I'll leave you with the menu."

Donatello wrestled a cigarette from the case and fumbled with his lighter. Slovika took the lighter and lit his cigarette. After a long drag, he pointed it at her. "You see? I tell you," he said with a wave of his bandaged hand. "Alphonse give buona bottle wine and best table. Is as I say, the politica di Hollywood. Now, look the menu. If you no can read it, I help you."

As she opened the padded folder, something across the aisle caught his eye.

Overly-tan, bleached-blonde, and heavily made-up, the woman's appearance demanded attention. Wearing white knee-high boots and tight hot-pink, she shared a table with a lanky man she seemed to be ignoring.

Donatello locked her in a visual embrace. He nodded and raised his glass. The woman flashed a smile and mirrored his actions. *Like I am her prisoner, she holds me captive. It is impossible to take my eyes away. From every pore, she screams,* "Make love to me!"

"What is this?" Slovika asked, pointing to a selection on the menu. Looking up, she caught her breath and the padded folder slipped from her hand. *That woman . . . soon she will come to him, or he will go to her. But either way, I will be alone.*

The waiter came back to the table. "And what will the lady have?" he asked, pen in hand, smiling at Slovika.

"The lady -- " Donatello interrupted, pointing across the aisle. "Ask will she like to join us."

The waiter looked first at the woman, then at Slovika, then back at Donatello.

"Ask will she like to join us," Donatello repeated.

"Yes sir," the waiter replied, then went to deliver the invitation.

Slovika gripped a wad of her paisley skirt. *I do not believe he does this, yet I am not surprised. If I could, I would kill him, but without him I am alone.*

The man sharing the woman's table stretched, then got up and left. Heads turned as she stood and straightened her short hot-pink dress, and followed the waiter across the aisle to Donatello's table.

"Well, *hel-low*. I'm Deborah Donaldson," she said in a breathy nasal whine. As she bent to extend her hand, her voluminous breasts, reminiscent of a baby's bottom suspended in a sling, nearly rolled out of her low-cut neckline. "And *who* might you be?" she asked with a sugary-sweet affectation, emphasizing certain words to enhance their effect.

Donatello's eyes widened. He coughed, then swallowed. Unable to take her hand, he held up the splinted mitt instead. "Donatello Dragghi," he replied, sitting back so his pale silk shirt fell open, revealing his sculpted torso.

She paused for a moment, staring at his chest. "Hey! Donatello Dragghi -- Deborah Donaldson. We have the same initials. We could use the same monogram," she said with a high-pitched squeal.

Donatello smiled. "Perhaps we will," he said, his voice smooth as warmed brandy.

"You'll have to excuse me, I have to manage my assets," she said, laughing and setting a long, thin handbag on the table. She wiggled the neckline to settle her breasts. Her dress strained at the seams as she slid into the booth beside him. "Since this is a place to see and be seen, I was looking for promising prospects -- you know, working the room, when you came in. I don't know *who* you are, but I do know Alphonse found a table for you almost immediately."

She leaned forward and ran a fingertip around her neckline. "*That* intrigues me. As I always say, it's good to get in on the ground floor, as it appears nobody around here has a bigger ground floor than you," she said, pointing a frost-white fingernail at him. She looked over at Slovika. "And who are you, honey?"

"A friend," Donatello replied before Slovika could answer.

"Oh, good. I thought maybe you two were, you know, *together*," Deborah said, laughing again. She unclipped a jeweled latch on her handbag, and took out a pack of cigarettes. Pulling one from the pack, she leaned toward Donatello.

He fumbled with his lighter, then turned to Slovika. "You will light for her?"

Glaring at him, Slovika grabbed the lighter, lit Deborah's cigarette, then slapped it on the table.

Deborah winked. "Thanks, hun." Turning back to Donatello, she caught him staring at her breasts. "Well, shame on you," she said, pulling up on the plunging neckline. "So, what's your sign? Bet you're a Scorpio."

"No. Leo."

"I should have guessed." She tapped her chin. "Hmmm. It could still work, depending on your rising sign. "You have an accent. So you're not American . . ."

He shook his head.

She took a long drag off the cigarette. "From France?" she asked, the smoke escaping with each syllable.

"No, Italia."

"A Leo, all the way from Italy." Her eyes sparkled. Wrinkling her nose, she pointed to the bandages. "What's wrong with your hand?"

"Broken."

"Broken? How'd you break it?"

Donatello mouthed a silent exaggeration of the word, "Mafia."

Deborah gasped and raised her brows. "What! What on earth happened?"

He shook his head again. "I no can talk of it."

"Oh, wow. That's too bad, because it's probably so, you know -- *dramatic*." She paused again and fluffed a mound of hair ratted at the crown of her head. "So, what brings you to LA?"

"I am attore e un regista."

"I don't speak Italian, silly."

Donatello shrugged. "Uh, actor and, how you say it, direttore?"

"Oh, um, director?" Deborah took another drag off the cigarette and tapped the ash into the ashtray. "*Fa-bulous*. Then you are in the business. I thought so. Are you working on anything?"

"My film, how you say, at the rating board waiting a . . ." He snapped his fingers. "A decisione the rating."

"Oh. Well . . . as you may have guessed, I'm a leading lady. But right now, I'm hosting a talk show. It's live here in LA. You'd be a *fa-bulous* guest. And of course, you could plug your movie." Deborah wiggled in her seat. "In fact, tomorrow we're taping a pilot for my show to go national. It'll be up against Mike and Merv."

Donatello stared blankly at her.

"You know, Mike and Merv? Surely you've heard of them."

He shook his head.

"Mike Douglas and Merv Griffin?"

He shook his head again.

"You've never heard of Mike Douglas and Merv Griffin? They're *only* the biggest talk show hosts on TV." She shook her head. "Well, anyway, like I said, I'd love to have you as a guest. You'd be just *fa-bulous*!"

10

LONG AFTER THE restaurant stopped serving, and most of the other patrons had gone, Donatello, Slovika and Deborah sat at the table littered with a stack of dishes, an overflowing ashtray and three empty wine bottles. A cloud of stale smoke hung in the air and the ceiling vibrated with a driving beat from the upstairs nightclub.

Slovika looked wistfully at the ceiling. *I wish to be there, dancing.* She dropped a spoon into a bowl of congealed lentil soup, then pushed it away. *For days I sit alone with them at this table.* Her stare wandered to Deborah's temples where unblended brown make-up met the faint dark roots of her platinum hair. To the thick black eyeliner concealing the bands of her false lashes. To the small lines painted to look like eyelashes, sinking into the creases under her eyes. To the frosted white lipstick covering a mouth perpetually in motion. *Her face like a mask -- talking, talking, always talking.*

Deborah's droning voice brought Slovika back to the table.

"Like I was saying . . ." She paused as the man who had been sitting at her table lumbered toward them, breathless and sweating. Wearing a cowboy hat and boots with jeans ripped at the knees, he sported thick sideburns shaped like lamb chops.

"There's a righteous party goin' on down the street at The Whiskey, the likes of which have never been seen on a Sunday night!" he announced with a thick Oklahoma drawl. He took off his hat and wiped the back of his neck with a napkin. "It's like a heathren paradise. They've even got the girls dancin' in the cages. Too bad y'all are missin' it."

Slovika stared up at him. *I would dance in a heathren paradise cage -- whatever that is.*

Deborah frowned. "Bob, I thought you would've outgrown caged dancing girls by now." She looked over at Donatello. "This is Bob, uh, Robert Morant. He's the drummer for The Time Season Band. Have you heard of them?"

Donatello shook his head and glared at Bob.

"They just got back from a European tour." With a wink in Slovika's direction, she added, "You know drummers, hun. They're all muscle and they've got great rhythm."

Bob nodded at Donatello and thrust out his hand. "Howdy," he said with a broad grin.

Donatello held up his splinted appendage. "Donatello Dragghi. I no can shake your hand."

"Whoa! What happened to you?" Bob asked.

"The Mafia," Deborah said before Donatello could answer.

"The Mafia?" Bob repeated loud enough that the few remaining diners turned and stared.

Deborah rolled her eyes. "Yes, the *Ma-fia*. It's supposed to be hush-hush, even though you just announced it to the whole Sunset Strip."

Bob stared at Donatello a moment, then his face lit up. "Hot damn! I thought you looked familiar. I didn't recognize ya without the greasy hair, and no . . ." he said, rubbing his chin where a stubbly beard would have been. "You're 'The Bounty Killer!' Far-freakin'-out!" He grabbed Donatello's other hand and ardently shook it. "Man, I love that movie. Especially the part at the end when you blew that whole town away, lock, stock, and barrel for hidin' the banditos. I saw it in London. Ya know, England -- not the one in Arkansas."

Donatello visibly warmed. "So, you like *The Bounty Killer*, eh?"

"Yeah man, yeah," Bob replied. He stepped back and stared at Donatello as if he had been taken by surprise. "But, dang . . . I thought you'd be bigger 'n that. You're like a little banty rooster."

Donatello turned to Deborah. "What he say?"

Taking a long drag off her cigarette, she shot a stinging look at Bob. "You'll have to excuse him. He's from *Okla-homa* and he acts like a hillbilly. I've tried working on his manners, but -- "

"Yeah, yeah, yeah. You're whippin' a dead horse with all that crap, Deb."

Deborah blew a cloud of smoke out her nose. "I believe, in spite of all my crap, you're living in my house and driving my car."

"It might be your car, but no matter how you slice it, it's *our* house," Bob said. "But that's got nothin' to do with nothin'." He drew himself up and stretched. "Anyway, I'm leavin' for Frisco in the mornin', so I'm blowin' this pop stand. You comin' or not?"

Looking desperately at Bob, Slovika made the sign of the cross over her chest. *Maybe this man will take the devil woman away with him. Please, Saint Sara e Kali . . . please . . .*

Deborah paused. "I have to stop by the studio."

"What? You didn't say anything about that."

"I know. I forgot my questions for tomorrow's show. I didn't think it would be a big deal."

Donatello leaned forward. "I take you."

Please, Sara e Kali, I will do anything . . .

"Um, I don't know," Deborah muttered, winding a lock of platinum hair around her finger. "I want to stay, but . . ."

Please, God.

"Come on, Deb," Bob moaned. "Make up your mind."

"Oh, alright." She leaned toward Donatello. "If you're *sure* you don't mind. Besides, while we're at the studio I can add your name to the guest list, and we can talk about what questions you want me to ask tomorrow."

"I no mind," he said with a broad flourish of his bandaged hand. "But I am not, how you say, promettendo, uh, promise."

Slovika sank against the table.

Deborah looked up at Bob. "Well then, I guess you can, as you say -- 'blow this pop stand.'"

"Well, then I guess I'll see you whenever." He turned to Slovika. "G'night, Miss," he said, tipping his hat. He snugged it on his head, then looked over at Donatello. "Hey, great meetin' ya, Mr. Bounty Killer," he said with a shallow bow. "Just don't let Deb suck you into any a' her BS. I guaran-damn-tee she'll try ta turn ya into a wuss."

Bob sauntered toward the door. He turned and mimicked the action of pointing a gun and shooting off a round, and Donatello pretended he had been hit in the heart.

Deborah took Donatello's hand. "You're probably wondering about me and Bob", she said, tracing her fingernail over the bandages. "We used to be, well...*married*. Actually, we still are. Sort of. We kind of love each other and everything, but now we're just like, you know, friends. I mean, I *really* love Bob, but we're not exactly compatible. Know what I mean?"

He shrugged, then frowned and shook his head.

"Oh, Donatello, don't be so judgmental." She paused a moment and her eyes widened. "Oops. I forgot. You're Italian, so you're probably Catholic and you can't help it."

11

BUCK FUMBLED WITH the lock on a hotel room door. After a sharp click, he swung the door open. He set the plastic-fobbed key on an end table and dropped the suitcase beside the bed. Then tossed his jacket onto a chair and pulled his tie through his shirt collar. "I'm beat." Slumping onto the edge of the bed, he kicked off his shoes. "Even in Hush Puppies, my dogs are barkin'."

Pauline hung her coat in the closet. "It's cold in here and it smells like an ashtray," she said, wrinkling her nose.

"Hotel rooms are always cold and they always smell like cigarettes," he replied, taking off his glasses and stretching out on the bed. "Why don't you turn up the heat?"

"This is the oldest hotel in San Francisco. Why can't we ever stay someplace new?"

"I like it here. Besides, my father would roll over in his grave if we went to another hotel."

Pauline sat down beside him. She pinched the bridge of her nose and closed her eyes. "Oh Buck . . ." Her voice cracked and tears streamed over her cheeks. "Steven is so . . . so alone. I wanted to stay with him and . . ."

"I know. Come 'ere." Buck pulled her onto the bed beside him and put his arm around her.

"How could he do this? Everything is such a mess. And that horrible Dr. Buehler . . ."

"Yeah. I'd love to kick his pompous -- "

"Buck!"

"Well, I would. But, dislike him or not, seems like he knows what he's doing."

"Steven . . . he's so thin and . . ."

Buck held her tighter. "But he's alive. That's what we have to hold on to. There's nothing more we can do tonight."

"I guess you're right." She sighed and her expression softened. "You know, apart from the neck brace and the goose egg above his eye, he looks almost like he did when he was little. Older and worse for wear, but still Steven."

Buck smiled. "His head shaved like that reminds me of the time he fell asleep with gum in his mouth and you had to cut off his hair."

"Yes, and the time he and Roy got into that glue that wouldn't wash out," she added. "And the stitches remind me of the time he fell off Copper when you were teaching him to ride. Boy, that was something."

Buck stiffened. "Yeah. That was something alright."

"I still don't understand why Copper acted like that. He was such a steady horse. Why do you think -- "

"Steven fell off."

"I know. But how? After all this time, you still haven't told me. I know Copper was too big for him, but -- "

"That happened a hundred years ago. Right now, I need to shut my eyes."

"Buuuck . . ."

"Shhhh." He put his fingers to her lips. "Hush little baby, don't say a word or papa's gonna buy you a mocking bird."

"Stop it. Be serious." She slapped his arm. "I want to know how it happened and you won't even talk about it."

"Ow! I am serious," he moaned, rubbing his arm. "I'm so tired, if you don't let me close my eyes, you're gonna be the proud owner of a mocking bird."

"Buck..."

"Hush," he whispered. "We saw Steven. He's alive. The hospital's taking care of him, and we'll see him tomorrow."

"Aren't you even going to undress and get under the covers?"

He shook his head. The rise and fall of his chest slowed to a languid rhythm. Like thread drawn by a needle, he was pulled into an ethereal chasm. Falling into a restless sleep, he wandered into a dream.

> A hot summer's day. A familiar place. And a boy on the knife's edge of manhood. A sound breaks the silence. The boy hesitates at an opening in a blackberry hedge. He dreads to look because he already knows what he will see.
>
> He parts the thorned branches. A fight -- a fight to the death. The old black rooster is locked in a losing battle with his son, the young red cockerel.
>
> A sinking feeling comes over him. He tries to turn away, but the sight holds him captive. First, valiant ritual posturing. Then the rivals engage amid a rising cloud of dust. Wings beat against the air. Spurs slash. Feathers fall. Blood spills.
>
> The boy feels a heavy hand on his shoulder. He finds his father standing beside him. Without speaking, he pleads for his father to stop the battle, but his father looks away. The boy knows the cruel law of nature. Only one will survive. The black rooster will be supplanted by his son.
>
> When the boy looks back, the old rooster lies dying, and the young red cockerel is gone. He turns to plead with his father again, but his father, too, is gone. His eyes fill with tears. But before the tears fall the boy has become a man.

Buck woke with a start, drenched in perspiration and Pauline gently shaking him. "Buck, you were having a nightmare."

"Yeah," he gasped.

"The one about the bridge?"

He shook his head.

"The staircase?"

He shook his head again.

"The roosters?"

He nodded. "I hate that dream. I always wake up feeling like a sniveling little kid." He looked at a clock on the bedside table. "Almost three. Still a long time 'til morning."

Pauline rested her head on his chest. "I'm dreading tomorrow, but I can't wait for it to come."

Lying motionless, he listened to rain striking the window. He rolled Dr. Buehler's words over and over in his mind.

Wine and heroin . . . psychological addiction . . . transient ischemia . . . hemiplegic paralysis . . .

Like sharp stones, he tried to smooth them. But no matter how he turned the words, they still came up jagged.

12

SLOVIKA STEPPED OUT of the bright hotel hallway into the lonely darkness of the suite. "Saint Sara e Kali, why you didn't answer? He sends me back in a taxi. Alone." She threw her purse and a key with a brass fob onto a chair and closed the door behind her.

Always lies. Always excuses. Never the truth.

A pale moon spilling in through the picture window cast a long shadow across the floor. She took the last cigarette from a box on the table by the window and struck a match. The sulfurous aroma hung in the air a moment as she pulled the smoke into her lungs. Staring past the shadowy courtyard to the streetlights below, she pondered the dismal enigma of her marriage.

He pretends to love me. I pretend to believe him. Maybe I won't pretend any longer.

The traffic light changed from red, to green, to yellow several times and the cigarette went out. She dropped it in the ashtray, then took the bottle of vodka from the table and wandered into the suite's darkened marble bathroom.

Slovika set the bottle on the floor beside the tub and drew a bath. Slipping out of her clothes, she let them fall to the floor, then stepped into the tub and sank into the steaming water.

Silent. Weightless. Still.

A stream of tears slid over her cheeks, down her neck, into the bath. She reached for the vodka. Turning the bottle in the twilight, she paused a moment, then drank what was left in a series of choking swallows. Warmth spread over her chest, filling the void left by her tears.

As the bath began to cool, Slovika pulled the plug and watched with inebriated fascination as the water swirled down the drain. Holding onto the faucet, she pulled herself up, stepped out, and slid into in a thick hotel bathrobe.

Still dripping, she staggered into the living room, dropped cross-legged onto the floor and switched on the television. The flickering light danced through the room. An advertisement for a tour company lauded the virtues of the region.

> "The mountains."
>
> "The sea."
>
> "Disneyland."
>
> "Grahman's Chinese."
>
> "The Brown Derby."
>
> "The Walk of Fame."
>
> "The Sunset Strip."

"The Sunset Strip?" She frowned. "There, I have been. Now I am here, alone."

She changed the channel and sat back against the sofa. A teenage beach movie burst onto the screen. Little more than one song and dance number after another, the movie featured the teens on the beach, in their bedrooms, at school, and on surfboards with staged scenery moving behind them.

"I no know what they say, but I know they have fun."

Then, in a stroke of irony, a young Deborah Donaldson appeared on the screen. "That girl . . . she look like the devil woman, Deborah," Slovika gasped, staring aghast at the television.

She jumped up. The room began to spin, she lost her balance, and fell back on the couch. She struggled to her feet again and threw off the robe. Cool air brushed against the dampness of her naked skin.

Staring into the mirror above the sofa, Slovika straightened her back and struck a wobbly ballet pose. "I show you, devil woman, who dance best." She mimicked the teenagers motions, adding flamencoesque flourishes of her own, dancing until she could no longer stand.

"I do!" she announced with a toss of her head, then switched off the television and collapsed, panting and perspiring, onto the sofa.

She pulled the robe over her like a blanket. Lying motionless, her breath and heartbeat surrounded her.

When Donatello is here, then I will hate him. But for now, I am happy.

The muffled sounds of passion crept into the room from the suite next door. A single tear slipped down her cheek. She tightened the robe around her and pulled a cushion over her head. Sinking deeper into the sofa, she curled her knees to her chest.

I am Gypsy. Roma. Nomad. But nowhere to go.

13

DONATELLO STOPPED HIS car at the gate of a deserted television studio.

"I'm glad I finally talked you into doing my show," Deborah said. "When I find my list of questions, then we can discuss what you want to talk about."

A bulky man stuck his head out a window in the guard station beside the gate. He shook his head and whistled at the car like it was an attractive woman. "Hot damn. Nice wheels," he said, stepping out of the booth and waddling around the sports car. "I never seen a Freeari before."

Donatello forced a smile. "Is not Ferrari. Is Lamborghini," he said with a dismissive wave.

"Oh . . . a Lambogeni," the guard said, taking off his uniform cap and rubbing his forehead. "Sure is cherry. Bet it cost a bundle. How much'd it run ya?"

"Evening, Frank," Deborah interrupted. Leaning over Donatello from the passenger side, her breasts nearly rolled out of the top of her dress. "I need something from my dressing room," she said, tugging on the neckline.

The guard bent beside the car window. "Miss Donaldson? It's kinda late . . ."

"It'll be fine, Frank," she said with a slight slur. "I have the famous Italian actor and director, Donatello Dragghi here with me. He's doing my show tomorrow. Will you please put him on the list?"

"Yeah, sure," Frank muttered, still ogling the Lamborghini.

"So, how much *did* your car cost?" Deborah asked as she unlocked the studio door.

"My uncle, Lorenzo, in San Francisco, he give to me." Standing behind her, Donatello brushed her hair away and kissed the back of her neck.

"*Dona-tello . . .*" Deborah said with feigned irritation. She flipped a switch that illuminated a small reception area and a long hall, then dropped the keys on a table beside the door.

He followed her inside. The door closed behind them with a dull thud.

"I'm sooo glad you agreed to do my show."

"Why you say this?"

"I told you, I'd pay at the restaurant and call it business if you'd do it." She spun around. "Now you owe me."

He shook his head. "I no, sono d'accordo . . . how you say, agree just because you pay."

"Anyway, we'll talk about it later. Right now, I've got to get rid of these," she said, unzipping her knee-high boots and kicking them aside. "Before I forget, I'll add you to the guest list. Where's that clipboard?" She shuffled a pile of papers on the table. "There it is. Now, something to write with. I can never find . . . oh, I know." She rifled through her handbag and took out an eyebrow pencil. Dropping the purse on the floor beside the boots, she held out the pencil. "Write your name. I'm too tipsy."

He raised his splinted hand.

"Okay then, how do you spell it?" she asked as her eyelids sank half-way closed.

"Ah . . ." he purred, pulling her toward him. "Donatello . . . it start with 'D.'"

"I know that, silly. I mean your last name."

"D-R-A-G-G-H-I," he recited as Deborah scrawled it on the bottom of the page.

"There." She picked up her keys and took his arm. "Now, to find those questions."

The click of his heels and the soft patter of her stocking feet followed them down the long hall. She waved toward a wide double door. "This is where we'll be taping." They passed several other rooms, then stopped at a door with a yellow star and her name stenciled above it. "As you can see . . ." She pointed with exaggerated affectation. "This is my dressing room."

Deborah unlocked the door, opened it and led him inside. He slipped his arm around her waist and kissed her.

She giggled. "Dona-tello." She motioned to a bar on one side of a massive mirror. "Why don't you make yourself a drink? It'll be just a minute. Then we can, you know, work on what you want to talk about."

Looking around the room, he caught his reflection in the mirror. He ran his fingers through the dark waves of his hair and arranged his shirt to frame the crucifix hanging over his bare chest. After another glance in the mirror, he sauntered to the bar.

"Might as well pour me one," she said.

He opened the sliding door on the bar and took out two glasses. Pushing several bottles out of the way, he took one out and looked at the label. "Cento cinquanta uno?"

Deborah looked up. "One-fifty-one? Nooo. Better not have that; it's like firewater. We'd never make it in the morning."

He put the bottle back. "No vodka?"

"No, silly, I like rum. And, um, I also like scotch. Or brandy. *Actually*, I like vodka too, but I don't have any. So make mine scotch."

Donatello nodded. "Sì, duo scotch." He took out the bottle, fumbled to get it open, and poured the liquor into the glasses.

Taking a sip, he choked back a cough and wandered to a lipstick-red sofa. He pushed two books and a record album aside and set the glasses on a low coffee table. Positioning himself so his shirt fell open, he reached over, picked up a book, and propped his feet on the table. Beneath the title, *Master of the Mind*, the monochrome visage of a man stared back at him. "Who this is?" he asked, pointing to the cover.

She turned. "Oh, that's Parker. He's on the show tomorrow."

Donatello opened the book and read random bits as he flipped through the pages. "This seem . . . how you say, lunatic."

"Parker is a visionary. He writes about consciousness and transcendence." She went and snatched the book out of his hand, then picked up the other book and the record album, and set them on a nearby chair. "You'll meet him. The record and the books are what the other guests are selling. But I guess you'll just be selling yourself." She giggled.

He picked up his glass and studied her through the amber liquid. "As you do, amore mio?"

Deborah stared at him a moment, then shook her head. "Where are those stupid questions? They were in a tablet, right here . . ." She moved a pile of papers, dropped them on the floor, and began rifling through another. "Found it."

Donatello ran his hand over the sofa. "Deborah, come. Sit," he said, lowering his voice and thickening his accent.

She wandered to the couch and sat down beside him. "Okay. First the drinks, then what you want to talk about." She picked up her glass and tapped it against his. "Straight up."

"Sì, straight up."

"To my new actor-director friend, Donatello." Looking into his eyes she feigned a kiss, then took a long drink and set her glass on the table.

Staring back at her, he set his glass down and pulled her beside him. Gripping her hair, he pressed his mouth hard against hers and kissed her.

She sat up, sputtering and squirming out of his grasp. "*Donatello*, you're *absolutely* lecherous!" she said, then wiped her mouth and straightened her dress.

He threw his hands into the air. "What means this, how you say, leche-roos?" He thought a moment. "Leche'? I am like milk?"

"No, silly," she said, pushing her hair back in place. "It means, you know, like over-sexed, or something."

He threw his hands in the air again. "Deborah, why you say this to me? That is why you bring me here, no? To make love to you? Everything about you tells me that is what you want."

She crossed her arms and frowned. "Well maybe. But it's not as if it's ... *inevitable*. In spite of what some people think, I'm *not* a slut."

Donatello leaned toward her. "We cannot, uh, how you say it? Cambiare ... change what they think. Why should we live by their rules?" He put his hand to her face and stared into her eyes. "Deborah ... you and I, we are the same. We are like stars that shoot across the sky. The others, they cannot understand." He reached behind her and slowly unzipped her dress.

"But ..." she whispered. "I don't know ..."

He touched his fingers to her lips, then traced them down her neck and slipped the dress off her shoulders. "I want only what you want, Deborah."

14

EARLY THE NEXT morning Pauline stood in front of a mirror in the hotel bathroom, rummaging through her purse. She pulled out a black eyebrow pencil and a lipstick. After drawing harsh lines over her brows with the pencil, she spread waxy Hollywood-red over her mouth. She pressed her lips on a tissue, stepped back, and stared at her reflection.

Five years. How much have I changed?

With a discontented sigh, she dropped the lipstick into her purse.

She jerked a comb through her jet-black hair, then stopped, examining a thin white stripe at the roots. "Should've dyed it. I'm starting to look like a skunk." Gathering her hair at the nape of her neck with one hand, she reached for a hairpin with the other. The ends came loose and she started over.

"Are you almost ready?" Buck called.

"I'm having a battle with my hair," she called back.

"Well, surrender so we can get going."

Biting her lip, she twisted her hair into a tight knot and quickly wedged in several hairpins. She turned her back to the mirror and held up a compact. The ends of her hair escaped again, and she pulled out the pins. She looked up to see Buck standing in the doorway.

"Pauleeeen, will you *please* come on. We're not going to a fashion show."

"It's not even eight o'clock yet. Visiting hours aren't until nine and we're only five minutes away."

"What about traffic?"

"Alright, ten minutes."

"But I'm hungry. I don't want to eat at the hospital. I want to eat at the restaurant in the lobby. And we still have to rent a car."

"Quit nagging. It's been five years since I've seen Steven, and I want to look decent. Why don't you go down to the front desk and ask about a car, and get a table at the restaurant?"

The archaic elevator door clanged open and Buck stepped out. His heels clicked on the polished marble floor as he made his way to the front desk. The middle-aged clerk finished writing a note, attached it to a key, and looked up. "What can I do for you, sir?" he said with a practiced smile.

"I'm Buck Harper, room 515. I need to rent a car. The rental place at the airport was closed when my flight got in."

"Just a minute." The clerk went into an office behind the desk.

Buck drummed his fingers on the counter and looked around the lobby. *Same as it was when I was a kid . . . but everything else in the world has changed.*

Like ghosts from the gilt age of San Francisco, the granite columns and scrolled ironwork seemed to sigh under the weight of their fading grandeur, and the thick brocade drapery to shroud the lobby from the passing of time.

The clerk came back to the desk. "I can take care of that for you, sir. Shall I charge it to your BankAmericard?"

Buck pulled his wallet out of his coat pocket. "No, put it on this one," he said, slapping a Diners Club card on the counter.

"It'll be about half an hour," the clerk said as he copied the numbers from the card onto a charge slip. He passed the card back to Buck. "Should I ring your room?"

Buck looked at his watch. "No, I'll be at the restaurant."

He put the card back in his wallet, strolled across the lobby and stopped at a raised platform cordoned off by a fat velvet rope.

A host in formal dress unclipped the rope. "How many in your party, sir?"

"Two. My wife will be down in a few minutes."

The host nodded, motioned to a small table covered in white linen and pulled out a chair. Buck sat down and the host left two menus on the table.

A short time later, a bent silver-haired waiter with a towel draped over his arm came by. He cleared his throat. "What can I get for you, sir?"

"Just coffee for now," Buck replied, handing him a dollar bill.

The waiter returned a few moments later. "Your coffee," he said, setting a cup and saucer, and a small tray of sparkling coins on the table.

Buck took a sip, then shook the tray to rearrange the coins. *They still wash the change . . . thank God some things stay the same.* He looked around the lobby again. *Dad, what would you think of the world in 1968? Airplanes. Taxis. Diners Club and BankAmericard. And renting a car at a hotel . . .*

He stared out the window at the sky -- a patchwork of luminous white against a backdrop of cerulean blue. In seconds, he traveled decades back in time. In that same hotel lobby, he saw the crowd, and heard the enthusiastic shouts and fervent applause echoing from the past.

Women in long dresses with high lace collars. Men in suits carrying straw hats or bowlers. His father Senator Harper on a platform behind a lectern draped with an American flag. And his mother Nell, and several other thin-lipped women standing behind him. And behind them, a banner espousing the virtues of Prohibition.

Senator Harper raised his hands to quiet the rumblings of the crowd. "My fellow Californians, it is the duty of every good citizen to employ all industry to further the banning of liquor from our state, and our nation. Using no small influence, I have done all within my power to advance the cause of temperance!" he said, punctuating his remarks with an upraised finger.

"I will continue, zealously and tirelessly, to exercise my liberty in the prevention of evil and the suppression of vice! As long as I am your senator, in this jurisdiction we will have no bootlegging!"

"Here! Here!" several in the audience yelled amid waving hats and placards.

"And no speakeasies!"

"Here! Here!"

"No blind tigers!"

"Here! Here!"

"And I shall even go so far as to punish car rental companies for their involvement in the transportation of criminals and intoxicating spirits!"

Another shout.

"Therefore, I have no hesitation, whatsoever, in asking for -- no, demanding your vote!" Signs waving and hats thrown into the air, the Senator bowed to receive their accolades.

Buck shook his head. *I heard him practice that speech so often, I could've delivered it myself . . . except I didn't believe it.*

"Buck?"

He looked up.

Pauline stood beside the table. "I'm ready."

He put down his coffee, got up, and pulled out a chair for her. Sitting down again, he smiled.

No speakeasies and no blind tigers. Strange, I met Pauline outside just such a place. The good girl who wouldn't go inside.

Standing at the ICU nurse's station, Buck looked down at his watch. "It's past nine."

"The nurse is with your son," the nun manning the desk said with an unwavering stare. "You can go in when she's finished."

Buck turned to Pauline. "I thought the night nuns were bad, but the day nuns sure go by the book. You'd think she was guarding Fort Knox."

"Shhhh. She'll hear you," she said under her breath

"So what. I don't care if she does."

"Be patient. If you make her mad, we might not get to see him at all."

"Well, maybe if you didn't take so long to get ready, I wouldn't have to be so doggone patient."

Pauline crossed her arms. "We also had to wait for the rental car, remember?"

"Yeah . . . yeah . . ." he muttered.

She rolled her eyes, and an image on the periphery of her vision caught her attention.

A thin, barefoot young woman and a scruffy child stood a short distance away, staring at them.

The young woman's russet curls boiled out of a center part, falling in tangled tendrils past her shoulders. Her ice-blue eyes, outlined in black, were cold as a winter sky. She wore an old coat, long and loose, in velvet the color of wine, with strands of beads around her neck, wrists, and ankles. The child's strawberry hair hung in long, matted ringlets under a patchwork cap. And a tiny velveteen jacket topped a sweater and torn corduroy pants.

Pauline bumped Buck's arm. "Look. That girl . . . staring at us . . ."

He started to turn.

"No, don't be so obvious."

He glanced over his shoulder. "Barefoot tramps. Like Dr. Buehler said, the city's crawling with 'em. I'm surprised the hospital would -- "

"Wait," Pauline whispered. "Maybe she's the one who sent the telegram." She snapped her fingers as if it could jog his memory. "What was her name?"

"Hell, I don't know."

"Here she comes." Pauline grabbed his sleeve. "For heaven sakes, if it's her, act like you're happy to meet her."

The young woman stopped in front of them. "Are you Steven's parents?"

Buck stepped forward. Forcing a smile, he extended his hand. "I'm Buck Harper and this is my wife, Pauline." After waiting a moment, he dropped his hand and buried it in his pocket.

The young woman's lips trembled as the child sniffled beside her. "I've been waiting since yesterday, but they won't even let me see him!" she cried.

"What's your name, dear?" Pauline said in an overly cheerful tone.

"Shara Brennan," she replied.

"Sharon, how pretty. I've always liked that name."

A frown spread across the young woman's face. "It's Shara."

Pauline brightened. "Oh, *Sarah*. That's even prettier."

"It's not Sarah or Sharon. It's Shara. S-H-A-R-A. Steven told me you were old, but I didn't know you'd be *ancient*!" She glared at them a moment, then grabbed the child's hand and stomped away.

Buck looked over at Pauline. "What the hell just happened?"

15

HARRY RAY, PRODUCER of "The Deborah Donaldson Show," paused at the studio door. He raked his fingers through his steel-gray hair, then pushed the door open. *Shouldn't be unlocked.* Going inside, he tripped over a handbag and a pair of boots. "What the . . . why's this stuff laying around?"

He set a copy of "The Hollywood Reporter" on a table by the door and picked up the purse. The smell of perfume wafted around him as he opened it.

"Deborah."

Looking at the guest list, he squinted at the illegible scribbling on the bottom. "What's that?" he muttered, then shoved the clipboard under his arm and grabbed the purse.

A muffled knock echoed in Deborah's dressing room through the unlatched door. "Hey, Deb, are you in there?"

"Donatello?" she groaned, peeling her face off the red vinyl couch. She wiped the drool from her chin and looked around the room. "Donatello?"

Another knock.

"What!" she snapped, swinging her legs over the edge of the sofa and struggling to get up. "God, my head . . ."

"It's Harry. Are you okay?"

"Yeah." Stepping into her dress, Deborah pulled it up just far enough to cover her breasts. Holding the dress with one hand, she pushed her hair off her face with the other.

Harry opened the door and looked inside. "Deb, I found -- " His eyes widened, taking in the scene.

Papers scattered over the floor. Lingerie and stockings hanging over the arm of the sofa. Two glasses and an empty bottle of scotch turned on its side on the coffee table. An ashtray mounded with cigarette butts. And Deborah -- her hair a tangled mass, mascara smudged under her eyes, lipstick smeared over her mouth, clutching the front of her hot-pink dress.

He froze, holding out the handbag. "You look . . ."

"Awful?" she asked, then grabbed the purse and tossed it on the sofa. "Nice to see you, too, Harry."

Clearing his throat, he pulled a pencil from behind his ear. "Yeah, I mean, no. I meant to say hungover." He held out the clipboard and tapped the scribbling on the bottom. "What's this?" he asked, feigning nonchalance. "Looks like it was written with a crayon."

She yanked it out of his hand and tossed it beside the handbag. "It's eyebrow pencil."

Harry replied with a slow nod.

Deborah stared vacantly at him. "Is Susie here yet?"

"Who's Susie?"

"The new make-up girl."

"Not yet. Since we're doing the pilot, do you think it was smart to fire -- "

"Relax, Harry." Deborah turned and the open zipper revealed the languid curve of her naked back. "I don't have time right now."

He sighed. "Deb, what happened? I'm no Pollyanna, but this looks, well . . . bad."

She looked over her shoulder. "I don't want to talk about it. Least of all to you."

"We've worked together for years. This is a big break for you."

"Come here, Harry." Holding her dress, she pointed to the door. "What does that say? Right there, under the star it says, 'Deborah Donaldson'. Deb-o-rah. Not Deb. Not Debbie. And *definitely* not Harry Ray! It's my show, and my life, and I'll do what I want."

A pained expression clouded his eyes. "But, Deborah . . ."

"What?"

"It's just . . ." He took a long breath. "Just don't throw it away."

Her eyes flashed. She swung back and slapped him, leaving a row of fingernail marks across his cheek.

Putting his hand to his face, Harry stared at her and cleared his throat. "Well then, Miss Donaldson, when the new make-up girl shows up, you better get busy. We've got a show to do," he said, then turned and lumbered down the hall.

"What a jerk! Like he thinks he's my father!" Deborah slammed the door. She flicked on the lights and dropped into the make-up chair. Globe bulbs bordering the mirror bathed the room in a soft glow. She pushed her hair off her face and stared at her reflection. "He's right about one thing. Even in this light, I look terrible."

She licked her forefinger and rubbed the mascara smeared under her eyes. "God, what a hangover. I should've stopped after the first drink." *Donatello . . . when did you leave? You didn't even say goodbye.*

She fell into the chair. *Why aren't men ever as hot for me in the morning as they were the night before? I thought this time it would be different.* "I always think it will be different."

What's happening to me? She sat up in the chair. *Maybe I should do that skin magazine. Give my career a boost.* "Harry's against it, but so what . . ." She gathered her hair on top of her head and let her dress slip. Seductively arching her back, she drew her knees up and pointed her toes. *Besides, stuff like that doesn't matter.* She pursed her lips and blew a kiss to her reflection. *Parker says it doesn't matter.* She let her hair fall. "But, somehow, it always seems like it does."

16

A BOUQUET OF flowers, an unopened card, and a complementary continental breakfast waited on a room-service tray near the picture window in Donatello's suite. The sun rising in the pale beige sky splintered through an opening in the curtains. Though it promised to be as unseasonably hot as the day before, an icy chill hung in the room. Worse for wear after the all-night business meeting with Deborah, Donatello reeked of acrid smoke, and his eyes were an angry red. Sitting in statuesque silence, Slovika glared at him from across the table.

"Why you no open you card?" he asked with a tentative smile.

Breaking a hunk off a freshly baked croissant, she dropped it on her plate, then tossed the rest back on the tray.

He flexed the fingers poking out of the bandages on his hand. *I think it is my neck she wishes to break.* Drawing a daisy from the bouquet, he reached across the table and pushed it into her hair. "This morning . . . you look beautifool, amore mio," he purred, thickening his accent.

Slovika pushed her plate away.

"Come, why you so angry?" he said with a pout.

She glared at him. "Why so angry? If you no know, why you give me flowers?"

He threw his hands into the air. "What? Now I no can bring you flowers? It was business, for the publicity . . ."

"Ah, so you do know." Slovika stood, yanked the daisy from her hair and threw it on the table. Stomping into the bedroom, she slammed the door behind her.

Donatello looked at a clock on a table beside the sofa. *Time to go. Now she is in the bedroom with my clothes.* He shook his head and made the sign of the cross over his chest. *Ave Maria. Why women are so difficult? For a Gypsy bride who will give me no trouble, she gives me more than plenty.*

17

PAULINE REACHED FOR the door to Steven's room in the ICU. "Finally, we get to see him."

Buck caught her hand. "I need a minute."

"What?"

"Please Pauline, I . . ." He ran his finger inside his collar. "It's been five years. I just need a minute." He took a long breath and closed his eyes. After a moment he looked up. "Okay."

She opened the door.

Hauntingly thin and ghostly pale, Steven sat up in bed, supported by pillows. His head was immobilized by a tortuous neck brace. Shadowy circles surrounded his eyes, and stitches punctuated stripes of dried blood on the side of his face, and the purple-green bruise on his forehead.

He looked up. A blank stare of incomprehension preceded a flash of recognition. One side of his face remained frozen, while the other twisted into a grimace.

Pauline rushed past Buck to his side. "Steven, oh, thank God you're alive. We've been so worried . . ."

He sank back against the pillows and looked away.

She stared incredulously at him. "There is nothing, nothing, you could ever do that would make us stop loving you. You know that, don't you?" She watched him a moment. "Steven?" She turned to Buck; he stood frozen in the doorway. "For heaven sakes, say something."

He cleared his throat. "I need to talk to Steven. Alone."

She looked at Buck, then Steven, then back at Buck. "We haven't seen him for five years, and you want me to leave? Why?"

"There's a waiting room down the hall. I'll come get you in a minute."

"I don't understand. What can you possibly say to each other that I can't hear."

"I *said*, I'll get you in a minute."

Buck stood at Steven's bedside. *Now that she's gone, I can't think of a damn thing to say. For god sakes, say something. Anything.* A vacuous silence hung in the room and the antiseptic air seemed asphyxiating. He looked up and cleared his throat. "Your doctor tells me you can write."

Steven replied with a feeble nod and struggled to reach a legal pad on the nightstand.

Buck winced. *I can hardly stand this.* He set the pad on Steven's lap and handed him a pencil. "I can understand you not wanting to see me. But your mother -- there's no excuse for worrying her the last five years. She didn't do anything to deserve that. Whatever's been between you and me, stays between you and me. We leave her out of it. Agreed?"

Steven nodded again.

Buck's expression softened. "What happened, son?"

Steven drew a long breath. His face wrenched with effort as he printed several words, then held up the tablet.

WhY Do you CARe

Buck rubbed his forehead. "What kind of answer is that? Why do you think I wouldn't?"

Steven sighed, then held up the tablet.

I OveRdosed

"I know, but how? I mean why?" Buck shook his head. "I don't know what I mean." He stared at the floor. "Steven, how could you do this to yourself? I don't understand. I thought you were smarter than that. But you can be such a hot-head."

Steven scratched violently on the notepad. He looked up, his eyes hard as glass.

LIKE FATHER LIKE SON

Buck's face flushed, his hands coiled into fists. "What do you mean? Why do you always -- " *Stop. Don't upset him.* He turned and stared out the window.

Silence descended in the room.

Parting the curtains, he stared into the Parrish blue sky, then down at the bustling street below. *How can people go about their lives like nothing's wrong, when here in this room, everything is?* He rested his forehead against the glass. *God, I'm begging you. I'll do anything . . . just help him.* "I'm sorry, Steven. It's just, I can hardly stand -- "

A strangled, gasping sound interrupted Buck's soliloquy.

He spun around.

Steven's eyes rolled back, and the color drained from his face. Buck rushed out into the hall. "Nurse!"

A few minutes later, Dr. Buehler hurried into the room, flanked by an intern. Shoving a clipboard at the intern, he picked up Steven's wrist and took his pulse. Pulling a small flashlight from a pocket in his smock, he lifted Steven's eyelid and shined the light in his eye. He looked up at Buck. "What happened?"

"We were talking. I mean, I was talking and he was writing, and then he just sort of fainted."

Dr. Buehler took the clipboard, handed the flashlight to the intern, and motioned for him to look. "Well?"

The intern shined the light into Steven's eyes, then turned to the doctor. "A seizure?"

Dr. Buehler shook his head. "Exhaustion." He made a note and looked over at Buck. "He needs to rest. You'll have to come back later."

"But my wife . . ."

"I'm sorry. Your son's welfare comes first. That's why I limited visitation." With a broad sweeping motion and a forced smile, Dr. Buehler ushered Buck out of the room.

Buck shuffled down the hall toward the waiting room. *You've really done it this time.* He shook his head. "You just had to talk to him," he said under his breath. *Then you stand there like an idiot. And when you do say something...*

He stopped at the waiting room door. Sunlight filtering through the leaves of a potted palm cast a striped shadow on the floor beside Pauline's chair.

She's going to tear into me like nobody's business. He pulled his glasses off and rubbed the bridge of his nose. *Think! Not an actual lie. Just bend the truth.* Putting his glasses on, he pasted on a stoic expression, went in, and rested his hand on her shoulder.

She spun around. "You startled me," she gasped. "What's wrong?"

"Nothing. Except Dr. Buehler came in and said Steven needs to rest. But we can see him again this afternoon."

"What do you mean, again? I didn't even get to talk to him."

"It's not my fault. It's that damn Dr. Buehler."

"What did you do? You had to talk to him alone. You upset him, didn't you?" she said, slapping his arm.

"Ow! No."

"Honestly, Buck! You infuriate me. It's been five years, and I had less than a minute with my son . . . my only child!"

"Aw, come on, Pauline. Don't get upset. Dr. Buehler said we can see him later."

She glared at him.

"How 'bout we get something to eat? Early lunch?" he said with a hopeful smile.

"You can't be serious. Our son is in Intensive Care. How can you even think about food?"

"Since we can't see him until this afternoon, there's no sense in waiting around here. Come on. Pork baos at the usual?"

18

HARRY RAY LOOKED at his watch. *Two hours 'til showtime.* He slapped a pencil on the tall table by the studio door. "Relax, Harry," he muttered, mocking Deborah's nasal whine. "Relax? How can I relax? It's the biggest break she's had in who-knows-how-long and she's about to flush it down the toilet." He planted his elbows on the table and dropped his head into his hands.

Why should I care? The Deborah Donaldson Show isn't even something I'd choose to produce. If I had a choice. At my age, I should just be glad I've got a job.

The click of heels echoed in the hallway. A tall, thin young man with a dark Prince Valiant haircut, and a long chiseled nose came toward him carrying a clipboard. Walking with an exaggerated strut, he wore orange and brown striped bell-bottoms, a matching vest, and a ruffled, bright orange shirt.

"Good god, Clive Barlow wearing day-glo. Glorified gofer," Harry muttered. *The friend of a friend, of a friend, from London. How he acquired the title of assistant floor director and what he actually does . . . who knows.* "Always carrying the clipboard with vital information no one ever needs. He guards that damn board with his life."

"Harry," Clive chirped with a stiff British accent. He dropped the clipboard on the table. "The guest list. You left it in

Deborah's dressing room," he said, tugging on the bottom of his vest and staring at the welt on Harry's cheek.

"Clive," Harry said, straightening his boxy tweed jacket. He scanned the list. "Parker. What's his last name, anyway?"

"Are you daft? It's just Parker."

Harry rolled his eyes. "The folksingers. Cal Jeffries. But what the hell's this?" he muttered, rapping the pencil on the scribbles at bottom of the page. "She came unglued when I tried to ask her about it."

"Another guest," Clive replied. "But there's been no sign of him."

"She added someone at the last minute? Why does she pull crap like this?"

"Deborah has always played this way Harry."

"But why does she always skin the cat? Why can't she have a nice safe talk-show, with nice safe talk-show topics, and nice safe talk-show guests?"

Clive shrugged again and fluffed the ruffles on his shirt. "I can assure you I have no idea."

Just then, a short, round young woman burst through the door and nearly knocked Harry over.

"Hey, watch where you're going," he snapped.

"Good morning, Mr. Ray," she breathlessly replied, brushing a lock of curly hair off her face. "Sorry I'm late."

Harry jerked on the front of his jacket. "Late? Who are you?"

"Susie, the make-up girl."

"Well, Susie, Deborah's in her dressing room. You better get busy. She's a mess."

"Yes, Mr. Ray," Susie said, then hurried down the hall.

Harry turned to Clive and shook his head. "Another friend of a friend, fresh from cosmetology school. She'll be lucky to make it in this business."

Clive raised one eyebrow. "She'll be bloody lucky to make it through the day."

"Careful Susie," Deborah groaned, straightening a towel covering her shoulders and a short, low-cut navy-blue dress. "Ow!"

"Sorry, Miss Donaldson. The pin got stuck," Susie said, pulling a curler the size of a frozen juice can out of Deborah's hair. She set the roller on a tray holding curlers, hair-pins, and other beauty accoutrements, and picked up a comb.

Deborah frowned. "Stop calling me Miss Donaldson. It makes me sound so *old*."

"Yes, Miss Donald -- I mean, Deborah," Susie replied, ratting the back of Deborah's hair.

Deborah picked up a hand mirror and poked at the mound. "It's still too flat. Give me the comb." Biting her lip, she fluffed the platinum mass.

There was a light tap on the door. Clive peered into the dressing room. "Your orange juice."

Deborah motioned for him to come in.

Clive set the glass on the coffee table. "The illustrious Mr. Woo at the cafeteria refused to put the egg in it. He told me, 'That's not remedy for hangover. If you want to ruin orange juice, do it yourself,'" Clive said in a bad imitation of an oriental accent.

Deborah's eyes flashed. "I should have him fired!"

"But he relented and gave me one." Clive took an egg from a pocket in his vest. He bent and cracked it on the edge of the coffee table, dropped the contents into the orange juice. He stood and tossed the shell into a trashcan. "Now, something to stir it with . . ."

Deborah passed him a rat-tail comb. "Use the skinny end."

He stirred the juice and gave her the glass. "There. Your hangover remedy."

She took a long drink. "Thank you, Clive. Have a seat. You can act as referee between me and Susie."

Clive dropped onto the sofa. "And offer a parliamentary 'here, here' when needed?"

"Exactly. Isn't that what assistant floor directors are for?"

"You already have your dress on. Isn't that a bit risky?" he asked.

"As you know, we're running late. I need your opinion."

"Alright, I'm keen to have a go."

"What do you think? Is my hair too flat?" she asked, fluffing the mound at the crown of her head.

Sitting back, he crossed his long legs and cocked his head to one side. "Oh, no. It's appropriately over-done."

"Okay, Susie. Spray it."

"Yes, Miss Donald-- I mean, Deborah." Susie picked up a can, shook it, and engulfed Deborah in a cloud of resinous spray.

Clive coughed, yanked a tissue from a box on the table, and covered his nose. "God, that stinks."

"We all have to suffer for beauty," Deborah said.

"I don't know why I have to suffer for it," he replied through the tissue.

"Because my beauty pays your salary. You're starting to sound like Harry."

"Point taken. Speaking of Harry -- I gave him the guest list. He inquired about the illegible scratching on the bottom."

"And you told him . . ."

"Someone you added."

"His name is Donatello Dragghi. I met him last night."

Still holding the tissue over his nose, Clive quizzically raised one eyebrow.

"Don't look at me that way, Clive. Donatello is a famous actor and director from Italy. He made *The Bounty Killer.* It's the biggest movie in Europe right now. I'm sure you've heard of him."

"No, I can't say that I have. But if he is the biggest actor in Europe, he'd be bloody gormless to do your show."

Deborah frowned and pointed a frosted fingernail at him. "Mark my words, Clive Barlow, Donatello will be here. Excuse me while I manage my assets," she said with a seductive wink, then stood, smoothed her dress, and wiggled the neckline to settle her breasts. "After all, if I don't manage them, who will?"

Clive tapped the comb on his knee. "Cheeky, Deborah . . . very cheeky," he replied with a disinterested stare. "But, given the dismal state of your marriage, and the disappearance of the mysterious Mr. Druggie, or whatever his name is, you're probably right."

"Oh, Clive, you're perfectly square -- just like an ice cube."

"But, if you think about it, Deborah," he said, pointing the comb at her. "Ice cubes are usually *rec-tangular.*"

19

"SO, THE USUAL?" Buck asked.

Pauline sighed. "The usual."

"The usual" wasn't far from the hospital. It was just off the main thoroughfare, near the Dragon's Gate by an alley that ran between the streets of Chinatown. Buck parked the rental car and fed the meter. He helped Pauline out and stepped over a stream of rainwater spilling across the sidewalk from a downspout.

"I don't see how you can even think about food when Steven is in Intensive Care," she said.

"I know, but we have to eat sometime." Buck took her arm and they hurried across the street.

Ignoring the incessant hawking of a flower-cart vendor, they passed through the Dragon's Gate, then walked up two bustling blocks on Grant Street. Neon signs and striped awnings advertised touristy shops and eateries, and streetlights shaped like dragons punctuated the sidewalk.

"Smells like Chinatown," she muttered as they waited for a cable car to pass.

Turning into an alley, it seemed they left San Francisco and entered another country. Brilliantly colored buildings with pagoda-style roofs rose several stories above the busy, narrow street. Awash in Chinese characters, a multitude of vertical signs flanked the crowded assemblage of apartments, businesses, and restaurants. Crates stacked with goods and produce spilled out of storefront shops and groceries, vying with street vendors for space on the perpetually wet sidewalk.

They went around a withered man selling bamboo toys from a cart. "There it is," Buck said, stopping at a tall crimson placard glittering with gold characters. Below it, almost as an afterthought, a small black and white sign simply read, "Ping's."

Pauline shook her head. "Ping's. Every time we're in San Francisco, we go to Ping's. If we're anywhere near San Francisco, we go to Ping's. Even if we aren't hungry, we go to Ping's. Just once I'd like to go to a regular restaurant instead of a Chinese take-out."

"Okay, okay," he muttered. "You always say that."

"What if she isn't even here?"

"She'll be here."

Bronze bells tied to the door clattered as they entered the familiar hole-in-the-wall take-out. The Chinatown smells intensified as the door closed behind them. An expansive menu painted in brilliant red -- Chinese characters above, English translation beneath -- covered a gloss-white wall. Chinese beauty queens smiled from years of calendars papering another, and a gallery of yellowed, fading photographs hung on still another.

"Nothing's changed. Except the rubber tree," Buck said pointing to a plant that stretched up to the ceiling and sprawled across the front window. "It was only about two feet tall the last time we were here."

The jangling bells brought the proprietress, a silver-haired china doll, to greet them. A broad smile spread across her face, and her eyes disappeared into the roundness of her cheeks. "Mr. and Mrs. Harper!" she shouted, then bowed, and the Harpers bowed in return.

"Ping Ho Chan. You're still here." Buck laughed. "I thought you would have retired by now. "

"I never retire!" Ping said with mock anger. "You finally come to see me. I always think, why Mr. and Mrs. Harper never come? I wait for you. Where you been?"

"Just haven't been to the city lately," he said. "I knew you'd never forgive us if we were in San Francisco and didn't stop by."

Ping nodded, then pointed to a fading photograph among the gallery hanging on the wall. Two men -- one Chinese and one Caucasian, wearing archaic clothes and top hats, sitting on a raised wooden sidewalk. "You see, your father is still here."

"Still sitting with your father," Buck replied with a melancholy smile.

Ping bowed again. "We never take that picture down. We never forget your father. How he help my father to stay in this country when they want to send him back to China," she said as if the words had been polished by years of repetition.

Buck stared at the floor. *Mother, in all her supposed propriety, hated the Chans. And that photograph. Dad stood up to the liquor industry, but he couldn't stand up to her.*

"So, you eat here or take to go?" Ping asked.

"Eat here?" Buck repeated, looking over at Pauline. "We didn't know you had a dining room."

Ping crossed her arms. "That because you never come to see me."

"Well then, we'll eat here," Buck said.

"Good." She smiled again. "Wait to see what I show you. We not open for lunch yet, but I make you something special." She motioned for them to follow her behind a thick black curtain that separated the take-out from the kitchen. Past the curtain, she led them through a darkened doorway, then down several steps.

Four generations of Chans labored in the windowless, cauldron-like kitchen. Ping shouted at them in a torrent of Chinese. A pretty girl in a Catholic school uniform looked up from a pile of receipts on a tall desk. A woman who appeared to be Ping's daughter glanced over a mound of shrimp. Four boys stopped folding fortune cookies at a small table. And two men, sweating in sleeveless t-shirts, paused while searing strips of meat in a large wok over an open flame.

They stood at attention facing the Harpers a moment, then bowed.

Buck and Pauline bowed in return. After another rush of Chinese from Ping, one of the men poured a ladle of broth into the wok, and all the Chans disappeared in a hissing cloud of steam.

"Now, come with me." Ping led the Harpers through another doorway, down several more steps, to a foyer that opened into a large, underground dining room, covered with gleaming gilt wallpaper.

Light streamed from golden lanterns dripping with tassels, hanging in military precision from the ceiling. Black lacquer frames surrounded cranes, dragons, and tigers carved from coral, jade, and mother of pearl. Tables draped in white linen stood at attention on the garnet carpet, and seemed to march toward a vanishing point at the far end of the room.

Ping took menus from a black table inlaid with a baby Buddha holding a peach, standing beside an aquarium that was home to three fat goldfish -- two gold and one black as luck demanded. She seated the Harpers at a table with a large lazy-susan on its center.

"Ping..." Pauline said, looking around the dining room. "It's just beautiful."

"We work and work for many years, until we can pay for it. Now here we are, and you have all to yourself for now. I know you like pork bao," she said giving them each a menu. "You know what else you want?"

Buck opened the padded crimson folder with a golden dragon embossed on the cover. Columns of Chinese characters and rows of English words paraded across the pages, along with a seemingly endless list of numbered specials and combinations. After several minutes, he shrugged and shook his head. "Too many choices. How do we decide?"

Ping took the menus. "Okay, I make you something special. Like I make for your son."

Buck looked up. "You've seen Steven?"

"Yes. Not too long ago. He come sometimes with a red-hair woman and a little one. Where is he?"

"Uh... he's not feeling well," Buck replied.

"Oh." Ping looked away. After a moment, she looked up. "We get you something to fix him," she said in a bright singsong tone, then bowed again to no one in particular and went back to the kitchen.

20

HARRY RAY STOOD at the back of the television studio watching the crew. Cameramen waited behind a trio of TV cameras pointed at a semi-circle of tall chairs. Gaffers wrestled with a tangle of electric cords. A production assistant rifled through a stack of cue cards. And a pair of security guards blocked access to the set. *Amazing, the manpower and hardwork it takes to create effortless TV magic.*

"The reality behind the fantasy," he muttered. "When the lights go on, the fantasy begins."

Soft footfalls, hushed whispers, and the rustling of robes echoed in the hallway. An ominous, mystic void seemed to settle in the studio, accompanied by the aroma of patchouli, sandalwood, and marijuana.

Parker came in with a group of his followers, shadowed by a half-cocked security guard.

Clive hurried down a row of steps bisecting the bleacher-like seating. "Harry, he's here," he said under his breath.

"Who?"

"Parker, old boy. That symphony in beige is Parker."

Wearing a long, loose caftan of un-dyed linen, Parker appeared to be all of a single non-descript color. Neither white nor blonde, his hair was a shade somewhere in between and cut so short it was almost shaved. His skin -- the color of sand. And his pale eyes -- not quite green, blue, or gray. It seemed that in his presence, color simply drained away.

"*That's* Parker?" Harry said, wrinkling his nose as if he had smelled something fetid. "He looks like a lizard."

Harry rapped on the dressing room door. "Miss Donaldson, that Parker guy's here."

A moment later, Deborah swung the door open. "What did you say?" she demanded, digging her nails into her hips.

"That Parker guy's here." Harry turned to Susie. "You've got your work cut out for you. He's the color of bleached putty."

Susie glanced hesitantly from Harry to Deborah.

"Guy! Parker's not a *guy*. And he's certainly not putty!" Deborah snapped.

"Well, whatever he is, he looks like a half-baked biscuit."

She crossed her arms. "Parker is transcendent."

"More like translucent," Harry muttered as he turned and lumbered down the hall.

Deborah stared after him, then slammed the door so hard it bounced off the latch and swung open again. "He makes me so mad! How can he be so stupid?" She threw herself into the make-up chair. "Parker? A half-baked, bleached-putty biscuit? He's *practically* god!" She crossed her legs and drummed her fingers on the arms of the chair. The tempo quickened.

"It's probably because Harry's so *old*!" Swinging her leg in time with the drumming of her fingers, Deborah's whole body jiggled. "I don't know why I let him talk to me like that." She looked up at Susie's reflection in the mirror. "What are you staring at? Get busy making me beautiful."

Susie sucked in her breath. "Yes, Miss Donald -- Deborah." She paused a moment. Hands shaking, she dabbed a wedge of sponge over a bottle of liquid make-up and patted it on Deborah's face. Then she stubbed a fat brush into a tin of loose powder. With awkward strokes, she swept the bristles over Deborah's face and brushed the powder across her mouth.

"*Su-sie*, watch what you're doing! I don't know why I ever hired you," Deborah said, spitting the powder off her lips. "Oh, give it to me." Grabbing the brush out of Susie's hand, she bumped the tin and spilled the pink-brown powder down the front of her dark blue dress. "Damn it, Susie!"

Susie stood trembling as Deborah frantically swiped at her dress, smudging the make-up into the fabric. "You're . . . you're not gonna fire me are you, Miss Donaldson? I need this job."

"No, but I should! And quit calling me Miss Donaldson. Don't just stand there, do something!"

Susie scrambled around the dressing room, then looked up and froze.

"Now what are you staring at?" Deborah snapped. Following the trajectory of Susie's stare, her eyes shot open. Parker stood in the doorway, flanked by his emaciated disciple Gregg and a blue-suited security guard.

The guard put his hands on his hips. "Deborah, are they -- "

Parker stepped around him and seemed to float into the room. "Deborah, I had hoped for a moment alone with you, but . . ." he said, glaring at the guard.

"They're my guests," she replied with a thin smile.

The guard looked suspiciously at Parker and Gregg. "Okay, if you say so," he muttered and tromped away.

Parker took her hand. "Deborah . . . why such chaos?" Staring into her eyes, his words came slowly, and hypnotically, like dripping water.

She looked down at the powder smeared on her dress, then back up at him. "I don't know, it's just my dress and . . ."

He put his finger to her lips, and with a serpentine wave of his hand, he seemed to erase her words, her thoughts, and all of her actions. "Why do you worry about inconsequential things?" An expression of concern creased his brow. "I have been so anxious for your transcendence . . . not only for the intransience it will bring to you, but also for the balance it will bring to Orion. Yet I often wonder about your sincerity."

"Parker, I'm sorry," she replied. "It's just, my new show, and I've been so . . ."

He dropped her hand and backed away. "Oh. Of course. I understand. The material world and the entertainment monolith still hold your heart," he said, staring at the floor.

She went toward him. "No, Parker, really . . . really, I want transcendence . . . "

He looked up at her and smiled. "Then, that is what I want also, Deborah."

21

THE CHINESE LEFTOVERS had vanished into their customary paper cartons, and the fortune cookies made their entrance, when Ping came to the Harpers' table carrying a flashlight.

"Come, I take you to someone who will fix you something for Steven," she said over the clattering of dishes and chattering of diners.

Buck looked warily at the flashlight. "But . . ."

"No but. You come," Ping ordered, motioning for them to get up.

"What about -- " he said, pointing to the leftovers.

"Come with me."

Reluctantly, the Harpers got up, and Ping led them to a small doorway masked by gilt wallpaper at the far end of the dining room.

"The doctor is in the underground," she said, opening the door and stepping into inky darkness.

"Doctor?" Buck repeated.

Pauline grabbed his hand and dug her nails into his palm. "I do *not* want to go down there."

He jerked his hand away and flapped it at her. "Shhhh. Ping will hear you."

"What if there's an earthquake or the flashlight goes out?"

"Look Pauline, I don't want to go down there either." He turned and bumped his head on a low beam. "Ow, damn it," he grabbed her hand. "Come on."

The Harpers tottered after Ping down a short flight of steps into dank, chill air, heavy with the smell of mildew and a hint of urine. Their footsteps and the sound of dripping water echoed in the quiet as they followed the bobbing beam of the flashlight.

At the foot of the stairs, Ping flipped a switch. Bare bulbs strung on an electric wire revealed a long, arched tunnel. A hodgepodge of brick, stone, and bedrock, propped up by cracking timbers, connected a shadowy, ramshackle labyrinth beneath the streets of Chinatown.

Ping stepped over a trickle of water running the length of the darkened passage. The Harpers followed her over the thin stream, then around a pile of empty liquor bottles and used syringes. She turned at a support beam leaning at an obtuse angle and went down a side tunnel. A ragged cat scurried from a pile of wooden crates and metal cartons. After several more turns, Ping stopped at a crooked doorway, cut in a wall made of crumbling brick and loose rock. "This it," she announced, then opened the door and went inside.

The Harpers hesitated.

"Buck, I absolutely *do not* want to go in there," Pauline said under her breath. "Let's go."

"I don't either, but we'll never find the way back by ourselves." He took her arm. "Come on."

Descending a few rickety steps, they entered the shop. Lit by a single bulb, the room seemed claustrophobic, and the smell of decay filled the air. Wooden drawers marked by yellowed labels paneled one wall. Boxes, tins, and bottles of peculiar medicinal preparations crowded the dusty shelves of another. And a garland of desiccated bird's feet hung like a macabre necklace above the counter.

Buck stepped back and the garland brushed against his neck. "Ugh!" he gasped, swiping at it.

Then, a rustling sound, and like an apparition, an old woman in a long brown robe came out of the shadows. Her head was shaved and her skin so pale it seemed almost translucent. The fingernails of one hand were so long, they curled into spirals. She beckoned the Harpers to come closer with a single twisting nail.

Ping bowed and stepped aside. "Mr. an Mrs. Harper, this is Hai Yen. She is Chinese doctor."

Buck drew back. "*She's* the doctor?"

Ping nodded. "If you tell her what is wrong, she will give you something to fix Steven. I translate for you."

"We're not sure what's wrong with him."

Ping related the response to the doctor, who replied in Mandarin. Ping turned back to the Harpers. "Hai Yen ask what is his symptom."

Buck glanced at Pauline. "He's, uh, having trouble with the nerves on one side of his body. Like a paralysis sort of thing."

After a flood of Chinese from Ping, the practitioner closed her eyes and ran a spiraling fingernail over her face. She pointed heavenward, a burst of Mandarin ensued, and she disappeared through a curtain at the far end of the shop.

"She say she know something to help," Ping said with a definitive nod.

"What is all this stuff?" Buck asked, waving around the shop.

"Some is plant. Some animal. And some secret thing, only Hai Yen knows," Ping replied. "She is best doctor in Chinatown. She know the old ways. Steven will get better. You see."

A short time later the doctor returned with a small bottle of a murky green tincture and an eyedropper. She took a notepad and pencil from a drawer beneath the counter and handed them to Ping. Another burst of Mandarin followed.

"She say you give him a few drop two time a day in a little bit of water, and he will get better," Ping said as she wrote.

"What is it?" Buck asked.

Pauline took his arm. "Yes, what is it?"

Ping translated and waited for a response. "She say from a plant. She does not know the English name."

Buck looked hesitantly at the tincture. "Please thank her. Tell her we're honored such a respected doctor would help our son."

Ping translated again. The practitioner bowed and put the tincture, eyedropper, and note into a small paper sack, then gave the package to Buck.

"A few drop two time a day. Steven will get better. You see," Ping said, wagging a finger at him.

Buck reached for his wallet, but the doctor had already vanished into the shadows. "We didn't pay her . . ." he said.

"No charge. On the house," Ping replied.

"But . . ."

"You know better. Your father make it so we can stay in this country. It is my way -- "

"Ping, you've already paid a thousand times over. Besides, you know my father didn't do it for money. He did it because he liked your father."

"I know. But that makes it all the more a debt we cannot pay."

Buck shook his head. "There's no point in arguing with you."

"You right," Ping said with a wide smile. "Come, I take you back."

The Harpers followed her out of the apothecary shop. Past the leaning timber. Down the labyrinthine passageway. Around the pile of crates and bottles. Up the ramshackle steps. And through the small door. Out of dank darkness, into the bright clatter of the dining room.

"At least let us pay for the meal," Buck said, blinking as his eyes adjusted to the light.

Ping shook her head. "Mr. Harper, you know better."

"I'm glad you slipped some money into Ping's pocket," Pauline said as they went out the Dragon's Gate. "I feel guilty eating there for free."

They stopped at a street corner, waiting for the light to change.

Buck juggled a carton of leftovers and the package from the Chinese doctor to look at his watch. "We went from high-noon to midnight and back again in a little over an hour."

Pauline shook her head. "Never in my life did I imagine I would go into the Chinatown underground. I didn't even know there was an underground. It's as if we traveled through the center of the earth and came up on the other side, and we never even left San Francisco."

The light turned green.

"That shop . . ." he said as they crossed the street. "Filled with who-knows-what kind of dried-up dead stuff. That would've made Rod Serling run for the hills."

"And the doctor . . . her shaved head and those nails like horrible noodles. I didn't know fingernails could grow like that."

They stopped at their rental car. Buck put the carton on the roof and unlocked the door, then set it on the back seat.

"What are we going to do with all that food? We can't possibly eat it and we don't have anywhere to keep it," Pauline said.

"I dunno. Give it to someone at the hospital." He passed the small paper bag containing the tincture. "Here. Take this."

"What do you want me to do with it?"

"Hang on to it."

"You aren't thinking of giving it to Steven . . ."

"Of course not. It's going straight in the nearest trashcan. Even if she is the best doctor in Chinatown, we don't have any idea what's in it."

"My thoughts exactly," Pauline replied, dropping the package into her purse.

Buck looked up at the sky, darkening as another storm blew in off the bay. "Look's like rain."

22

HARRY LOOKED OUT at the studio from behind a backdrop on the set. A waterfall of voices resonated in the large, open studio as the audience began filling the bleacher-like seats.

Mixed bag. Tourists. Average folks. "And the old-time Hollywood regulars," he muttered, watching a group of elderly women in garish make-up sitting in the front row. "Still waiting for that big break."

More than the usual number of LA crazies. Way more. He watched Clive and the floor director, trying to control the crowd. *Earning your pay today, Clive, old boy.* He shook his head. *This is going to be a nightmare.*

Harry felt a tap on his shoulder.

"Having a reflective moment?" a middle-aged man with perfectly trimmed jet-black hair and a pencil-thin moustache asked. He wore a well-tailored charcoal suit that suggested he worked for the government.

Harry sighed. *Cal Jeffries. Only a little less irritating than Deborah and her basket-case friends.* "Just licking my wounds, sorting my worries and thinking about retiring in Tahiti."

"That bad?" Cal asked, taking a pen from inside his jacket.

"Not really. The audience is past capacity with people left over, we've got the crazy guru and his crowd, and Deborah added another guest last night who hasn't shown up yet."

Cal peered around the backdrop at the audience. "Wild group."

"Roar of the greasepaint and smell of the crowd," Harry muttered with a shrug. "Most of them are here to see that Parker character -- the maharishi, or guru, or whatever the hell he is. Apparently you can't separate him from -- "

"His lemmings?" Cal offered. "I'm looking forward to sparring with him. Thanks for the invitation; I'm assuming it was your idea."

"Don't mention it. Gotta have some balance between 'America's Little Sweetheart' being just hip enough to be interesting and throwing herself off a cliff into complete insanity. I'd bet, if anyone was betting, that Deborah's lost her mind. But her ratings usually prove me wrong." Harry paused, staring at the audience. "I've lived here all my life but, ever since the riots at Pandora's Box, I don't understand this town anymore." He looked up. "Hey, Cal, here's a news flash for you -- under all the phony Hollywood tinsel, guess what? There's real tinsel."

Cal laughed and took a small note pad from another pocket. "That's a great line. I'll give you credit the first time I use it."

A bell rang.

Moments later, Deborah came in with Susie, followed by Parker and his companion, Gregg, who was now shirtless.

Harry tapped Cal's arm. "Catch up with you later." He hurried behind the backdrop to the other side of the set and pulled Deborah aside. "What are you wearing . . . or not wearing? What happened to your dress and where are your shoes?"

"I changed my mind. And as you can see," she said, pointing a bare foot toward him, "I'm not wearing any. This is more in line with the theme of today's show."

"That's not from wardrobe."

Deborah put one hand on her hip. "I know," she said, waving the other over the short, beige caftan. "Parker's most trusted disciple, Gregg, let me borrow it."

"You're wearing some guy's shirt to tape the pilot? And he's going to stand around topless?"

"It's not a shirt," she said, smoothing the embroidered fabric over her torso. "It's a tunic. This is the look I want for my new show."

"Yeah, but the sponsors want Debbie Donaldson, 'America's Little Sweetheart' -- not some hippie-chick, wing-nut."

Deborah rolled her eyes. "Oh, Harry, relax." She took Parker's arm, and Susie and Gregg followed them to the set.

The bell rang again.

"Places!" the floor director shouted.

Clive hurried toward Harry. "The riff-raff Parker brought with him . . . we don't have enough seats and we can't get rid of them. They're stuck to him like glue. You try to move them and they go bloody ballistic."

"The guy Deborah invited -- tell me he's here."

Clive shook his head. "No sign of him."

Harry paused. "Okay. Push the chairs on the set back. We'll put the riff-raff on the floor at Parker's feet -- like kids sitting around Santa in a Perry Como Christmas Special. Keep the folksingers where we planned -- on Deborah's left. Put Parker next to her on the right. And Cal next to him. Leave the end seat for what's-his-name. Then, if he doesn't show, we can pull the chair off the set at the last minute."

23

AS THE HARPERS trudged down the hall toward the Intensive Care Unit, the institutional green walls and the antiseptic air seemed to close in around them. Passing the waiting room, something caught Pauline's eye. She tugged on Buck's sleeve. "You go ahead. I'll be there in a minute."

"What? I thought you couldn't wait to see Steven. You practically bit my head off this morning when Dr. Buehler kicked me out."

"I'll be just a minute."

"Don't take too long. The good doctor might change his mind again," Buck said, then continued down the hall.

A distant elevator chimed as Pauline peered into the waiting room. The young woman with the long russet curls and the child sat facing the window. The child sat beside her, holding a tattered book upside down.

Goodness, what was her name? Pauline pinched the bridge of her nose. *How could I forget . . . Shara.* She brushed her hands over her coat and smoothed her hair, then went into the waiting room.

A stale, smoky smell, redolent of incense and hemp hung in the air. Shara sat staring at a view distorted by rain as the child pretended to read.

Pauline cleared her throat.

Shara looked up. Freckles dotted her cheeks and blonde eyelashes fluttered above her ice-blue eyes, outlined in black and reddened by tears.

She looks like a schoolgirl -- much younger than I thought. Pauline forced a smile. "Do you mind if I sit down?"

"It's a free country," Shara said. "At least it's supposed to be."

Pauline sat across from them on a hard, vinyl-covered chair and settled her purse on her lap.

As the child pretended to read the book, Shara crossed and uncrossed her legs several times while twisting a lock of hair around her finger. She dropped her hair and fidgeted with a button on her burgundy velvet coat, then went back to twisting her hair. Her motions, abrupt and erratic, seemed almost like spasms.

"I'm sorry I misunderstood your name this morning," Pauline said.

"That's okay," Shara replied with a shrug. She turned the child's book upright, then began twisting her hair again. "I'm used to it. Everyone messes it up. My mom must've been drunk when she named me. Sorry I said you're ancient."

Pauline forced a smile. "Have you been waiting long?"

Shara took a sip from a flimsy paper cup with pop-out handles. "Long enough to have three refills of this yucky free coffee." She wrinkled her nose and set the cup on the vacant seat beside her.

The child looked over the top of the book. "Mommy sad."

"Oh?" Pauline replied.

Shara's lips trembled. "It's . . . it's been two whole days, and they keep hassling me, and they won't tell me anything." She sniffed and ran her fingers through her hair. "It's like, I'm freaking-out . . . ever since Steven overdosed, everything is so messed-up, I can't handle it. I thought when you guys got here -- "

Just then, the lights flickered, thunder crashed, and lightning tore the sky. Pauline and Shara jumped. The child screamed and dropped the book, bolted off the seat and scrambled underneath.

Shara reached under the chair, her sleeve bumped the cup and spilled the coffee. "Damn it!" she snapped.

Another flash of lightning. A clap of thunder. And the crying child backed further under the chair.

Shara dropped to her knees on the floor. "It's just thunder," she said, then grabbed the child's arm and yanked it. "I *said* come on!"

The child screamed, and she burst into tears.

Pauline moved to a chair beside them and rested her hand on Shara's shoulder. "It's alright, dear. It's just a storm."

Shara jerked away. "I know. I'm not stupid!" Throwing her hands into the air, a fresh stream of tears came. "I've been waiting all day! They won't let me see him! And they won't even tell me if he's alive!" she shrieked between sobs.

Pauline sat back and fumbled in her purse. She took out the paper bag holding the Chinese medicine, set it on the chair next to her, and pulled out a tissue. "Here."

Shara grabbed it and wiped her eyes. "Those stupid Nazi-nuns and that ego-maniac doctor! He's such a jerk!" Another flood of tears came. She blew her nose and twisted the tissue into a knot.

"I hate to say it, but that makes two of us. He kicked my husband out of Steven's room this morning. I only had a few minutes with him."

Shara looked up; streaks of eyeliner ran down her cheeks. "You saw Steven?"

"Yes. Only for a minute."

"But you saw him? And he's alive?"

"Why, yes, dear. Worse for wear, but he's alive."

Shara coaxed the child out from under the chair and sat down next to Pauline.

"You have a beautiful little one," Pauline said. "How old is . . ."

Shara pulled the child onto her lap. "He's three," she said, taking off his patchwork cap.

Gracious, he looks like a girl. "Three? What's his name?"

"Donovan." Separating his matted, golden-red hair into strands, she wove them into a loose braid.

"Donovan," Pauline repeated.

"I named him after Donovan, the musician. He used to be my favorite singer."

"He's not anymore?"

"No," Shara said, wrinkling her nose. "Now I'm into Dylan. But luckily, I still like the name," she added as Donovan settled against her, sucking his thumb.

"I do to. It's a wonderful name. He looks almost like Steven did at that age. Except he has your coloring."

"Like father, like son," Shara said, brushing a stray curl away.

Pauline caught her breath. The elevator chimed again. *My God, she said that as if it was nothing at all.* She froze, looking at Donovan. *Steven's son. My grandson. Dirty. Barefoot. Frightened.* She looked over at Shara. *And she's his mother.* "Then you're Steven's . . ."

"Girlfriend," Shara replied. "We live together."

Try to appear casual. "Oh. And how old are you, dear?"

"Eighteen."

Pauline's jaw dropped slightly. *Eighteen? Three? Dear God, she was only . . .*

Donovan sniffled. "Who da wady, Mommy?" he said with his thumb still in his mouth.

"She's your grandmother," Shara replied.

"Wha's a gwamodder?" he asked, looking quizzically at Pauline.

"I'm your daddy's mommy. But you can call me Gramma." Pauline paused, recalling the family picture above her kitchen sink. *Grandmother. Somehow that one word makes the picture complete.*

Buck drummed his fingers on the desk at the ICU nurse's station, staring at another militaristic nun.

"If you'll wait for just a minute," she said.

She looks like Charlton Heston in a habit. "That's all I've been doing since I got to San Francisco."

"As I said, just a minute."

Several minutes passed.

The nun returned. "Your son is resting now. Dr. Buehler's orders are, he is not to be disturbed," she said with an authoritarian tone. "He had an unfortunate *incident* this morning. You can visit again tomorrow."

"Damn," Buck grumbled under his breath.

"Excuse me?"

"Sorry. What the hell am I supposed tell my wife? She hardly even had a chance to see him," he said, waving toward the waiting room.

"Well, I'm sure I don't know, sir," the nun said with a huff. "Perhaps the truth might be in order."

Buck shook his head and shuffled down the hall. *Can't let on I had anything to do with it. Blame it on Buehler. Why not? It's not an actual lie and Pauline can't stand him.*

He stopped at the waiting room door.

Pauline, that girl and the kid . . . talking like they've known each other all their lives. Play my cards right and I'm off the hook. He went in and sat down across from them.

"What's wrong?" Pauline said.

"Nothing. Except Dr. Buehler said Steven can't have any more visitors today."

"What? Why?" Pauline and Shara said in unison.

Steady . . . "The nun at the desk said, Dr. Buehler said, Steven needs to rest. We'll have to come back tomorrow."

Pauline looked suspiciously at him. "Why?"

Don't flinch . . . "Hell, I don't know. That's what she said."

Shara rolled her eyes. "Great. Just great. I hitchhike all the way over here again for nothing."

There was an awkward pause as Buck, Pauline, and Shara stared at each other.

"Well, that's that," Buck announced, brushing his hands together as if he had finished an unpleasant task. "No sense in waiting around here."

Pauline turned to Shara. "Can we take you somewhere, dear? You two can't hitchhike in the rain."

"Um . . ." She glanced out the window. "We could use a ride back to Berkeley."

24

HUNGOVER AND IRRITABLE, Donatello rolled past a police car and a disheveled gathering on the sidewalk outside the gate of the television studio. He slid his sports car to a stop. A barefoot girl in a short crocheted dress with a pentagram painted on her forehead blocked the driveway. Flashing a seductive gap-toothed grin, she draped herself over hood of the car, dragging an armful of bracelets across the paint.

"Porca vacca cavolo! Get away!" he snapped, waving his splinted hand at her.

The guard leaned out of the booth. "Hey, I told you to beat it!" he yelled at the girl.

She smirked and rolled her eyes, then sauntered off.

The guard manufactured a smile. "What can I do for you, sir?"

"The Deborah Donaldson Show," Donatello grumbled.

"Ah, 'America's Little Sweetheart,'" the guard said with a wistful look. "I'm sorry, there aren't any more tickets for her show. The studio's full -- past capacity. And as you can see, there are lots of fruitcakes still waiting to get in," he added, pointing to the gathering on the sidewalk. "All over the place. On the street. Crawling under the gate. Climbing over the fence. We had to call the cops."

"But Deborah expect me. I am guest on her show."

"Your name?"

"Donatello Dragghi," he replied, drumming a staccato rhythm on the steering wheel.

The guard pulled a clipboard off the wall and scanned it over the top of his glasses. "Nope. You're not on the list."

Donatello slapped the steering wheel. "The fat man last night -- he put me on!"

"Oh, must've been Frank. Well, I can call -- "

"Sì! Sì! Call!"

The guard picked up the phone.

Looking heavenward, Donatello kissed his thumb, then made the sign of the cross over his chest. "American, così stupido," he said under his breath.

A few minutes later the guard leaned out of the booth. "They're waiting for you Mr. Dragghi," he said, then pressed a button and raised the gate. "It's the second studio on the left. Have a nice -- "

Before he could finish, Donatello gunned the engine, shoved the car into gear, and left a layer of rubber on the driveway.

"Places everyone! We'll have to go with what we've got," the floor director yelled, rapping a conductor's baton on a music stand.

Just as Clive was about to drag the extra chair off the set, footsteps echoed in the hall. Donatello swaggered in, wearing a champagne-colored sharkskin suit with a black silk shirt open half-way down his chest.

"Donatello! You came!" Deborah gushed.

"Ciao, amore mio," he said with a smile that seemed to charge the atmosphere with electric sexuality.

Clive motioned to the vacant chair beside Cal. "Please have a seat."

Donatello made his way around Parker's entourage sprawling on the floor and sat down.

"Places!" the floor director shouted, waving the baton. "All right everybody! Deborah! High-beam smile!"

White-hot TV lights flooded the studio with smell of ozone. A red lamp on top of the center camera flared and the director counted down the seconds.

Five.
Four.
Three.
Two.
One.

He pointed at Deborah. "You're on!"

The show's theme song, a big band version of a surf song, erupted from overhead speakers. Deborah looked into the camera and flashed a wide smile. "Welcome to the Deborah Donaldson Show!"

A crewmember held up a card reading: APPLAUSE! And another waved wildly to energize the audience.

"Let's welcome our guests. This is Parker, founder of The Orion Institute in Big Sur. And the author of the sure-to-be bestseller, *The Master of the Mind*." She held up his book, and the camera came in for a close-up of Parker's face on the cover.

The cue card went up again. Enthusiastic applause filled the studio.

Parker placed his hands together and took a shallow bow. The red light moved from one camera to another. Deborah turned to Cal. "And Calvin Jeffries," she announced with a noticeable lack of fanfare. "The conservative philosophy and religion reporter for the LA Examiner," she added, holding up his book.

The crewmember hoisted the cue card. There was a tepid response.

"Now," she said with a magician-like wave. "Let's welcome Donatello Dragghi, the star and director of the *fabulous*, soon-to-be released motion picture, *The Bounty Killer*! He's already taken Europe by storm and he's about to do the same thing here. Let's give him a real Hollywood welcome!"

Donatello stood and bowed. He smiled and waved, and the audience burst into applause, cat-calls and whistles.

Deborah motioned to the folk trio, standing behind a row of microphones to one side of the set. "And our musical guests, Blowin' in the Wind!"

"Let's thank 'Blowin' in the Wind' for their *won-derful* acoustic version of 'Ride That Wave,' the theme song from my movie, *Beach Balls and Bongos*," Deborah gushed, holding up the folk singers' record album.

The folk singers dropped into a deep bow and sprang up again. As the audience applauded, the female singer gave her tambourine a gratuitous rattle.

"Cut to commercial!" the floor director shouted, and the lights on the cameras went out.

The trio maneuvered around Parker's followers and sat on the vacant chairs in the semi-circle. Susie came and dabbed powder over Deborah's nose and forehead as Clive traded the record album for Parker's book.

"Deborah! High beam!" the director shouted a few moments later, then counted down the seconds again.

The light on the center camera flared and Deborah flashed a toothy grin. "Welcome back. We're talking to Parker about the Orion Institute and his *fantastic* book, *Master of the Mind*. Parker, tell us all about it."

"Deborah, you've been to Orion," he said with a perplexed stare. "You know the principles and you've read *The Master of the Mind*."

"Well, yes. But tell the audience."

"As you know," he said in an odd drone, "and as I illuminate in *Master of the Mind*, we each have our own existence -- separate and isolating. But at Orion, in the simplest sense, I teach the unification of an individual into the collective existence of the divine. By getting out of our own separate, isolating minds and offering our individual, eternal, internal selves to the universal collective consciousness, we can find true freedom -- or what I call the art of the mind."

Cal cleared his throat. Leaning forward, he clasped his hands together. "In essence, did you just say that you teach people to go out of their minds?"

Deborah frowned. "No, he did not say that." She twisted in her chair. "Parker, please go on."

Parker turned to the audience. "As I explain in my book, the life you create for yourself in this sphere or time-space continuum, will be either a work of art, a masterpiece, your magnum opus. Or a cheap cookie-cutter, assembly-line version of the substandard existence the unenlightened consider . . . *normal*."

He stared at Cal a moment, then looked at the audience. "At Orion, we practice the art of the mind. Evolving. Eternally evolving. Expanding consciousness by mastering the mind. Deborah, may we demonstrate a foundational Orion principle -- the first step to the unification of a soul into the divine?"

"Why, of course," she replied as Harry and the floor director exchanged perplexed glances.

Parker motioned for his entourage to stand. "Any in the audience, who wish to, may join us."

A few audience members came down from the bleachers and the folksingers got out of their chairs.

"Pair off and face one another." Parker waited as the participants positioned themselves. "First, call yourself into awareness. Let your true self to come to the forefront and just *be* . . . honest . . . real . . . everything you are, and everything you wish to be, right now, in this moment. The past is a vapor and the future exists only as a thought. Don't allow yourself to hide. What you see in front of you is far less real than what actually is."

He paused a moment. "Look deep into each other's eyes, into the eyes of the soul. Call that person's soul into awareness. Don't hide from each other. Break down the walls, tear down the judgments, take down the façade and allow the other person in. Can you do it? Can you stay fully aware, fully real, fully united, here in the now? It is more difficult than it seems, because the ego often runs from the reality of the now." With a flourish of his hand, the white-hot TV lights glinted off a massive diamond ring on his little finger.

"Awareness . . ." he continued. "Can you see it in their eyes? Awareness of nothing? Awareness of some things? Awareness of all?"

As the participants stared at each other, more than one person began crying. And one woman began to wail. She broke from the group and rushed out of the studio, leaving her partner standing alone.

Tears filled Parker's eyes. "Awareness . . . it can be exhilarating or excruciating." He paused a moment. "And so very often, it is both."

25

THE HARPERS WAITED with Donovan beneath a dripping gable on the doorstep of a brown-shingle house in Berkeley. Trees, just beginning to blossom, shuddered against the rain and a cold wind blowing in off the bay. Buck shifted the box of Chinese leftovers, then turned and looked down the street to the fuzzy outline of Alcatraz, shrouded in fog. "Nice view," he said.

"Mommy, hungwy," Donovan whined as Shara rummaged through her crocheted handbag.

"Found it." She pulled a key from her purse. "I'll get you something to eat in a minute."

"Hungwy, Mommy . . ."

"It's my friend Roxanne's house," Shara said, unlocking the door. "We just sort of permanently crash here." She opened the door, looked in, then abruptly closed it again. "You can put the Chinese stuff down, and I'll take Donovan," she said with a nervous flip of her hand.

"Why, we wouldn't think of it," Pauline replied.

"No, really."

"Pauline, maybe we should -- " Buck began.

"Nonsense."

Shara took a deep breath. "Well, okay . . ." She swung the door open and the Harpers followed her into the darkened house.

An electric guitar wailed from a turntable. Jim Morrison joined in, screaming, the chorus of "Light My Fire." Pungent smoke and incense choked the air. Peace signs and daisies hung from a mobile on the ceiling. Worn oriental rugs covered hardwood floors. Nouveau lithographs and fluorescent posters -- psychedelic announcements in swirling script from the Fillmore, Cow Palace and Avalon Ballroom, papered the walls.

In the center of the room, a mattress, spread with tapestry. And languishing on the mattress, a woman in her mid-thirties wearing a faded blue kimono and a man perhaps ten years younger, lying beneath a sheet.

The woman glanced up. "Oh, Shara, ish you," she slurred.

Shara looked back at Buck and Pauline. "That's Roxanne," she said under her breath. "But I don't know who the guy is. The kitchen's this way." Taking Donovan's hand, she stepped around a pile of clothes beside the mattress and hurried to a narrow hallway.

Pauline looked helplessly at Buck.

He shifted the leftovers from one arm to the other. "Satisfied?" he whispered. "Maybe this'll teach you to mind your own business!"

They followed Shara around the mattress, down a hall stenciled with a mural of Ché Guevara, into the kitchen. Beer cans, liquor bottles and garbage climbed out of a trashcan onto the cracked linoleum floor. Shara set Donovan on a stool at a counter, sticky with grime and stacked with dirty dishes. She moved a chipped bowl crusted with dried oatmeal and set it in the sink. "You can put the Chinese stuff there," she said, pointing to the vacant spot on the counter.

Buck pushed a skillet out of the way, set the box down, then stepped back beside Pauline, who stood like a statue in the center of the room.

"Mommy, I hungwy," Donovan whined again.

Shara sighed. "Okay. I'll make you something." As she opened a cupboard and pulled out a plate, a pair of roaches joined together at the back end fell onto the counter, then separated and scurried away.

Pauline caught her breath. Clasping her hand over her mouth, a tiny squeal snuck out.

Angry voices echoed from the living room. "I can't help it, they came walking right through! How was I supposed to know?" Roxanne screeched.

The man's voice reverberated, "I'm outta here, you stupid mother -- "

"Mom-mie! Hungwy!" Donovan screamed, kicking a cabinet door and bursting into tears.

Then the front door slammed. The wailing guitar stopped, and the stereo needle scratched across the record. A few moments later, Roxanne came and slouched in the kitchen doorway. "Thanks a lot. He took off," she slurred. She brushed an earring made from the eye of a peacock feather off her face and the frayed kimono shifted, falling open over her bare breast. "You really know how to wreck a good time," she muttered, straightening the kimono and staggering into the kitchen. "Wha's this?" Peering into the box of leftovers, she opened a paper bag with a pagoda printed on it and pulled out a small carton. "Oh, Shinese." She looked up at Shara with a dejected stare. "You went to Shinatown without me?"

"No, I was at the hospital. They brought it," Shara replied, motioning to the Harpers.

"Oh." Roxanne put the leftovers back in the box and turned to Buck and Pauline with a look of surprise. "Who a' you?"

"They're Steven's parents."

Roxanne shrugged. She shuffled to the refrigerator, yanked the door open and pulled out a bottle of milk. "You're lucky I found him when I did, 'cause he almost croaked." She took several long gulps from the bottle, shoved it back in the refrigerator, closed the door, and staggered out of the kitchen.

"Don't mind her," Shara said, shaking her head. "She's super weird when she's stoned."

―――∞―――

Berkeley merged into Emeryville, and the freeway passed a soggy spit of land sandwiched between the road and the bay. Rain turned to drizzle and blue sky broke through the clouds.

"Looks like the mudflat scavengers have been busy," Buck said nodding in the direction of a group of make-shift sculptures constructed from debris left by the outgoing tide. "There's the Red Baron. And the windmill. The guy with the head made out of a tire. Don Quixote and his horse. Hey, look, now there's a space ship, and one of those peace sign things, and 'End War' made out of driftwood."

He looked over at Pauline; she stared straight ahead, lost in thought. "Hey, did you hear me?"

She shook her head. "Um, no, I didn't."

"I said, the mudflat scavengers have been at it again."

She nodded.

Silence settled in the car again.

"Hand me my wallet, will ya'?" Buck said as they came to a toll booth on the Bay Bridge. "It's in my jacket pocket."

Pauline pulled out his wallet and gave it to him. He slid the car to a stop and paid the toll. The attendant waved as they drove away.

She turned to Buck. "Did you notice how quiet he is?"

"The tollbooth guy?"

"No, Donovan. He's three years old. Normally you can't keep kids quiet at that age."

Buck drummed a dirge-like rhythm on the steering wheel, as the traffic on the bridge came to a halt. "No, I didn't notice. Except when he was screaming."

"Surely you must have."

"No, Pauline, I didn't. I was busy trying not to see everything I saw."

"What?"

"The mattress in the living room. All the stuff hanging on the walls. The guy under the sheet. That Roxanne woman and her sagging kimono. Not to mention the roaches. It was like we went into another world."

Pauline grabbed his sleeve. "We have to do something. We can't let him live like that."

The muscles in Buck's neck tightened. "Pauline, like it or not, Steven is an adult. We don't -- "

"Not Steven. Donovan."

Buck turned and stared at her. "Pauline, that kid is none of our business." He turned back to the road. "You can't go around picking up all the strays in the world. We've got enough trouble with Steven right now without adding that kid to it."

"But -- "

"Pauline, please."

"Buck, 'that kid' . . . is your grandson."

26

PARKER PLACED HIS hands together and bowed. "You, in the studio, who experienced the first Orion Principle are beginning an ascension out of the individual, and transcending into the collective consciousness of the divine."

Gathering his caftan around him, he took his seat. His entourage and some who had been sitting in the bleachers, sat at his feet.

"May all of you continue to experience a transcendent reunion with your inner self," he said with a grandiose wave.

Donatello shook his head, He took his gold cigarette case from his pocket. *Why he goes on and on? If he talks the whole show, why Deborah asked me to come?* Holding the case in the crook of his arm, he managed to take out a cigarette. Cal produced a lighter, leaned over, and lit it for him.

"Grazie," Donatello said under his breath as he slid the case back in his pocket. Slouching on the stool, he crossed his legs and took a long drag. The smell of burning tobacco wafted over the set. He watched Deborah watching Parker, balanced on the edge of her seat almost to the point of falling off. *As if he hypnotizes her, she looks at him like he is god.*

"As you can clearly see," Parker droned. "Those who participated have gone into another sphere."

"Looks like they're all still here to me," Cal said with a dry chuckle.

Donatello half-heartedly nodded and took another drag off the cigarette. Blowing smoke out his nose, he tapped the ash onto the floor beside his chair.

"Oh, you may still see our outer selves," Parker replied. "But we, the eternal, internal we, have gone on to another sphere. But you," he added, glaring at Cal, "are like an unenlightened person holding a frog. The frog sheds its skin, and you are left holding the empty visible remains. And you, being unenlightened as you are, have no idea where the transcended frog has gone."

"But frogs don't shed their skin," Cal said with a dead-pan stare. "That's a flawed metaphor, if ever there was one."

Deborah crossed her legs and drummed her fingers on Parker's book while wiggling a bare foot. "Parker is speaking metaphysically. Will you *please* let him finish?" she said in a terse tone, as her talk-show façade began to crack.

With another dramatic flourish of his hand, Parker waved Cal's comment into oblivion. "Never mind, Deborah. His statement is just as irrelevant as he is."

"Is it sort of like what goes around, comes around?" the female folksinger asked.

"Not exactly." Leaning forward in his chair, Parker absently twisted the diamond ring on his little finger. "Most people will never reach the circularity of enlightenment. They are not even aware of it's existence, though it is both within them and around them, simultaneously."

"Circularity?" Cal said with a frown. "Circular logic gone to seed. I won't insult your intelligence by assuming you actually believe that -- it's utter nonsense."

Parker's eyes darkened. "Nonsense? In a sense, it is just another form of sense, isn't it?" He shook his head. "Like you, the caterpillar is unable to comprehend how the butterfly can become a moth."

"You obviously flunked biology. Let alone that butterflies don't turn into moths, and frogs don't shed their skin . . . what makes you think a caterpillar can comprehend anything?"

"Will you *please* shut up and stop interrupting!" Deborah snapped.

Parker raised two fingers in a saint-like affectation. "I need no help defending myself, Deborah. Love is my defense. And I have nothing to hide." He turned to Cal. "To you, and those in your deficient sphere of *un-being*, I admit nothing. In your narrow existence, you will never understand." Tears clouded his pale eyes. "Do you want to know the truth?"

"That would be refreshing."

"Then I will tell you." He motioned to the crowd on the floor. "They are dying and I must save them."

Cal half-smiled. "God complex?"

"No, god."

"Well, not *god*," Deborah said with a nervous giggle. "You mean a form of god."

"No, Deborah, I mean god." Parker stared down the bridge of his nose at her. "This would not be so incomprehensible to you, if you had extracted yourself from this soul-draining entertainment monolith and the incessant lure of fame, given your offering, and immersed yourself in the truth of Orion."

Harry slapped his forehead. He made a rolling motion at the floor director, and the show's theme song burst from the speakers.

"Cut to commercial!" the director shouted.

Harry summoned Deborah with a wave She slid off her chair, and stepped around Parker's entourage.

Harry took her arm. "Tell me I didn't just hear him say he thinks he's god. What the hell's he talking about? The sponsors aren't going to buy this crap."

Deborah looked away. "I don't know. I mean, I *know*, but I didn't think he would be so -- "

"Insane?" Harry offered. "And since his crowd is here, we can't just get rid of him."

"What should I do?" she moaned.

Harry tapped his chin. He motioned to Clive. Clive came and joined them.

"Emergency," Harry said. "Switch seats. Put the Italian guy next to Deborah, then Parker, then Cal."

Clive nodded. "Right."

Harry turned back to Deborah. "Remember, it's your show. Get the focus off Parker and on the other guests, and keep it there."

"Places!" the floor director shouted.

"But, Harry -- " she whined.

Harry lifted her chin with a forefinger. "You can do it. You're 'America's Little Sweetheart.'" he said, leading her back to the set.

"Deborah, you're on!"

As the first bars of the theme song filled the studio, she pasted on a thin smile. "Welcome back to the Deborah Donaldson Show. We're talking to the *fa-bulous* Italian movie star, Donatello Dragghi. So, Donatello, tell us about your new movie, *The Bounty Killer*."

"Why you don't ask him?" he said, waving his splinted hand in Parker's direction. "You already talk to him the whole show."

She forced a strange-sounding giggle. "You're so funny. Really. Tell us about your movie."

He shrugged. "*The Bounty Killer*, it is, how you say, stuck with the puritani at the rating board. They say too much blood. Too much sex."

Parker leaned forward. "Sex, being a form of love, I can understand. But in the age of seeking peace, how do you justify the violence?"

Donatello looked at Deborah. "I no know what he says."

She drummed her fingers on Parker's book again. "Justify is like, um, explain. He asked you to explain the violence in your movie."

Donatello turned to Parker. "My film, it is what it is," he said with another shrug. "Everyone know, bad publicity e' good publicity, no?"

Parker rested his hand on Donatello's arm. "You may be rich, and you may be famous, but it seems in all your hypocrisy, you have nothing intelligent to say. In fact, *you* are the only cloud standing in the way of your own, obvious brilliance."

He brushed Parker's hand away.

"Excuse me," Cal interrupted. "Speaking of justifying hypocrisy . . . aren't you well past the age of being trustworthy -- you know, 'don't trust anyone over thirty?' And that rock on your finger? Seems a bit gaudy for someone who doesn't live in this world." He shifted in his chair. "And your followers calling you 'master'. Justify *that* if you can."

"Hmmm," Parker said. "Which shall I justify for you first? The master of the mind? The mind of the master? Or the mind over which I am master?"

"You better get a check-up. Sounds like you've got a bad case of cranial rectitus," Cal said with a laugh.

"I won't dignify that with a response." Parker waved as if he was whisking away a fly. "You are both Philistines."

Cal looked over at Donatello and laughed. "Seems that we've been slain by the jawbone of an ass."

"*You* . . ." Parker replied, glaring at Cal, then Donatello. "Are two sides of the same flawed perception."

"But *you* . . ." Cal blurted, "are crazy!"

A collective gasp. Deborah looked anxiously at Harry. He shrugged and shook his head.

"Everyone knows there is a fine line between madness and brilliance," Parker said. He pointed to Donatello. "In this man's sphere of influence, perhaps he is brilliant. But in the macrocosm of time-space, he is a fool. This ring you keep staring at," he added, holding it toward Cal. "It was a gift. Though why that concerns you, I cannot imagine. And if my disciples wish to call me 'master,' what of it? Though I have searched the universal consciousness, I cannot find any reason to discourage them."

Cal leaned forward. "The real question is, who decides? What is brilliance and what is madness?"

Parker shrugged. "There is no mystery. People. Society. The government. They all try to decide. But an infinite, eternal man is god and decides for himself."

Donatello sat back in his chair. "This god-man, he is a man like you are?"

"No. A god like I *am*."

Silence hung like an anvil cloud in the studio. Harry looked at his watch, then waved wildly at the floor director and drew his forefinger across his neck.

"Tell me . . ." Parker rested his hand on Donatello's thigh. "Do you believe? Am I god?"

Donatello pushed his hand away. "Man is not God." He shifted in his chair, his shirt fell open, and his gold crucifix slipped out.

With a bird-of-paradise affectation, Parker reached for the cross. "They say, that man was."

Donatello snatched the crucifix from his hand. "Sì. But you are not that man."

27

THE HARPERS SAT at a small table by a window in their hotel room, picking at room service Crab Louie salads, and shrimp cocktails.

Buck looked over at Pauline and frowned. *Grandson. That one word complicates everything.* "It's practically wilted," he muttered, pushing the salad around with his fork. "We should've at least kept the leftover pork baos."

"It's not that bad," Pauline said.

He set the fork down. "I wanted to go out." He pulled a chilled shrimp off the side of the glass, dipped it in blood-red cocktail sauce, and shoved it in his mouth.

She crossed her arms and stared at him. "We could have gone out, but you can't talk in a civil tone about anything more serious than the weather."

"Me? You're the one who's upset." He leaned back in his chair. "You still haven't answered my question. It's not unreasonable -- how do we know Shara's telling the truth?"

"Why do you always have to be contrary?"

"Pauline, please. Let's not argue."

"Why would she lie?"

"I don't know. Why wouldn't she? You saw how they live."

Pauline stabbed a slice of boiled egg with her fork. "You just don't want to see it."

"See what?"

"That Donovan is your grandson."

Buck slouched in his chair. "Ordinarily I'd be happy to find out I was going to be a grandfather, but . . ."

She set her fork down. "But what?"

"It's not that I don't want Donovan to be my grandson." He paused, shaking his head. "Shara sent the telegram. She lives with Steven. She's been hanging around the hospital for three days waiting to see him. No one does that unless . . . it doesn't take a genius to figure it out."

"Then why -- "

He pulled off his glasses and set them on the table. "It's just . . . I don't want . . ."

Pauline looked puzzled. "Don't want what?"

"Any of this."

"What do you mean?"

"Well, let's see. For starters, my son, who I haven't seen in five years, overdosed on drugs. And I don't know when, or if, he's going to get better. How 'bout that?" he said, raising his voice. "And he's living in a house with not one, but two . . . two women gone feral. How 'bout that?" His voice grew louder. "And there are who knows how many other guys hanging around doing who-knows-what to who-knows-who! How 'bout that?" Louder still. "And all of it coming straight out of the blue, without warning!" He slammed his fist on the table. "How 'bout that!"

"Calm down and lower your voice. The whole hotel will hear you."

"I don't care if the whole damn world hears me!" He looked up at her. "Not to be *contrary*, Pauline, but what happens next? What if Steven doesn't get better? Are we going to take care of him? How are we going to do that? And for how long? What about Shara? And Donovan? Are they all going to live with us? Not to mention -- who's footing the bill for all of it?" He stared out the window. "It's not fair. Why do I, I mean we -- at this stage of our lives, why do we have to pay for everyone's mistakes?"

She took his hand. "I don't know. But this is not a stray dog we're talking about. That dirty, frightened, barefoot little boy is Steven's son -- our grandson. And we have to do something."

He looked up at her. "Like what, Pauline? Kidnap him? Go to the authorities? Damn it, I just -- "

"Buck, we have to."

He pulled his hand away and ran his fingers over his crewcut. "I know, Pauline. I know."

28

EARLY THE NEXT morning, Shara peered around the corner at the nun manning the ICU nurse's station. "If anyone gets to see your dad today, it's gonna be us," she whispered to Donovan. "That nun looks really mean. You hide out while I try and find his room, then we'll sneak in and see him."

Shara led Donovan to the waiting room and settled him on a chair. "Wait here."

"I wan my daddy," he said in a loud voice.

Shara clapped her hand over his mouth. "I know, but we have to be really quiet." She pulled a stuffed monkey which was missing an eye and most of its fur, and a tattered book from her long, crocheted purse. "Here's Mikey and your book. Play quiet, okay?"

"Awight," he said with a pout.

"I'll come get you in a minute." Turning, Shara noticed a small paper bag on a nearby chair. "What's that?" She picked up the package and opened it. Inside she found a note, a small bottle, and an eyedropper.

> For Steven—
> Put little bit in glass of water two times a day. He will get better.
> Love, Ping

Shara looked up. "Ping? *His parents went to Chinatown yesterday...*"

"Wha's it Mommy?" Donovan asked, swinging his legs and bouncing the monkey on the arm of the chair.

"I don't know, but I think it's for your dad." Taking the bottle out of the bag, she turned it in the fluorescent hospital light. "It's like, I was supposed to find it, or something." She opened the bottle, put her finger over the opening, then touched the green elixir to her tongue. "Not too bad," she said, wrinkling her nose.

Shara tucked the note in the pocket of her jeans, closed the bottle and dropped the package into her purse. She got up and peered around the corner. The nun on duty got up from her chair and went through a door behind the desk. "Coast is clear. Wait here for me, okay?"

"But I wannu see my Daddy," Donovan whined.

"Shhhh," she said, flapping her hand at him. "I need to find out which room he's in first. Then I'll come get you. So, don't go anywhere, and don't talk to anybody."

He frowned. "Okay."

"Promise?"

Pushing his lower lip out, he nodded. "Pwomise."

Shara hurried past the nurse's station, then crept down the hall. She passed several rooms, glancing at the names on the doors. *Margie Meyers. Barney Tindale. Where is he?* She scurried past another door, then stopped. *Steven Harper.*

She paused a moment, then opened the door, pulled back the drape, and slipped inside. The room was dark, except for a crevice of light coming in from the hall. The metronome beeping of a heart monitor, and the smell of antiseptic made the room feel cold and forbidding.

She caught her breath

Steven sat up in bed, sleeping. His breath came slow and shallow, almost as if he wasn't breathing. And his faded green hospital gown had come untied and slid off his shoulder.

Shara slumped into a chair beside the bed. She stared up at the monitor recording his heartbeat. *How close did you come to stopping it forever?*

She lightly touched his cheek. "Steven?"

No response.

She shook his shoulder.

Again, no response.

She traced a fingertip over the dark hair on his forearm, then over his hand, drawn into an infantile fist.

Can't you feel it?

Prying his fingers open, she entwined them with hers. With all her strength, she dug her nails into his hand. Her fingers turned crimson, and her knuckles white. After a moment, she let his hand fall back onto the bed. A shiver ran through her as she watched his fist close again.

God, this is real . . . it's not a dream . . .

She sat back. The beeping of the monitor filled the room. A single sob escaped her and tears spilled down her cheeks. "What will happen to Donovan?" she whispered. "And what will happen to me?"

KRAK!

"AK! Sniper! One o'clock! Stay down! Get off the road!"

Remember, stay low. Head down. Breathe.

Eric! Call in location to fire base! We need an artillery launch of beehives to dust these dinks"

KRAK! KRAK!

"Fire from four o'clock! Get to the river! Run!"

"Head down, Eric!"

Head down. Stay low. Breathe.

BA-ROOOM!

"Incoming mortar!"

118

God, can't hear! Mortar! Shit!
KRAK! KRAK! KRAK!
More fire! "Eric! Look out!"
"Eric?"
Wet -- blood! My blood? His blood! -- don't look . . .
BOOOM! BOOOM!
More mortars! Run! Don't look back . . . keep breathing. Breathe! Breathe!
KRAK! KRAK! KRAK! KRAK!
God, they're following! Run! Stay low . . . breathe . . . breathe . . .
BAARROOOM!
Thank god, the river . . . M-16 overhead . . . blood in the water . . . My blood? Eric's blood! Jesus . . . Breathe . . .
"Damn! My foot!"
Caught! On what? Branches! Shit! Come on . . . let go! More fire! From where? Damn it! My leg! Sinking! Can't breathe!
KRAK! KRAK! KRAK!
The river . . . pulling me . . . pulling me under . . . running over me . . . running through me . . . can't breathe . . . can't breathe . . .
Can't bre --

Steven woke gasping, struggling against the neck brace holding his head and the dead weight of his body. Closing his eyes, tears slid down his cheeks, and he sank back against the pillow. *God. It's real. I'm not dreaming . . .*

Shara shook him. "Steven, it's me. You were having a nightmare."

He drew a sharp breath. *Shara?*

"Steven?"

He looked up at her. His mouth twisting into a grimace, and a rivulet of saliva trickling down his chin, he tried to speak her name.

"God, Steven..." Tears filled her eyes again, and she looked away. "How could this happen?"

She can hardly look at me. He motioned for a pencil and legal pad on the nightstand.

She put them on his lap and he began writing.

I FORGOT WINE AND HEROIN DONT MIX

"Come on, Steven, this is no time to kid around."

NOT KIDDING

She watched him a moment. "So, how do you feel?"

NOT MUCH

"Steven, quit joking. Really, how do you feel?"

TIRED BAD HEADACHE HOW DO I LOOK

"You look like Frankenstein -- with the stitches and..." She motioned to the neck brace and monitor. "Does it, you know, hurt?" she said, lightly touching the side of his face.

NOT TOO MUCH

Another awkward silence.

"Oh... I almost forgot. Ping, from Chinatown, made you some kind of medicine or something." Shara pulled the note from her pocket and passed it to him, then rifled through her purse and took out the bottle.

Steven read the note and looked skeptically at the bottle.

"Want to try some?"

He shook his head.

"Why not? Maybe it'll help."

NOT IN THE MOOD FOR SURPRISES

"Okay. I'll put it in the nightstand in case you change your mind," she said, then opened the drawer and dropped the package inside.

HOW DID PING KNOW

"I think your parents told her. They gave me and Donovan a ride home yesterday. And they gave us a bunch of Chinese food. So I figured -- "

He fumbled to tear the page off the tablet. Shara reached over and did it for him, then repositioned the pad on his lap.

YOU MET THEM

"Yeah."

YOU WERE HERE

"Yeah. Almost all day yesterday, and the day before that, and the night Roxie found you. But those Nazi nuns and that stupid-jerk, Dr. Buehler, wouldn't let me see you."

THREE DAYS

"Almost four, if you count today."

A slight smile twisted half Steven's face.

I THOUGHT YOU GAVE UP ON ME

Shara shook her head. "Give up on you? Me and Donovan have been hitchhiking back and forth everyday to see you."

Steven's face contorted.

YOU HITCHHIKED WITH DONOVAN

"Well, yeah. What was I supposed to do? The bus takes *forever*. I didn't have money for a cab or a babysitter. And I couldn't leave him with Roxie -- you know how she is . . ."

WHERE IS HE

"In the waiting room."

ALONE

"Steven, don't look at me like that. He's not alone. He's got a book and Mikey the Monkey to keep him busy."

A STUFFED TOY

The color drained from Steven's face. His head fell back on the brace.

"Hey, are you okay?" Shara ran her hand over his forehead. "Steven? Talk to me."

CANT TALK

The pencil slipped from his hand.

"Steven?"

No response.

Shara watched him a moment. "I guess I better go so you can rest," she said, then got up and went to the door. "Donovan can see you next time." She paused again, blew a kiss, and closed the door behind her.

Steven looked down at the notepad on his lap, listening to the beeping of the monitor and the sound of his breath. *I can see it in her eyes. How long before she says goodbye?* He sank against the pillow. *Without her I'm nothing. No one.* He tore the page off the tablet and stared at the edge. *Turn me sideways and I almost disappear.*

29

THE HARPERS CAME upon Shara in a hallway near the ICU nurse's station, and she fell into Pauline's arms. "It's . . . it's such a drag," she sobbed. "Like an unbelievable bummer."

Pauline looked helplessly at Buck. "Has something happened to Steven?"

"No," Shara moaned. "I mean, nothing new. It's just, the whole thing . . . he's so messed up!"

"But Steven is -- "

"Okay. If you call *that* okay," Shara said with another flood of tears. "I hitchhiked all the way over here again and snuck into his room. Then, like, after just a few minutes, he told me to leave. That he needed to rest."

"Told you?"

"I mean wrote. He can't even talk."

Pauline glanced up and down the hall. "Where is Donovan?"

"He's in the waiting room." Shara sniffed and wiped her eyes with the back of her hand.

"Alone?"

"That's what Steven said -- I mean wrote, then it was like he practically fainted."

Pauline took Shara's arm. "Well then, let's go to the waiting room and talk this over."

Donovan looked up from under his book, opened tent-style over his head, as Shara came into the waiting room with Buck and Pauline. She picked up his stuffed monkey and flopped onto a chair next to him, while Buck and Pauline sat down across from them.

"That's one way to read," Buck said with a chuckle.

Donovan pulled the book off his head and made a grasping motion for Buck.

"I think he wants you," Pauline said.

Buck looked up. "Me? You want to sit with me?"

Pushing out his lower lip, Donovan nodded.

Buck tugged on the knees of his pants, then held out his hands. "Okay, climb aboard."

Donovan scrambled down off the chair and onto Buck's lap. Settling against Buck's chest, he began sucking his thumb and twisting his strawberry-blonde hair around his finger. "I wan da book an Mikey," he said with his thumb still in his mouth.

"Here." Shara tossed the partially bald monkey to Donovan, then passed the book to Buck.

"This must be Mikey," Buck said, looking askance at the stuffed toy. "And this must be a reject from the candy-striper's cart."

Shara frowned. "It's not a reject. It's his book from home. He likes to pretend he can read."

"Oh." Buck pursed his lips and nodded. "'The Sun Also Rises?' Isn't that a bit advanced for a kid his age?"

Donovan took his thumb from his mouth. "My daddy wead to me." His lips trembled, then he burst into tears. "I wan my daddy . . . I wan my daddy . . ." he wailed.

Shara buried her face in her hands. "Come on, Donovan. Stop it. I told you they won't let us go in there."

"I wan my daddy! I wan my daddy! I wan my daddy!" he screamed.

"Buck, maybe they'll let you take him to Steven's room, just so he can see him," Pauline said.

"It's worth a try," Buck replied. "Hey, Donovan, how 'bout we sneak into your dad's room?" he said, feigning excitement and exaggerating a smile.

"Wait a minute. I didn't say to go sneaking around. I meant ask at the desk. You can't break the rules, they might -- "

Buck stared at her. "Not let us go in at all? Pauline, sometimes it's better to beg forgiveness, than ask permission." He looked at Donovan. "If we're going to see your dad, we have to be like big boys. Real quiet and no crying. Can you do that?"

He sniffed and nodded.

"Okay, let's go."

Carrying Donovan, the stuffed monkey and the book, Buck skirted around the nurse's station with his back to the desk.

"Sir? Can I help you?" the nun said.

He looked over his shoulder. "I'm going to Steven Harper's room. I'm his father."

"He's resting now."

"If it's alright with you, I'll just sit quietly until he wakes up."

"That will be fine. The room is rather small. You can leave that big package here at the desk if you like."

Donovan squirmed. Buck tightened his grip.

"That's okay," he said, shuffling away. "It's a present for my son."

"Well, alright," the nun replied, though he was nearly around the corner.

Buck paused at the door to Steven's room. "Remember, we have to be big boys," he said under his breath.

Donovan nodded, then Buck opened the door.

"Daddy!" he squealed.

Buck slapped his hand over Donovan's mouth. "Shhh! Your dad's asleep," he whispered. "We have to be quiet so he can rest."

Donovan looked up, his eyes like saucers.

"Can you do that?"

He nodded.

"Good." Buck slowly took his hand away. "What do you say we read until your dad wakes up?" Sitting in the chair beside the bed, he settled Donovan on his lap, then opened the book. Several dog-eared pages fell out. "How about let's make it up as we go along?"

Donovan nodded again, then slipped his thumb in his mouth and nestled against Buck. He closed his eyes and within moments he was asleep.

Buck set the book on the foot of the bed. He looked over at Steven. *Daddy?* Then down at Donovan. *Hell, even I can see the resemblance. Wide forehead. Broad nose. Square jaw with a slight cleft.*

Watching them sleeping, the stillness of the room, the softness of their breathing and intermittent beeping of the monitor took their toll. Buck yawned. Closing his eyes, he followed them into a dream.

"It's so stupid." Shara wiped her eyes with the back of her hand, then pulled her knees up and sat cross-legged on the waiting room chair. "I had to sneak into Steven's room like a freakin' burglar. "They won't let me see him, and they won't even tell me how he is, because we're not related. But we *are* related. I'm his girlfriend!"

"You're not married," Pauline said.

"Married?" Shara repeated as if she tasted something sour. "What's that got to do with anything?" Her shoulders sank. "I can't believe he's so messed up. Not to mention, they shaved off his hair. Now he looks like he's back in the army, or something."

Pauline stared at her. "His hair? If that's what you're worried about, it grows back, you know. I had to cut all his hair off more than once when he was little. Trust me. Things have a way of working out, including hair."

Shara sighed. "I guess you're right." She uncrossed her legs and sat forward. "I guess I might as well grab Donovan and split."

"Split?"

"You know, take off. Hit the road. Get going."

Pauline stiffened. *She can't. She can't take him. You simply cannot let her take him.* "If you want -- I mean if it would help . . . we can keep Donovan with us," she said as if it was a question.

There was a prolonged pause.

Shara bit her lip. "Ummm, are you sure?"

Dear God, am I sure? "We'd be glad to."

"It's not permanent or anything..."

Stay calm. "No, of course not. Just until everything settles down."

"Wow. Cool. Thanks," Shara said with another sigh. "It's not like I don't, you know, want him around or anything... it's just... I'll leave some of his stuff." She turned her purse upside down, shook it, then sorted through the contents and set an indiscernible wad on the chair beside Pauline. "That's it." She stepped back and hooked one thumb around the strap of her purse, and the other through a belt loop on her jeans. "I guess I'll see you when things settle down." Then she smiled and waved, and walked away.

Pauline stared at the mound of Donovan's belongings on the chair beside her. She picked up a tiny velveteen jacket. Holding the dirty, worn fabric to her face, she closed her eyes. *The first time I saw him, even then, somehow, I knew my own flesh and blood.* She dropped the jacket onto her lap. *Now what? Looking after a three-year old boy at my age. I can hardly imagine...*

Several moments passed. She gathered Donovan's things, then stood and smoothed her dress. Slipping past the nurse's station, she hurried down the hall to Steven's room. She silently opened the door and pulled back the curtain.

All three sleeping...

Steven. My dear, dear son. We almost lost you. Bruises -- fading. Cuts -- healing. The dark hollows under your eyes will fade with time. But what will heal your heart?

Donovan. Your son, my grandson. Who are you, little one?

And Buck. It seems I've known you all my life. How will we cope with the changes that are here at our door?

Buck woke with a start. "Pauline?" he groaned.

She bent beside the chair and whispered, "I have something to tell you. Now don't get upset... Shara left Donovan with us."

"But Pauline, I thought we decided..."

"Shhh. Regardless, she left him."

Just then, Steven moaned, stirred, and opened his eyes.

Pauline went to his side. "It's okay, dear. Everything's fine."

Looking hazily up at her, he reached for the tablet.

She patted his arm. "Don't worry. Shara left Donovan with us. We'll keep him until you're better."

He exhaled a deep sigh.

"We need to get back home to check on the animals. We left in such a hurry we didn't have time to arrange for anyone to watch them. There was a rockslide on the highway, so we had to fly. We'll get Donovan settled at our house and we'll all drive back in a day or so."

Steven nodded. A slight smile turned one side of his lips. Sinking back against the pillow, he closed his eyes again.

30

DONATELLO LEANED BACK and rolled down the window in his sports car. Resting his elbow on the opening, he took a long breath. The highway turned toward the ocean, and cool salt air chased away the heat, smog, and smell of the city. Hanging low on the horizon, the sun cast golden brushstrokes over the water.

"You see, I tell you. LA is lunatic," he said with a broad wave. "Is good to go, no?"

Slovika sat silently, staring out the window. Her jaw set like iron, her eyes were fixed like amber glass. The wind whipped strands of her hair around her face and rippled the sleeves of her blouse.

"We no be home before dark," he said. "At least six hour to San Francisco and hour to wine country."

No response.

I will pretend innocence. I am, after all, an actor. "The drive, it is beautifool, no?" he said, thickening his accent. "Why you are so quiet, amore mio? Come, why you no talk?"

More silence.

Donatello shook his head. *I hate to be alone . . . but to be with her is almost to be alone.* He reached over to touch her hair but she caught his hand. Their eyes locked. He sighed and turned away.

More than an hour passed and miles of scenery went by before Donatello noticed Slovika's jaw soften. The icy silence in the car melted into a cloud of gloom. In place of anger, sadness surrounded her like a shroud.

It may be as the scriptures say -- my sins, they are as scarlet, but I feel a truce is coming. "You are hungry?" he asked. "If you want eat something, I take you someplace nice."

Silence. A few more miles passed.

I am undaunted. "When you want to eat?"

She shrugged.

Ah, a start.

"Where we are?" she asked.

A truce! At last! "The next town is only little way," he said with a nonchalant wave and blasé stare.

"We eat there?"

"If you like."

She nodded.

He exhaled an audible sigh. *Absolution . . .*

At the edge of the next town, Donatello turned off the highway. Alongside the exit a large, glowing sign with a burned-out letter announced:

SHELL
GAS FOOD LODGING
NEXT EXIT

31

"EIGHTEEN-A," BUCK MUTTERED, shuffling down the airplane isle. He stopped at the eighteenth row, took a newspaper from under his arm and slid into the window seat.

Pauline settled Donovan beside him, took off her coat and sat by the aisle.

"Maybe you can hide his clothes with your coat," Buck grumbled, wedging the newspaper into the seat pocket in front of him. "But there's nothing we can do about his hair."

Pauline sighed. "Let Grandma fasten your seatbelt," she said, rummaging under Donovan for the end of the strap. With a click, she secured the belt, then draped her coat over him like a blanket. "There. All set. Now you're ready for your plane ride," she said, fastening her belt.

Donovan wrestled the stuffed monkey out from under the coat. "Gwamma? Where da pwane going?"

"Don't you remember? We're flying to Sacramento. Then from there, we'll drive to our house," she said with exaggerated cheerfulness.

"I wan my daddy."

"Oh dear. But it'll be fun." She looked over at Buck. "It'll be fun, won't it?"

"Yeah, it'll be fun, alright." Buck shook his head and looked out the window.

"Why Mommy an Daddy don't come too?"

"Your daddy's getting better at the hospital, remember? And your mommy . . . well . . . you're going to stay with us while things get sorted out."

"What thing, Gwamma?"

Buck turned and stared at her. "Yeah, Pauline, what things?"

She took a deep breath. "Oh, like where everyone is going to live. Things like that."

"Gwamma?"

"Yes, baby."

"Will da party people come to you house too?"

"Who are the party people, honey?"

"Da people who get stoned. Do Gwampa an you get stoned?"

Pauline raised an eyebrow. She looked over at Buck. "We . . . we don't do that."

"Why not?"

She pinched the bridge of her nose. "Oh dear. It's . . ."

Buck sat forward. "It's bad. That's why."

"But Mommy an Daddy get stoned."

"It's bad for them too. Maybe now they won't be so dumb. At least I hope your Dad won't."

Donovan looked up at him. "Why?"

"Because he ended up in the hospital."

"Why?"

Buck shook his head. "By doing bad things and being stupid."

Donovan's lips began trembling. Just then, the roar of the engines engulfed the cabin. He screamed and buried himself under Pauline's coat.

"Honestly, Buck! You upset him."

"Damn it, Pauline, the boy needs to know the truth," he said over the din of the engines. "Steven was stupid. Just plain stupid."

"That may be, but Donovan doesn't need to know the whole truth about everything right this minute. Goodness sakes, he hardly knows us." She patted the sobbing mound beside her. "It's okay, baby. Grandpa is just worried about your dad. Grandpa's sorry." She glared at Buck. "Right?"

"Yeah, Grandad's sorry."

She pulled Donovan from under the coat. "You see." She looked into his eyes. "Grandad didn't mean it."

He sniffed and wiped his nose with the back of his hand. "Weally?"

Pauline smiled. "Really. Now it's all settled. In a minute we'll take off and we'll be up in the air. And we'll have a nice airplane ride, then we'll stop for ice cream on the way home."

Donovan's eyes brightened. "Ice cweam?"

"Yes. And when we get home, you can play with our dog. He needs someone his size to play with."

"A dog?"

"His name is Tailor. I know he's going to like you."

Buck pulled the newspaper from the pocket, sat back and opened it.

ASSASSINATION IN MEMPHIS
CIVIL RIGHTS LEADER MARTIN LUTHER KING JR SHOT

His jaw dropped. "Someone shot him," he said under his breath.

Pauline looked up. "What?"

"Martin Luther King. Somebody shot him."

"Good heavens." She pulled Donovan close and covered his ears. "Why on earth would anyone do a thing like that? That's awful, how..."

Buck shook his head. "I don't know. Says there's rioting in Boston, Chicago and Detroit." He dropped the paper onto his lap. "Ever since JFK was assassinated it's been one thing after another. Like the whole damn world's on fire."

Just then, a svelte brunette stewardess in a red and orange mini-dress, red knee-high boots and a fishbowl-shaped cap came by. "Please fasten your seat belt," she said with a practiced smile, looking intently at Buck. "We're almost ready for take-off." She paused. "Sir? Your seat belt?"

"Oh, uh, yeah." He folded the paper and shoved it into the seat pocket, then pulled the belt across his lap and secured it.

"We'll be serving refreshments once we're in the air," she added, then continued down the aisle.

Engines racing, the plane began to taxi. Buck glanced at the runway, black and glistening with rain, then at Donovan, sucking his thumb with his head on Pauline's lap. He looked at his hands, large, wrinkled, and weathered with age. Then at Donovan's, small and smooth. *It'll be his world soon. What kind of mess will we leave him?* He made a fist and stared at the the knobbiness of his knuckles. *Me, raising a kid his age. Who am I kidding?* He looked over at Pauline. *And her. Who's she trying to fool? Herself I guess.* Turning back, he rested his head against the glass. *And Steven? How will we . . . god, I can't even think about it.*

Squinting into the late afternoon sun, Buck maneuvered his station wagon around a steep turn. "Almost home," he said as the shadow cast by the rearview mirror fell across his face like the mask of a bandit.

Pauline stretched her legs. "Boy, will it feel good to get out of these shoes. My feet are numb." She looked down at Donovan, sleeping on the bench seat between them, and stroked the strawberry-red tangles of his hair. "His life is certainly going to change."

Buck draped his wrist over the steering wheel as the road leveled to a gentle grade. "Ours already has."

"Fortunately, I kept Steven's bed made, just in case he came home, and we still have some of his toys up the attic."

Buck pulled the station wagon to a stop at the entrance to their property. He got out, unlatched the scrolling iron gate, then put his thumb and forefinger in his mouth and whistled. A few moments later, a wire-hair terrier came bounding toward him. Barking and wagging his stubby tail, the dog jumped into his arms.

Donovan woke. "Gwamma?" he whimpered, rubbing his eyes.

"It's okay. We're home."

His eyes shot open. "A dog!" he cried, struggling to sit up.

Pauline smiled. "That's Tailor."

"Twailor!" he gushed, sliding out the open door of the station wagon. "Gwampa! Gwampa! I wannu pway wiff da dog!"

"Okay, " Buck said. "But be careful. He doesn't know you yet. Hold out your hand . . ."

Buck put the dog down. He sidled over to Donovan. Amid the onslaught of wags and wiggles, Donovan fell backward, giggling as Tailor mercilessly licked him.

"Okay, come on you two," Pauline said. "Get back in the car."
Just then, a white horse trotted by.
"Buck, look. Nahlah's out," Pauline said, pointing to the mare.
"What in tarnation . . ." he muttered.

The horse trotted toward him and stopped a short distance away. She tossed her head, then threw her tail up over her back and galloped off.

Eyes wide, Donovan scrambled to his feet and started after her. "A horse! I wannu pway wiff da horse!"

Buck grabbed his arm, then picked him up and planted him on the front seat. "Oh no you don't. She might hurt you." He motioned to Tailor. "You too."

The dog jumped in, and he closed the door behind them.

"Wonder how Nahlah got out," Buck muttered as they rolled over the circular gravel driveway toward the house.

Rounding the bend, Pauline looked up to see a stocky Appaloosa devouring a pale green branch in her rose garden. Pink petals fell like cracker crumbs as he moved from one branch to another.

"Buck! It's Chief! He's eating my rosebushes!" she shrieked, sending the dog into another chorus of barking.

Oblivious to the thorns, the horse moved with abandon from one bush to another.

"Buuuck! Do something! He just took the head and shoulders off my 'Mr. Lincoln!'"

"Doggone him. He must've let Nahlah out. How'd he get the gate open?"

"He's too smart for his own good, that's how. Are you going to do something, or just stand there!"

Buck looked down at his tweed jacket and dress pants, then raked his fingers over his crewcut. "I can see what's left of my day going down the drain," he muttered. "You drive the car up to house, and I'll take the horses out to the pasture. Then I'll ride Chief back up to Alma's in the morning."

32

A RAMBLING ROSE, just beginning to bud, climbed up the front post and hung over a porch spanning the front of the Harpers' log-framed house. Pauline drove past the front entrance and pulled to a stop near the back door.

"While Grandad takes care of the horses, we'll get you settled," she said, holding the car door for Donovan and Tailor.

"But I wannu pway wiff da horse," Donovan said as he slid across the seat, and the dog scrambled out after him.

Pauline pulled a paper bag filled with his things from the back seat of the station wagon. "I know, honey, but she's so big, she might hurt you. Grandad will show you what to do." She closed the car door, and they shuffled across the driveway.

Tailor ran ahead and bounded through a worn leather flap covering an opening in the bottom of the back door. "Twailor hab a door?" Donovan asked, looking up at Pauline.

"Yes, he does," she replied, then swung the back door open, switched on a light and led Donovan into the laundry room. She dropped the sack beside the washing machine. "New clothes are in order, but in the meantime, we'll wash these."

"I wan Mikey," he whined, making a grasping motion and pointing to the stuffed monkey at the top of the bag.

"And we'll buy you a brand new teddy bear."

"I don wan a Teddy Bear. I wuv Mikey," he said with a sniffle.

Pauline smiled. "Just like your dad. Loyal to a fault," she said, then gave him the monkey. "Now let's go see your new bedroom."

She took Donovan's hand, and led him up the stairs and down a short hall, with Tailor following. The bedroom door creaked on its hinges as she opened it.

Donovan's eyes brightened. "A cowboy woom," he said, pointing to the boot and spur wallpaper. "An a cowboy bed," he added, motioning to the wooden wagon wheel serving as a headboard. He looked up at her. "I wike da cowboy woom, Gwamma."

"I'm glad. It was your daddy's room." She went to the window, turned the latch and pulled up on the bottom casement. Fresh air flooded in. She sat on the bed and pulled him up beside her. "We still have some of your daddy's toys in the attic. We'll get them down for you to play with."

"Wha's a attic?"

"It's sort of like a room at the top of the house, up by the roof."

"I wannu see da attic."

"We'll go up there later."

"Dere's wots of books." Donovan pointed to a bookshelf mounted on the wall across from the bed. He looked down at the floor and sniffled. "I wike it when my daddy wead to me."

"Well then, we'll read lots of books together."

"Wha's dat?" he said, pointing toward the window.

"Oh, that's a telescope."

"Wha's a tewestope?"

Pauline smiled. "I forgot -- so many questions. You look in it at night and you can see lots of stars. In the summertime, we put it out on the front porch. Your daddy liked to do that."

"Can we wook at da stars?"

"When it gets dark, if it's not too cold."

Tailor jumped onto the bed beside Donovan and licked his nose.

"I wike him, Gwamma."

She smiled. "He likes you too."

"We don't hab a dog at Woxie house."

"You mean Roxie's?"

Donovan nodded. "Where do you an Gwampa sweep?"

"Sweep? Oh, you mean sleep. Our bedroom is just down the hall."

"At Woxie house, my mommy an daddy, we all sweep togedder."

"Since your mommy and daddy aren't here right now, you get the bedroom and Tailor all to yourself."

"When are my mommy an daddy coming?"

"I don't know yet, but pretty soon we'll have it all figured out."

"Sometime when da party people came over to Woxie house, they twied an make me get stoned, but daddy maked them stop."

Pauline sucked in her breath. "Those people aren't coming here. But, even if they did, your granddad and I would never let them do that to you."

Donovan's lips quivered and he began to cry. "I wan my daddy."

"Oh, dear. I know, honey." Pauline blinked several times as tears welled in her eyes. She pulled him onto her lap and held him close. "I miss him too. More than you could possibly know."

"Hungwy, Gwamma," Donovan whined.

Pauline pulled out a chair at the kitchen table. "Okay, you sit here while I make dinner." As he scrambled up, Tailor curled into a ball under the table.

"What would you like?"

He shrugged.

"Um . . . how about pancakes? You like pancakes, don't you?"

"Wha's pantake?" he asked, kicking the table leg.

"Goodness. You've never had pancakes?"

He shrugged again.

"We'll fix that right now." She tied an apron around her waist and set a cast iron skillet on the stove.

Buck came into the kitchen. "The horses are in the back pasture for the night," he said, wiping his hands on a pair of muddy overalls.

"Take those off and put them in the laundry room," Pauline said, wrinkling her nose. "You'll track mud all over the house. How on earth did you get so dirty?"

"Chief was rolling in the vegetable garden when I caught up with him. Now I'll have to till it all over again." He unhooked the overalls, shimmied them down to his ankles, and stepped out. "What's for dinner?"

"Breakfast," Pauline said. "Bacon, eggs, and pancakes."

"Nothin' wrong with that," he said, draping the muddy garment over his arm.

"Donovan's never had pancakes."

"What? Never had pancakes?" Buck looked over at him. "You're in for a treat. Your grandma makes the best pancakes in the whole world."

"Weally?" he said, bouncing in his seat.

"You bet."

Pauline smoothed her hair as she went into the kitchen. The smell of bacon and maple syrup lingered in the air. "There were a few more tears, but he finally dropped off to sleep. Tailor is up there with him."

Buck patted his stomach. "I've got to hand it to you. You rustled up some real good grub."

"If you don't mind breakfast for dinner."

"Breakfast is good anytime, day or night." He wiped his mouth with a napkin, and set it on the table. "It was touch-and-go for a little bit, getting him to try the pancakes. He's got a strong will, but he's not unreasonable."

Pauline looked up. "Like Steven?"

"Yeah. A lot like Steven."

Drifting out of a dream, Buck ran his hand over the side of the bed. "Pauline?"

He looked at the clock on the nightstand. "Twelve-thirty. Where'd she go?"

He yawned and stretched, then got up and padded down the hall. The door to Donovan's bedroom stood ajar. Looking in, he found Pauline sleeping beside Donovan, with Tailor stretched out at their feet.

Buck shifted his weight and the floor creaked. The dog flipped over and looked up at him.

"Why's everybody in here?" he whispered.

Tailor cocked his head to one side as if he wanted to answer.

Buck went to the window and slid it closed. He paused a moment, watching them sleeping and stroking the dog's curly coat. "Keep an eye on them, okay?" he said, then went out, closing the door behind him.

33

EARLY THE NEXT morning, Donatello sat atop a flat boulder overlooking a languid stream flowing through his vineyard near the coast in Northern California. Dappled sun filtered through cottonwood leaves just beginning to open, and tufts of new grass filled the air with the scent of spring. Watching the stream slipping around a fallen tree, his mind wandered.

"Slovika . . . why you no smile?" he asked. "Why you always so angry."

"Smile?" She took a hairbrush from her purse, then threw the handbag on an upholstered bench in their darkened bedroom. Wearing a short black chemise, she sat on the bed and yanked the brush through her hair. After several strokes, static built up, and her hair began to levitate.

Donatello sat down beside her. "Look, your hair, it flies."

She dropped the hairbrush, crossed her arms, and stared at him. "Why you say this? Maybe I am too ugly for you," she said with a petulant frown.

He put his arm around her and lowered his eyes, looking up at her through his thick, dark lashes. "No, amore mio, you are beautiful."

Slovika pushed him away. "If it is as you say, then why you no make love to me since we are in LA? Maybe the devil woman, Deborah, or someone else you want."

Donatello reached for her. "Slovika, please. It mean nothing. It is business . . ."

She jumped up off the bed. "You spend night with her, and is business. But me? Your wife? You no make love with me!" She grabbed the hairbrush and flung it, shattering a crystal vase on the nightstand.

"Now look," he said, motioning to the lamp. "Is you I want, but . . ."

"But?" She glared at him.

He shrugged and shook his head.

"You see, you no can answer," she snapped, then stomped out of the bedroom, slamming the door behind her.

Leaning back against the rock, he looked up at the clouds changing shape and his mind wandered again. The voice of his father's stodgy cousin Lorenzo, whom he called Uncle, echoed in his mind. With a dismal sigh, he was there again in the library of Lorenzo's stately San Francisco townhouse, sitting across from him in a high-backed leather chair, drinking warm brandy.

"Dona, I love you like you're my own son. I only want what's best for you." Lorenzo drummed his fingers on the arm of the chair. "You look so miserable. Have you been taking your medicine? You know your father will ask."

Donatello frowned and shook his head. "No. I no want take it. Make me always sleepy. And feel sad."

"Dear God, if you're like this when you're not taking it, I can't imagine what you'd be like if you did. Maybe there's something else, some new drug or something. I could get you an appointment. Besides, your father wanted me to find you a doctor."

"I no want go the doctor. I no want anyone to know."

Lorenzo looked up at him. "Dona, I think you're playing with fire. If anyone sees you having a seizure, they're sure-as-shit going to know. Have you had one since you've been here?"

Donatello paused, then shook his head. "No." He stared into the amber liquid in his glass. "I just want go back Italia."

"I know you're homesick, but you can't go back. You haven't been here that long. Give it a chance." Lorenzo paused, sipping his brandy. "You know, up north in the wine country near Napa . . . ah, molto bella," he said, pressing his fingertips together and kissing them. "I swear, it's so much like Siena, you'll have to pinch yourself to be sure you're not dreaming. Almost like home. Take a little trip there with Slovika and see. I'll pay for it."

A chill breeze blew through the valley. *Lorenzo, I am here, but is not like home.* Donatello winced at the cold and the dull ache that seemed to surround him. He slid off the rock, and followed a path beside the creek, upstream to a narrow, moss-covered footbridge. The weathered-gray planks creaked under his weight as he crossed over the stream.

There, the path ascended out of the shade, onto a terraced, sun-bathed hillside covered with wire-topped scaffolds and grapevines. He stopped to study a new leaf on an old vine. *The wine will be good this year? Or I lose money I don't have? The fortuneteller did not say.*

"So, you went on a trip to wine country and now you want to buy a vineyard," Lorenzo said, sitting in the same chairs, several weeks later. He tapped his cigar over a silver tray, then brushed a stray ash off his velveteen smoking jacket. "This vineyard has a name?"

Donatello leaned forward. "Sì, Mondscheinberg Cellar. German for, how you say, moonlight hill. In summer, the moon, it shines on the vineyard."

Lorenzo sighed and shook his head. "Ave Maria, Donatello. What do you know about growing grapes? The family business is law and politics. You already disregarded your father and became an actor. Now you're going to disrespect him again and become a vintner?" He puffed irritably on his cigar.

"Uncle, the vineyard is old. Planted the turn of the century. Old enough, they say, to make buono wine by itself," he said with a hopeful smile. "My father would see the uh, saggezza . . ." He snapped his fingers. "The wisdom."

Lorenzo looked skeptically at him. "Then why is it for sale?"

"The son of the Austrian who plant it, he play the cards, how you say . . . gioco?"

"Gamble?" Lorenzo offered.

"Sì. He gamble all his money. Then he ipotecato, uh, morte' . . ."

Lorenzo shook his head. "Dona, I wish you'd learn English. You mean mortgage?"

"Sì. He mortgage the vineyard, and he gamble that too. Uncle, I wish to buy it and grow wine. But how I can do it? Until *The Bounty Killer* is release, I have no money."

Lorenzo raked his fingers through the salt and pepper waves of his hair. "You know . . ." He pointed a stout forefinger at him. "Anyone else would be glad just to be alive after a round with

Caggiano. You're lucky he only broke your hand. But not you. You're miserable. And when you're miserable, guaranteed, you'll make everybody else miserable too. And being here in California, I don't think you've ever been more miserable."

Donatello looked dejectedly back at him. "Uncle, I do as you say, and go the wine country. Now you treat me like bambino."

"Oh, alright. If it will make you happy, I'll loan you the money," Lorenzo said with a sigh. "It's close enough that I can keep my promise to your father to watch out for you, but it's far enough that you won't drive me out of my mind." He reached over and patted Donatello's cheek. "Of course, you know I'm only kidding."

Nearing the top of the hill, Donatello looked out over the valley. Past the patchwork of Mondsceinberg's gnarled vines. Past a rock-walled cave carved into the hill that cellared fresh casks and dusty bottles. Past a neighboring vineyard. Past the cottonwoods on the valley floor. Through a stand of redwoods to the vast, blue Pacific.

He stared down at the bandages on his hand and stretched his fingers over the splint. *Will it ever heal? Lorenzo was right. The vineyard, it does not make me happy. Slovika, she does not make me happy. Maybe I never be happy, if I cannot go home.*

34

THAT SAME MORNING, Buck stopped at a gate that opened to a wide expanse of pastureland. Stretching more than forty acres, the pasture dipped like a bowl, bordered by ponderosa pines, sequoias, and valley oaks. Though the sun was shining, the scent of rain lingered, and in the shadows snow still held its icy grip.

With a length of rope hidden behind his back, Buck opened the gate, put his thumb and forefinger in his mouth, and whistled. "Nahlahhhh . . ."

Both Chief and Nahlah looked up from grazing. Buck picked a handful of grass and waved it at them. "Come on . . ." he said in a saccharine tone.

Nahlah watched him a moment. She tossed her head, and trotted toward him, then stopped a few steps away.

"Come 'ere."

She bobbed her head and pawed at the ground.

"Nahlahhh . . . don't do this to me."

She took a step closer.

"You've had a little vacation. Now, come on," he said, waving the grass at her.

A few more steps.

"Good girl." He dropped the rope over her neck, tied it in a slipknot, and pulled it tight. "Gotcha." Leaning against him, she rubbed her face on his chest and lipped his over-alls.

"Alright, I love you too. But I need to get you back in your stall so I can catch your Appaloosa boyfriend."

He led the mare from the pasture to the barn. Her hooves echoed on the wooden floor, and the smell of hay and damp earth surrounded them. He lead her to her stall, slipped the rope off, slapped her on the rump, and closed the stall door . "Now for the rebel."

Buck found Chief blissfully rolling on a fresh gopher mound at the far end of the pasture. He stomped toward the horse with the rope tied into a crudely improvised bridle.

He slid the bridle over the horse's blocky head. "Okay, let's go. It's not like I've got nothing better to do than ride you back home."

Chief scrambled to his feet and shook a cascade of dirt off his back.

He led Chief out of the pasture, past the barn to the driveway. "Dang you're fat," he muttered. "Alma needs to cut down on your groceries." He scrambled onto the Appaloosa's wide, mud-caked back.

Just then, Pauline came out of the house. "I see you caught him."

"Yeah." Buck pulled on a pair of worn leather work gloves and straightened his hat. "Don't expect me back any time soon."

"I know." She crossed her arms. "Because when you go to Alma's, you need to figure in time to visit . . ."

He nodded. "And visiting with Alma, when done correctly, can take hours." He jabbed Chief with his heels. "Now, get going you old glue-bucket."

Pauline waved as they ambled off toward the road with a slow, rolling gait.

"You're like riding a horse-hide recliner," Buck muttered, settling into the lazy rhythm.

They sauntered out onto a two-lane road that wound through the foothills to the summit of the Sierras. The hollow sound of Chief's hooves echoed on the pavement. Birds chirped tentatively from the Manzanita bushes, and a pair of red-tailed hawks circled in the crisp, cloudless sky.

The morning sun warming his back, Buck looked down at the rope lying across his weathered glove and his mind wandered. He was there again, in the pasture teaching Steven to ride. *He was only a little older than Donovan . . .*

Two horses, standing side by side. Steven, sitting on one, while Buck climbed onto the other.

"Daddy, I want to hold the reins," Steven whined, reaching for the leather straps.

"No. You're too little to ride by yourself," Buck said, winding the reins tethering Steven's horse, around his hand. "Copper's too big for you."

"I am not too little. I can do it."

Buck frowned. "I said no."

"Dad-dy . . ."

"No. Now hold on to the saddle horn."

"But -- "

"Damn it, Steven, I said no!" Turning, Buck jabbed his heel into his horse'dess side. The horse leapt forward and broke into a gallop.

"No!"

Copper bounded alongside.

Buck desperately gripped the reins. *Slipping! God, no!* They slid out of his hands, burning the flesh off his palm. In several strides, Copper passed his horse by.

"Steven! Hold on!"

"Daddy!"

With agonizing clarity, he recalled Steven's scream as he slid off the saddle and crashed against a fencepost. But all that followed was clouded and hazy, as if it had happened in a dream.

"Steven's cast will be off in a month or so. Young bones heal fast," the doctor said with a reassuring tone. "I *know* you know better than to wrap reins around your hand, let alone not wearing gloves . . ."

Buck lowered his eyes.

The doctor patted his shoulder. "You're mighty lucky you didn't lose a finger."

Buck came to with a start as Chief turned off the road and broke into a trot on a wide cobblestone driveway. "Whoa! What-are-you-do-ing?" His voice bounced in time with the choppy stride. "You-won't-get-go-ing-'til-you're-al-most-home!"

He jerked back hard on the makeshift reins. Loose cobblestones rattled under the horse's hooves as he slowed to a walk.

They passed a massive sequoia, and went around an imposing iron gate, ornamented with scrolling acorns and oak leaves. Immobilized by rust, the gate had not moved in several lifetimes.

Around a bend in the drive, Alma Richardson's stone mansion came into view. Built of granite quarried from the surrounding foothills, the mansion looked out over acres of rolling pastureland, and the rugged peaks of the Sierras. Reminiscent of a woman once beautiful, who lost her charm as she aged, the house and the grounds wore decades of neglect like a shabby overcoat.

Buck rode around to the back door where he found Alma's pick-up parked nearby. He slid off the horse, reached through the window, and honked the horn. The blast sent a multitude of sickly stray cats and kittens running for cover under the rotting boards of the back porch.

A moment later an elderly woman, less than five feet tall from the jack-knife bend in her spine, threw open a torn screen door. "What!" she screeched.

Buck held out the rope. "Hey Alma, I think this belongs to you."

She stared blankly at him, while smoothing strands of yellow-white hair that had come loose from the braids circling her head like a halo.

"Chief. He got out again," Buck said, waving the end of the rope. "I brought him back. Don't you want him?"

Still no response.

He shook his head. *She's just gonna stare at me.* "I guess I'll put him back in his stall and see if I can rig up something that'll hold him."

"That'th a good idea," Alma said with a cartoon-like lisp. Her tongue poked through a gap where her front teeth should have been. "Just go ahead and sthee what you can do," she said, then turned and went back into the house as the screen door closed behind her.

35

DONATELLO FOLLOWED A footpath to the top of the hill where a lichen-dappled rock wall surrounded the Romanesque mansion of Mondscheinberg Cellars. He opened a small iron gate and crossed a wide brick driveway. Statuesque valley oaks flanked a broad portico at the mansion's entrance. As he ambled up the steps, a dull ache settled low in his pelvis. He opened the tall front doors and wandered through an expansive foyer to the kitchen.

The aroma of simmering chicken stock filled the air.

Polishing silverware at a large, work-worn table, Lupe, his sturdy middle-aged housemanager, looked up when he came into the room. "You're up early," she said, smoothing her black hair, tarnishing to gray, into a thick chignon.

He slumped onto a chair at the table beside her.

She watched him a moment. "Are you okay? You don't look well. And you haven't been yourself since you came back from LA." She wiped her hands on her brightly colored apron. "Maybe you're coming down with something. Let me feel your forehead."

He leaned back in the chair. "Lupe, I am bene . . . uh, fine."

She pressed her fingers over his brow. "You're not feverish, but if you don't feel well, maybe we should call Uncle Lorenzo."

Donatello shook his head and hunched over the table. "No. We call enough. He already nag all the time."

"Why don't you go upstairs and lie down? I'll call you when lunch is ready."

Donatello shrugged, got up and sauntered out of the kitchen.

He went into a small bathroom tucked beneath the massive stairs framing the mansion's entry and closed the door. Flipping up the burl-wood toilet seat, he unzipped his pants. A slight burning sensation singed his groin. Staring into the toilet bowl, milky-apricot preceded a clear yellow stream.

Ave Maria. He closed his eyes. *What is wrong? There is no hope I imagine this. It only gets worse.* He zipped his pants, yanked the gold-plated lever, and watched the water swirling out of the bowl. Standing in front of a marble vanity, he turned on the faucet. He stared at his reflection in a gilt-framed mirror, rubbed a bar of soap over his hands, then let the water rinse the suds away. *I wish soap will wash it away.*

Donatello closed the bathroom door and went into his study. He sat down at a large mahogany desk and leaned back in his chair. The heady scent of narcissus and hyacinth wafted in through an open window. Fumbling with his cigarette case, he managed to pull one out. He put the brown paper to his lips and struck a match. The sulfurous aroma and the smell of burning tobacco mingled, masking the scent of the flowers.

I must call Lorenzo. Winding the chain of his crucifix around his finger, he stared at the phone. *No. It still may go away.* Then, another vindictive ache. He shook his head. *Deborah, why you do this to me?*

He kissed the cross, then picked up the phone.

It rang several times. "Hello," a gruff voice answered.

"Uncle Lorenzo, is Dona."

"Oh, Dona," Lorenzo replied. "Good to hear from you. What is it this time?"

"I . . ." Donatello began.

"Speak up. I can hardly hear you."

"I need doctor."

"You had a seizure?"

"No."

"Well, I'm glad you're finally coming to your senses. I already looked up a specialist -- someone who treats epilepsy."

"No. I have . . . something else wrong."

"Have what?"

"I think I get something . . ."

A stony silence, then Lorenzo cleared his throat. "So, do you think you got this *something* from a woman?"

Another silence.

"Sì."

Lorenzo exhaled a long breath into the receiver. "Dona, I thought when your father arranged your marriage to Slovika . . . well, I thought you'd at least try to act like you're not insane. Who gave it to you?"

"I no want say." Another pause. "Actress I meet in LA."

"Oh, an actress. After all the mess with Caggiano's mistress, you got involved with an actress?"

"She is married. I thought she is safe."

"Mary, mother of God, Dona. Married?" Unintelligible words flooded the receiver. "A seizure specialist isn't going to fix that. Let me think a minute."

Another silence.

"Okay. There's a clinic here in the city -- the Free Clinic. Trust me, to them stuff like that is no big deal."

"But, Uncle, *The Bounty Killer* . . . I no can go . . ."

Lorenzo sighed. "Oh, yeah, right."

More silence.

"Okay. I know a guy who might be able to help. He got into a beef with the law for writing bogus prescriptions for San Francisco socialites. But he might still have his connections."

"Grazie, Uncle Lorenzo."

"Dona, you should be more careful. This isn't Italy. There are a lot of nuts running around. With your knack for getting into trouble, guaranteed, they'll find you."

Looking heavenward, Donatello rolled his eyes. "Sì, Uncle."

"I know you hate it when I nag. But I don't want you to get into anything you can't get out of. You could be in over your head before you know it. Besides, what will your father think? You know how he is -- if anything happens to you, he'll have my head on a platter."

A little more than an hour passed.

The phone rang in Donatello's study. He jumped off the couch and grabbed the receiver. "Ciao . . ."

"Dona, it's Lorenzo. I got hold of the guy I was telling you about. He can get you a round of antibiotics. He also said, anyone you've been with -- I mean Slovika, not the slut who gave it to you -- she needs a round too, symptoms or not, just in case."

Donatello sank into the chair at his desk. "Sì, grazie, Uncle. But Slovika, she no need it. I have not sleep with her since we are in LA."

36

"CRAZY OLD WOMAN. Who the hell does she think she is, anyway?" Buck muttered. "Ordering me around like a hired hand." He kicked a loose cobblestone as he shuffled toward the barn, pulling Chief along behind him. They passed an immense pile of aging bottles, rusting tin cans, rotting wood, and cardboard heaped next to an archaic incinerator. He shook his head.

"Junk pile. Big as ever. It's like a damn dump around here." *Must've been here all her life and probably before. Nothing ever leaves this place, unless it goes up in smoke.* He took off his hat, slapped it on his thigh, and put it on again. "Sure as hell, she's got a crazy streak."

Buck swung the wide barn door open. The smell of hay, horse manure, and old leather hung in the air. He tossed his hat on a nail, pulled off his gloves and dropped them on a bale of hay. Then led Chief to his stall, untied the makeshift bridle, slapped the horse on the rump and closed the door. "Alma needs to get a padlock for your stall." Sliding the pin into the latch, the lonely sound echoed through the cavernous structure.

"Now, something to hold it with . . ."

He found a length of rusted chain, and a twisted piece of baling wire in a dusty wooden crate opposite the stall. He wound the chain around a post, then through the latch and secured it with the wire. "There," he said, tugging on the chain as Chief hung his head over the stall door. "That should hold you. But you're smart and you've got all day to figure out how to bust out of here."

Buck pulled a handful of alfalfa from a bale near the stall. Chief stretched for it, flapping his thick lips. Buck rubbed his forehead, then gave him the hay. "Why do you want to go roamin' all over the country anyway? This is a nice place. Sure, it's a little dusty, but..."

He paused. The haunting silence closed in around him. The only other signs of life in the barn were another of Alma's stray cats, and her litter of kittens, and a nest of barn owls high in the rafters.

"Never mind, I know. You're lonesome."

Chief bounced his head up and down, leaning toward the hay bale. Buck patted his neck.

"No wonder you're so fat. I bet all she does is feed you."

Watching the dust swirling in a triangular wedge of golden light filtering in through a small window, Buck saw fragmented images of all the work and sweat that once took place in the barn. In a whirlwind of memory, he saw them all again -- the cowboys, ranch hands, and vaqueros.

> Trinity, Frank, Joe, and Mel -- the cowhands who stayed in the bunkhouse. And Jack the farrier -- at the forge, making horseshoes. And Rico, Lancho, and Angel -- the migrant vaqueros who camped down at the river.

"Frank and Trinity taught me to ride," he said under his breath. "So many years have passed... Lancho's the only one who's still around. He must have been just a teenager when he came. Don't think we've said more than two words in ten years." Buck paused a moment. "And the German cook... what was his name? Oh yeah, Uncle Otto. Haven't thought of him in ages."

Then, another recollection. An odd image.

A woolen vest draped over a chair in Alma's entry and a wooden cane resting at the foot of her stairs.

"Uncle Otto . . . I wonder . . ." He smiled. *Sure. Makes sense. I should've figured it out before.*

All the cats scattered again as Buck stepped onto a loose board on Alma's back porch. "Dry rot's gonna eat this place alive," he muttered, avoiding the rotten wood near the threshold. He rapped a knuckle on the door

"Come on in," she called.

Yanking on the rickety screen, he braced himself for the parlor. Diffused sunlight spilled in through a dirty picture window, drenching the parlor in a golden glow that faintly alluded to the mansion's former elegance. The musty smell of neglect hung in the air. Dusty bags, boxes, and bits of things took up every available space. Along with newspaper. Stacks and stacks of newspaper. As if the house, its occupant, and all the contents had been stained the color of aged newsprint.

"Damn firetrap," Buck said under his breath, making his way around the hodgepodge to the living room. *Place never changes. The first edition of the Sacramento Union -- the oldest daily in the west -- is probably buried in one of the stacks.*

He pushed a half-crushed shoebox filled with string and lace out of the way with his foot and sat down on a threadbare sofa. It sank under his weight, and he found himself sitting uncomfortably close to the floor. "Chief's all tucked in," he said, setting his hat and work gloves on the arm of the couch. "And, since I'm here, you can hang up the party line," he added, motioning to a receiver sitting to one side of the telephone.

Alma frowned and dropped it onto its cradle. She settled herself on a chair draped with the makings of a quilt, its inspiration long before forgotten. She crossed her legs, revealing a pair of men's work boots. "It'th good of you to visit," she lisped, smoothing her Annie Oakley-style blouse and split riding skirt.

He shook his head. *Looks like she rode into the twentieth century on a buckboard.* "Actually, Alma, I didn't come to visit. I brought Chief back, remember?"

"Never-the-leth, here you are," she said with a gap-toothed smile.

Buck squirmed irritably on the sofa. "Chief let Nahlah out again, and he rolled in my vegetable garden which, by the way, I had just finished tilling."

"Oh? Well, he'th a character." Alma paused a moment, looking at Buck with a suspicious stare. "Where did you and Pauline go? You were gone quite a while."

"And the party line went dead?"

She crossed her arms and frowned.

Buck looked down at his lap. "Um, we went to visit a long-lost relative in San Francisco."

"You don't usually leave that thuddenly. Ith everything okay?"

"Yeah, sure." Buck took a deep breath. *I hate the question that'll probably come next and the conversation that usually follows.*

"That'th good. How'th Steven?"

Bingo. He forced a smile. *In this case, I'm not above telling an out-and-out lie.* "He's fine."

"Doing well?"

One lie leads to another. "Very well."

"I don't generally care for kids, you know. But, I've alwayth liked him. You're lucky he'th a good boy. Speaking of San Franthisco, did I tell you my niece'th daughter turned into a beatnik?"

Buck fidgeted on the sofa. "Yes, Alma, you told me. But I think they're called hippies now."

"Oh. Then she turned into a ippie."

"That's hippie. With an 'H'."

"Don't be perthnickety. Anyway, she went to San Franthisco and she justh dithappeared . . ."

The conversation twisted and turned until the grandfather clock in Alma's foyer chimed twelve. Being spry for her age, she abruptly jumped up. "You musth be hungry. I'll get you thomething," she said, then vanished into the kitchen.

"Alma, no! Don't go to any trouble," Buck called, frantically trying to free himself from the sofa. But it seemed to swallow him like quicksand. *Don't want anything from that kitchen!* "It's getting late and I really should be going."

"It'll be just a minute . . ."

Alma returned carrying a tray with two bottles of Diet Rite cola, and two cans of tuna with forks stuck in them.

Buck sank back on the couch. "Now Alma . . . you shouldn't -- "

"Nonthense," she said, setting the tray on a stack of newspapers beside the couch.

"I really have to go. Pauline will be fixing lunch."

"That'th not very neighborly."

Think, damn it, think! Hey, throw out Uncle Otto and see if he catches anything. Buck looked up at her. "I bet you really miss Uncle Otto."

She shifted nervously in her chair. "Why would you thay that?" she said with a puzzled expression,

"You two were pretty close, weren't you?" he said as if it was both a question and the answer. "I bet you really miss having him around, if you know what I mean," he added with a wink.

"Well! I never!" she huffed.

"Sure you did. Uncle Otto was your lover."

Alma blanched, then blushed, and threw her hand over her mouth.

Buck sat back and crossed his arms. "Well, well, well. I wasn't sure until now."

37

THE BACK DOOR screeched on its hinges as Buck came into the laundry room. He hung his hat on a hook and dropped his gloves on top of the washing machine.

"Buck..." Pauline called from the kitchen. "Since you're home from Alma's, can we get Steven's toys from the attic?"

"*We* really means *me*, doesn't it?" he called back.

Pauline met him at the foot of the stairs.

Buck pulled off his glasses and rubbed the bridge of his nose. "Alright, where's the toy box?" he said, wrapping the wire earpieces around his ears again.

"Where it's always been. Under the window at the gable end."

"Anything else while I'm up there?"

"No, just the toys. Lunch will be ready in a little while."

"Good. I'm starved. I almost had to eat at Alma's."

"What? Just the thought of that kitchen is enough to turn a person's stomach. How'd you get out of it?"

"I dug up the memory of her German cook, Uncle Otto. She got so flustered, she forgot all about lunch. And thanks to the political craftiness I inherited from dear old Dad, for the most part, I managed to scoot out from under the wrath of the victim."

"Why would that upset her?"

"He was her lover."

"You're kidding. How did you know?"

"The idea came to me in the barn, while I was tucking Chief in," he said, unfastening his overalls. He wriggled them down to his knees and stepped out. "One time my dad sent me over there for something. The door was unlocked so I went in, but when I yelled for Alma, no one answered. I remembered seeing Uncle Otto's vest and his cane at the foot of her stairs. I thought that was kind of strange, but it didn't register until today. Since she was trying to force-feed me a can of tuna, I figured I might as well test my theory." Buck glanced around. "Where's Donovan?"

"He's in the living room playing with Tailor."

"I'm surprised he's taking this so well."

"We had a few more tears, but Tailor helped console him. I think his world has been so shaky, even though everything is new . . ." She shook her head. "I don't understand how Steven could do this. I thought we raised him better than -- "

Buck put his finger to her lips. "It doesn't help. Things aren't the way they used to be. And maybe they never were." He kissed her forehead. "I'll go get the toys."

Buck yanked on a thick cord hanging from the ceiling in the upstairs hall. A trap door opened and he pulled down another set of stairs. The wood creaked under his weight as he lumbered up the steps, into the dry, dusty attic. At the top, he flipped a switch. Stark white light from a bare bulb replaced the soft amber glow filtering in through a small window at the gable end.

"Stuffy as ever," he muttered with a cough. Stepping around the cartons, bags, and boxes stacked near the stairwell, he looked up at an antique lantern and wooden ironing board hanging from a beam. *Pauline's got a new ironing board and now we use a flashlight. Why do we keep all this old junk, anyway?*

Passing a stack of photo albums, Buck paused at an aged book and ran his hand over the tooled leather cover. "The Harper family Bible," he said under his breath. Then he noticed a nearby cardboard box and pulled away the brittle masking tape that had come loose from the top. He opened the carton, moved a sheet of newspaper, and took out a porcelain plate ornamented with a picture of a pheasant, bordered by a band of oak leaves and acorns. "Mother's dishes." He set the plate back in the box.

He looked past several rusted coyote traps hanging from a nail to a saxophone and clarinet. *The sax and the licorice stick . . .*

He wandered over and swept a cobweb off the curving brass of the saxophone, then picked up the clarinet. The instrument bent slightly as he brushed away a film of dust. Holding it to the light, he examined the mouthpiece, then twisted off the barrel. *Cracked cork and chipped reed.* He slid the pieces together again. Putting his lips to the mouthpiece, he placed his fingers over the keys, then closed his eyes and breathed lightly over the reed. The note fell flat. Tears welled in his eyes.

Just then, a noise at the foot of the stairs startled him. He set the clarinet down and wiped his eyes.

"Buuuck . . ." Pauline called. "Lunch is almost ready. Did you find the toys?"

He cleared his throat, then turned and saw the toy box. "Uh, yeah. Found 'em."

38

SEVERAL DAYS LATER, Donatello sat at the desk in his study, staring at a ledger and a stack of bills. *The more I look, the taller it grows. The taller it grows, the more I despair.* He ran his fingers through his hair, then dropped his head into his hands. "I follow the advice -- no use my money if I can use money of someone else. Now I have no agent. No work. I no more can borrow, and I cannot pay." *I am 'The Bounty Killer.' It should not be this way.*

A knock on the door startled him. Lupe peered hesitantly into the study and cleared her throat.

Donatello looked up. "Sì?"

"Yoshio wants to see you."

"Why?"

"Um, I don't know. He just wants to talk to you."

Donatello frowned. "Where he is?"

"I think he's in the greenhouse."

Donatello went out the back door of the mansion and walked briskly across the driveway. Warmed by the midday sun, the air held a hint of the summer inferno to come. "Interruptions, always interruptions," he muttered. "But maybe I am thankful to be away from money problem."

Situated on a rise across from the mansion, the glass-walled greenhouse looked out over a terraced orchard of cherries, peaches, and apples.

He stomped over a flagstone walkway in front of the greenhouse, startling a sparrow splashing in a puddle between the stones. Yanking on the door, hot, humid air, and the smell of wet bark mulch came upon him like a tropical storm.

"Yoshio . . . Lupe say you want talk to me . . ." he called, stepping over the raised threshold. He waited, watching the condensation running in thin rivulets down the glass.

No reply.

He went around rows of slatted tables holding vine cuttings and vegetable seedlings. Passing through a curtain of clear plastic strips, he went into another room as long and wide as the first. There, large containers of specimen plants waited for the last frost to pass.

"Yoshio . . ." he called again, taking a long breath of the oppressive air.

No reply.

Going through another plastic curtain, he came to the last room. A large turbine at the far end spun cool air into the greenhouse. Stopping in front of the fan, the breeze chilled the perspiration beading on his skin.

"Yoshio?"

Wandering back the way he came, Donatello flung the greenhouse door open and stepped out of the humidity into the warm, dry air. Just then, a stocky oriental man wearing overalls and a coolie hat came out of a storage building, pushing a wheelbarrow.

"Yoshio," Donatello called, flapping the front of his shirt to release the moisture. "Lupe say you want talk to me."

Yoshio set down the wheelbarrow. "Yes, Mr. Dragghi," he said with a slight bow.

Donatello frowned. "What you want?"

Yoshio pushed off the coolie hat. It hung over his back by a cord. "It's spring."

Donatello stared blankly at him. "Sì, sì. Spring."

Yoshio stared back at him.

Looking heavenward, Donatello kissed his fingertips and rolled his eyes. "I know the season. You bring me here to tell me this?"

"It's past time to hire the laborers."

"Laborah? What is this, laborah?"

Yoshio took a noticeable breath. "Workers. Workers to tend the vineyard. I can't do it all myself. Especially since you have me working on the gardens around the house."

"Then get them," Donatello said with a dismissive wave.

"They will need to be paid. They won't work for free."

Donatello shrugged. "Sì. Of course. Pay them."

"But, Mr. Dragghi, I'm supposed to get paid once a week and it's already been two weeks . . ."

Donatello put his hands on his hips and glared at Yoshio. "You no be paid? Why, Lupe, she did not pay you?"

Yoshio looked down and scuffed at the ground.

"Okay. I find what is the problem." Donatello shook his head, then crunched back across the gravel, toward the house. Stomping up the steps, he threw the door open. "Lupe!" he shouted over the din of a vacuum cleaner, then followed the sound into the living room. "Lupe!"

She jumped, spun around and turned off the vacuum. "Oh, you startled me!"

"Yoshio say for two week he has no be paid," Donatello said with a hawk-like stare. "Why you no pay him?"

She glanced at the floor for a moment, then looked up at him. "There was no money."

"Not in household account?"

She shook her head.

"Then . . . you be paid?"

She shook her head again.

"Why you don't tell me?" He slumped onto dark brown couch and sank into the leather. "I remember. You tell me this already." He paused a moment, then looked up at her. "Lupe, perdonami . . . forgive me. You and Yoshio will be paid."

Donatello went back to his study. He closed the door and wandered to the window. Staring out at the vineyard, he rolled his forehead on the glass. *What am I to do? I cannot call Lorenzo. I must crawl to my father.*

He went to a marble mantle above the massive fireplace across from his desk. Studying a group of photographs, he picked up a picture of three smiling boys in school uniforms, posing at the base of a sculpture. *Micha ... Leo ... me ...* "Will I ever equal my brothers?"

He set the picture down, and picked up an aged sepia-tinted photograph of a distinguished-looking man. "Papa ..." he said under his breath, lightly tracing his fingertip over the glass. "I wish I make you proud. But I must call."

He set the picture back on the mantle, went to his desk, and picked up the phone. "Operatore internazionale. A call to Italia, uh, Italy per favore."

39

DEMETRI DRAGGHI PICKED up the phone on a nightstand beside his bed, in his villa overlooking the Mediterranean. "Sì?" he said in a gravelly voice, glancing at a clock beside the phone. *11:25? Who would call at this hour?*

"Papa..."

"Donatello?" Demetri switched on a lamp, illuminating bedroom walls finished in marble. "Something is wrong?"

"You were sleeping?"

Demetri sat up in bed. "Not yet. You sound troubled, my son. What is it?"

Donatello cleared his throat. "Papa... I need to borrow -- "

An audible sigh. "I should have known. Did I need ask?" Demetri picked up a torn air-mail envelope and tapped it on the edge of the nightstand. The rhythm quickened as he re-read the postscript on the letter that came in the envelope. He ran his fingers through his hair. "With you, Dona, it is always money. Never do you call otherwise."

"Papa," Donatello said. "This is not true."

"Ah, my son, but it is." Demetri dropped the envelope and picked up the letter. "Your Uncle Lorenzo writes to tell me you will be needing money." He paused. "How does he know this? Is it because you have asked him too?" He set the letter back on the nightstand.

"But Papa..."

"He also tells me you have no work, *and* you have no agent. *And* the vineyard cost more than you had. *And* he told you not to buy it. *And* you borrowed the money from him. *And* you did not tell me." Demetri squeezed his fingers together and rocked his hand back and forth. "Why, why, why you do this to me, Dona?"

"But, you loaned the money to make *The Bounty Killer*. Now, all over Europe, it is success and you make the money back."

"But the movie cannot be released in America."

"Oh, Papa..."

"You no 'oh Papa' me!" Demetri exhaled sharply. "I send you to California to straighten out, but instead it all starts again. Always the same. One step from disaster. I ask Uncle Lorenzo to let you stay with him, to protect you in case Caggiano breaks his promise not to kill you. But do you stay with him? No. You buy a vineyard. Quite an extravagance for a man who has no income!" he shouted into the receiver. "And I buy you a bride, a beautiful Gypsy girl, so you will keep your hands to yourself. But does she satisfy you? No. No. No. *And* Lorenzo tells me you don't take your medicine."

"The medicine make me sleepy."

"Reckless, Dona! Reckless! And Lorenzo tells me in the postscript, not only do you sleep with a married actress... she gives you a disease! I send money, money, and more money, but it all starts again!" Demetri shook his head and waved his hand through the air. "Why you do this to me, Dona? Why you can't be good like your brother?"

"Why you always bring up Leo? And why does Lorenzo tell you all this... and about Deborah?"

"Ha!" Demetri said with a sharp exhale. "Maria madre di Dio, then it is true!"

"But Papa..."

A prolonged silence.

"Alright, Dona. You are my son. I can't give all the money you need, but I will do what I can."

Demetri hung up the phone. He sat, staring at the floor. *Now, sleep will not come for hours.*

He got up, pulled a robe over his silk pajamas, and picked up the letter. Wandering out of the bedroom, he went down a long hallway to his office. He slumped into the chair at his desk and buried his face in his hands.

"Dona, Dona, Dona. I love you, my son, but you make me crazy."

Several minutes passed. Demetri sat back and switched on a lamp. *Somehow I must help him. But he has burned more bridges than a man can build.* He flipped open a leather address book. Page after page, he studied the entries. *Nothing. Is there no one who can help him?*

Drawing his finger over the names on the last page, he paused, then sat back in his chair. "Beletski Yacov. The investment banker living in Milan. He has had no dealings with Dona. Or Caggiano that I know of. Perhaps."

The next morning Demetri sat in his office, watching the hands on an ornate clock on his desk. *Wait until 9:30.* "I cannot appear too anxious," he said under his breath. At 9:25 he picked up the phone and dialed a Milan number.

After several rings, a gruff male voice answered. "Yes?"

"Demetri Dragghi. You are Beletski Yacov, the investment banker?"

The man took a long, loud breath. "No. How did you get this number?" he said, his voice rasping as a cheese grater.

"A friend. Benito Maggiore. He gave to me."

"Ah, my good friend, Benito." The voice warmed. "He gave you my private number. Maybe you misunderstood. My name is Yacov Beletski, not Beletski Yacov," he said between noticeable breaths. "Since you are a friend of my dear friend, Benito, what can I do for you?"

"My son, Donatello Dragghi, he is director of the film, *The Bounty Killer*. Perhaps you hear of it?"

"Hmmm. Yes. I believe I have."

"Donatello is in California, in San Francisco. And *The Bounty Killer* is hold up at, how you say, the American rating . . . rating . . ."

"Ratings board."

"Sì. They say too explicit sex, and too violent."

"Mmmm . . ." Yacov muttered. "That could be good in the long run," he said with a bit more interest.

"But since the movie is not released, Dona . . . he needs money."

"Who doesn't?" Yacov said with a gravelly chuckle.

"But Dona is not well known in California."

"Oh, I see. This is where I come in." Yacov paused; his breath filled the receiver. "Why didn't he call me?"

"Benito . . . he is my friend. Dona doesn't know him."

Yacov sighed. "Alright. Since you're a friend of Benito. I'll be stateside in a few days. First, I'm going to New York. When I'm finished there, I can meet with Donatello in San Francisco. My secretary will make the arrangements."

"Grazie. If ever there is something I can do for you . . ."

"Don't worry." Yacov laughed. "There will be."

40

MORNING SUN FLOODED into the Harpers' kitchen as Pauline wiped sticky fingerprints from a cabin-shaped tin of syrup.

"Breakfast is ready," she called, setting the tin back on the table.

A few minutes later, Buck lumbered in and sat down. "You're chirpy this morning. Where's Stev -- I mean Donny?"

She smiled. "He's upstairs with Tailor. You're doing it too."

"What?"

She set a plate of bacon, eggs, and waffles on the table. "Calling him Steven. And it didn't take long to shorten Donovan to Donny, did it?"

Buck picked up the cabin-shaped tin. "Been awhile since we've had the cabin instead of a bottle. He already had breakfast?"

"Yes and he ate like a horse."

Buck drizzled amber syrup over the waffles. "With your cooking, he'd be a fool not to."

"Oh, I almost forgot. I called the hospital."

He sliced a wedge out of the waffles. "And?"

"They're transferring Steven out of intensive care in a day or so."

He set the fork down. "That's good news."

Pauline looked up. Her eyes sparkled. "Yes, it is."

"When you smile like that, you're pretty as a picture. Come 'ere." Buck pushed his plate aside and pulled her onto his lap.

"Your breakfast will get cold."

"Who cares."

"But what about the rest of the waffles?"

"Let 'em burn."

"You don't mean that."

"Oh, yes I do." He kissed her and rubbed the stubble on his chin over her neck.

"Buck! That tickles!"

"I know. I meant it to."

She kissed his forehead. "Well, you old bear."

"It's good to see you happy."

"It's good to be happy," she replied with a sigh. "It's been a long time." She hugged him, then got up and straightened her apron. "Now finish your breakfast."

Tailor wandered into the kitchen, wagging his stubby tail.

"Do you want your waffle?" she asked.

The dog sat on his haunches and pumped his forelegs. Pauline tore off a piece tossed it to him. After a soft flap of his muzzle, it was gone. "I'm taking Donny shopping later," she said, tossing another bit of waffle.

"How come?"

"That should be obvious. He needs some decent clothes."

"Then I'll take him to Tony's."

"Tony's?" Pauline repeated. "The feed store?"

"Yes, the feed store. If you take him downtown, guaranteed, you'll run into Carolyn Cox, or another one of your friends, and she'll weasel the whole story out of you. Then about a half hour later the whole county'll know. Besides that, a boy needs clothes he can get dirty. He needs flannel shirts, jeans, and overalls. And nobody's got more of 'em than Tony."

The sound of boot heels echoed on the dusty plank floor of Tony's Feed and Hay. Cobwebs filled in the angles of the rafters, and the air was thick with the smell of alfalfa, molasses, and leather. Buck and Donny sauntered through the large, converted barn until they came upon a stack of folded denim. Donny waited patiently as Buck rifled through the pile until curiosity overcame him, and he wandered away.

"I thought there were some kid-sized over-alls around here somewhere," Buck muttered. He pulled a tiny pair out of the stack and held them up. "They look about right. Wonder if they'll shrink? Pauline will be t'd-off if they do. Better ask Tony." He ambled toward the counter. "Hey, where's Tony?" he called to a man at the other end of the store.

"Loading the delivery truck," the man yelled back.

Just then, Tony burst through a swinging door and made his way to the counter, where several customers were waiting. When they saw him coming, they quickly formed a line. From opposite directions, Buck and Alma stepped in line at the same time.

"Hello neighbor," she said pushing in front of him. "I'm ordering hay. How 'bout you?"

"Just stocking up on a few things," he replied, holding the overalls behind his back.

Tony positioned himself at an antique cash register. "What'll it be?" he asked the first man in line.

"Ton a' oat hay."

Tony ran his hands over his jet-black hair, then drew a pencil from an empty tin of Bag Balm and licked the lead. "Want it delivered?" he asked as he printed the man's bill.

"No, I'll load it."

"He writes the prettiest bills in the county, bein' the new owner and all," a weathered rancher said to the man behind him.

"Just takes 'im awhile to do it," the other man replied, shifting his hands in the pockets of his dusty overalls. "I'm still mad at Gus for sellin' the store to him in the first place. Can't find a damn thing in here anymore."

"Hell, Floyd, it's been two years . . ." the first rancher said.

The other man shrugged in response.

Tony rang the rancher's order, speared a copy of the receipt on a spindle, and looked over at the next in line. "What'll it be?"

"Balling gun. Can't find 'em since you moved everything around," he grumbled.

Tony frowned. "They're right where they've always been." He stepped from behind the cash register and the line of customers followed, leaving Buck and Alma standing by the counter.

"How'th Pauline?" she lisped.

"Fine."

"And Steven?"

Buck stared at her. *God, I hope she doesn't ask about Donny. How do I explain a grandkid coming out of nowhere with long hair and ratty clothes?* His eyes shot open and he glanced frantically around the store. *Donny!*

"Well, ith he okay, or not?"

"He? Uh, who?" Buck stammered.

Alma grabbed his shirtsleeve. "Steven. Ith he alright?"

"Yeah, uh, sure . . . 'scuse me," he said, prying her fingers off his sleeve.

Just then, he felt a tug on the back of his pant leg. He turned to see Donny waving a half-eaten candy bar and rubbing his nose with chocolate-covered fingers.

"Gwampa! Gwampa! Wook!" he mumbled with a mouthful of chocolate.

"Where've you been?" Buck snapped.

"Well, ith Steven okay or not!" Alma blurted.

"Yes, of course, he's okay."

"Why didn't you justh thay so."

Buck grabbed Donny's hand. "Come on."

Alma stepped in front of them. "Justh a minute. Did that little girl call you Grandpa?"

"Um . . . well . . . uh . . ."

"Buck Harper, did I, or did I not, hear that little girl call you grandpa?"

He took a long breath. "Uh, yeah."

"Then she muth be Steven'th daughter."

He sighed. "That would be the logical assumption, except *she* is a *he*."

"What?" Alma waved a bony finger at him. "What the devil do you mean?"

"His name is Donovan," Buck said with a definitive nod.
"What?"
"Alma, you sound like a broken record."
She stared at Donovan. He smiled back at her with chocolate-coated teeth.
"But the hair..."
"I know," Buck said. "But we checked, and he's definitely a he."
"She, I mean he, lookth to be three or four. Why didn't you tell me Steven ith married and hath a girl -- I mean boy?"
Buck paused. "Well, he's not exactly married..." He smiled. "It's sorta like you... and Uncle Otto..."

41

DONATELLO STOOD AT the entrance of an Italian café near Grant Avenue in San Francisco, known for decent food and opera-singing waiters. The air was heavy with a half-century of garlic and wood smoke. Murals of the Italian countryside painted on the cracked plaster walls had faded to sepia.

He looked at his watch, then irritably scrutinized the patrons. *The man's secretary said to meet him here at half-past twelve . . .*

Cold air rushed into the stuffy, crowded foyer through vinyl-padded doors as a vagrant man with long straggly hair, ripped jeans, and bare feet wandered in.

"No shirt. No shoes. No service," a middle-aged hostess said, pointing at him with a pencil.

He pulled on his dirty tie-dyed t-shirt as if to prove that she couldn't be talking to him.

"No shirt. No *shoes*. No service," she repeated, pointing to his feet.

"I just wanna use the can," he muttered.

"Restrooms are for customers only," she said, waving toward the door.

"Can't a guy even take a piss?"

"Not here, you can't."

Shaking his head, the transient turned and ran into a hulking man wearing a dark topcoat and carrying a briefcase.

"Watch where you're going," the large man snapped. Then they danced around each other a moment before the vagrant shuffled past him, out the door.

The man with the briefcase lumbered to the reservation desk. "How long?" he said between rasping breaths.

The hostess stared at him. "Excuse me?"

"How long to be seated?" he said, combing long strands of oily black hair back over his bald spot with his fingers.

"At least half an hour," she tersely replied. "Shall I add your name to the list?"

"Yes. Yacov Beletski. B-E-L-E-T-S-K-I."

The hostess scribbled his name and picked up a stack of menus. "Mahoney . . . party of eight!" she shouted, then turned and nearly ran into Donatello. She caught her breath and blushed. "Mahoney?" she asked in a thin, wavering tone.

He shook his head.

Just then, the Mahoney party converged on the reservation desk. The hostess squeezed Donatello's hand. "Don't go away, I'll be right back."

Waving to the Mahoney party, she bumped into Yacov. Then, like a rite of passage, the rest of the party ran into him in one way or another as they followed her to their table.

Donatello stepped forward. "Yacov Beletski?"

"Of course," he replied with a frown. "And you must be 'The Bounty Killer.'" He straightened his topcoat and adjusted his tie, then stepped back and looked at Donatello. "Hmmm. I thought you'd be taller."

Donatello glared at him. "And I think you will be on time."

"Patience may be a virtue, but promptness? In this case, considering it's a thirty-minute wait, maybe not."

Donatello shrugged. "We will see."

"She just told me it's a thirty-minute wait."

"We will see," he repeated.

Moments later, the hostess returned. Donatello swaggered to the desk. Placing his hands over the list of reservations, he tilted his head to read her name tag. "Janice . . . like your name, you are beautifool, amore mio" he said, thickening his accent and staring deeply into her eyes. "You have a table for me, Janice?"

She blushed. "I think I can find something."

42

"YOU WERE WORRIED about me running into Carolyn, but you ran into Alma," Pauline said as she untied her apron. "That must have been something."

"It was something, alright," Buck replied. "But I managed to get her out of our hair, at least for the moment. Come 'ere." He led Pauline into the living room, flopped onto the couch, and pulled her down beside him. "Speaking of hair -- it has to go."

"What?"

"Donny. His hair has to go. He can't live here looking like a girl," Buck said, drumming his fingers on the arm of the couch.

"But we can't just -- "

"Oh yes we can. Shara more-or-less deserted him. And Steven is in no condition to object. I'll take him to the barbershop."

"You can't take him there," Pauline said. Look what just happened at Tony's. They're worse than a bunch of gossipy old women."

Buck frowned. "Well regardless, he's gotta have a haircut. If I can't take him to the barbershop, then you'll have to do it."

"Let me take your shirt off. Gramma's going to cut your hair," Pauline said, forcing a smile.

Donovan squirmed as she pulled a torn, tie-dyed T-shirt over his head and tossed it on the tiled bathroom floor. *That has an appointment with the incinerator.* She patted the seat of a low stool in front of the dressing table. "Come sit down," she said, lifting him onto the stool. "Are you cold?"

He nodded.

"Then we'll turn on the heater." She pushed a button and a row of gray-white elements embedded beneath a grate on the wall began to glow, and a warm electric smell radiated in the room. "Let's put something over you," she said, draping a hand towel around his shoulders.

Pauline picked up the comb and scissors. "Okay, here we go." *Dear God, his hair's probably never even been combed, let alone cut.*

Donny looked skeptically at her. "I don wan a haircut, Gwamma."

Look confident. "I know, but I promise it won't hurt."

Soon, the comb was caught in a long strawberry-blonde tangle. Pulling the comb out, she gingerly tugged in another spot. *Don't think this is going to work . . .*

He began whimpering. "Ow, Gwamma."

"I'm sorry. It hurt a little, didn't it?"

Donny sniffed and nodded.

Pauline put the comb down. "Maybe I can do it with my fingers." Separating the matted strands, she froze. Miniscule creatures hid in the tangles, and yellow-brown eggs were affixed near his scalp. She caught her breath, jumped back, and flapped her hands. "Buuuck!"

Donny screamed, slid off the stool, and scrambled under the dressing table as Buck rushed into the room.

"What! What's the matter?" he blurted.

"He has lice!" she shrieked, pointing at Donny, cowering under the vanity.

Buck sighed. "Lice? Is that all? I thought it was something serious. With all the roaches crawling around back home, it's not too surprising he's got bugs living in his hair."

"That's an awful thing to say. What should we do?"

Buck rubbed his forehead. "I'll get the horse clippers. While you shave off his hair, I'll run down to the pharmacy and get the stuff that kills the eggs. I better get some for you too, since you slept in his room. Then I'll stop by Tony's and pick up some farm-boy clothes."

43

THE HOSTESS SEATED Donatello and Yacov at a window table overlooking a busy street corner. While Yacov polished his flatware with a napkin, Donatello alternately traced his splinted fingers over the red-checkered tablecloth and pulled slivers of melted wax from a Chianti bottle acting as a candleholder. He looked up as a server went by singing and carrying a tray loaded with plates of bubbling lasagna.

Yacov glanced at his watch. "Too bad you can't use the same magic you used on the hostess to scare up a waiter," he said with a grating exhale.

Madre di dio, he breathes like a beast. "I no am God," Donatello replied. "Charm, it does not work so much on men."

Just then, a young server came to the table. Blithely singing part of an aria from Tosca, he poured ice water into their glasses.

"Not bad," Yacov said.

The server looked at him with a curious expression.

"Your voice. It's not bad," Yacov repeated.

The server smiled. "Thank you," he sang to the tune of the aria.

"I'm in a hurry. First, I'd like a salad..."

"I just fill water glasses and clear tables," the young man sang.

"Then get our waiter," Yacov demanded.

The server frowned. "Fine," he said in a terse monotone, abandoning the tune.

A few minutes later a mandolin-strumming troubadour and a waiter came to the table. "Can I get you something from the bar?" the waiter asked over the vibrato of the mandolin and the noise in the café.

"No. Just coffee," Yacov replied.

The waiter turned to Donatello. "And for you?"

"Same."

The young server returned with their coffee. He set a pitcher of cream beside a small caddy holding packets of sugar, a jar of grated cheese and the wine list. With a toss of his head, he resumed the aria as he stomped away.

Donatello took three packets of sugar from the caddy. Holding them with his bandaged hand, he shook the packets, and tore off the ends.

"That's a hell of a lot of sugar," Yacov said. "I thought Italians like their coffee strong and black."

Donatello stared at him. *The fire-breathing bastard almost demand that I hate him.* "This not Italia coffee," he said, then shook the packets again and sprayed the white granules over the table.

The waiter and troubadour came back to the table.

"We've, uh, had a little accident," Yacov said with a slight grin, motioning to the sugar.

"Yes, I see." The waiter snapped his fingers and caught the attention of a passing busboy. As the musician played, the busboy swept the sugar and the wax from the Chianti bottle into a small dustpan.

The waiter leaned forward and pointed to the wine list with his pen. "Have you seen -- "

"We're ready to order," Yacov interrupted. "I'll have steak. New York. Rare. And a green salad with Roquefort."

The waiter smiled curtly, and set down a steak knife by Yacov's fork then turned to Donatello. "And for you?"

"Ravioli."

"Anything else?"

Donatello shook his head. The waiter motioned to the troubadour, and they went on their way.

Yacov took a long swallow of black coffee. "What did you think about them postponing the Oscars because of the assassination?" he asked, dabbing his mouth with a napkin. "And cancelling Cannes for all those protests?"

Donatello shrugged. "Since I no get, how you say, Academy nomina . . ."

"Nomination?" Yacov offered.

"Sì. Since I no get nomination for best foreign film, I no care if they postpone. *The Bounty Killer*, it make more lira than all the other film, messi insieme . . . uh, how you say it, combine? Especially the winner, 'War and Peace' -- so long and boring." Donatello looked up. "What is this -- assination anyway?"

"A-*sass*-in-nation," Yacov replied. "Martin Luther King Jr., the civil rights leader. He was tragically shot -- assassinated -- in Memphis."

Donatello shrugged. "Sì. he was grande uomo, uh, a great man. It makes no sense." Looking down at Yacov's steak knife. "America the beautiful can be dangerous."

Yacov rubbed the back of his neck. *My god, this will be a strange investment.*

"This country, is molto strange."

"Can't argue with you there." Yacov paused a moment, then took another swallow of coffee. "Your father tells me you bought a vineyard. That's gotta be a money pit. You have experience with viticulture?"

Donatello looked blankly at him.

"You know . . . growing grapes?"

"Some."

"This vineyard has a name?"

"Mondscheinberg."

"Ah, Mondscheinberg . . . moonlight mountain. I've heard of it. I don't think they've put out a decent wine in decades. So, you're making moonshine up on moonlight hill, huh?" Yacov said with a throaty chuckle.

Donatello stared at him.

"You know, moonshine? Corn liquor?"

No response.

Yacov shook his head. "Oh hell, forget it. It was a joke. You look so gloomy, I thought maybe you could use some humor. Guess you're homesick, huh?"

Donatello glanced at the sky. "Here, is so cold and, how you say it . . . gray."

"Gray? Boy, are you in for a shock this summer, baby," the banker said with a laugh. "As the old saying goes -- there's no colder winter than a San Francisco summer."

"What means this?"

Yacov shook his head again. "Just a saying. When the rest of the country warms up in the summer, San Francisco gets colder. Or at least it seems that way." He took a sip of coffee. "Your father tells me you're looking for lira."

"Why he tell you that?"

"I'm an investor. Lending money is what I do. You *do* need money, don't you?"

"Why you think -- "

"Look, *Donna*, I'll make this short. Judging from what your father said, I don't think you can afford to be choosy."

"My name is no Donna."

A haughty smile spread over the banker's face. "Oh? Your father called you that when he asked me to bail you out. Nice man, your father. Although, like a lot of parents, seems like his devotion might be misplaced."

"My father, he call me *Dona* not Donna."

"Then what should I call you?"

"Donatello."

Yacov leaned back in his chair. "Well, uh, Donatello, we might as well put all the cards on the table. After your father called, I developed a sudden curiosity about Italian ex-pats, like yourself. So I asked around. I found out you're here because you got in trouble with an Italian MP. The name Caggiano rings a bell? If not, the bandages on your hand should help jog your memory."

In one explosive motion, Donatello threw his napkin on the table, jumped to his feet, and sent his chair crashing to the floor behind him. "Caggiano! He is ass! Damn him to hell!" he shouted as nearby diners turned and stared.

Yacov reached and grabbed his sleeve. "Sit down."

Donatello glared at him.

"I *said*, sit down!"

Taking short, sharp breaths, Donatello jerked his arm away, pulled up his chair, and sat down. "Damn him to hell!" he said under his breath. "He want to ruin me, and my father!"

Strands of greasy hair slipped off Yacov's bald spot as he grabbed Donatello's splinted hand and pulled him closer. "You're lucky if I don't break it again. You, of all people, should be careful about doling out damnation," he grumbled. "Truth is, you touchy bastard, everything was fine until you helped yourself to Caggiano's mistress."

Donatello wrestled free from the banker's grip and rubbed his hand. "Why I shouldn't? Meika, she is too good for him. And my father, he could be Caesar compared to that dog."

As the other diners returned to their conversations, Yacov pushed his hair back in place. "Why do you Italians always want to revive the Roman Empire? Mussolini's kids probably thought the same thing about their father."

Just then, the waiter came with a wide tray. "Anything else?" he asked, setting their plates on the table.

"The check," Yacov replied.

The waiter nodded and backed away.

Yacov stabbed his salad with his fork and pushed a large wad of lettuce into his mouth. Still chewing, he sliced off a hunk of steak, mopped it in the crimson juices, and shoved it in with the salad.

Donatello poked at a ravioli. *The beast and his bloody meat make my stomach turn.*

Yacov pointed at Donatello's plate with his knife. "Ravioli, just likka you Nonna used to make back home in Italia?" he said, mocking an Italian accent.

Donatello stared down at the pasta pillows, swimming in a red sauce. "No. Nothing like she make."

"Be that as it may . . ." The timbre of Yacov's voice deepened. "We're not here to talk about the food."

Donatello looked up. *By the change in his voice, and the look in his eye, I sense the offer will be butchery.*

Yacov sliced another chunk off his steak. Staring like a predator, he speared the oozing beef and pointed it at Donatello. "I'm known for being a shrewd, heartless bastard. And I've been told more than once that my heart is black as the ace of spades. But I have a fondness for opera, as you may have guessed by my choice of restaurants -- though they mostly mutilate it here," he said as the juices ran down the fork, staining the cuff of his starched white shirt.

"Uh . . ." Donatello pointed to the banker's sleeve. "Your meat, it drips."

"Damn." Yacov dropped his fork and dabbed at his cuff with a napkin. "I'll be honest. You don't impress me, but the effect you had on the hostess did. I have connections with a group of venture capitalists. If anyone knows how to package a deal, it's me. With the right proposal, I can get all the money you want. So, here's what I'm thinking -- an adaptation 'Faust' -- my favorite opera. Updated. With ripped jeans, long hair, and rock n' roll."

Donatello frowned. "Faust?" he said, shrugging and shaking his head. "Why you want do that? That opera, so old, and, how you say it . . . deprimente?"

"You mean depressing? I thought Italians love opera. Especially depressing ones. 'Faust' has it all. Life. Death. Salvation and damnation." Yacov chuckled. "And you're big on damnation. The point is, a friend, a Broadway investor -- he says hippie musicals are gonna be big. Real big. He's opening one in a couple of weeks. An extravaganza called 'Hair' or something . . ."

"Hair?" Donatello muttered. "Why he calls it that?"

"I don't know. Point is, he insists hippie musicals are the next big thing. It's only a matter of time before someone makes the leap from stage to cinema. I figure we might as well jump first. And if we do an adaptation, basically the plot's already written. Just update the language and music, then add the long hair and electric guitars."

Donatello sat back. "But I am actor and regista di film. Not singer or cantante di opera, or director of theater," he said with a shrug.

"Look, I know a guy -- Roland Van d'Vrie. He's done it all in musical theater. Actor, director, composer. He's even done a couple of movie scores. A real virtuoso. You two can collaborate. And if you can't sing, we'll cast the other parts with people who can."

"Why you think I do this?"

"It's the golden rule, baby. He who has the gold makes the rules. I think two million-five should do it. I'll give you, say, 500 Gs up front to start the ball rolling. And another 500 when it's in the can."

"And percent of box-office?"

"That was my offer -- take it or leave it. As I said before, I don't think you have a choice."

The waiter came by again. "If there's nothing else . . ." he said, placing a padded folder on the table.

Yacov shook his head.

The final blow. Donatello drew a long breath. *I am at the butcher's mercy. He is right. I have no choice.*

Baring his teeth, Yacov yanked the last bite of steak off his fork and seemed to swallow it whole. "Of course, all the usual deadlines and penalties will apply." He pushed his plate away and leaned back in his chair. "But if you don't think you can do it . . ."

I cannot do it, but I need his money. I am an actor. I must make him believe I can. "Sì. The usual deadline and penalty," Donatello said with a nonchalant wave.

"Good. Done and done." Yacov dropped his napkin on the table and picked up the check. "I'll pay it."

The cafe's swinging doors thudded behind Donatello as he shuffled out onto the sidewalk. Pulling his leather jacket tight around his chest, he looked up at the sky. *Darker than before. Cold like the silver-gray of the Mediterranean in winter. But here, it is spring.*

The doors thudded again.

"So, where you parked?" Yacov's rasping voice echoed from behind.

Donatello nodded toward a hill.

"My car's up there too. Let's walk. If we have an agreement, I can have my office draw up the papers and contact Van d'Vrie."

Donatello nodded. "Sì. Draw the papers," he said, staring down at the sidewalk.

They paused at an intersection, then crossed the street, and started up the hill. Just then, two girls in white go-go boots and bright mini-dresses bounded out of a nearby shop.

"Look out!" Yacov said as Donatello ran into one of the girls, sending her sprawling to the sidewalk.

She sat stunned for a moment, looking up at him. Then her eyes shot open and her jaw dropped. "You're that Italian guy!"

"Pardone," he said, reaching down to help her up.

"'The Bounty Killer!'"

He smiled and bowed. "Sì."

"Oh, wow!" her young friend gushed. "Who is he?"

"He's an Italian movie star!" the first girl squealed, bouncing up and down, while staring at him. "I saw your picture in my mom's Italian Vogue! She thinks you're, like, the coolest. Wait 'til I tell her! She'll be so totally jealous!"

"Far-out!" the second girl said, bouncing along with her friend.

The first girl beamed at Donatello. "Wow! You're a total fox. You look even cooler than your picture. Can I have your autograph?"

"Sì," he replied, flashing a wide smile. "But . . ." he added, shrugging and holding up the bandaged mit.

"That's okay. Just make it look like an autograph." The girl pulled out a pen, then rifled furiously through her day-glo plastic purse. She looked over at her friend. "Do you have any paper?"

The other girl shook her head.

"Darn it! He's a movie star, and I don't have any paper."

Yacov watched the girls with greedy fascination. "Here. I have some," he offered, opening his briefcase and tearing a sheet from a ledger.

"Gee thanks!" the first girl gushed.

Donatello took the paper, scrawled a signature, then gave it back to her.

"So, what's his name?" her friend asked.

The girl shrugged. "I don't know, but he's famous! Wait 'til I tell my mom!" She pressed the autograph to her chest, then clasped her friend's hand and they skipped away.

Donatello looked over at Yacov.

With a faraway stare, the banker seemed to be calculating the girl's attraction into dollars.

Donatello smiled. *Ah, I think my fortune turns. I come back from the grave. The butcher's greed traps him. He is at my mercy, but he does not know it. Yet.*

44

PAULINE MADE HER way over the gravel driveway to the barn, sidestepping mud puddles left by an early morning rain. The musty smell of wet hay and horse manure accosted her as she went through the double doors. She found Buck in back, cleaning Nahlah's stall.

A perfect way for a heathen to spend a Sunday morning. She stepped onto a piece of plywood by the stall door to avoid soiling her brown and white pumps, then cleared her throat. "Donny and I are leaving."

Buck dumped a shovel-full of muck into a wheelbarrow. "Wha'd you say?"

"I'm going to church and Donny's going to Sunday School."

He moved the wheelbarrow and looked up at her. "You're kidding."

"What's wrong with that?"

"What isn't? Donny? Sunday School? With everybody back home sleeping around and getting stoned? And everyone at the church . . . bunch a' pious hypocrites. Why do you want to put him through that?"

"Buck!"

"Well?"

"He needs a religious education. Everyone does. You *could* come with us, you know. Your religious training could use a little refreshing."

He dumped another shovel-full into the wheelbarrow. "Look Pauline, most of the time I try to please you. But forced religion, for no other reason than 'just because' -- on that, I'm not budging. Either you believe it, or you don't. And I don't. And I'm not going to act like I do. Give me one good reason why I should."

"I would think, after all that's happened, you'd be at least a little bit grateful."

He planted the shovel into a pile of manure and stared at her. "Grateful? For what? That it didn't turn out worse? Anyway, who says I'm not. Grateful's in the eye of the beholder."

Pauline threw up her hands. "Buck Harper, honestly! If you had been a church-going man, maybe your son would have been a church-going son, and none of this would have happened."

He rested his arms on top of the shovel. "Oh, now the truth comes out. You're not going to try pinning this whole thing on me, are you?"

She straightened her coat. "Steven used to go to church until he figured out you weren't going -- and like father, like son," she said with a frown.

"Who's to say if I went to church, it would've changed anything? Just listen to the news or read the paper. There are plenty of fathers who go to church and do everything they're supposed to, and their kids still run off, just like ours did. You can't force religion on people." He yanked the shovel out of the muck, scooped up a load and pitched it into the wheelbarrow.

The small off-white church, complete with steeple, could have been cut from a postcard and placed in a vale of aspen alongside an old highway. A sunbeam shining through the clouds illuminated the church and a row of daffodils blooming in a window box, as if God himself was smiling.

Pauline and Donny stopped at the door of a shoebox-shaped Sunday School building behind the church. "You got into something, didn't you?" Licking her fingers, she rubbed a smudge on his cheek. "Fiddlesticks. It's not coming off." She straightened the collar of a knit shirt that matched his corduroys, and took his hand. "Oh well, let's go."

He looked up at her. "Gwamma?"

"What, baby?"

"I don wannu go in dare."

"You'll be fine. There will be coloring and games. And you'll even have a little snack. Just be good and listen to the teacher." Taking a deep breath, she straightened her coat and opened the door.

The teacher, Mrs. Cox, and the other children looked up when they came in. "Well, Pauline, hello," Mrs. Cox said. "I heard you had a little guest."

Pauline forced a smile. *Wonder who told her. Maybe Buck was right, I can almost hear her staring.* "This is Donny," she said as he disappeared into her sky blue coat.

Mrs. Cox bent and held out her hand. "Hello, Donny."

He buried himself deeper.

"Donny, don't be rude," Pauline said, extracting him from the fabric cocoon. "Say hello to Mrs. Cox."

"That's alright," she replied. "This is probably new to him."

Pauline sucked in her breath. "Probably so. Donny, go play with the other children." She led him toward a knee-high table spread with crayons and paper.

"Children should be with their parents. Whenever possible, that is. How long will he be staying with you?"

"We're not sure."

"How does Buck feel about having a little one around? It's been ages since I've seen him at church."

"Hmmm." Pauline stiffened. "I haven't seen your Tom around much either."

Buck shot upright from rummaging in the refrigerator and quickly closed the door. "I'm not doing anything," he said with a guilty stare as Pauline came into the kitchen.

She dropped her purse, her Bible, and Donny's Sunday School papers on the counter. "Honestly . . ."

"What? I didn't do anything. I even changed my clothes..."

She draped her coat over the back of a chair.

He cleared his throat. "So, how did Donny do in Sunday School?"

"That Carolyn Cox! What a witch!"

"Oh, Carolyn," Buck said with a long exhale. He wiped his forehead and slouched against the refrigerator. "You mean that with a 'B'?"

Pauline frowned. "As a matter of fact, I do."

"I thought you two were friends. What did she do now?"

"She can be so... she acted like Donny had fleas. Like there was something wrong with him. Like he should be in a freak show."

"What did you expect, Pauline? That's the way they are down there. I tried to tell you..."

She crossed her arms and stared at him.

He stepped away from the refrigerator. "Well, they are. Why did you think they'd be any different just because it's you?"

"I told you. I think Donny should have a religious education. And we agreed -- "

"No, Pauline, *we* never agreed on anything. You decided. I tried to tell you, but you wouldn't listen."

"You're probably right. Anyway, your grandson already has a little girlfriend and he won a prize," she said with a dismal sigh. She pulled a small blue plastic-covered Bible from her purse, holding it by a handle attached to the spine.

"Sounds like he did okay then."

"He won the Bible for learning a memory verse."

"What was the verse?"

"Jesus loves all the children of the world."

"I thought you said Carolyn treated him like a freak?"

Pauline slumped into a chair at the kitchen table. "Maybe I over-reacted. Maybe she wasn't any different than she always is. Maybe I'm the one who's a freak. I don't know... everything's upside down and nothing's simple anymore."

He picked up the little book and flipped through the thick pages. "'The stories of the New Testament.' Donny's a smart kid. He's got a good head on his shoulders."

Buck dropped into his chair in the living room and propped his feet on the ottoman. Donny came in with Tailor.

"I heard you won a prize," Buck said.

Donny nodded.

"How'd you like going to Sunday School?"

"I wiked it, Gwampa."

"Do you wanna go next week?"

Donny nodded again.

"Turn on the TV for Grandad, okay? Gramma will have lunch ready in a little bit."

Donny shuffled to the set and turned the knob. A staticky hum and gray snow filled the screen.

Buck shifted in his chair. "Change the channel."

Donny paused, puzzling over the knobs.

"It's the top one."

Donny turned it; the snow disappeared, replaced by a man on a crowded putting green, and the hushed voice of an announcer.

"Gary Player could take the tournament if he wins this round. It would be his third win . . ."

"That's good. We'll watch golf."

Buck pulled on the knees of his ranger-green work pants, and Donny scrambled onto his lap. "Wha's dat, Gwampa?" he asked, pointing to the TV.

"That's golf."

"Wha's goff?"

"It's a game where you try to hit that little white ball into the hole, and you get lots of money if you win," Buck replied.

"Oh." Donny settled against him, while Tailor stretched out beside the chair. "Do you pway goff, Gwampa?"

"Not very well." Buck picked up a newspaper from the end table and shook it open.

PROTESTERS HOLD COLUMBIA UNIVERSITY HOSTAGE
STUDENTS TAKE OVER ADMIN. BUILDING

Beneath the headline, a photograph of hand-painted signs and angry, shouting faces.

"Gwampa, wha's dat?" Donny asked, pointing to the picture.

Buck straightened his glasses. "Uh, those people . . . well, they're not happy with the way things are, and they're really mad, and they want everybody to know about it."

"Why?"

"Well, we don't know why. It has something to do with folk not liking one another and some want to make a building that separates black people and white people. And at this school the black and white people got together to say they didn't like that idea. Now the black and white people are fighting each other for some reason. I have to agree with your Grandma. "Everything's upside down and nothing's simple anymore." What they all need is a real good spanking cause they're acting like a bunch of little children."

Donny paused a moment, then looked up at him. "But, Gwampa, Mrs. Cox said, 'Jesus wuvs all da widdle childwen of da world.'"

45

PARKER WANDERED THROUGH a doorway beneath a staircase, into the spacious, timber-framed great-room of the Orion Institute. The rustling of his long, draping caftan, and the soft footfalls of his bare feet whispered in the stillness. A stone fireplace, rising two stories, divided one wall. Empty bookcases bordered another. Windows, stretching from floor to ceiling, were either cloaked with heavy drapes, or boarded over, and the darkened room devoid of furniture, except for a row of threadbare theater seats, and a group of worn, mismatched couches.

Gregg, Parker's most trusted disciple, licked his forefingers and ran them over his eyebrows which met in the center, then got up from one of the sofas, and went over to Parker, sitting on another. "Parker? Is something wrong?"

"I received a nagging letter from my publisher," he replied with a frown, passing it to Gregg.

"Oh?" He paused to read the letter, then looked up. "I don't understand."

"They're threatening to shelve the second book for lack of sales on the first. They expect me to promote it, which to me, is the same thing as selling my soul." Parker fidgeted with a loose thread on the scrolling embroidery bordering the sleeve of his caftan. "Damn," he muttered as the thread came loose, and part of the design unraveled.

"I'll have one of the girls fix it." Gregg said.

"I thought being on Deborah Donaldson's show, would satisfy them." Parker shook his head. "But the publishers want more. Always more. More publicity. More sales. And they want it all immediately. As you know, enlightenment is the opposite of immediate."

Gregg nodded and gave the letter back to him.

"I don't live in their world. Nor do I wish to." He folded the paper into a tight square and put it in a pocket of his caftan. "Is it possible to take the awareness of Orion to the center of the universe without selling my soul in the process?"

Gregg thought a moment. "There is only one who could, and fortunately, you are that one."

"Yes," Parker said. "I am." He went to a tall window and pulled back a thick drape. Brilliant sunlight burst into the room. "To placate them, I sent a request to that Philistine reporter, Calvin Jeffries, for an interview, and he has accepted."

"But . . ." Gregg began.

"Yes, I know. I'm taking a chance." Parker fidgeted the diamond ring on his little finger. "Most likely, he will try to make me look like Mephistopheles."

Gregg rested his hand on Parker's shoulder. "True. But in the end, Mephistopheles transcends and prevails."

46

A YOUNG MAN in a crisp navy blue blazer and tan chinos, with a boxy camera hanging from his neck, wandered into the secretarial pool of the *Los Angeles Examiner*. The repetitive ka-chunk, ka-chunk, ka-chunk of a teletype machine accompanied the clicking of typewriter keys and dinging of carriages. And the smell of overflowing ashtrays made the large, open office seem stuffy and small.

He paused at the desk of an elderly woman. "Afternoon, Millie."

She looked up. "Quinton?" Her fingers stopped scuttling over the keys. "What are you up to?"

He ran his hand through his sandy hair. "I'm a little bit nervous. I've got an appointment with Mr. Jeffries. I think maybe I landed an assignment."

"That's wonderful, Quinton. Don't worry, Cal's fair, unlike some of the slackers around here. If you do a good job, with his recommendation, you'll be on staff in no time."

He looked at clock on the wall. "Thanks, Millie. Gotta run."

Quinton sidestepped her trashcan and continued past several more desks to a glass-paneled office. He straightened his blazer, then tapped on the door. Cal Jeffries stood and motioned for him to come in. Quinton opened the door, went into the chilly air-conditioned room, and closed the door behind him.

Cal straightened his tie and tugged on his pin-stripe shirt, then looked at his watch and smiled. "Quinton. Good to see you. On time and you brought your camera. Have a seat." He motioned to a chair beside his desk.

"Thanks, Mr. Jeffries," Quinton said, settling himself on a dark chair, rubbed to bare wood in places. "A Scout is always prepared."

Cal watched him a moment, then sank into a worn leather chair behind his desk. "Call me Cal. You were a Boy Scout?"

"Eagle Scout, actually."

"Good." He folded his hands on his desk. "How's your father? Haven't seen him since the Alumni Dinner."

"Dad? He's okay. Making lots of money buying up ocean-front real estate."

"He was voted 'Most Likely to Succeed,' or he should have been. How does he feel about you getting into the news game?"

"Not exactly happy. But he foot the bill for my journalism degree, and he hasn't made any moves to stop me. All bark and no bite, I guess."

Cal sat back. "What I have in mind is -- let's say out of the ordinary for a fledgling reporter. It'll require the ability to think on your feet, street-smarts and perhaps a crazy streak. But if you pull it off, I can guarantee you a position here at the Examiner. And since the Newspaper Guild's on strike, it wouldn't surprise me a bit if you could write your own ticket at any news room in the city."

Quinton raised an eyebrow. "Sounds too good to be true, to which my father would say, 'then it is.' So, what is it?"

"I just got an invitation to interview that guru, Parker, at his Institute up in Big Sur. You've heard of him?"

Quinton shrugged. "Sure. He has a lot of buzz around campus among the turned-on, tuned-in and dropped-out crowd."

"Have you heard of Anthony Campanella?"

Quinton shook his head.

"He was a singer, and he owned a nightclub in Las Vegas."

"What's that got to do with Parker? And me?"

Cal sat back. "The property up in Big Sur belongs to Anthony, or it used to -- Parker claims Anthony gave it to him. Anyway, after hanging around Parker awhile, Anthony disappeared for . . . oh, I guess it's been almost two years. I don't have any proof of anything, just a niggling that won't go away. I want to know what happened."

"I still don't see what that has to do with me."

"Parker is obsessed with gathering followers. But he's also secretive. For instance, no one knows where his money comes from. No one knows where he comes from. In fact, no one knows if Parker is his first name, his last name, or if it's his name at all. And for all anyone knows, he could be a murderer. He's offered me an interview at the Big Sur property."

"I still don't -- "

"I want you to come with me to the interview as my photographer, then find an opportune moment to defect, just like you're a convert. See what you can find out. About Parker. Who he really is. What he's really about. What kind of existential stew he's cooking up there. And about Anthony. Where'd he go? What happened to him? Is he still alive?"

Cal paused, watching Quinton. "I think we can throw him off-guard. You're young and fresh-faced enough that you won't send up any red flags by joining up. And being an Eagle Scout, you're resourceful enough to have a reasonable chance of staying one step ahead of him."

Quinton fidgeted with the strap of his camera.

"It's a great opportunity -- could be the story of a lifetime. But it's not without risk."

"Go on."

"Although Parker claims to be a purveyor of peace, sources tell me he's drugged people who get in his way, or don't agree with him. They take an unplanned trip, if you know what I mean. Not to mention the questions about Anthony's disappearance. I don't think he's violent, but . . ."

Quinton sat back in his chair. "I see what you mean."

"Think about it."

The room was silent, but for the muffled clicking of typewriters, ringing of phones, and chunking of the teletype from the outer office.

Quinton took a long breath. "My father always talks about risk, opportunity and reward. No risk. No opportunity. No reward."

He thought a moment longer.

"Okay. I'll do it. Color me in."

47

"BUCK, WAKE UP," Pauline whispered, shaking him.

"What?" he gasped.

She pulled out a loose curler, re-rolled it and stabbed it with a plastic pin. "I think Donny's coming down with something."

"What time is it?"

"Five."

Buck grimaced. "Five AM? Nobody comes down with anything at his hour."

"See what you think."

"Oh, alright." He threw off the covers, swung his feet over the edge of the bed, and slid into his slippers. Yawning and rubbing his eyes, he followed Pauline into the darkened bedroom.

"I think he has a fever," she whispered.

Buck rested his hand on Donny's forehead, then motioned to her, and she followed him out into the hall. "He feels okay to me."

"But he was over-tired and cranky last night. Do you think I should call the doctor?"

"Come on, Pauline. It's five in the morning and he doesn't even feel hot. Why wouldn't he be cranky? His father's in the hospital. His mother took off. He's in a strange house, with strange people. Going to a new Sunday School. Meeting everybody and the teacher treating him like he's got fleas. Plus that whole lice and hair-clipper business. That'd be enough to piss anybody off. Besides, we're going to the hospital today. Steven will want to see him."

"I don't think Donny should go. Steven wouldn't want us to bring him if he's not feeling well. Why don't you go this time, then we'll all go next time?"

"Pauleeen..." Buck moaned. "It's a three-hour drive. I don't want to go by myself. How about nobody goes 'til Donny gets better?"

"How can you say that? Steven is expecting us. He's all alone in San Francisco, in the hospital. And remember, Dr. Buehler said we have to keep his spirits up."

"Geeze, Pauline, you sure know how to lay on the guilt."

She stared at him.

He frowned. "Aw, nuts. Okay, I'll go."

Later that day, a quick rap echoed on the door to Steven's hospital room.

"Good morning. How are you feeling?" Dr. Buehler said as he went inside.

Steven shrugged one shoulder.

The doctor took a file from under his arm and paged through it. "Good news. We're transferring you out of ICU today. You won't be needing these anymore," he said, motioning to the monitors. "You've made all the progress we expected and then some." He pushed up his tri-focal glasses. "So, more good news -- we'll be releasing you in a few days. I'm sure you're anxious to get out of here."

Steven's jaw dropped. Half his mouth hung misshapen and unmoving. He motioned for the legal pad.

Dr. Buehler passed it to him and he scratched out a response.

WONT I GET BETTER

"It's possible, with time and therapy, you'll regain more function." The doctor looked into his eyes. "You're a lucky young man, Steven. Lucky to be alive. It could easily have gone... the other way." He looked down at the file. "Meanwhile, you'll need physical therapy and long-term care. But we don't do that here.

Our objective was to stabilize you and put you on the road to recovery."

I ThOuGht I woULd GeT WeLL

"You have a few choices. We can transfer you to a nursing facility. Or, since you're a veteran, they may take you at the VA hospital. Or you can go home. I'll make recommendations based on what you decide."

Steven scribbled a few words, then tears filled his eyes, and he dropped the pencil on the tablet.

BuT I THOuqHT

Dr. Buehler cleared his throat and patted Steven's shoulder. "I need to continue my rounds. I'll check back later."

The doctor hurried out and closed the door behind him. A deafening silence fell in the room. Steven touched the neck brace holding his head. Then looked down at his hand, drawn up like the lifeless foot of a bird, clutching a roll of fabric. He threw off the covers, and stared at his leg, and the foot turning in toward the other. His head dropped back on the brace.

Then it's permanent. A choking sob caught in his throat, and he sank into the bed. *And this is my life.*

"I have a message for you from Dr. Buehler," the nun on duty at the ICU nurse's station said.

"What now?" Buck muttered as he shook the rain from his umbrella onto the polished hospital floor.

The nun passed a folded piece of paper to him.

He unfolded the note. "He wants to see me? Why?"

"I'm sorry, sir, I don't know," she replied with a sympathetic smile.

Buck shoved the umbrella under his arm, then began the long, lonely march to the Physicians' Building. He found Dr. Buehler's office deserted, except for the stiff receptionist who sat encased behind her glass partition.

"Buck Harper," he announced.

"Have a seat. Dr. Buehler is making rounds. I'll page him."

Buck slumped onto a hard chair. After a moment, his mind wandered. *I'd take all of it back, if I could . . .*

Steven breezed into the kitchen, his dark hair tousled and his cheeks flushed. Turning a chair backwards, he sat down at the table across from Buck. "I'm done cleaning the stalls," he said, flexing his arm. "Anything else?"

Buck looked up from the newspaper. "Nope, that's it. What're you going to do now?"

"Meet Roy in a little bit and go cruisin' in Sacramento."

"Cruising? You know how your mother feels about that. Be careful down there. And don't get into trouble."

Steven rolled his eyes and flexed his arm again. "I've got a little time. Wanna' arm wrestle? It's been awhile . . ."

Buck set down the paper. He stared at Steven. *I can still take him.* "Sure. If you think you're man enough."

Steven pretended to spit on his hands, then rubbed them together. "Yeah, I'm man enough."

"Alright." Buck pushed the paper out of the way. He clasped his fingers, then turned his palms out, cracking his knuckles. "Best two out of three?"

Steven looked sideways at him. "Okay."

"You call it," Buck said.

Making mock gestures as if preparing for a boxing match, they planted their elbows on the table and grasped hands.

"Go!" Steven shouted.

Their arms and eyes locked.

Buck set his jaw. *Let him think he's got me, then . . .* Steven's arm hardened, and Buck felt his own wrist waver. He tightened his grip. *When did he get so strong?*

Steven took the advantage, inching his father's hand toward the table. Buck's arm began to shake, and his heartbeat quickened. *He's never won, unless I let him.*

"You give?" Steven seemed unfazed by the effort.

Buck's whole body trembled. He leaned into the struggle. *He can't win.* "No. How 'bout you, kid?" he sputtered.

"Kid? Who you callin' kid?"

Then, an instant, Steven broke the set of Buck's wrist and slammed his hand against the table.

God! Feels like he ripped my arm off!

Steven swung a rock-solid leg around the seat of the chair, then stood and brushed his hands together. "Who's the kid now, old man?"

Old man? "Old man!" Buck reached across the table, grabbed Steven's shirt, and slapped him.

Steven froze.

His heart racing erratically, Buck released his grip. He collapsed back on the chair, flushed yet pale, cold yet sweating. *What's wrong with me. I almost hit him.*

A look of incredulity clouded Steven's face as he shrugged his shirt back into place. "What'd you do that for?" He paused. "Dad? You look like you're gonna pass out, or have a heart attack, or something. Are you okay?"

"I'm fine," Buck said with a wheezing breath.

"You look terrible."

"So, now you're a doctor?"

Steven reached for him. "No, I'm your son."

Buck blocked his hand. "I said, I'm fine. Now get out of here . . . go on . . ."

And within a month he was gone.

Buck abruptly came to himself.

Dr. Buehler stood over him with a file under his arm, his hands clasped in front of him, twirling his thumbs. The doctor motioned for him to follow. He stood, straightened his tweed jacket, and followed the doctor into an examining room.

Dr. Buehler closed the door. "Have a seat," he said with an unusually warm tone. "I trust you had a pleasant drive?"

"Not bad."

"I have some good news. We moved Steven out of intensive care, and we'll be releasing him in a few days."

"Releasing him?" Buck repeated while fidgeting with the hem of his jacket. "But he's not well yet," he said as if it was a question.

"True. But his condition is stable."

"And you're going to release him? Just like that?"

"As I've said all along, beyond getting him stable, further recovery will hinge on physical therapy, and his body's ability to heal or compensate for the damage. Plus how well he can adapt emotionally and his will to recover. But none of that requires a hospital. It's critical that he maintains a positive attitude and keeps fighting. There have been some amazing recoveries, even in cases we thought were hopeless."

Buck stared blankly at the doctor. It seemed that all the blood drained into his shoes. "But, you . . . you can't release him, he can hardly function."

Dr. Buehler opened the file and began paging through the papers. "I understand Steven is a vet?"

Buck nodded.

"If you insist he remain hospitalized, I can try transferring him to the VA. They do long-term care. Casualties of war, etcetera. But I have to warn you, it's tough over there. Not for the faint of heart." He paused again. "Or, if the VA can't take him, a convalescent hospital might. But neither one would inspire much hope in a young man." Dr. Buehler closed the file. "My suggestion? If he were my son, I'd do whatever I could to take him home."

Buck found Steven's room in a remote corner on an upper floor next to a linen closet. *Looks like they already forgot him.* He opened the door and looked in.

Steven's face twisted into a one-sided frown as he tried to squeeze a rubber ball with his lifeless hand.

Buck tapped on the door.

Steven looked up. The ball slipped from his hand and rolled onto the bed.

"Can I come in?"

Steven nodded, then watched the door a moment. Positioning the legal pad on his lap, he wrote a few words.

WHERE ARE MOM AND DONOVAN

"You know your mother -- she thought Donny was coming down with something. She swore he had a fever. Oh, uh, we started calling him Donny. It just sort of happened. Hope you don't mind."

Steven shook his head. Swallowing hard, he picked up a tissue and wiped beads of perspiration from his forehead, then dabbed a trickle of saliva off his chin.

An awkward silence settled in the room.

Buck took a deep breath. "You got promoted to a private room. But there's hardly enough space to turn around in here."

Steven scrawled on the pad.

NOT PLANNING TO HAVE A PARTY

A weak smile turned the corners of Buck's mouth and he looked down at the floor. Setting his umbrella on the foot of the bed, he squeezed past the chair to the window and parted the curtains. Dark clouds hung in a slice of sky sandwiched between two building, and a gasp of steam rose from a narrow asphalt roof. He turned back. "Not much of a view."

HAVENT SEEN IT
THEYRE RELEASING ME

"Yeah, I know. I talked to the doctor." He paused. "This is going to be a long haul. Do you know what you want to do?"

Steven sucked in a breath. He sat frozen a moment, then scratched furiously on the paper.

HOW SHOULD I KNOW

"This is serious business, son. It's no time to fool around. You'd better think about it, because it won't be long before . . ."

Steven's face reddened. Anger flashed in his eyes. He flung the legal pad onto the tray table, sending a pitcher of ice water splattering across the floor.

A passing nurse in a starched white uniform rushed in. "What happened here?" she demanded, looking accusingly from Buck to Steven, and back again.

Buck cleared his throat. "There's been a little accident."

"I'll say! It's not as if housekeeping has nothing better to do than clean up after temper tantrums!" She glared at Steven a moment, then spun on her heels and stomped away.

Steven slid down in the bed. Tears spilled over his cheeks. Saliva ran from the corner his mouth, and one shoulder shook with silent sobs.

Buck pulled a chair beside the bed. He sat down and took Steven's functional hand. "It's okay, son. It'll all be okay."

Looking desperately into his father's eyes, he shook his head.

"Yes it will," Buck said with a determined stare. "Somehow it will. We have to believe that."

Then, a deep sigh and Steven's breathing settled into a slow, shallow rhythm. After several minutes, he fell into a restless sleep, and Buck pulled his hand away.

There was a light tap on the door.

"Housekeeping," She stopped. "Should I come back later?"

Buck motioned for her to come in. She quickly mopped up the spill, then left and quietly closed the door behind her.

Oblivious to the passing of time, he stared at a shadow stretching across the floor. The past, present, and future swirled into one. *Who am I? The father? The grandfather? Or the son?* He looked over at Steven. *And who are you? I see my hands in your hands. My face in your face. My life in another body. I should know you like I know myself, but I swear, I don't know anything about you.*

Evening closed in and lights came on in the hall.

He brushed his fingers over Steven's cheek.

Steven woke with a start. His forehead furrowing and lips contorting, tears pooled again and a strangled sound came out.

Buck took his hand. "Shhhh. Steven, don't. Take it easy. It's going to be alright, son. I promise. It'll all work out."

He motioned for the notepad.

Buck passed it to him.

He paused, then printed a few words.

CAN I COMe hOMe
 ANd bRiNg ShaRa with me

48

"I'M BEAT," BUCK said, handing Pauline his jacket.

"It's so late, I was beginning to worry," she said as she hung it in the coat closet. "Why don't you sit down and I'll bring you some coffee?"

"That would be great."

"Are you hungry?"

"No, I stopped at a drive-in."

As Pauline went to the kitchen, Buck sauntered into the living room. He flopped onto his chair and put his feet up on an ottoman. Tailor crawled into the chair beside him. The soft gurgling of the percolator drifted in from the kitchen, joining the ticking of the mantle clock and random sparking of the fire. Settling deeper in the chair, he kneaded the dog's curly coat, and watched lucent flames licking the blackened logs and glowing embers gasping for air.

A few minutes later, Pauline came in and set the coffee on a table by his chair. He picked up the cup and took a drink, then held it close to his face and breathed in the aroma. "How's Donny?"

"Asleep. It was a false alarm."

"Figures."

Pauline smoothed her checkered housedress and sat on the sofa across from him. She pulled an embroidered pillow cover from a basket, took out a needle, and began stitching. "Now that we're settled, tell me everything."

He set the cup back on the table. Tailor yawned and squeezed out of the chair. "They transferred Steven out of ICU."

"Well, that's wonderful," she said, drawing an indigo thread through the fabric.

Buck rested his forearms on his knees. "There's more."

She stopped stitching and looked up at him.

"Good news and bad news. Maybe it's all good . . . or, I don't know, maybe it's not so good after all."

"Well, for heaven sakes, what is it?"

"They're releasing Steven in a few days."

"That's good. What's the bad news?"

"They're releasing him in a few days."

After a moment's hesitation, her eyes shot open. "But he's not . . ."

"Bingo." Buck dropped his head into his hands. "And that's just part of it."

"But how can they release him?"

"Dr. Buehler said Steven is stable, but he will need physical therapy. And depending on how that goes, he may need long-term care. The hospital doesn't do any of that. He said the VA or a convalescent hospital might take him. Or we can bring him home."

"What does Steven want? Did you ask him?"

"He wants to come home."

"Then it's settled. We'll bring him home."

Buck sighed and sat back in his chair.

Pauline frowned. "You're against it, aren't you?"

"No, I'm not." He looked up at her. "It's not as simple as that."

"Buck . . ."

"This is serious, Pauline. Think about it. We don't know the first thing about physical therapy or taking care of someone in his condition. I haven't seen any physical therapists hiding in the woods around here, have you?"

"But, really, what choice do we have?"

"Really? I haven't even had a chance to think about it. Before we can bring him home, we have to figure everything out."

"Like what?"

"Like, how are we going to get him into the house? He'll be in a wheelchair. We have steps up to the doors. And once he's inside, where's he going to sleep? The bedrooms are upstairs. And what about getting him dressed? And bathing? Can we even get a wheelchair into the bathroom? We need to figure all that out, plus who knows what else, before he comes home."

"Do you have any ideas?"

"So far, I figured I'll have to build a ramp up to the house, and he'll have to sleep downstairs."

"You said that was part of it. What's the rest?"

Buck took a long breath. *Here goes.* "He wants to bring Shara with him. I don't understand it. Maybe it's misplaced loyalty, or maybe for Donny's sake . . ."

Pauline stared blankly at him.

Countdown to detonation . . . tick . . . tick . . . tick . . .

She dropped her embroidery and jumped to her feet. "But, they're not married!"

And the explosion. "He says he feels responsible for her."

Pauline planted her hands on her hips. "If he feels so responsible for her, what business did he have getting involved with her in the first place? She was fifteen years old. Fifteen! He could have been arrested. Not to mention getting her pregnant! She more-or-less abandoned Donovan. What makes Steven think she won't do that to him too?"

Buck shook his head. "Geeze Pauline, I don't know. I'm just telling you what he wants. I'd rather see him come home by himself and concentrate on getting well and doing what's best for Donny."

"They absolutely cannot live here unmarried. What will people think?" She frowned. "But since, pure-as-the-driven-snow Carolyn Cox knows about Donny, the whole church probably knows."

Buck sighed. "Probably."

"And since Alma knows, the whole county probably knows."

"Probably."

"Then it really doesn't matter, does it?"

"Look Pauline, if you believe they should be married to live here, then they should be married. Because that's what you believe, not because of what anyone else thinks."

"I don't know what I believe anymore." She crossed her arms. "What do you think?"

"I'm exhausted. And right now, I don't give a damn what people say, and I don't give a damn what they think. Especially down at the church. They can do, and think, and say, whatever the hell they want."

"You can't mean that!"

"Ah, but I do. With all my heart."

Pauline glared at him, then got up and left the room. He heard her stomp upstairs, and he heard the bedroom door close behind her. He slid down in the chair.

I better manufacture a change of heart, or I'll be sleeping on the couch until I do.

Succumbing to the hypnotic, metronome ticking of the clock and panting breath of the fire, Buck drifted into a memory. He heard the ghost-like echo of his father's voice.

> *"Propriety, son. Your mother's right. Propriety's the important thing. The mere appearance of it can fix almost anything . . ."*

"I beg to differ, Dad," Buck said. "All the propriety in the world won't fix this mess."

49

NOON-DAY SUN SLIPPING through openings in the thick drapes and boarded-over windows, cast blades of light across the floor in the great-room of the Orion Institute in Big Sur.

"Come, sit." Parker gathered his caftan, then sat on a low chair and motioned for Cal Jeffries to sit across from him.

Cal hesitated, looking askance at the chair, draped with coral-colored fabric and sprinkled with rose petals.

"Please," Parker said, waving toward the chair.

Cal unbuttoned his suit jacket and sat down.

At their feet, ragged wanderers gathered along with Parker's robed followers, sitting on oriental carpets spread over the floor. Some had shaved heads and some did not. Off to one side a man in a white turban sat plucking the strings of a sitar.

A resinous cloud hung above the gathering. Bouquets of fragrant flowers, bowls of pungent incense, and the scent of patchouli on unwashed bodies made the space seem almost claustrophobic. One of the wanderers lit a joint and handed it to Parker. The heady smell joined the odorous cacophony, and it seemed that the room itself was humming along with the sitar's drifting harmonics.

The gathering crowded in until there was no room in front of the chairs. Cal ran his finger around his collar, then straightened his tie. "Can you tell them to back off? It's getting kind of close in here."

Parker motioned to his minions, but none of them moved. "Calvin," he said with a dip of his head in the direction of a young man standing off to one side. "You took it upon yourself to bring a photographer?"

"Yes," Cal replied, drawing a fingertip over his mustache. "Parker, meet Quinton Bradley."

Quinton held up his camera and nodded.

"I was so surprised that you asked me to come, I wanted to capture the event for posterity. You don't mind," Cal said as if it was a question.

"Why would I?" Parker replied. "I want the truth about the Orion Institute told to the world. I asked you here with the hope that you would help me in that pursuit. You will tell the truth, won't you?"

"I try to. How about you? Will you tell the truth? The whole truth?"

"And nothing but." Parker leaned forward in his chair. His eyes narrowed as he twisted the diamond ring on his little finger. "The whole truth. Always."

"By the way, can we get a portrait of you . . . to run with the article?" Cal asked.

"Of course," Parker said with a grandiose wave. He sat upright, squared his shoulders and turned slightly in his chair. Crossing his legs, he smoothed his caftan, then put one arm across his waist and rested the elbow of the other on it. Holding the joint in an exaggerated pose, he looked seductively into the camera.

"Do you want to get rid of that?" Cal asked, pointing to the joint.

Parker rolled his eyes. "Of course not. I have no intention of hiding the essence of who I am."

"That's your essence?"

Parker frowned. "Of course not. But it is symbolic."

Cal shrugged, then motioned to Quinton. "Okay. Go ahead."

Taking a pencil from his jacket Cal flipped open a notebook and started scribbling in the tablet. He looked up. "What truth do you want to tell me today?"

Quiton's flash bulb popped searing Parker's face in white light.

"All truth, the totality of truth," Parker replied as his followers nodded and exchanged knowing glances.

"All. That's a tall order and broad spectrum," Cal said. "You want to narrow it down to something we can cover in an afternoon?"

Parker smiled. "No. Whatever I say -- it will all be the truth. And so, it will be all truth."

"So help you God?"

"So help me -- me, myself and I -- the holy trinity of a self-made, god-man."

Cal nodded. "I get it."

"Of course you do not, 'get it', Calvin. But you will serve my purpose."

"And what purpose is that?"

Quinton took another picture.

"What I said -- to expand the truth of Orion from the center of the universe, to the ends of the earth."

"I'm anxious to hear that truth," Cal said. "But first I'd like to talk about Anthony Campenella."

Parker cocked his head to one side and stared at him. "You waste no time in pursuing your objective to entrap me."

"As I said, I'm here to get the truth."

"Then, go on. Ask your questions."

Cal took a deep breath. "Anthony Campenella owned -- or owns this property, the property now occupied by the Orion Institute. Are you renting, buying, was it a gift, or are you . . . squatting?"

"Of all the subjects in the universe, you choose such a tiresome one. So typical of you," Parker said with a dismissive wave. "It's not a matter of renting or buying, giving or taking . . . or *squatting*." He looked up at the ceiling with a far-away stare. "Instead, let's talk about Anthony -- the man. A most enlightened being. Perhaps the most gifted, charismatic, and physically striking, yet spiritually cognizant men I have ever met. A combination not often found in a single individual."

"All individuals could be considered single," Cal replied with a slight smirk.

Parker frowned. "Again, so typical of you. Hardly worth a reply, but I will continue. For example, Anthony understood the transcendent perception of consumption and possession."

"Consumption and possession? I'm assuming your definition will be different than mine."

"He understood that humans, being mortal . . . ephemeral . . . evanescent . . . transitory, cannot actually *own* anything. We can only possess or consume for a time or a season. Possession lasts for a time, or a season, while the things that are consumed are gone in an instant."

With a broad flourish, Parker waved across the expanse of the room. A flashbulb popped as Quinton took a photo.

"This property, that Anthony once possessed, I now possess." Glaring at Cal, Parker held his hand toward him. "And this ring you keep staring at, that he once possessed, I now possess. Anthony understood that perception."

"You speak of him in the past tense. Why? Surely you know there have been questions."

Parker closed his eyes. "Anthony is on a journey. He is not, now, within the sphere of my presence. I haven't seen him for some time, so I speak of him in the past, when the spheres of our consciousness intersected and we were together."

"You say he's on a journey, to . . . where?"

"A journey within himself. Following wherever his eternal, internal self leads him."

Quinton snapped another picture.

Cal shook his head. "So, he left a successful career as a singer and nightclub owner to follow himself around? Like a cat chasing its own tail?"

Parker frowned again. "Calvin, you truly are a master of the pedestrian metaphor."

Cal half-smiled. "Actually, I believe that would be a simile. But regardless, the question remains."

"My book, *Master of the Mind: The Journey to Orion*, is, as the title suggests, about the journey to Orion, to the truth found within. Anthony is on that path. But I don't know where on the physical earth his journey may have taken him. The path within is never linear -- one event following another like a strip of film.

Internal and external events happen concurrently, therefore the truth of circularity is to find peace while traveling many divergent roads at the same time."

Cal shifted in his chair and crossed his legs. "Parker, what do you mean by circularity? I read your book and I must admit, in spite of myself, I found some elements intriguing."

"You damn me with your faint praise. But I will acquiesce to answer the question." Parker formed elegant circles with his thumbs and middle fingers and Quinton snapped the picture. "The universe, both internal and eternal, is made of spheres. Spirits leave the world, or sphere, in which they dwell and become a soul. That soul takes on a body and comes into this sphere, to this limited third-dimensional expression of reality, or time-space continuum -- the terms are interchangeable."

Holding up a forefinger, Cal scratched on the notepad, then looked up. "Okay, go on."

"The internal universe is much darker and more complex than the external. Spheres of consciousness. Spheres of attraction. Spheres of avoidance. Polarity and perception. Actually the sphere of perception itself is simply an on-off grid." He stared at Cal. "And as I have said before, for some people the grid is off. Eternally off."

"But what does all this mean, say to an 'Average Joe'?"

Parker shook his head. "To the 'Average Joe'? Nothing. Because they have no cognizance that the transcendence, or expansion of the mind, exists. Even among those who do have awareness, many can only access the first three, or possibly four, of the seven spheres of consciousness. For that reason, the last, seemingly divergent perceptions of science, art and spirituality can only be truly accessed by deep meditation, or for those seeking a quicker entry into the divine -- psychedelics, or pharmacology."

"But -- "

"If the government had not overstepped its own boundaries by outlawing harmless substances, people would be free to find the path into the spheres of divine creativity . . . into the art, science, ecstasy and true sexuality that are within them and around them at the same time."

"True sexuality? As opposed to . . ."

"True sexuality -- both physical *and* spiritual."

A thin young man, his hair hanging like long brown corkscrews around his acne-scarred face, leaned against Parker's chair and rested his head on Parker's lap.

After adjusting the lens on the camera, Quinton took the picture.

Cal paused a moment. "You . . . young man," he said to the boy. "How old are you?"

The boy looked up at Parker.

"Tell him," Parker said.

"Sixteen," the young man replied.

"Where are you from?"

He looked at Parker again. Parker nodded. "Ohio," the boy said.

Cal scratched on the notepad. "Do your parents know where you are?"

The boy fell silent, staring at the floor.

"Don't you think they're worried about you?" Cal continued.

Parker glared at him and rested his hand on the young man's shoulder. "You don't have to answer."

Cal looked down at his notes. "That brings me to my next topic. It's been said that you have a taste for . . . let's call it switch-hitting."

"It's not a matter of taste." Sitting upright, Parker took his hand from the boy's shoulder. "The truth is, I am called to strip those seeking enlightenment to their essence, so they can be re-born into the divine. Simply put, males have more difficulty with the perception of dominance and submission than females. The feminine enters into the spheres of the spirit more easily than the masculine. Because of their fluid quality, females adapt . . . like water poured through a screen. But man is like rock, which must be broken into sand before it can pass through the grid."

Cal sat back. "And you're just the one to break them?" He turned to Parker's followers. "Have any of you ever thought that you mean nothing to him? That maybe he's just using you?"

Some looked at each other. Some shrugged. Others shook their heads. A few seemed to contemplate the question. Quinton snapped another picture.

"How can I use those who have given themselves freely to me?" Parker motioned to his disciples. "This young man beside me, and many of these, have been utterly rejected by your world. What difference does it make to you, in your tiny, little, self-serving life, what happens to them? What concern is that of yours?" He paused. "What do you expect them to do? And where do you expect them to go? In their circumstance, what would you do?"

"How should I know? I have no idea what their *circumstances* are."

Parker's eyes glistened and a single tear slid down his cheek. "I see you have no answers. Only more questions. A myriad of accusing questions, but not a single answer." He paused again. "They are all welcome to live in my house," he said, stretching his arms over the gathering. "Would they be welcome in yours?"

Cal looked down and scribbled on the notepad.

Parker motioned to Gregg. Then Gregg nodded to an attractive, pubescent girl with a shaved head, sitting on the floor. She got up, smoothed her short, sheer tunic, and stood beside Quinton. Taking his arm, she pressed herself against him and kissed his cheek. He shook his arm from her grasp and took another picture.

"You see, Calvin, I have no need to use them," Parker said with a wave. "I give myself to them, and they give themselves to me . . . and to each other."

Gregg nodded at the girl again. She put her arm around Quinton's neck and kissed him again. Laughing, he shrugged and moved away.

Parker smiled. "We at Orion are surrounded by masses of humanity who have little, or no, notion of their divinity. Actually all men are god to some degree. Only a very few have luminosity enough to have any awareness of it." He looked into Cal's eyes. "And as I have said, most are not aware of it at all."

Cal wrote on the tablet. "Okay then, how about Deborah Donaldson? Is she aware of her divinity or is she part of . . ." He glanced down at his notes. "You called it 'the soul-draining entertainment monolith.'"

Parker folded his arms. "Deborah is an antecedent. An iconoclast. A paradox. Living as a woman, in a sphere of sexual freedom that is most often inhabited by men. Because society has decided that such liberation is unacceptable for a female, and looks down upon it, she lives in a lonely place, out of her element and ahead of her time."

"But despite all her exposure to the espoused truth, she hasn't left the monolith. Why?"

Parker looked away.

"And the Italian movie star . . ." Cal glanced at his notes. "Donatello Dragghi. On her show, he more or less, ironed your caftan. It didn't seem that you made a dent in converting him either. Is he aware of his divinity?"

Parker stiffened and looked down the bridge of his nose. "Perhaps. He lives in a form of old-world quasi-circularity, which is different, but not entirely opposed to the spherical reality we practice here. Though on the surface he appears unaware, I believe he is not as far from the freedom found in the truth of Orion as it might seem. The only thing blocking his path to enlightenment is the empty shell of a dead religion he clings to. The symbol of it hangs like an anchor around his neck."

"So many words. Why can't your truth be plain and simple, like do unto others -- something even a child can understand?"

Gregg motioned to the girl. She giggled and smiled, then kissed Quinton again. With a sideways glance at Cal, he allowed her to take his hand. Cal inconspicuously nodded, then watched as the girl led him away.

"You see? Even your young photographer friend is embracing the truth of Orion."

"Young men are easily swayed. I don't think Orion is all he'll be embracing."

Parker's eyes hardened. "Always the glib reply." He sat back in his chair. "Coming into the universal consciousness is like coming face to face with god. Becoming like god. And then becoming god. Nothing could be more simple. Anyone can understand, if they wish to."

Cal rubbed his forehead. "If that was simple, I'd hate to see complicated."

"The truth of Orion seems complex only to those who choose to remain ignorant. With the decision to embrace enlightenment comes understanding. Either all that I say is true, or it is all a lie. Black or white. Simple as that. And these..." Parker waved toward the sprawling group. "They will attest that I speak the truth. From the beginning that is what I told you. All of this has been chronicled in my book. Now I have nothing more to say."

Parker got up, bowed to his disciples and turned to Gregg. "See him out." He walked, barefoot, across the greatroom and disappeared through the doorway beneath the stairs.

50

THE DOOR TO Steven's hospital room swung open.

"Daddy!" Donny squealed, running to the bed as a half-smile spread over Steven's face.

"Hold on there pardner," Buck said. "Let me help you up."

As he hoisted Donny onto the bed, Pauline came into the room.

"Wha's wong wiff you mouth, Daddy?" Donny asked, settling next to Steven.

"That's why he's here, honey," Pauline said. "The doctors are trying to fix him."

Donny looked up at her. "How did he get bwoke, Gwamma?"

"He's not broken. He wasn't feeling well and the doctors are helping him get better. We'll talk about it later," she said, patting Donny's head. She turned to Steven. "Donny's been so anxious to see you. He talks about you all the time."

Steven ran his hand over the stubble of Donny's hair, then reached for the dog-eared legal pad.

WHAt HAppeNed

"We had to shave it," Pauline said.

"I had wice!" Donny announced with a wide grin, bouncing his feet on the bed. He scrambled to stand. "Daddy, at Gwamma and Gwampa's we hab a dog name Twailor! An a horse name Nawah!

An I hab my own bedwoom wiff wots of books an cowboy wheels!"

Buck cleared his throat. "Uh, he means he had lice. He's staying in your old room with the wagon-wheel bed. Now we have a little wire-haired terrier named Tailor. And you remember, Nahlah, the mare. She's still around."

WANt TO See THEM

Steven looked up, his eyes questioning.

"Of course we want you to come home," Pauline said.

"You gonna live wiff Gwamma and Gwampa too, Daddy. I wike it dere," Donny said, jumping up and down on the bed.

Buck caught him and sat him on the edge. "No jumping," he scolded.

Steven paused, then scratched on the paper.

What about ShARA

Pauline stiffened. "You're welcome to bring her. But you can't live in our house, unmarried."

Steven looked over at Buck.

"We want you to come home, son, but if you bring Shara, you'll have to be married." He folded his hands. "That's your mother's decision and I support it."

Steven stared up at the ceiling, then looked over at Donny. After a moment, he began writing again.

Then I WANT SHARA to HAVe A ReAL WeDDiNG ANd I wANt RoY to Be BeST MAN

51

AFTERNOON SUNLIGHT ILLUMINATED Steven's hospital room. He settled the legal pad on his lap, then stared at the blank paper. *I can't propose with my mouth sagging and spit running down my chin.*

Grimacing, he printed several lines. Then ripped the sheet off the tablet, threw it on the floor, and started over. After numerous attempts, he printed three short paragraphs and tore off the page. Sinking back against the pillow, he stared up at the ceiling.

Am I doing the right thing? Or will it be another mistake in a long line of mistakes?

Just then, Shara came into the room.

Steven, tore the page from the tablet, crumpled it, and hid it under the covers.

"Wow! They stuck you way out in the middle of nowhere. I had to ask three different nuns before I found one who knew where you were." She planted a kiss on his cheek, then dropped her crocheted purse at the foot of the bed. "What's all that?" she asked, pointing to a mound of wadded paper and used tissue on the floor.

He shrugged one shoulder.

Shara squeezed past the bed, looked out the window, and wrinkled her nose. "Ugly view. How long have you been here?" She threw herself into the chair, splayed her jean-clad legs out in front of her, and watched the legal pad for his answer.

He printed his response, then wiped the saliva away with a tissue.

COUPLE DAYS

"I would have come sooner, but it's like, you know, really hard to get over here from Berkeley. And anyway, they wouldn't even let me see you. Besides, I figured your parents would want you all to themselves."

THEY BROUGHT DONOVAN

She looked around the room. "Really? Where are they?"

THEY WENT HOME

"When?"

FEW HOURS AGO DONOVAN'S HAIR IS SHORT AS MINE NOW

Shara looked aghast. "What? How come?"

HE HAD LICE

She frowned. "Lice? How'd he get lice?"

Steven sighed.

"Has anybody else been to see you?"

He shook his head and tore the sheet from the tablet.

Shara paused a moment. "Hey, check this out." She pulled off a beaded velvet house slipper, held her foot toward him, and wiggled her toes. "Black nail polish. Roxie ripped it off a drag queen at the beauty college. Like it?"

Steven nodded.

"I did my fingers black for Vince's birthday party, but it already came off. He and Vickie had the most *outrageous* party. What a blast! It lasted two whole days and they had a band and everything. They said to tell you they missed you. Everybody was *totally* wasted. You would have been proud of me -- I was completely smashed. I can't even remember most of it."

Steven watched her put the slipper on again. *Proud? Is that true? Would I ever have been proud she was wasted?*

"Hey, are you okay? You look like you're gonna cry or something."

He took the proposal from under the covers and passed it to her. She looked down at the wrinkled paper, then back up at him. "Steven? What's wrong?"

ReAD IT

"Come on. Talk to me."

I CaNT

"Steven..."

Shara wandered down the deserted hospital hallway, then sank onto a bench across from a row of elevators. A small niche in the wall held a statue of the Virgin Mary, holding the Baby Jesus. *He's breaking up with me. I could see it in his eyes.*

Struggling to swallow the lump that had formed in her throat, she smoothed the wrinkled paper over her thigh.

SHARA
I wish I could write A poem oR siNG a SONG. BuT I Can't eveN talk. theRes NothiNG left iNside me anymoRe. I'm soRRy I made A mess of eveRythiNG. If I Could I would do it ALL DIffeReNtLy. Now the ONLY thiNG thAt mAkes seNse is to move BACk home.

"I knew it!" Shara crushed the paper and dropped it onto the bench beside her. She closed her eyes and a stream of tears ran over the freckles on her cheeks. *Steven, don't leave...*

Moments later, Shara felt a light touch on her knee. She jumped and looked up to see a small, white-haired woman in a pale peach coat standing in front of her. The woman opened her purse, pulled out a tissue and pressed it into Shara's hand. "Don't worry, dear.

The Blessed Virgin sees, and knows." With an angelic smile, she pointed to the statue. "Whatever the trouble is, if you ask, she'll help you. My husband was very sick, but I prayed to The Virgin, and now the doctor says he's getting better."

Shara blew her nose into the tissue, which smelled of breath mints. "But I'm not Catholic."

The woman put up a gnarled finger. "Shhhh. Trust and believe," she said with a wink, looking up at the statue. "She sees and she knows."

A bell rang and the elevator door opened. The woman smiled again, then slipped inside. The doors closed and she seemed to vanish like an apparition.

Shara looked up at the statue, then closed her eyes.

"Dear Blessed Virgin," she whispered. "My name is Shara and my boyfriend, Steven, is here in the hospital. I know you don't know who I am, because I never really prayed before." Her lips trembled. "If Steven leaves me, I don't know what I'll do. I'm trying to trust and believe. Please . . . please . . . help me."

Shara opened her eyes. She spread the note on the bench beside her and continued reading.

> I Love you And I wAnt you to come with me, but my pARents wont let us LivE THeRe unLess we're mARRIED. Its Not A fAIR tRAde, but if youLL Give me youR FutuRe, ILL GIve you my nAme.
> Steven

Her jaw dropped. *Married?* She looked into the face of the Virgin. "He *is* leaving, but he wants to take me with him. Thank you, Blessed Virgin! Thank you!"

Shara folded Steven's proposal, put it in the pocket of her jeans, and wandered back to his room. She paused a moment, then opened the door.

He looked up.

She smiled and rushed to his side. "Yes, Steven! Yes!"

52

SHARA PACED AROUND the living room of the brown-shingle house. The chords of Buffalo Springfield's "For What It's Worth" echoed from the turntable. She stopped at the front window and parted the ramshackle blinds. A long-haired man in a poncho wheeled by on a bicycle, and a multi-colored VW Bug rolled down the street. She let the blinds fall back into their usual state of disrepair, then went to the mantle and picked up a photograph of two shirtless young soldiers in jungle khaki, posing in front of a temple. *Steven . . . you made it through Viet Nam, but now . . . what if you don't get better?*

She set the picture back on the mantle and wandered into Roxanne's bedroom. Tugging on the top drawer of a beat-up dresser, she yanked it open and rifled through the clothes. "There it is," she said under her breath. "She won't care if I smoke some." She took out a baggie of weed and a small stone pipe, then shoved the clothes back in the drawer, and went into the living room.

Sitting cross-legged on a mattress in the middle of the room, she took a pinch out of the bag and pressed the brittle leaves into the bowl. Then lit the pipe and took a long drag. The smell, like burning coffee, filled the room. She pulled Steven's proposal from her pocket and read it again as she exhaled. *I already said yes, but . . .*

Her head began to hum.

I should tell Roxie. But I already know what she'll say.

Shara stood in front of a full-length mirror mounted on the coat closet door. "She'll go like this . . ." Putting her hands on her hips, she affected a haughty stare. "'*Sha-ra*, how can you be so *stu-pid*?' or '*Sha-ra*, why on earth would you do that?' or '*Sha-ra*, you never know what the hell you're doing.'" She rolled her eyes at her reflection, then flopped down on the mattress again.

"She really knows how to lay it on. I hate it when she does that." *Why should I care what she thinks anyway?* Listening to the deafening hum in her head, she watched the paper peace signs and daisies gently swaying on the mobile hanging from the ceiling. *I'm getting married and I just want someone to care.* "Maybe Vickie knows where she is."

Wearing a patched velvet coat with a matted fox collar, Shara walked across a thin strip of lawn to the neighboring house. She unclipped several scraps of paper from a clothespin nailed to the gate, and paged through the messages as she went up the walkway. Pausing on the front porch, she looked out to Alcatraz in the bay. *An island doesn't cry . . .*

Squaring her shoulders and stiffening her jaw, she rapped on the front door.

A short, chunky woman wearing a lime-green flowered muumuu and a puka shell necklace answered. "Oh, Shara, hi," she said with a lazy stare, took a drag off a brown cigarette, and blew the smoke out her nose. Leaning against the doorframe, she tapped the ash onto the porch.

Shara handed her the scraps of paper. "Voodoo Spirit is still looking for Scott -- she left three notes. And some guy named Barney wants a couch. How come you aren't reading your messages?"

Vickie took the notes and glanced back over her shoulder. "Vince and I are acting like we're not home. We're grading exams," she said, pointing to a red pencil poked into a twist of her wiry gray hair. "Gotta satisfy the educational-establishment machine."

Without losing her grip on the cigarette, Vickie straightened her yellow granny-glasses, stuck her thumb down the neckline of her muumuu, and scratched the hollow between her pancake-flat breasts. "I just happened to see you coming. What's up? How's Steven?"

"Uh, he's better, I guess," Shara said, staring at Vickie's faint moustache. "I just got back from the hospital."

"Did he get the feeling back?"

Shara shifted her weight. "Not yet."

"Bummer. Guess Roxie found him just in time." Vickie looked from side to side. "Where's Donovan?"

"Steven's parents are keeping him."

"Oh, before I forget . . ." Vickie reached behind the door and pulled out a pair of knee-high suede moccasins topped with fringe, that laced up the side. "Are these yours?"

Shara shook her head.

"Somebody left them at the party. I thought for sure they were yours. They don't fit me. Want 'em?"

"Uh, yeah, sure," Shara replied with a shrug, taking the moccasins. "I'm looking for Roxie. Have you seen her?"

"She said something about going somewhere." Vickie snapped her fingers. "Oh yeah. I think she went to the city with that guy she met at the party. Hey Vince, what was his name?" she shouted toward the dining room."

"Who?" came the muffled response.

"The guy Roxanne went to San Francisco with. He played drums at your party."

"Um . . . Carl something."

"No, the other guy. Carl's the bass player. The one from Oklahoma who lives in LA."

"Oh, him . . . uh, Bob, I think."

Vickie turned back. "She's with that drummer, Bob. You met him."

Shara frowned, fidgeting with the fringe on the boots. "I don't remember." Her voice wavered. "Do you know where they are? I really need to talk to Roxie."

"I think Bob's staying at Carl's place in San Francisco. They're playing a gig tonight at a club or something. Hey, Vince, do you know Carl's number?" Vickie yelled.

"Yeah, just a minute . . ."

Shara looked back at Alcatraz and bit her lip. *Islands don't cry . . .*

A few minutes later Vince lumbered to the doorway. He handed Shara a scrap of paper with a phone number scrawled on it.

"Thanks," she said, staring at the paper.

"Good to see you," he replied. He rubbed his dark, pointy beard, tightened his thinning ponytail, and went back the way he came.

Shara looked up. "Hey, Vickie, can I use your phone?"

53

SHARA STARED DOWN from the smoke filled L-shaped balcony of the nightclub to the stage and crowded dance floor below. The balcony vibrated with the music erupting from the stacks of speakers flanking the stage. The air was heavy with the smell of weed and tobacco. Diogenes Lantern Works swirled to the beat with a light-show of fluid shapes and colors that spread up the back wall and on to the ceiling.

The guitarist fell to his knees and tore at the strings as the organist bashed out the melody. The drummer, bass player, and percussionist matched the ferocity with a driving beat. After exploding into an extended crescendo, the music stopped. A momentary silence, and the audience broke into applause. The musicians bowed several times, then disappeared backstage. Muffled voices reverberated like the sound of falling water, replacing the din of the band. Moments later a KPFA disc jockey announced, Jefferson Airplane's 'Somebody To Love'. The song blared through the nightclub.

Shara pushed an aluminum ashtray out of the way, then glanced around the balcony at the bar, three deep with people waiting for drinks, and at the tables filled with raucous partiers. *Come on, Roxie...*

A tall waitress with wild black hair came to Shara's table wearing a microscopic bikini, cowboy boots, and fringed leather chaps. She took a pencil from behind her ear and pulled an order pad from the waist of her bikini bottom. "Hey," she said, tapping the pad with the pencil. "Are you ready to order?"

"Not yet." Shara tightened the worn fox collar of her coat and twisted one leg around the other. "I'm waiting for my friend. I'll order when she gets here."

"Tables are for customers. And as you can see," the waitress said, pointing to the overflowing bar, "there are tons of people who want a table."

"My friend is with the band. She said she'd meet me when they take a break."

The waitress planted her hand on her bare hip. "If I had a buck for every time some jerk said they're with the band, I could quit my job and move to Hawaii." Rolling her eyes, she stomped away.

Shara hung her arm over the balcony and looked down into the crowd. *Where is she?*

A man at the next table pulled a pouch of Bugler from a pocket in his patched denim jacket and a packet of Zig-Zag papers from his jeans. He nodded at Shara. "Hey, Red, want one?" he said, holding up the tobacco.

"Um, okay."

The man rolled two cigarettes. As he got up and went to Shara's table, a couple quickly took his place. He flicked the cover on his lighter, lit both cigarettes, and passed her one. "Mind if I sit down?"

Shara took a drag, then coughed. "Actually, I'm waiting for someone."

"Why the hell didn't you say so? Now I lost my table."

"My name's not Red, and this tastes like crap" she said, stubbing the cigarette out in the ashtray.

"If I wanted your opinion about the smoke, I'd ask for it, you stupid bitch." Thrusting up a middle finger, he stomped off toward the bar.

A few minutes later, Roxanne sauntered to the table and flopped down across from Shara. "Hey, where'd you get the joint?" she said, motioning to the ashtray.

"It's not weed." Shara frowned. "It's super-crappy tobacco. Where were you? The waitress has been hassling me. And the guy who gave me the cigarette flipped me off. And I had to thumb a ride. And panhandle enough to get in. But you're still gonna get me backstage, right?"

Roxanne looked down at a backstage pass, hanging from her neck by a cord. "I can't."

Shara's face fell.

"Sorry. They're really tight with them tonight. They announced the show on that new station, KSAN, this morning, and all of a sudden everybody in town showed up. But, hey, at least you got in." Roxanne paused. "You're really decked out -- mostly in my clothes, I might add. Except the moccasins. Where'd you get them?"

"Vickie. Somebody left them at Vince's party. So, you really like that Bob guy?"

"Yeah. You met him, remember?"

"Actually, I don't remember hardly anything about that night."

Roxanne laughed. "Trust me, you met him. You were so smashed. He said you're really cute when you're stoned."

"What's his sign?"

"Sagittarius."

"What's his rising?"

"I don't know. Who cares. I'm not gonna marry him. Besides, you can be incompatible with someone, zodiac-wise, and it can still work, at least temporarily. You and Steven are proof of that. But here's the most outrageous part. You've heard of The Time Season Band?"

Shara nodded.

"He's the drummer!"

"What? You're kidding."

"No. Bob is really good friends with Carl, so he's been jammin' with Carl's band. He's flying back down to LA in a few days to start rehearsing for their next album and . . ." Roxanne paused, flashing a smile.

"What, Roxie? What?" Shara said, her eyes wide, leaning closer.

"He asked me to go with him. But that's not all."

"Come on, Roxie, tell me."

"He said you can come too, and he said he'd buy you a ticket!"

Shara's eyes popped open. "You're kidding? Really? Wow! Cool! That'll be a total blast!" She froze. "But . . ."

Just then, the waitress reappeared. "So, what's it gonna be?" she grumbled, thumping the pencil on the pad, and looking at Shara and Roxanne with an ill-tempered stare.

"I'm with the band, so I'm only here 'til the next set," Roxanne said, conspicuously winding the cord suspending the backstage pass around her finger.

"Yeah, well, what about you?" the waitress demanded, turning to Shara. "Somebody better order something quick or I'm calling the bouncer."

"Oh, all right." Roxanne pulled a wad of bills from a pocket on her embroidered satin blazer and threw a dollar on the table. "Bring us a beer and keep the change."

The waitress looked down at the bill, then shook her head and went back to the bar.

"What's with the chaps? And dig that crazy hair," Roxanne said, pointing over her shoulder with her thumb. "It's like she thinks she's Annie Oakley or something." She settled back in her chair. "So, what's up?"

"Uh, oh yeah." Shara fidgeted with the sleeve of her coat, while staring at the floor.

"Hey, what's wrong? You were all excited a second ago."

Shara took Roxanne's hand. "Roxie, there's something I need to tell you."

"I figured that when you asked me to meet you."

Shara cleared her throat and began again. "There's something I need to -- "

"You already said that."

She closed her eyes and sucked in her breath. "Steven asked me to marry him."

"So?" Roxanne said, extracting her hand. "You blew him off, of course . . . right?"

"No. I told him I would."

"What!" Roxanne shrieked with a look of horror as the couple at the next table turned and stared.

"So, what do you think?"

Roxanne slouched in her chair. "Unless you're a complete idiot, you already know what I think."

Just then, the waitress returned. She set a tall glass down with a thud, sloshing some of its contents on the table. "Anything else?" she said with a scowl.

Roxanne waved her away.

"Well?" Shara said, watching the effervescence ebb from the spilled beer. "Aren't you going to say anything?"

Roxanne grabbed the glass, took a gulp and looked reproachfully at her. "Personally, I think you're crazy. How could you?"

"I love him."

"Oh my god. I can't believe I'm hearing this. You don't want to get married, do you?"

"No, but . . ." Shara paused. "Steven's moving back home."

Roxanne's eyes hardened. She shook her head. "And his parents are making you get married."

Shara looked up at her.

Roxanne threw her hands in the air. "I can't believe this. He's so stupid! First he knocks you up. Then he overdoses. Are you going to let him ruin the rest of your life? I knew I should've kicked him out before you got hung up on him."

"Don't say that! You know how freaked out I've been ever since he overdosed." Shara buried her face in her hands. "Why does my life always have to be such a drag?"

"Mark my words, if you think your life is a drag now, just wait. As soon as Steven gets back up there with his parents and his good buddy, Roy, he'll turn out to be just as square as they are. And then you'll be trapped."

"But what about Donovan? He's taking Donovan with him."

"So what. Let Steven and his parents keep him. You didn't actually want a baby. Steven was the one who talked you into having him in the first place."

"It wasn't that, I just . . . I don't know how to be a mom."

"Like, whatever. Anyway, that wasn't what you said." Roxanne frowned. She slid the beer to Shara. "One day you'll wake up, like most women do, and discover that men don't think about anyone but themselves. Then you'll wonder why you wasted your life. I'm telling you -- no, I'm begging you, don't do it. I mean, if it's a man you want, there are men everywhere. Dime a dozen. Trust me. You're beautiful and you can do better."

"But I prayed, and the Blessed Virgin answered my prayer."

Roxanne's jaw dropped slightly. "What? You can't be serious."

"I prayed and she answered."

"You must be trippin'. You're even crazier than I thought. You think some religious fairy godmother answered your prayer? And you're gonna throw your life away based on that?"

Shara looked out over the balcony. "God, Roxie, I don't know. I think I might be Catholic."

"Catholic? *Sha-ra*, no one *thinks* they're Catholic. Besides, when have you ever known what the hell you're doing?"

"Never, I guess. It seems like my life always just happens to me."

"That's why I have to figure everything out for you," Roxanne said with an acidic tone. Her eyes narrowed. "Who found you wandering around Golden Gate Park after your sleaze-ball, alcoholic mother ditched you?"

Shara rolled her eyes and sank in her chair. "Here we go again."

Roxanne leaned closer. "And when did I find you?"

"When I was fourteen," Shara said with a long sigh.

"And who taught you about 'Dialing for Dinners?'"

"You."

"And how to panhandle when necessary?"

"You."

"And how long have you been living off me and my trust fund?"

"Four years." Shara looked up at her with a blank, catatonic stare. "Why do you always rag on me like this?"

"I'm not ragging -- I'm just being myself. Why do you always act like a moron?"

Shara's lips trembled. She let out a shrill cry and fell forward onto the table, wailing uncontrollably, and gasping as she sobbed.

People on the balcony turned and stared.

"Shhhh! Shara, stop it! Do you want them to kick us out?" Roxanne said, shaking her.

Shara pushed her away. "I hate you!"

The waitress returned with an enormous bouncer. "Do we have a problem here?" he asked, crossing his arms over his chest.

"No, she's just upset," Roxanne said as Shara wailed. "Her grandmother died."

"Well, tell her to keep it down," the bouncer snapped. "This's a nightclub, not a funeral parlor. People come here to get drunk and have fun. And they don't want anybody crapping on their parade."

"Yeah," the waitress added with a smirk.

"Tell your friend to straighten up, or she'll be upset outside on the sidewalk." The bouncer jerked his head in the direction of the bar, then he and the waitress went back the way they came.

"Come on, Shara," Roxanne said under her breath. "Everyone's staring."

Shara looked up, her eyes red and her cheeks tear-stained. "I don't care!"

Roxanne yanked a napkin from a holder on the table, pushed it into Shara's hand, then sat back and stared at her. "Quit acting like a freak and pull yourself together."

Shara jumped up, "You're such a bitch! I hate you!" she shrieked, then stumbled around a nearby table and rushed out the exit door knocking over the glass of beer. The amber liquid ran across the table, into Roxanne's lap. She lurched from her chair, swiping at the wet spot spreading over the crotch of her jeans.

Just then, the band came back onstage to round of enthusiastic applause. Bob pointed a drumstick toward the balcony and smiled at Roxanne. He tapped the sticks together three times, and the band broke into a throbbing wall of sound.

Roxanne shook her head. "Wonderful. Now it looks like I peed my pants." She ripped a wad of napkins from the holder and went after Shara.

Roxanne pushed the exit door open and stepped out into the cold night air on Sutter Street. The frenetic sounds coming from the nightclub muffled as the door closed behind her. Scanning the darkened street, she saw Shara running down the hill. "Shara! Shara! Come back!" she yelled.

Shara turned. "Shut up! You stupid bitch! I said I hate you!" she shouted, then tripped on a crack in the sidewalk, and tumbled into the street.

Roxanne ran to her. "Shara! Are you okay?"

She pulled herself up off the pavement and sat on the curb, sobbing. "Do I look okay?" she snapped, holding up her scratched palms. "I skinned my knee, twisted my ankle, scraped my hands, *and* scuffed my new moccasins!"

Roxanne sat down beside her. "Shara, I'm sorry. I just -- "

"Shut up! I hate you!" Shara looked up and wiped her eyes. "Why do you always have to say stuff like that?"

Roxanne brushed a red tangle off Shara's face. "Come on, don't be mad. I said I'm sorry. I was only trying to help. I just don't want you to do something you'll regret." She put her arm around her. "Come down to LA with Bob and me. He's really fun, and we'll have a blast. And besides, who knows what will happen."

54

PAULINE PUT DOWN a newspaper crossword puzzle as Buck came into the bedroom and sat on the edge of the bed. Donny and Tailor scrambled up between them.

"Gramma and I have things to talk about. You and Tailor go play," Buck said, patting Donny on the head.

"What things Gwampa?"

"Big people stuff."

"Whas da big people stuff?"

"You and Tailor go play in your room for awhile, then we'll go outside and play catch."

"C'mon Twailor." Donny slid off the bed and trudged out of the room with the dog following along behind.

Buck punched his pillow, pushed it up against the headboard, and flopped down next to Pauline.

"How on earth can we have a wedding?" she said. "Steven is still half paralyzed and he can't talk."

"I don't know. You're the one who said they need to be married."

"Buck . . ."

"Okay, okay." He thought a moment. "Assuming Shara says yes, we'll keep it simple."

"But where?"

He paused, then his eyes brightened. "Hey, how about the hospital chapel? It'll be a piece of cake, relatively speaking. Steven wants Roy to be best man. Someone'll be maid or matron of honor, and someone'll give Shara away. We can get flowers from the hospital florist and rent tuxedos someplace nearby. And if you want a tip of the hat to matrimonial tradition, Donny can be ring-bearer."

"Matrimonial tradition?" Pauline gripped the chenille bedspread. "Buck, this whole thing . . . it's so seedy -- like a bad dream." She pulled on the chenille and the fabric ripped. "Now look," she moaned, holding up the fuzzy wad. "I tore the bedspread."

"Take it easy. The bedspread was old, anyway."

"But what about a ring?"

"Steven can give her his grandmother's ring."

"Buck, you can't be serious. Your mother's engagement ring is like a diamond doorknob. Shara might pawn it."

"We've always said we were keeping it for him."

"But it's worth a fortune. "

Buck shook his head. "Pauline, a promise is a promise."

"Promise? In this case, I hardly think our keeping a promise is the issue. Shara doesn't strike me as the kind of person you could trust to give you the right time of day, let alone give her word and have it mean anything. She's so . . . and what on earth is she going to wear? She can't possibly wear white. Donny's proof enough of that. But if she doesn't, then -- "

"Pauleeen, please. Don't nit-pick. We're keeping our promise to Steven, not Shara. No matter what, it won't be perfect. So, for his sake, let's just try and get everybody to the altar. Okay?"

She took a long breath. "Alright."

"If Shara goes through with it, we go ahead with our plans. And if she doesn't, then none of it matters."

Buck swung the back door open and squinted into the sun. "Donny . . ." he called. "Let's play catch . . ."

Donny came running with Tailor bounding beside him.

Buck handed him a leather glove almost as big as he was. "Stand in the middle," he said, motioning to a circle of lawn surrounded by the driveway.

Tailor followed Donny onto the grass.

Buck gave the ball an easy underhand toss.

Donny scrambled to catch it, but it rolled out of the glove and fell between his feet. Tailor rushed in, grabbed it, and trotted away. Donny looked up with a dejected stare.

"Tailor! Drop it!" Buck shouted.

The dog dropped the ball and flopped down at the edge of the lawn.

"Don't worry, you'll get the hang of it," Buck said as he went to pick it up.

Donny threw the ball, but it arced toward the ground.

"Gwampa, wha's da big people stuff?"

"Huh?"

"Da stuff you an Gwamma talk about."

"Boy, have you got a one-track mind." Buck tossed the ball directly into the center of Donny's glove, but it bounced over the side. "We were talking about your dad coming back here to live."

Tailor grabbed the ball and ran off with it.

Donny looked up. "Wha about my Mommy, an Mommy fwiend Woxie?"

Buck pulled off his hat and rubbed his forehead. "Your dad is going to ask your mom if she wants to come too."

"Wha about Woxie?"

Buck put his hat back on and crossed his arms. "Roxie's staying right where she is."

Donny stared down at the ground a moment, then looked up at Buck with a serious expression. "I don wike Woxie."

Buck smiled. "I don't either. But, you know what? I like you."

Donny smiled back. "I wike you too, Gwampa."

55

HIGH ON A bluff overlooking the ocean, Parker and Gregg sat on a pew-like bench made from a redwood log. The afternoon sun hung low on the horizon as they shared a bowl of raw snow peas and bean sprouts, while sipping on glasses of Blue Nun.

"That was quite an interview yesterday," Gregg said with a long exhale.

"Yes, quite." Parker took a pea from the bowl and leaned back on the bench. "But Mephistopheles did not transcend and prevail as you suggested I would. Calvin Jeffries is very much alive and well, and as influential as ever." He held the bowl out to Gregg.

Gregg took a few snow peas, then took a drink of wine.

"Is it possible he's right?" Parker said. "That the truth of Orion has had no affect on either Deborah Donaldson, or the Italian? And I'm only using the people who come here searching for enlightenment?"

Gregg shook his head. "Don't be ridiculous. Some things take time. As you said, how can you use someone who gives themselves freely for you to use?"

Parker spun around with a bird-of-prey stare. "Now I'm ridiculous?"

"Parker... no. I meant it rhetorically. Being god, of course, you can't *actually* be ridiculous."

Parker sat back. "Alright."

"I only meant -- "

"I know what you meant."

Gregg brightened. "But Calvin Jeffries certainly can't see the world the same as he did before. I believe he had an epiphany, leaving Orion without Quinton, his young photographer friend. Quinton is beginning his journey -- he's going to stay. DoPenny has seen to it. She told me he came to the very edge of himself."

"And no one can bring a man to the end of himself like DoPenny can," Parker said, refilling their glasses. "The streets of Las Vegas have never produced a more willing protégé. I'm thankful to Anthony for finding her and bringing her to me."

"She's easily led, and she always answers her master's call," Gregg added.

Parker stared blankly at the ocean. "But still, it seems that there should be something ... more." He sighed, shook his head, and took a few more bean sprouts from the bowl. "Did you know that, transcendently, my birthday falls on the day of the summer solstice?" He dropped the sprouts into his mouth.

Gregg raised his glass. "Then we must have a party."

"Do you know what gift I'm giving myself?" Parker said, placing his hands on his chest.

"How could I?"

Parker set his glass on a flat stone beside the bench, then turned to the main house of the Institute and pointed to the roof. "I'm building a deck there, over the second floor, against the turret. And between those two second-story windows ... a door leading to the deck."

"Yes, I see. It would have a mind-blowing view of the ocean."

Parker smiled. "Well put. I met a man who will build it for me as an offering. He said he can have it finished in time for the solstice."

"Then it's cosmically perfect."

"Yes. I have decided to invite exactly ninety-nine guests."

"Why ninety-nine?" Gregg asked.

"The number is symbolic of illumination, enlightenment, divine communication, true awareness and cosmic love. The numerological equivalent of Orion, and therefore, utterly perfect."

"Oh." Gregg nodded.

"An artist in Berkeley has offered to design the invitations. Again, as an offering. I'm calling the event, 'The Summer Solstice Cosmic Convergence.'" Parker paused a moment. "How much blotter do we have left?"

"Acid?"

"Yes, of course."

"You dropped the last two."

Parker thought a moment. "Call down to Laguna Beach and have some sent up for the party. Also . . . get some hash, Blond Leb if they have it and some Michoacán weed easy on the seeds and stems."

Gregg stared at the ground. "So, you've been planning this -- "

"For awhile."

Gregg frowned.

"Don't worry," Parker replied, patting Gregg's knee. "I've been planning it by myself. No one knows, but you and, of course, me. 'The Summer Solstice Cosmic Convergence' will kill many birds with one stone. I'm inviting Deborah, giving me another opportunity to release the gilded bird from her cage."

Gregg cleared his throat. "Um, wouldn't it be releasing the bird from her gilded cage?'

"You *do* understand that, in this case, it's the bird that's gilded."

Gregg thought a moment. "Oh, yes, of course."

"And I want to invite the Italian actor I met on her show."

Gregg crossed his arms and sank against the bench. "Why?"

"Must I always explain myself to you? As he said on Deborah's show, 'even bad publicity, is good publicity'-- for my book, I mean. And publicity aside, he interests me."

"But why?" Gregg said with a petulant frown.

"Oh, alright. He presents a challenge. Nothing more. You know how to contact the gilded bird. I think she will know how to find the Italian."

56

VICKIE PARTED STRANDS of deep purple beads hanging in the arched doorway of her living room. She motioned for Shara to follow. A soft clatter echoed in the room as the beads closed behind them.

Rhythmic chords of "Scarborough Fair" and the fragrance of sandalwood incense filled the room. Day-glo origami cranes hung from a mobile on the ceiling. And a split-leaf philodendron stretched across the picture window, while a nearby pathos plant drooped in its macramé hanger.

"Come. Sit," Vickie said, patting the seat of a blocky gray-green couch. She tapped the ash off her cigarette into a standing ashtray ornamented with a stylized leaping stag.

Shara smoothed a short skirt made from a pair jeans, then sat down beside her on the hard, unforgiving cushion. "What's wrong with your plant?" she said, pointing to the pathos.

Vickie looked up. "Oh, someone poured beer in it at the party. Guess it didn't like Falstaff," she said with a shrug.

"That's a drag. I like that plant. Do you think it'll make it?"

"Probably. Pathos are pretty indestructible." She moved a glass bowl filled with more origami cranes, then propped her bare feet and stout, unshaven legs on the coffee table. "What happened to you?" she said, pointing to the hot-pink, Mercurochrome-tinted scrape on Shara's knee.

"I got in fight with Roxie at the nightclub her boyfriend was at, and I tripped on the sidewalk."

"About what?"

"Steven asked me to marry him, and I said I would."

"Well, what did Roxie say?"

"Can't you guess? She thinks I'm insane."

"Why? I've always liked Steven. He's a great guy. You could do a hell of a lot worse."

"That's weird. Roxie said I could do better."

Vickie took a long drag off her cigarette. "Spoken by Roxie, whose long-term relationships last less than a month. It's none of my business, but you don't seem very happy for someone who's about to get married. Maybe that's what she means."

"Maybe." Shara looked away. "It's just like, it's all happening too fast."

"Then why are you doing it?"

"His parents . . . and Donovan, I guess. But I love Steven -- at least I think I do, and I feel like if I don't marry him, I'll lose him."

"Where's it happening?" Vickie asked with a sympathetic smile.

"At the hospital chapel, since Steven's still . . . you know. His parents are setting it up."

"So, what are you wearing?"

Shara shrugged. "Who knows."

"Hey, I have this bitchin' white lace outfit you can borrow. It's one of my favorites. Or at least it was when it fit me." Vickie laughed. "Actually, it never fit me -- just wishful thinking. I keep hoping I'll get skinny enough to wear it. Anyway, it's a little bit risqué without being too slutty. I'll show you in a minute."

Shara twisted a lock of hair around her finger. "Um, maybe, if I can't find anything else."

"Well, thanks a lot. You haven't even seen it."

"Sorry. I didn't mean it that way."

Vickie stubbed her cigarette out in the ashtray. "So, is Roxie at least going to show up?"

"No. She got totally pissed-off that I wouldn't take off and go down to LA with her and Bob. I bet the only reason she hasn't kicked me out of the house yet is because she's hanging around with him all the time. How could I go? I already told Steven I'd marry him."

"If she goes completely off her rocker, you can always stay here."

Just then, Vince parted the beads and slouched in the doorway, eating a cashew butter and avocado sandwich. "Want one, Shara?" he asked with one side of his mouth bulging.

She shook her head.

"We're talking about the wedding," Vickie said.

"What wedding?" he asked.

Vickie rolled her eyes. "Steven and Shara's."

Vince went in and sat next to her. "So, how's it going?"

Shara sank against the sofa. "Terrible. My so-called best friend isn't even coming, and now she hates me. I don't know what I'm wearing, who'll be my maid of honor, or who'll give me away. And I'll probably have to hitchhike to get there."

"How about Steven's parents? Won't they come get you?" Vince asked between bites.

Shara sighed. "I don't know. I'm pretty sure they hate me too. I feel like they think I'm the one who made Steven overdose, or something." She fidgeted with a seam on the sofa. "I just wanted somebody to care that I'm getting married, and Roxie's the only one I thought might kinda care."

Vickie took her hand. "Shara, honey, we care, right?" she said, turning to Vince. "We could do it -- father of the bride and matron of honor . . . couldn't we?"

"Would you?" Shara asked.

Vince shrugged, then shoved the rest of the sandwich in his mouth. "I guess," he mumbled. "I just never thought of myself as being old enough to be her father, is all."

"How about older brother?" Vickie asked.

Vince wiped his mouth with the back of his hand, stood, and pointed into the air. "Never fear, Vince and Vickie are here!"

Vickie patted Shara's knee. "See, hun, we've got it all figured out. It's a package deal. He'll be your big brother. I'll be matron of honor. And now you've even got a ride!"

57

THE PHONE RANG in a long, single story house on a curving street in Pacific Palisades. The hollow sound echoed around the Polynesian-style room, over the tiled floor, and through an open sliding glass door.

It rang again.

The muffled sound resonated on a sunny patio surrounding an amoeba-shaped swimming pool with a slide and lava rock waterfall.

And rang again.

Lying on a redwood chaise lounge, Robert Morant looked over at Roxanne, sunbathing on a chaise beside him. "Better get it. Might be 'bout rehearsal," he said with his gravelly drawl. Just as he got up, the phone fell silent. He adjusted the waistband of his cut-offs, pulled his cowboy hat down over his eyes, and stretched out again. "Whatever happened with y'all's red-head friend, Sarah who was gonna come down with us?"

"You mean Shara. We had a fight that night at the club, remember?"

"I thought y'all were best friends?"

Roxanne straightened her bikini top. "I don't know. Maybe because I didn't get her a backstage pass."

"Hell, I coulda got 'er backstage, pass or no pass. You shoulda told me. She's real cute. Woulda been a gas."

"Yeah." Roxanne sighed and flipped onto her stomach. "So, Bob, whose house is this, anyway? You say it's yours, Deborah says it's hers . . ."

He rubbed his bicep, tattooed with the Lone Star of Texas,. "Beginnin' at the beginning, it was Deb's. She was just movin' in when I met 'er. Back then she wouldn't shack up, so we got hitched. And since I was bringin' in more dough, seemed like the gentlemanly thing to, you know, take care 'a the bills and the house payment." He took a long breath. "Everything was fine 'til she got mixed up with that bag 'a spiritual nuts and they started bleedin' her. The head nut job started tellin' her what ta do and what ta think, and how dad-gum spiritual she is, and hittin' her up for cash. You know, the whole lunatic cult-leader thing."

"Since you two aren't really together, why are you still playing the knight in shining armor?"

Bob pushed his cowboy hat back and looked wistfully at Deborah, sitting with Clive and Susie on the other side of the pool. "I feel kinda sorry for her now, 'cause she ain't exactly a spring chicken. She's not gettin' much work, and what she does get don't pay like it used to." He shrugged. "But she might get a break with her talk-show."

Roxanne turned onto her side. "Do you still love her?"

"I s'pose I could if she gave me any encouragement."

"Then why hang around?"

"Hell, why not? Since I'm payin' for most ever'thing, I figure I might as well get a bang for my buck -- no pun intended."

The phone rang again.

"Back in a minute." Bob got up and sauntered across the patio, through the doorway, and down a short hall to the kitchen. He picked up the receiver on a pink, princess-style phone that seemed out of place with the dark Polynesian décor. "Yeah?"

"Who is this?" a hesitant male voice asked.

Bob took off his hat, rubbed his forehead, and put it on again. "Well, who's this?"

"Uh . . ." The voice cracked. "Parker, master of the Orion Institute asked me to call for Deborah Donaldson. Is she there?"

"Huh?"

"I want to talk to Deborah Donaldson."

Flip-flop footsteps echoed on the tiled floor behind Bob. Clive came into the kitchen carrying a tray with three tall glasses. He set the tray down next to a cutting board, sticky with juice seeping from the carcass of a pineapple. "Sorry to disturb, but Deborah ordered more Piña Coladas," he said with his clipped British accent.

Bob cupped his hand over the receiver. "Hey, Clive, tell Deborah her guru's toady, Gregg, is on the phone."

Wooden tikis scowled from either side of a bamboo bar with a palm-thatched roof. Sitting on a tall rattan stool, Deborah turned to Susie, sitting beside her. "Did I ever tell you the bar was a prop from my second movie, *Tiki Tango*?"

"Yes, Miss Donaldson," Susie, her make-up girl, replied.

Deborah fluffed the ratted platinum mound at the crown of her head. "I've been thinking about changing my hair. Maybe not so big and blonde. What do you think?"

Susie thought a moment. "Um, I like your hair now, but maybe it would be pretty the other way . . . too, I mean. But, not like it's not pretty now . . . because it is."

"What?" Deborah said with a frown. She paused. "Oh, you mean just for a change."

"Yeah," Susie said with a long sigh. "Just for a change."

Deborah swayed on the stool and caught herself on the bar. "Well, like I was saying . . . everyone in this town is playing games. Head-games. You might as well get used to it. If you want to make it in this business, you have to learn how to play better than they do. Take Harry, for instance. He tries to act like he's everybody's father. As if you have to do what he says just because he's so *old*. Did you ever notice that regardless of what's happening in the studio, no matter how much time we have, he's always in a huge hurry -- like he's about to have a heart attack?" She put her hands on her hips. "'Better hurry up, we've got a show to do,'" she said with a gruff look, imitating Harry's voice. "I hate it when he does that. That's how he plays his head-game -- making everybody rush around so they don't have time to figure out why they're letting him boss them around."

Deborah looked up as Clive came toward them. His rubber sandal twisted, he lost his balance, and stumbled slightly.

"Have a nice trip?" she asked with a snicker.

He frowned and straightened his shirt, printed with Polynesian flowers. "Cheeky, Deborah. Very Cheeky."

She crossed her arms. "Okay, since I'm so *cheeky* -- knock-knock."

He stared at her.

"Come on, Clive . . . knock-knock."

He looked over at Susie.

"You're supposed to say, 'who's there,'" she offered.

"Oh, blimey. Alright. Who's there?"

"Harry," Deborah replied.

Clive stared at her.

Susie giggled. "Say, 'Harry who.'"

Clive shook his head. "Okay, Harry who?"

"Better Harry up, we've got a show to do," Deborah replied as she and Susie burst into a chorus of laughter.

He looked blankly at them.

"It's a *joke*, Clive," Deborah said, rolling her eyes.

He crossed his arms. "You call *that* a joke? It's juvenile at best and hardly funny."

She put one hand on her hip and wagged a forefinger at him with the other. "It might be juvenile, Clive Barlow, but mark my words, the next time Harry Ray says that, you'll laugh your head off."

"I'll keep my head, thank you. Even if he said those exact words, to the letter, it still wouldn't be funny."

Deborah looked quizzically at him. "Hey, where are the drinks?"

"Oh, I almost forgot -- you're wanted on the blower. Something about the unlikely combination of a guru and a toad."

Deborah stared at him. "What?"

"The blower, uh, the phone. You're wanted on the phone."

"Back in a minute, Susie." Deborah stood and her sarong slipped. "Oops. Time to manage my assets," she said, wriggling the top back into position.

She traipsed, barefoot, past the pool, through the door, and down the hall. Just as she went into the kitchen, Bob shoved a hunk of pineapple into his mouth. He motioned to the receiver.

"Your guru's toady is on the phone," he said with juice oozing from the sides of his mouth.

"Bob . . . the pineapple was for the drinks." She shook her head and picked up the phone. "Yes?"

"Deborah, this is Gregg. Parker . . . he asked me to call."

"Oh, Gregg, hello," she said, brightening. "Is Parker there? Why didn't he call? He usually does."

"He wanted to, but he's not in the right space, metaphysically." Gregg paused a moment. "He received a vision for a spiritual event. A cosmic convergence on June twenty-first, the night of the summer solstice which also, transcendentally, happens to be his birthday. You can imagine the cosmic significance."

"Ohhhh, wow, yeeees," Deborah replied.

"Parker is calling this event 'The Summer Solstice Cosmic Convergence.' He's inviting a spiritually significant number -- exactly ninety-nine enlightened guests. He wants you to be among them." Another pause. "But you have yet to complete your transcendency. This event could also converge with the consummation of your enlightenment. He wants very much for you to go on to the next sphere that night. Can you be here to celebrate with us?"

"Yes. Of course."

"Then the only thing lacking for Parker to proceed with his plans for you is an offering."

"Oh. I'll put it in the mail as soon as possible."

"Excellent. Parker will be pleased to be with you on that most cosmic of nights. Also, the Italian actor -- the one he met on your show. Ask him to come with you."

"Donatello?" Deborah drummed her fingers on the counter. "I think I can figure out how to contact him. I'll ask around."

"Wonderful," Gregg replied. "Watch for the invitations."

58

SITTING AT THE desk in his study, Donatello slid a sheet of carbon sandwiched between two sheets of paper into an antique typewriter. He spun the roller several times. *I have the beast's money. Now I must give him a script. Faust, if you will indulge me, somehow I will give you redemption.*

He sat back and stared at the typewriter.

"Ave Maria, I pound my brain, but l'ispirazione evade me. I must have something to show the butcher's puppet when he arrives."

He drew his hands down his face, and his features warped like the mask of tragedy. A pain stabbed his broken hand. "Porca vacca," he moaned, stretching his fingers over the splint. *Always, Caggiano haunts me.*

He stood and wandered to the stone fireplace and looked at the photographs on the mantle. He picked up the picture of his father. "Please, Papa, help me."

He paused a moment, then slapped his forehead.

"Grazie! Of course! Why I no think this before? The butcher did no say what time or place." *Film in Morocco, and change the setting to a western, same as The Bounty Killer. It may be the butcher's money, but the movie will be mine.*

Donatello set the picture back on the mantle, kissed his fingertips, and pressed them to the glass. He went back to his desk. "I give the banker "Faust" such as he has never seen." He began pecking on the typewriter using one hand and one finger poking out of the bandages on the other.

```
INT. BEDROOM - NIGHT
   A desperate, man (FAUST) sitting on a bed in a
cheap room above a bar in the old west.  Beside him
on the bed, an open Bible and a Colt 45.  He looks
at the Bible as sounds of revelry echo from the bar
below.


                    FAUST
            (Picks up a pistol. Cocks it and
       puts it to his head.)
       I search and search, but the answer to
       the riddle of life eludes me. If death
       won't come to me, I will go and find it.
       Mephisto, come. Help me.
```

Just then, there was a knock at the door. Slovika peered into the room. "Lupe say you want me."

"Un minuto," Donatello replied, raising the finger on his splinted hand. He punched out a few more letters, slid the carriage, and looked up. "Come in."

She crossed her arms and went into the room.

"I must work. I need you do something."

She looked skeptically at him. "What?"

"Is Lupe and Yoshio, payday." He passed two envelopes to her. "Give to Lupe. She will give to Yoshio." He paused a moment. "Slovika, you have been to Morocco?"

She shook her head.

"Perhaps we go together. I make my new movie there. I bring you too, if you like."

59

LATE AFTERNOON SUN spilled in through a stained glass window, casting a random pattern of rose and violet in the hushed confines of the hospital chapel. A faint flowery scent wafted into the compact space as Pauline straightened a bow on a bouquet of white daisies and yellow roses. Pulling back the cuff of her glove, she turned her watch to the light. *Almost time.*

She smoothed her glove back into place. Looking up at a crucifix hanging above the altar, she gripped the back of a pew. The thick oak had been darkened by countless hands clasped in prayer. Staring into the face of the suffering Christ, tears pooled in her eyes. "Steven's wedding, and nothing is the way I hoped it would be," she whispered. "Forgive me, Jesus. I should just be grateful he's alive."

She glanced at Donny, sitting near the aisle, playing with a new stuffed bear. *And for Donny. He's brought so much joy to our lives.*

"Gwamma . . ."

"What is it, honey?"

"I wan my Daddy."

She patted his head. "I know. He'll be here in a little while. Play with Boo Boo while we wait." She stopped to straighten the collar of his tiny suit jacket. A voice from behind startled her.

"Hey, Mrs. Harper!" Roy Bartman, Steven's childhood friend, bounded in wearing western boots and a white cowboy hat with a tuxedo that strained over his bulging thighs and biceps.

"Goodness, Roy, you gave me a start," Pauline gasped, her gloved fingers fluttering over her heart.

Roy pulled off his Stetson and pushed his hair into place. "We finally made it. The Bay Bridge was backed up half-way to Tahoe."

"Woy!" Donny squealed, scrambling off the pew and running toward him.

Roy scooped him into his arms. "Donovan? You got your hair."

Pauline looked up in surprise. "You know each other?" she said, glancing from Roy to Donny and back again.

"Sure," Roy said. "Steven's my best friend -- how could I not know Donovan?"

Just then, Roy's petite wife, Terrie, came down the aisle and stood beside him. "When you said you had to hurry, Roy, I didn't think you would leave me standing in the elevator."

Pauline forced a smile. *Now for the customary pleasantries . . .* "Why, Terrie, hello."

"Hello Mrs. Harper," she replied. "My mother has your grandson in her Sunday School class."

"Terrie, dear, how is your mother? I didn't see her at church on Sunday."

Terrie shifted her weight and smoothed her short, crisp dress. "She went up to the cabin with my father."

"Oh? And your sister, Carrie?"

"She went with them."

"And how are you?"

Roy stepped between them. "Tell you what, Mrs. Harper, she's better than fine! Tell her, Terrie. Tell her the news."

She glared at him.

Pauline pasted on an expectant look. *Oh dear. Probably the unhappy tidings I heard through the church's prayer chain . . .*

"Then, I'll tell you," Roy gushed. "Terrie's got a bun in the oven!"

Pauline manufactured another smile. *What on earth do I say?* "Well, my goodness. A baby. How wonderful."

Roy put his arm around Terrie and pulled her close. "Yeah, it is wonderful, isn't it, honey?"

She pushed him away. "That's easy for you to say. You're not the one who's going to swell up like a whale."

Pauline and Roy stared awkwardly at each other.

He sighed. "Guess I'll go see if the groom's finished dressing."

An unsettling blend of men's cologne and disinfectant hung in Steven's hospital room. He sat on the edge of the bed as Buck tried to pull the sleeve of a stiff tuxedo shirt over his paralyzed hand.

"At least you're not in the neck brace anymore." Buck slid the shirt off, stepped back and rubbed his forehead. "Can you straighten your hand out at all?"

Steven shook his head, staring at the infantile fist gripping a roll of fabric.

Buck took off his tuxedo jacket and draped it over the back of a chair. "Don't worry. We'll do it." He pulled the chair alongside the bed and sat down.

Don't worry? Steven sighed. *My father has to dress me. Stay strong. Have to stay strong.*

"Maybe if I get rid of the cloth, I can work the sleeve around your fingers." Prying Steven's hand open, Buck extracted the roll of slightly fetid fabric. "It practically took an act of congress to get the hospital to let us use the chapel. I even had to resurrect the memory of your dear, departed grandfather and all the dough he donated."

After a few moments effort, Buck worked Steven's fingers through the French cuff and pulled the shirt on. "There. Hope it's worth it."

Watching his father fasten the cuff-link, Steven felt the room closing in around him. *Worth it? Shara is all that's left of me.*

Buck stood and pulled a white bowtie around the shirt collar and fastened it. "Now for the bottom half," he said, whisking away a sheet covering Steven's naked lap.

Steven stared down at his legs -- one normal and the other beginning to atrophy. Tears welling in his eyes submerged the room into a blur.

Just then, the door flew open. "Hey! Is the groom ready yet?" Roy said, bursting into the room.

Steven looked up. Their eyes met. Roy froze, and his jaw dropped as a tear slid down Steven's cheek.

First my father, now Roy, sees me naked . . . shriveled . . . crying.

Roy lowered his eyes. "Uh, sorry, Steven. Guess I'll come back later," he said, holding his hat in front of him like a shield as he backed out of the room.

60

SHARA GOT OUT of the elevator and slumped against a sterile, white hospital wall. Vince and Vickie came and stood beside her. The doors closed again with a clang and the whirr of a distant motor.

"Why'd we get off here? The chapel's not on this floor," Vickie said, pushing up her pink hexagon glasses and fluffing the sleeves of her formal floral muumuu.

Shara shrugged and glanced at the statue of the Blessed Virgin, tucked into the niche in the wall across from the elevator. "I just felt like it."

A gargantuan orderly in a white lab coat rushed past pushing a gurney, the wheels rattling like branches caught in a windstorm. He stopped and stared at the trio a moment, then shook his head and quickly rattled away.

Shara sank further down the wall.

"Never mind him. He's a troglodyte. What a jerk, staring like that," Vickie said with a frown. She motioned to Vince. "Come here, Renaissance man."

"Yes, ma'am," he said, standing at attention. "Watch it Shara, the whacked-out earth mother hasn't finished primping her moon-children yet."

"Oh, hush." Vickie tucked a loose strand into his thinning ponytail. "Let me straighten your shirt. The collar's disappearing." Pulling up on the collar, she tugged on the bottom of his brocade vest, then fluffed his drapey sleeves. "Vince, sometimes you're a total pain in the ass, but when you're dressed up, you look fine as wine."

"Thanks, earth-mom," he said with a slight bow. "How about the knickers and tights? You want to check them too?" he asked, pointing the toe of his burgundy ballet slipper.

"They're okay, moon-child." Vickie looked over at Shara. "Now for the bride."

A middle-aged couple dressed in tailored tweed came to the elevator.

"Peace, man," Vince said with a smile.

The man shot a contemptuous glance at him. "Why they allow those kind of vulgar people in a Christian hospital..."

The woman wrinkled her nose. "They're dirty, smelly, half-naked and barefoot."

Vince stepped forward. He arranged himself in ballet's third position and pointed into the air. "Speaking of Christ, may the Baby Jesus shut your mouths and open your minds."

The couple gasped. The elevator door opened. Taking his wife's arm, the man stomped inside, pulling his wife along with him. "Damn Hippies!" he snapped, punched the button, and the door closed.

Vickie rolled her eyes. "So much for Christian kindness. I don't think we smell."

"But we *are* vulgar," Vince said with a low chuckle. "And you two aren't wearing any shoes."

Vickie turned to Shara. "Honey, what's wrong? You look all weirded-out."

Shara held up the hem of an antique-white lace tunic with long bell-shaped sleeves, and lace bell-bottom pants beneath it. "I bet she was talking about me."

Vickie smoothed the lace over Shara's thin shoulders. "Don't pay any attention to them. What do they know," she said, repositioning a halo of yellow ribbons and white daisies circling Shara's hair. "Besides, Janis Joplin has an outfit just like it." She stepped back. "Wow, Shara. You look outrageous. When Steven sees you, he'll be totally blown away."

Shara sighed. "I dig the outfit and everything, but maybe it should be less, you know . . . see-through."

"Why?"

Shara frowned. "Because I think I might be Catholic?"

Vickie shook her head. "Honey, if you were Catholic, trust me, you'd know. Anyway, the lining's strategically placed. You can't *actually* see anything."

Vince slouched against the wall next to Shara. "Shara might be right," he said, rubbing his beard and studying the lace. "To the casual observer it would appear the bride is, essentially, naked. All the skin peeking out here and there, makes it a nice fleshy shade of off-white, just shy of pornographic. And the suspense makes it sexier than if there wasn't any lining at all." He crossed his arms. "But, being Catholic, of course, you don't want to do anything to t-off the Deity."

"Vince!" Vickie snapped. "Quit playing with her head. Shine him on, Shara. I've got a pipe and a little weed in my purse. Want to smoke some in the bathroom?"

She shook her head. "I'd probably freak out."

"Don't worry," Vince said with a sardonic smile. "The wedding'll be over in a minute. You won't feel a thing. But then, you'll be hooked for -- "

Vickie planted her hands on her hips. "Vince!"

"What's the matter now?"

"You're being *totally* unhelpful."

Just then, the elevator door opened again and a tall, imperious nurse in a starched white uniform stomped out, followed by the gargantuan orderly. The nurse stared at them like a hawk watching a family of rodents. "What are you doing here?" she said. "There have been complaints about people loitering."

Vince stepped forward. "We're not loitering, we're waiting. Besides, it's a free country."

The nurse's eyes narrowed. "This is a hospital, not a circus. And we don't allow vagrancy."

Vickie motioned to Shara. "Her boyfriend's a patient, and

they're getting married in the chapel."

"Married?" the nurse said with a suspicious stare. "What's his name, and what room is he in?"

"Steven Harper," Shara stammered. "Room 617, I think. They keep moving him."

The nurse took a pad and pencil out of her uniform pocket. "Then go to his room, or go to the chapel," she said, scribbling on the tablet. "There is absolutely no loitering allowed."

An intercom crackled overhead.

"Nurse Praxell . . . you're wanted in admitting . . ."

The nurse looked up at the intercom, then glared at them. She spun on her heels and stomped down the hall with the orderly hurrying after her.

Vince took Vickie's arm. "Come on, let's split before we get busted by the hospital Gestapo."

"You guys go ahead," Shara said. I'll be there in a minute."

"Honey, are you sure?" Vickie asked.

Shara nodded. "Yeah. I just need some space."

Vince punched the button, and the elevator opened. He and Vickie got in, and the doors clanged closed behind them.

Shara slumped onto the bench near the statue of Mary and looked into the eternally tranquil face of Mary. "Dear Blessed Virgin," she whispered, gripping the hem of the tunic. "Thank you for answering my prayer. You probably already know I told Steven I would marry him. But I'm scared. Blessed Virgin, please help me. I don't know how to be married. Please show me what to do."

She sat motionless, staring into the statue's vacant eyes. "Please . . ."

Several minutes passed.

Shara sank against the bench. *Guess the virgin's busy.* She got up and went to a picture window next to the elevators. Looking out over the city, she pressed her forehead against the glass.

Maybe Roxie's right. This is a mistake.

Vince stopped in the hallway outside the chapel. "Go on in. I'm going to hang out here awhile."

"Okay." Vickie shrugged. "Guess I'll plant myself in a pew."

Vince wandered past a vacant room, stopped, and went inside. Glancing over his shoulder, he pulled a flask from his vest, unscrewed the cap and took a swig.

Just then, Roy sauntered by. "Vince?"

Vince coughed, sputtered, and spun around. "Roy? You scared the crap out'a me!"

"Hey, sorry. I was just passing by."

Vince stepped back and studied Roy from head to toe. "Righteous hat. Looks like you turned into a hardcore cowboy since you moved back up to the foothills."

Roy eyed Vince's drapey sleeves, ballet slippers and knickers. "And you turned into a ballet dancer."

"Touché. Ala Vickie," Vince replied, fluttering his sleeves and placing his feet in first position.

"What're you doing here?" Roy asked.

"Acting as the bride's big brother and giving her away."

"How'd that happen?"

"Vickie."

Roy nodded. "Nuff said."

"How about you?" Vince asked.

"Best man."

Vince held out the flask. "Want some?"

"Sure. Upholding best man tradition -- showing up drunk." Roy pushed back his hat and took a long drink. His eyes shot open. "Damn, that's strong," he wheezed.

"So, what've you been doing since you vacated the domestic bliss at Roxanne's house and moved back up to the sticks? You know, she's still pissed . . ."

"I went back and finished my last semester at UC Davis."

"What's your major?"

"Veterinary medicine. Large animal. I'm going into practice with my father. In the meantime I married Terrie, the girl I was going with before." He took another drink and passed the flask back.

"So, how's marriage been treating you?" Vince asked.

"Could be better."

"That sure-as-hell's the truth." He held up the flat bottle. "To Steven and Shara." He took a drink, then passed it back to Roy. "Speaking of Steven, how is he?"

"Okay, I guess . . . haven't had a chance to talk to him."

Vince passed the flask. "A guy in his situation could really go down the tubes -- emotionally, that is. But on another level, in an anthropological-psychological sense, the whole thing's amazing."

Roy took a drink, then looked up at him. "What?"

"All the gyrations everyone's going through for something no one really wants -- there will be the usual maudlin observations about marriage in general, and a tepid recitation of the vows -- hardly seems worth it. I predict the apex of the whole affair is right there in that little bottle."

Roy wiped his mouth with the back of his hand. "Better go see how the groom's gettin' along." He passed the flask back, pulled on the brim of his hat, and straightened his tie. "Pleasure drinking with you, Vince," he added with a bleary smile.

"You too, Roy. It's been real copasetic. We should do it again sometime soon."

Roy found Terrie waiting for him in the hall.

"Where've you been?" she snapped.

"I was in there," he replied, deepening his voice and pointing over his shoulder with his thumb. "Why?"

"They're waiting for Steven and Shara."

"Then they weren't waiting for me, were they?"

"Well, I've been looking for you." She crossed her arms and stared at him. "You've been drinking."

"Oh, don't get all in a lather."

"I *told* you I didn't want to come, but you insisted. Then you leave me standing in the chapel, staring at Mrs. Harper like an idiot, while you go who-knows-where."

"I thought you liked the Harpers."

"I did until Steven ran off and turned into a dope-fiend."

"Watch it. He's my best friend," Roy said, pushing past her and stomping down the hall.

She stomped along behind him. "What were you doing in there, anyway? And who were you talking to?"

Stopping at the elevator, he punched the button, and spun around. "Alright. I was talking to Vince, Steven and Shara's next door neighbor."

"You mean Roxanne's neighbor. They live in Roxanne's house."

Roy threw his hands into the air. "Whoa. Hold on. Vince is Steven and Shara's neighbor. And, yeah, since they live in Roxanne's house, he's her neighbor too. But she's not here. And as far as I know, she isn't even coming."

Terrie glared at him.

"Look, I broke up with Roxanne and I married you. And that better be the end of it." He shook his head. "Ya know, this's a hell of a time to bring up all that old crap. Now, if it's alright with you, I'm gonna go see if Steven's finished dressing."

61

CAL JEFFRIES SAT by an expansive picture window in a crowded surf-side restaurant on Monterey's Cannery Row. Watching the waves sliding onto the rocky shore, he ran a finger over his thin black moustache and straightened his alpaca golf sweater.

He looked up as a young man came toward the table wearing a wrinkled oxford shirt and rumpled khakis.

"Good to see you, Quinton," Cal said, taking a pencil and small notebook from his pants pocket. "I thought Parker might be holding you hostage."

"Thank god, Neil De Vaughn's serves steak," Quinton said, dropping onto a chair. He set a crumpled brown-paper lunch bag on the table and slid it to Cal.

"Besides appearing like a frat-boy on a three-day bender, you're looking a little thin and smelling a little . . . ripe."

Quinton ran his fingers through his tangled blonde hair. "You'd look thin and smell ripe too, if you were lodging in a house with who-knows-how-many people and only one functioning bathroom, while surviving on a diet of raw snow peas and a yellow gruel-like substance made of mung beans. Not to mention, I've been wearing the same clothes since I got there."

"Mung beans?"

Quinton shook his head. "I don't know what that is either, but after a few days of it, I think I'd rather have a bowl of bull crap."

Cal laughed. "Hungry are we?" He pushed a basket of sourdough bread and a plate with pats of butter across the table.

"No kidding. I had to hitch a ride from Orion. Get me the biggest steak they have, plus everything that comes with it."

"And the turtle soup?"

"You bet." Quinton grabbed a slice of bread, slathered it with butter, and shoved it in his mouth. "Nice sweater," he said with his mouth bulging.

"It's an Arnold Palmer for Robert Bruce. If only my game was as good as the sweater."

Quinton swallowed the wad of bread. "Going golfing?"

"After."

"Pebble Beach?"

Cal nodded, then opened the paper sack and took out several rolls of film. "You've been busy. Enjoying yourself?"

"No. Taking pictures and investigating. I can't help it if investigating involves -- "

"That girl?"

"Girls."

"Well, at least you're putting your Stanford journalism degree to use. But I doubt my frat brother's thanking me for giving you the assignment."

Quinton buttered another piece of bread. "Right now my dad's just glad I've got a job." He took a large bite, then shoved the rest into his mouth.

Cal tapped his notebook with the pencil. "Any highlights, other than what you got on film?"

Quinton struggled to swallow. He took a long drink of ice-water. "I'm Parker's new prototype for spiritual transformation -- even though, as he's fond of telling everyone, I'm in the lowest possible sphere of enlightenment. There hasn't been any more about Anthony Campanella. Or anything beyond what you saw at the interview -- that goes on all the time. But everybody's been busy. I don't think anyone will even notice I'm gone."

"Busy? Doing what?"

"Parker's throwing a big bash to celebrate his birthday -- on the night of the summer solstice. Supposed to last a couple of days. He's got a guy doing construction on the main house to get ready."

Cal stared out the window at the waves. "A party . . ."

"For some cosmic reason, he's inviting ninety-nine guests -- two being that blonde bombshell, Deborah Donaldson, and an Italian movie star Parker met on her show down in LA."

Cal nodded. "Yes, I was there that day and met him. He seemed normal enough. Do you think there's anything to the party, story-wise, I mean?"

Quinton shrugged. "Could be. In his caring, cult-leader way, Parker's been strong-arming Deborah for an offering -- I'm assuming to pay for the party. A pretty good chunk of change from what I hear through the grapevine."

"What grapevine?"

"The girl grapevine. Given a little encouragement, they don't mind talking."

Cal smiled. "Are you game for a little more? Like staying around for the party?"

Quinton thought a moment. "All right. Get me a hotel with room service for the night. I want to run up a huge tab, sleep in a decent bed, get my clothes cleaned, and take a shower."

"Okay. Deal. Just promise to keep your head on straight, and don't go native on me when you get back to Orion."

"Right . . . Soooo . . . what's been going on back at the office?" Quinton said.

Cal smiled. "Lots. Everybody's gone ga-ga over that portrait you took of Parker at the interview -- his publisher called and wants to use it in a promotion. And the top brass at The Examiner want to put it, and the article, into syndication. I brought a copy of the contract for you to sign. It's pretty standard, but you can have your father take a look at it when you get back. In my experience, The Examiner's been fair and flexible."

Quinton's mouth dropped "Wow . . ."

"The jokers in the office dubbed the portrait, 'The Quintessential Parker Picture,' then shortened it to, 'Quint Park Pic.'"

Quinton laughed. "'Quint Park Pic.' Sounds like a headline from Daily Variety."

Cal chuckled. "You'll be happy to know, you're going to see a nice bonus with your next check."

"Your kidding, Really?"

"Mmmm hmmm. We're both getting a lot of mileage out of it."

62

PAULINE LOOKED UP as a balding hospital chaplain breezed into the chapel, followed by a plain, harried-looking woman.

"Chaplain Edward Florenoy, and my wife, Carole," he said, motioning to the woman as she sat down at a small upright piano. He looked around the room. "I've been a chaplain for twenty-four years, but I don't recall ever doing a wedding here. Typically I'm called upon to comfort patients and families, and to perform the last rites." He wrinkled his nose to stop the slide of his thick horn-rim glasses. "You must be the mother of the bride," he said in a pained, yet patient way, while holding out his hand.

"I'm the mother of the groom."

With a baffled expression, the chaplain dropped his hand. "Oh. The mother of the unfortunate young man. Forgive me. I've been a little taken aback since the hospital asked me to officiate. I was taught in seminary to minister 'both in season and out of season,' and this certainly is out of season."

Pauline's mouth tightened.

Chaplain Florenoy adjusted his bifocals and pulled a stack of note cards from his suit-coat pocket. "The rest of the wedding party? Have they arrived?"

She shook her head.

The chaplain stepped up to the lectern, nodded to his wife, and she began a droning piece on the piano. A nun, a nurse and two aides came in. Their hushed voices echoed between the faltering chords.

Vickie fluttered toward the altar.

"Bickie!" Donny called, scrambling off the pew to meet her.

"Hi. I'm Vickie, matron of honor," she said, nodding at the chaplain and smiling at Pauline. "Donovan, what happened to your hair?"

"Gwamma cut it. I had wice."

"Wice?" Vickie thought a moment. "Oh, you mean lice."

The minister looked up. "Lice? Someone has lice?"

Pauline sighed. "No. No one has lice."

"Yes I did, Gwamma. I had wice," Donny said, looking up at her.

Vickie giggled. "That's not a big surprise. No one at Roxie's house is exactly Mrs. Clean."

"Bickie, Mommy an Daddy are getting marry!"

The chaplain looked over at Pauline. "Mommy? Daddy? Then the young couple have already started their family . . ."

Pauline steadied herself against the altar. "Yes, I'm afraid so."

Chaplain Florenoy pushed up his glasses. "Well, that is a new wrinkle. I'm sorry. Under the circumstances, marrying them would seem to convey that I -- "

Pauline held up her hand. "Please, Chaplain Florenoy. I can't help the circumstances. If you won't do it for my son's sake, or my sake, then for my grandson? Will you do it for him?"

The minister glanced at Donny. "All right. For your grandson. As the scriptures say, 'of such is the kingdom of God.'"

Vince sauntered in and wandered toward the altar. "Big brother of the bride," he announced.

"And the big brother's wife," Vickie said.

"Anthropology and English Lit professors, respectively," Vince added, crossing his arms.

"Professors?" the chaplain sputtered.

"At Berkeley," Vince replied.

The chaplain stared first at Vince, then at Vickie, then back at Vince. "You're the bride's brother?" he asked with a rattled expression.

"Actually, only acting as. Since the bride and groom more-or-less permanently crash next door, and our house functions as an unofficial meeting place and message board for all the free spirits who float around the neighborhood, you could say, I'm like a one-size-fits-all older brother."

The chaplain scrunched up his face. "What?" He motioned for his wife to keep playing. "Then the bride is here?"

Vince looked from side to side. "I don't see her, do you? I was waiting out in the hall, but I got tired of waiting."

"She said she needed some space," Vickie chimed.

"Space?" the chaplain repeated.

"You know, she needed time," Vickie added. "To think things over. After all, it's a big decision."

"Time? Hasn't she decided yet? The wedding should be starting any minute."

Vince smiled. "Not without the bride it won't."

Steven gripped the arm of a wheelchair with one hand while staring at the contour of the other, lying beneath a small, light blue blanket spread over his lap.

Sitting in a chair across from him, Buck fidgeted with the coins in the pocket of his tuxedo pants. "I know you weren't crazy about wearing pajama bottoms. But I just couldn't get the tux pants on. Besides, with the blanket over your lap, no one'll know the difference. They'll just think you're cold." He paused. "Hey, look on the bright side. At least it's not pink."

The bright side? Steven shifted his weight. *Who cares if it's blue? It's a damn baby blanket from the pediatric ward.*

Buck positioned a fresh legal tablet on Steven's lap. "There. You'll probably be the first person in the world to write 'I do.'" He rubbed his forehead. "Wonder where Roy went? I told him to stick around."

Just then, there was a knock on the door and Roy peered in.

"Hey, speak of the devil. Where've you been?" Buck said, getting up from the chair.

"Hanging around," Roy said as he came into the room.

Buck handed him a small velvet box. "The ring. Just give it to the chaplain when he asks for it."

Roy opened the box. His eyes popped open. "Holy smokes. Where'd you get it? Must've cost a fortune."

"It was his grandmother's," Buck replied. "Steven, I better check in with your mother. You know how she is." He turned to Roy. "Can you wheel him down to the chapel?"

"Sure, Mr. Harper."

As Buck closed the door, Roy put the velvet box in his pocket. He sat down and took off his hat. "Who would've thought when we were kids, that everything would turn out this way. Everything seemed so simple back then."

Steven looked up with a questioning expression.

"You going off to war. Coming back. Meeting Shara. Having Donovan and getting married. And me, being with Roxie. Then marrying Terrie. And now -- I didn't have a chance to tell you, she's pregnant."

Steven half-smiled.

Roy sighed and looked down at the floor. "But I don't even know if I love her." Resting his elbows on his knees, he fidgeted with the brim of his hat. "And who would've thought that you, my best friend, would end . . ." He looked up, his eyes glistening. "I"m sorry, Steven. I just never thought it would turn out like this."

Buck and Pauline stood at the altar with the chaplain as Roy wheeled Steven into the chapel. Vince and Vickie sat in the front pew with Donovan. Nuns and nurses in the pew behind. And Terrie, sitting by herself in back.

"I'm assuming this is the groom?" Chaplain Florenoy asked.

"And the best man," Roy replied.

The minister whipped a handkerchief from his pocket and wiped his forehead. "So, we're still waiting for the bride." He conspicuously looked at his watch, then nodded to his wife. She began another plodding piece on the piano.

Roy rested his hand on Steven's shoulder and whispered, "Don't worry. Shara loves you. You know how she is. She might be late, but she'll show up."

Several minutes passed. Hushed conversations echoed in the room.

The chaplain glanced at his watch again. He looked as though he might say something, then shook his head and paged through his note cards again.

More time passed.

Steven looked up and a one-sided smile spread over his face. Shara stood waiting in the chapel doorway.

63

AS THE FIRST chords of the wedding march swelled in the chapel, Vince walked Shara to the altar. A collective gasp rose in the small congregation as light shining through the lace created a diaphanous silhouette from the slender lines of her body.

Chaplain Florenoy's eyes shot open, and Mrs. Florenoy picked up the tempo. The closer Vince and Shara came, the more the chaplain's face flushed, and the faster his wife played.

"What the . . ." Buck whispered.

"Oh, dear Lord," Pauline said under her breath. "She's barefoot and almost naked."

Vince deposited Shara between Vickie and Steven, then sat down in the front pew with Donovan.

The minister coughed and cleared his throat. "We've all arrived, so let's begin." Staring up at the ceiling, he began a disjointed recitation of the wedding text.

"Dearly beloved . . ."

"We are gathered in the presence of God . . ."

"Marriage is not to be entered into lightly . . ."

"If anyone has reason to object . . ."

With a pained expression, Chaplain Florenoy looked at Shara. "Will you take this man to be your husband? To love, honor and obey? To keep him in sickness and in health?" He paused. "For as long as you both shall live?"

She closed her eyes and took a deep breath. "I will."

He turned to Steven. "Will you take this woman to be your wife, to love her and honor her, for as long as you both shall live?"

Steven sat motionless, staring at the tablet on his lap, then pushed it onto the floor.

"Steven?" Shara said, her voice hollow as an echo in an empty building.

He looked into her eyes. With one side of his mouth sagging, he slowly said, "Sha-ra . . . I w-w-ill."

64

THE SWEET SCENT of a blooming Plumeria bush wafted in through an open window as Deborah wandered into her sunken living room. She found Roxanne lying on the shag carpet with her head on a cushion and her feet propped up on the sofa, reading a book.

"What are you reading?" Deborah asked.

Roxanne tilted her head back and looked up at her. "*Hell's Angels: The Strange and Terrible Saga of the Outlaw Motorcycle Gangs.* Bob let me borrow it."

"Oh. Where is he?"

"Rehearsal."

"When's he coming back?"

Roxanne slid her feet off the couch, turned around and sat cross-legged, facing Deborah. "He didn't say."

"Why didn't you go with him?"

Roxanne set the book down. "I decided I'd hang around here instead."

"Groupies always hang around," Deborah said, shaking her head. "Are you already tired of him? Or is he already tired of you?"

Roxanne's eyes narrowed. "That's none of your business."

"You're hanging around in *my* living room, with your feet on *my* couch, sleeping with *my* husband. That makes it my business."

Roxanne got up and planted her hands on her hips. "The way he tells it, he's hardly your husband, unless you want something."

Deborah caught her breath. Her eyes flashing, she swung back and slapped Roxanne across the face. Roxanne lost her balance and fell back on the sofa.

Just then, Bob came through the front door, carrying a stack of mail. He paused a moment, staring at them. "What's goin' on here?" he asked, tossing the mail onto a long stereo console.

"Your groupie friend had the nerve to insult me in *my* house!" Deborah shrieked.

"I did not!" Roxanne cried, holding her hand to her cheek. "But even if I did, she started it!" Jumping off the couch, she bunched up her fists and lunged at Deborah.

Bob stepped between them. "Hey, don't blow a gasket. What's it all about?"

Deborah stared down at the carpet. "Nothing. I need to talk to you is all."

"Well, talk, then."

She crossed her arms and glared at Roxanne. "Not in front of her."

Bob sighed. "Roxie, split for a minute, will ya?" He nodded in the direction of a nearby hall. "I'll take ya out to dinner after."

Roxanne scowled at Deborah, then sauntered down the hall.

"Okay, Deb, what?"

"How long is she going to hang around?"

"Come on, cut the crap. Out with it. Whadda ya want this time?"

"I want to borrow some money."

"Borrow?"

"Yes, *borrow*."

"How much?"

She sidled up against him and looked into his eyes.

He pushed her away. "Quit horsin' around. How much?"

"A thousand."

"A grand? No way."

She frowned. "Why not? You've got plenty of money."

"Because you never pay me back, and you'll probably give it to that nut-job, Parker."

She looked away.

"That's it, isn't it? What's he want it for this time?"

"My transcendency."

"What?" Bob laughed. "I'd rather use a thousand bucks to light the barbeque."

Gripping his faded Hawaiian shirt and looking pleadingly up at him. "But Bob, don't you care about my spirituality at all? Parker is planning a cosmically significant event. He's inviting ninety-nine enlightened guests."

Bob pushed her away again. "Am I one of 'em?"

"No, not after you called him a pompous pork-brain right to his face. It's supposed to be just me and Donatello. Parker invited him specifically."

"I think a hundred's a cosmic number, too. One more won't make any difference."

"But you're not invited . . ."

He crossed his arms. "Here's the deal. I'll give you the dough, but I'm taggin' along. Don't worry, I'll stay out of his way He won't even know I'm there."

Deborah thought a moment. "Okay, deal." She shook his hand, then turned and traipsed down the hall.

Bob grabbed the stack of mail off the stereo and dropped onto the sofa. Paging through the letters, bills, and magazines, he found a manila envelope addressed to Deborah with a Big Sur postmark.

Speak a' the devil. He turned the envelope over. "Oh, bummer. Parker didn't seal it." Chuckling, he flipped up the metal prongs, and slid them through the grommet. "Let's see what Mr. Turd-head's been up to." He took out two invitations, printed in swirling, psychedelic color. Then he pulled out a short note. "Looks like it came from a monastery," he muttered, squinting to decipher the calligraphy.

283

Dearest Deborah,

    As the natural world begins its journey back into winter, the summer solstice draws us to experience its power, incarnating spirit into matter. I greatly desire that you and your Italian friend join me at a cosmic gathering on my birthday, the evening of the summer solstice. I also hope the consummation of your enlightenment will be part of this cosmic convergence. Come celebrate June 21st, the longest day of the year, with me. Enclosed you will find the invitations. All that's lacking in your journey to transcendence is your offering.

PARKER

"What a dip stick." Bob dropped the note and picked up an invitation. "Hmmm. Silk-screened. Shouldn't be too hard to bootleg."

He looked up as Roxanne came into the room.

"Are we still going out to dinner?" she asked.

"Yeah. Wanna go for ride first?"

"Sure." She leaned over to look at the invitation. "What's with the handbill?"

Bob passed one to her. "That, mi amiga, is a ticket to a trip. Actually, it's an invitation to a party."

"Whose party?" She paused to read the invitation. "The Summer Solstice Cosmic Convergence? Sounds cool."

"You know, that guy, Parker, who has the Orion Institute up in Big Sur? It's at his place."

"*That* Parker? Are you kidding?"

"Nope. Deb's as hung up on that spaz as a side a' beef."

"But he's supposed to be real super-spiritual."

"Depends on what you mean by spiritual. Long-story-short, he invited Deborah, and she wants me to foot the bill. I ain't cosmically significant enough to get an invite, but somehow-or-other my cash is."

Roxanne gave the invitation back to him. "Does everybody have to pay?"

"I dunno, but he expects Deb to. He probably thinks she's rollin' in change. I figure if ninety-nine's good, a hundred-somethin' will be even better. I'm gonna bootleg a few to pass around to liven things up a bit. Wanna go?"

"Sure." Roxanne thought a moment. "Hey, can I send one to my friend, Shara? Maybe it'll help patch things up between us."

"Why not? The more the merrier. In spite a'the fact Parker's a total jerk, he throws a bitchin' party. Should be a blast."

"So, how are you gonna bootleg them?"

"I know a guy with a silk-screen shop in Santa Monica. He's like a silk-screen guru -- best in the Southland. He does all the posters and handbills for our local gigs. I'll fire up my Indian Black Hawk and we'll ride down there, then run up ta Malibu for pu-pu platters and coffee grogs. And after that, over to the Whisky a Go Go for drinks an' dancin'. How 'bout it? Ever been to the Tonga?"

"Tonga?"

"The Tonga Lei. Polynesian bar and restaurant. Bamboo roof. Giant tiki torches in front. Rattan. Coconuts. The whole bit. Looks like Robinson Crusoe built it. Did you ever see Deborah's movie, *Tiki Tango*?"

"Yeah, but it was really dumb."

"Don't let her hear you say that -- she thinks it's fine art. Anyway, they filmed the restaurant scene at Tonga Lei. If ya saw *Tiki Tango* then you've seen the Tonga."

"Oh. So it's like Trader Vic's in San Francisco. That was one of my mom's favorite restaurants. She used to take me there all the time."

Bob shook his head. "Tonga Lei is the *real* Polynesian palace. That other place is a knock-off."

"It is not. Vic's is the real one."

Bob crossed his arms. "Look, Roxie, since I'm buyin', for once, can ya just humor me?"

65

CHAPLAIN FLORENOY HELD up a fold-out Polaroid camera. "Everyone, closer..." he said, motioning to the wedding party posing in front of the altar. Steven in his wheelchair. Roy standing on one side. Shara on the other, with Vince and Vickie beside her.

Vickie fluffed the sleeves of her muumuu as Vince placed his feet in third position. Roy took off his hat, Shara smoothed her lace tunic and Steven stared into the camera.

The chaplain motioned again. "Closer... everyone smile..." He looked up from behind the camera. "The groom is *not* smiling."

Roy waved. "He can't. His face doesn't work."

Chaplain Florenoy took a long breath. "Then everyone else smile... good..."

The flashbulb flared.

"There," he said with a sigh.

A collective exhale as the wedding party relaxed, waiting for the picture to slide out of the camera.

"Got it." The chaplain set the curled photograph on a pew beside several others. "The bride, groom and groom's parents?" he asked, turning to Buck.

Vince, Vickie, and Roy stepped away. Pauline, Shara, and Buck with Donny napping on his shoulder, positioned themselves around Steven's wheelchair.

"Okay . . . smile . . ."

Another flash. Moments later the picture slid out of the Polaroid.

"Any more?" the chaplain asked, with an impatient glance at his watch.

"No that's fine," Buck said.

Chaplain Florenoy gave Pauline the camera as Buck handed him a check. He folded it and put it in his pocket, then took his wife's arm. "Carole and I should be going."

The Harpers followed them into the hall. "Thank you for agreeing to officiate." Pauline brushed her fingers over Donny's forehead, still sleeping on Buck's shoulder. "For his sake."

The chaplain straightened his glasses. "Like I said, 'in season and out of season.'"

The Harpers watched the chaplain and his wife get on the elevator, and waved as the doors closed behind them. Buck leaned over and kissed Pauline on the cheek. "Well, Mrs. Harper, we did it."

Tears filled her eyes. "Yes, Mr. Harper, we did. Do you want me to take Donny for awhile?"

"Sure."

Buck settled Donny on Pauline's shoulder, then stretched. "If that Florenoy character would've said one more time how he was supposed to minister 'in season and out of season,' hinting at how 'out of season' everything was . . . well, it's a good thing he left when he did. I was gonna have ta give him a piece of my mind," he said, smacking his fist into his palm. "I would've liked to punch that sanctimonious bastard, but he was taking the Polaroids."

"Shhhh," Pauline said under her breath. "You'll wake Donny."

"He could've at least acted like it was a joyous occasion."

Pauline nodded in the direction of the chapel. "Come on, tiger."

"When did your parents start calling him Donny?" Shara asked with a frown. "His name is Donovan. And how come they didn't ask me, or at least tell me, they were going to cut off his hair?"

He shrugged one shoulder. With his good hand, he took the hem of her tunic and held it up to the light. "Sex-y. I li-ke it," he slurred.

Shara looked up as Buck and Pauline came toward them. She yanked the tunic out of his hand.

Buck stopped beside Steven's chair. "How long have you been able to talk?"

Steven swallowed hard. "For a f-ew day."

"Why didn't you tell us?"

"I wan to be a su-prise."

"Well, it sure the hell was. Your mother was about to faint."

"Me?" Pauline said. "What about you?"

"Well, me too. But how? Dr. Buehler said there was nothing more he could do."

Steven wiped the saliva off his chin with a tissue. "I de-cide to try the herb."

Buck, Pauline and Shara all looked at each other. "What?" they said, almost in unison.

"The Chi-nee med-i-cine from P-ing. I took it an the feel-ing started to come b-ack in my face."

Pauline's mouth fell open. "I completely forgot. How on earth..."

"Sha-ra brought to me."

The Harpers looked over at Shara.

She shrugged. "You left the package on a chair in the waiting room. I found it and figured out it was for Steven. So I gave it to him." She turned to Steven. "But you said you didn't want to try it."

"When the doc-or said there was no m-ore h-ope, I fig-ure I ha no-thing to l-ose."

Buck ran his finger around the collar of his tuxedo shirt. "Looks like I need to take another trip to Chinatown."

Buck eased his station wagon into a parking space near the Chinatown gate. Fumbling in the pocket of his pants, he found two dimes, then got out and slid them into the meter. "That should do it."

He hurried past a flower cart, stopped, and went back. He looked over the array of blooms. "She'll like these," he said, picking out a bouquet of red carnations. "How much?" he said to an elderly Chinese man, sitting beside the cart.

"Two-fifty dollar. You're going to party?"

"Nope. Wedding." Buck pulled his wallet from his pants pocket. He took out a five-dollar bill. "Keep the change."

He hurried into the alley and stopped at Ping's storefront. The brass bells jangled as he opened the door.

Ping looked up from the vertical characters on a Chinese newspaper. "Mr. Harper!" she said with a broad grin. "You come back so soon!" She paused, staring at him. "You go to party?"

"No, a wedding." He held out the carnations. "For you."

Ping took the flowers and inhaled their fragrance. "Very pretty. And smell nice too. But why?"

Buck paused a moment. "You always said your family owed my father a debt that couldn't be paid." He lowered his eyes. "Now, I have one too."

She looked puzzled. "What you mean?"

"Steven. His face was paralyzed, but he took the medicine you gave us and now he can talk. I just came from his wedding," Buck said as tears welled in his eyes.

Ping quickly looked away.

Thank god she won't let me lose face. "The doctor said there was nothing -- " His voice cracked. He blinked several times and hardened his jaw. "So, if it hadn't been for you . . ."

"Oh. I see." Ping paused. "He is all well now?"

"Not entirely. He still can't walk or use one of his arms."

Ping nodded. "I tell Hai Yen. She will fix something more for him."

"I appreciate it, but I need to get back," Buck said, turning toward the door. "I just wanted to tell you."

"You at the old address. I send to you."

"But Ping, this time I have to pay . . ."

A smile spread over her face. "It okay, Mr. Harper. I know. Now we both have a debt we cannot pay. So we even-steven!"

289

66

BOB STEERED HIS Indian Black Hawk motorcycle into the parking lot of a corrugated metal building housing a silk-screen shop, ceramic studio, and glass foundry. The parking lot radiated the hot, oily smell of sun-baked asphalt. A VW Bug, a dented Corvair, two beat-up bicycles, and a homemade skateboard were parked in the lot.

He cut the engine on the skirt-fendered bike, then swung his leg over and flipped the kickstand.

"Wow. That was like riding on a chainsaw," she said, sliding off and shaking the tangles out of her hair.

He patted the seat. "You'd growl too if you'd been around since 1950. I rode 'er all the way out here from Oklahoma. My old man prob'ly don't even know his bike's gone."

"How could he not know?"

Bob laughed. "He's got cars, boats, and motorcycles to burn." He took Roxanne's arm. They stepped over the weeds growing through cracks in the pavement and followed a trail of crayon-colored spills, splatters, and footprints leading from a battery of steel garbage drums to the silk-screen shop.

He stopped. "Hey, while we're in there, don't say anything, okay. If that beef-brain Walrus gets anywhere near a woman, he can talk the back leg off a donkey. Act like you're stuck up, and let me do all the talkin'. I know it'll be tough, but you can do it."

"Walrus?" Roxanne repeated.

"The guy who owns the shop. His name's Russell. Russ for short. Walrus is his nickname. Get it -- Wal-rus?"

Roxanne laughed. "Alright. I promise I won't talk."

Bob opened a glass door made opaque by dust and scratches. He held it for her and they went inside.

Layer upon layer of paint splattered the studio -- inky handprints on the walls and footprints on the floor. Psychedelic posters, a collection of calendars, and photographs of surfboards, motorcycles, and bikini-clad women ornamented the unfinished drywall dividing the space. Overhead fans kept the pungent vapor of acetone and linseed circulating. The muffled zip of rubber squeegees and clatter of wooden frames vied with Jimi Hendrix' version of "The Star Spangled Banner," blaring from speakers hanging from the ceiling.

"Hey! Walrus! Goo goo g'joob!" Bob shouted through a doorway cut in the wall.

A skinny young man in a paint-covered T-shirt came through the opening, carrying a sheet of paper. "What's up?" he asked as he grabbed a stapler hanging by a cord and added the paper to a collection of receipts, invoices, and purchase orders stapled to the bare drywall.

"I got a job for Walrus," Bob replied.

"Walrus!" the young man shouted. "Customer!"

"Be with you in a minute," a deep voice called back.

The worker went back through the doorway. A few minutes later, a large man came in wearing bib overalls covered in multi-colored stains, with sandals that looked like they were made from hunks of sod. He wiped his hands on a rag and pushed a paint-tipped coil of frizzy red hair off his face.

Pausing, Walrus looked at Roxanne from head to toe, seeming to undress her with his eyes. "Hey, baby, you got a name?" he asked with a wide, gap-toothed smile.

She shrugged and glanced at Bob.

"Her name's Roxanne."

"Hi, Roxanne," Walrus said, rubbing a keg-shaped belly that strained the seams of his over-alls. "What's your sign?"

She hooked her thumbs in her pockets and looked at Bob again.

He stepped forward. "Hey, Walrus, I want ya' to do somethin' for me."

"Do you know how to surf?" Walrus asked, still staring at Roxanne.

She shook her head.

"For a chick, she doesn't talk much. Usually you can't shut 'em up."

"She's shy."

"I like shy women . . ."

"Hey, Walrus, look at me," Bob said, waving at him. "I want ya ta bootleg a bunch of these." He passed him an invitation.

Walrus slowly took his gaze off Roxanne. "A handbill?"

"It's an invite to a party up in Big Sur on the summer solstice. It's 'sposed to be a blast. Can you do it?"

"Hmmm. Yeah, I can copy it. But it won't be exact." He looked back at Roxanne. "Are you going?"

"Sure, she's goin'," Bob replied. "With me."

"Oh. Know any other chicks that're going?"

"Yeah, there'll be plenty a' chicks there. Now, can ya do it?"

"How many do you want?"

"Uh . . . how 'bout a hundred?"

"Sounds bitchin'," Walrus said. "Mind if I bootleg some for myself? Stick 'em up around town in the head-shops, and -- you know."

Bob shrugged. "Sure. Go ahead. The more the merrier. How long'll it take?"

Walrus studied the invitation again. "Uh, four-color . . . rush job . . . hundred-plus copies." He looked up. "Three days."

"Can't you do it quicker?"

"Maybe two, if I pull an all-nighter."

Bob turned the Black Hawk onto the Pacific Coast Highway, heading north toward Malibu. "Hang on!" he shouted to Roxanne, then dropped down two gears and rolled the throttle, laying down a layer of rubber as he roared onto the highway.

A salt ocean breeze merged with the wind whipping around the motorcycle as the rumble of the engine surrounded them. Palm trees, prickly pear cactus, iceplant, and yucca dotted the embankment on the eastern side. And on the west, the vast silver-blue Pacific.

A short time later, they passed a mobile home park, a tile-roofed Mission-style church, several apartment complexes painted in pastel colors, and a community of small houses on the ocean side of the highway. Leaning, wall-to-wall, against each other, they appeared to have been blown slightly off-plumb by the incessant wind.

Past the houses, Bob rolled into the parking lot of a Polynesian restaurant with a bamboo roof and giant tiki torches flanking the entrance. He stopped the bike, cut the engine, and looked back over his shoulder. "This is it. The Tonga Lei. Get ready ta take a Polynesian trip chowin' on pu-pu platters and drinkin' coffee grogs."

67

A HULKING ORDERLY lifted Steven from his wheelchair onto the hospital bed. "You want that off?" he asked.

Steven looked down at his tuxedo shirt. "Na now," he slurred.

The orderly nodded, then backed away and closed the door.

Pauline settled Donny at the foot of the bed, covered him with the blue pediatric blanket, and tucked it in around him. "He must be exhausted." She draped his tiny suit coat over a hanger. "Just a few smudges. They should come right out." She turned to Steven. "You and Donny looked so handsome in your tuxedos."

He half-smiled.

"I'm so glad you're coming home. I can't begin to tell you how good it's been for your father and me, to have you, and now Donny, in our lives."

Steven looked up at her. "E-ven Da-d?"

"Oh, my, yes. Even your dad. He might grouse a bit, but trust me, he feels the same -- about both of you."

"What a-bout . . ." Steven looked down at his hand.

Pauline put her finger to his lips. "It won't always be this way, dear. You're going to keep getting better and better. But you should rest now. You'll need your strength for tomorrow."

He closed his eyes and settled back against the pillow.

A short time later Buck came into the room. "I've been looking all over for -- "

Pauline led him out into the hall.

"What are you doing up here?" he said.

"Steven was tired and Donny's still sleeping. Did you see Ping?"

"Yeah. She's going to get more of that Chinese medicine and send it to the house."

"I feel just terrible," Pauline said. "We never even considered giving it to him. Thank God I didn't get a chance to throw it away. And thank God Shara found it and gave it to him."

Buck yawned.

"Tired?"

"Way past tired."

"Me too."

"What do you say we take Donny, go back to the hotel, and get a good night's sleep?"

"What about Steven?"

Buck glanced into the room. "Looks like he beat us to it."

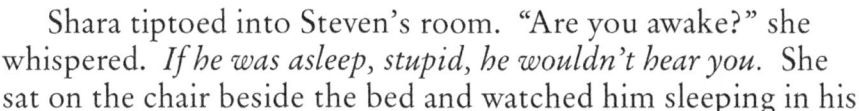

Shara tiptoed into Steven's room. "Are you awake?" she whispered. *If he was asleep, stupid, he wouldn't hear you.* She sat on the chair beside the bed and watched him sleeping in his rumpled tuxedo shirt with his bowtie askew. She cocked her head to read a note on the legal pad, lying on his lap.

> Steven dear –
> Shara is still downstairs with your friends, so we're taking Donny to the hotel with us. We'll be back in the morning. After they release you we'll go to Berkeley to get your things and pick up Shara.
> Love,
> Mom, Dad, and Donny

Shara sat back. *They took Donovan and they didn't ask me . . . or even tell me? Am I even his mother anymore? Do I even matter?*

Shara wandered back into the chapel. Vince, Vickie, and Roy sat on the front pew, talking, while Terrie sat in the pew behind them, frowning. Vickie looked up. "There she is. Hey, Shara, where'd you go? What happened to Steven?"

"He was tired," she said with a sigh. "His mother took him back to his room, and his father went to Chinatown."

Vince raised one eyebrow. "Chinatown?"

"It's a long story."

Vickie glanced around the chapel. "Where's Donovan?"

"Steven's parents took him back to their hotel. I don't know whether to be pissed off or grateful." Waving toward the doorway, light refracted off her wedding ring.

"Hey, let me see." Vickie reached for Shara's hand. "Wow, what a rock! I bet it's worth a fortune. I didn't know Steven had that kind of cash."

"He doesn't. It was his grandmother's," Roy chimed.

"Well, it's still a rock." Vickie slumped back in the pew. "So, what's next?"

"Next?" Shara asked.

"You can't have a wedding without a reception. Unless you elope, or get married at the courthouse."

Just then, a small grizzled man rapped on the open door of the chapel with a knobby knuckle. "Housekeeping . . ." he announced in a gravelly voice, pushing a cart of mops, brooms, and cleaning supplies into the room.

Another authoritarian nurse came and stood beside him.

"Wedding's over," the janitor said with a stiff nod. "Time to call it a day. They popped your pretty balloons, and now it's time to leave before they carry you all away -- to jail, that is. So you better beat it," he added with a smile, missing several teeth.

"Very funny," Vince said, rolling his eyes.

The nurse stepped forward. "No. Very serious. The chapel was rented for the afternoon." She looked at her watch. "It's now five o'clock and if you don't leave immediately, I will not hesitate for one instant to call the police."

Vickie paused a moment, then brightened. "Hey, let's have the reception at our house!"

Vince, Roy, and Shara stood beside the dining room table as Vickie parted the beads hanging in the doorway. She set a small cake decorated with flower power daisies beside a Pyrex mixing bowl filled with punch. Stepping back, she ran her fingers through her wiry gray hair. "Okay, it's ready," she said with a grin.

"Honey, don't you want anything?" Roy asked.

"No," Terrie replied, sitting stiffly in the living room on Vickie's blocky green sofa.

"Come on, honey, have something."

She crossed her arms and glared at him. "In case you forgot, Roy, I'm pregnant, and I don't want to vomit."

Vickie rolled her eyes. "The cake's not *that* stale," she said under her breath. "'Youth for Nixon' establishment-conformist types really piss me off. They always rain on everyone's parade." She looked over at Roy. "Not you of course -- you're cool." She shook her head. "I mean, it was so far-out, like a weird cosmic coincidence or something. The bakery was still open. And that kid didn't pick up his birthday cake. And they managed to change 'Happy Birthday Chucky' to 'Happy Wedding Shara' without messing up the flowers. And the flower-power daisies match the daisies on her headband."

"Cake and punsch for the newlywed?" Vince slurred.

"Sure," Shara replied.

Vickie cut a piece of cake, put it on a chipped handmade plate, and set it on the table.

Roy ladled punch into a ceramic mug. "For the bri -- " He hiccupped. "Bride," he said, passing the mug to Shara.

Shara took a long drink. Coughing and sputtering, she looked at the cup. "Tastes like cough syrup."

Vickie giggled. "Vince triple-spiked it. Hope you don't mind."

"Mind? Why would she mind?" Vince said. "You better hurry, Shara, if you're gonna catsch up. We already had some while we were in the kischen."

She looked at the mug, then downed the contents.

Vince motioned to Roy. "Pour her another one."

Roy took the mug and refilled it. "Too bad Steven isn't here," he said, passing it back to her. "But it's really great, he can talk."

"Yeah. Guess I'll have to drink enough for both of us. To Steven," Shara said, then downed the second cup in several gulps.

"So, how does it feel to be married?" Vince asked. "No groom at the reception, let alone no honeymoon. And Steven looks like he got yanked through a knothole backwards."

"Vince, quit it," Vickie said. "Don't bum her out."

Shara brushed her hair off her shoulder. "It's okay, Vickie. Right now, being married feels great. And it's feeling better all the time."

"Maybe it's too har . . ." Roy hiccupped again. "Oops, hard," he said, bracing himself against the table. "Sorry. I dunno, I guess I'm getting . . ."

"Smashed?" Vickie offered. Dissolving into a giggling, muumuu-covered mass, she slumped onto a nearby chair and stretched her bare feet out in front of her.

More punch," Shara said, holding out the cup.

"She's skinny as a rail, but she sure can drink," Roy said, refilling the mug. He passed it back, then dropped onto a chair beside Vickie, and they disintegrated into inebriated laughter.

Vince arranged himself in a wobbly ballet pose. "Didn't I tell you, Roy?" he said pointing into the air. "Just as I predicted, the apex of the whole affair is the liquor."

Streetlights flickered to life in the gathering twilight as Shara and Vickie leaned against each other on a strip of grass sandwiched between the two houses. "Your daisies are drooping," Vickie said, attempting to re-position Shara's floral halo.

"Thas not all thas drooping," Shara slurred. "I feel like . . . like I'm gonna crash."

Vickie pulled her close and hugged her. "The wedding was so far-out, Shara. When Steven said 'I do', I thought I was gonna pass out. I'm so happy he can talk, it blows my mind. And you look outrageous in that outfit. If you want, you can keep it."

Shara held out the bottom of the tunic. "Thanks."

Vickie stared blearily at her. "What now?"

"Steven's parents are picking me up tomorrow morning. I have to finish packing."

Tears filled Vickie's eyes. "I'm gonna miss you, Shara. You're like the daughter I never had. We were just starting to get tight, and now you're leaving. I have your new address and phone number, and you have ours. I'll always be here for you. Promise we'll stay in touch?"

"Yeah, I promise."

"Oh, I almost forgot." Vickie reached into the pocket of her muumuu and pulled out a piece of paper folded into an origami crane. "Roxie called this morning and asked me to give you a message." She passed the crumpled crane to Shara. "The crane is symbolic of . . . well, I forget, but it means something. Anyway, I thought it might soften the blow."

"Blow?" Shara muttered as she straightened the bill. "Vickie, the grass is spinning. I need to crash."

"I know. Me too." Vickie hugged Shara again and kissed her forehead. "Come for breakfast in the morning. I make a bitchin' hangover omelet."

Shara nodded, then staggered across the lawn toward the house. Fumbling with the key, she unlocked the door and went inside. She closed the door and dropped onto the mattress in the living room. *Terrific. Another person who wants to be the mother I never had.*

She unfolded the origami crane and struggled to focus on the writing. "Perfect." She threw the note on the floor. "Roxie's hates me. Steven's messed up. Donovan turned into Donny. And now I'm married!"

She flopped back on the mattress and closed her eyes. Her body seemed to float. Then fall. Then spin. Then float. Then fall. Again. And again. And again. She opened her eyes. The room itself seemed to be floating and spinning.

She clasped her hand over her mouth.

Great. Now I'm gonna barf...

68

LATE THE NEXT morning Pauline stood on the porch of the brown-shingle house with several grocery bags folded under her arm. She glanced up at a pair of sparrows chirping on a telephone wire. As she rang the doorbell, one flew away.

Minutes passed. She rang the bell again. No answer.

She went back to the station wagon, parked at the curb. Buck waited in the front seat with Donovan and his stuffed bear while Steven sat in back with a jacket covering his pajamas.

"There's no answer. Maybe she's not home," Pauline said.

"She's pro-bly still a-sleep," Steven slurred.

Buck looked at his watch. "It's 11:35. I figured since we took so long at the hospital, she'd be ready to go."

"I wan my mommy," Donovan whined, bouncing his feet on the seat.

"I'll try again." Pauline went back and knocked.

A muffled voice came from inside. Several minutes later Shara opened the door. The wilted daisy halo sat crooked on her head, and the lace outfit twisted around her as she leaned against the doorjamb.

Pauline looked away. *Now the lining isn't covering anything!*

"What time's it?" she asked, rubbing her eyes and straightening her clothes.

"Almost noon," Pauline replied.

"Guess I overslept." Shara wandered back into the living room and flopped down on the mattress.

Pauline followed her. "Did you finished packing?"

Shara pulled the flower headband from her hair and dropped it on the floor.

Pauline's mouth tightened. "Have you started yet?"

She pointed to a small stack of bags and boxes by the front door.

"At least you've done some. I brought a few grocery bags." Pauline took the sacks from under her arm. "Is there much more?"

"Mostly just clothes. The rest is Roxie's, or at least she thinks it's hers. She has this annoying habit of always -- as she says, 'just being herself,'" Shara said, shaking her head. "Which means doing whatever she wants no matter what happens to anybody else. But she did leave me this." She grabbed the crumpled paper off the floor and passed it to Pauline.

Pauline set the bags down and read the note. "'Shara, leave the key with Vickie.'"

"After four years of being, what I thought was best friends, almost sisters -- no goodbye. Not even 'it's been nice knowing you.' Nothing. Just 'leave the key with Vickie.' She might as well of said 'don't let the door hit you in the ass on your way out.'"

"It's hard to lose a friend," Pauline said, forcing a smile.

"Friend? She hasn't even spoken to me since I told her I was getting married. Let alone come to my wedding." Shara put her hands over her face. "God, I have a headache."

"Maybe in time she'll understand."

"How can she? I don't even understand." Shara got up and yanked a torn kimono from the arm of an easy chair and threw it onto the mattress. "That's Roxie's," she said, then retrieved a tiny Hawaiian shirt from behind a cushion. "This is Donovan's."

Pauline shook open a paper bag and dropped the shirt inside. Turning, she noticed a poster pinned to the wall. A wheel divided into pie-shaped slices. Unable to decipher the cryptic images, she looked closer. Taken in by the signs, the stars, and the positions of the naked bodies, her eyes traveled the entire circumference of the night sky. Her eyes shot open. "What on earth is that?"

"What?" Shara asked, rifling through a stack of record albums in a wooden crate beside the stereo.

"That," Pauline replied, pointing to the poster. "I, I thought it was a star chart."

Shara looked up. "Oh, that. It's the positions of the zodiac. Roxie's really into all that stuff. She wants to do all the positions. It's like, she thinks she's some kind of astrological sex goddess or something. She really puts the whore in horoscope."

Shara passed a small stack of records to Pauline. "Those are Steven's. I'm gonna go change." She stood and ambled down the hall toward the bedroom.

Pauline paused, staring at the poster. *What could 'all that stuff' be?* She looked around the room. *I remember the first time I saw this place. Roxanne and the man under the sheet. The smell. The garbage. The roaches. Why would anyone live like this? Why would my son?* She pushed the hairpins tighter into her French knot and picked up the grocery bag. "Shara?"

"Just a minute..."

Pauline followed the sound to a back bedroom. "There you are."

Wearing embroidered jeans and an oversized dashiki shirt, Shara picked up her crocheted purse, and shut the drawer of a battered dresser. "This can go in the bag, even though I don't know where I'll ever wear it," she said, tossing the lace outfit to Pauline.

"Now for our room." Shara went into the bedroom across the hall. "Oh, yeah..." She pulled a thumb tack out of the wall that held a piece of paper. She passed the paper to Pauline. "Steven wrote that the morning he overdosed. I think he's really talented."

Pauline stared down at the wine-stained page.

A violet sky standing in exile
A violent sky stands in exile
Souls twist in time like a witness tree
Young men smoke carnelian dreams
And the old again will sing
Of a far strange country

"I didn't know Steven wrote poetry." Pauline held out the paper and pointed to a line scrawled at the bottom. "What does that mean?"

Too late I ride the Dragon

Shara looked up. "Oh, uh, Steven was smoking heroin. It's called chasing the dragon. He must have known he was overdosing -- so, 'too late,' and he'd have to ride it out -- so, 'I ride the dragon.' At least that's what I think he meant. He has a whole book of poems and drawings. I'd show you, but it's already packed. I told him he should go to school and learn more about art and writing, but he hardly ever listens to me."

She wandered to a bare, stained mattress and untangled a long patchwork dress, a denim skirt and a peasant top from a faded beach towel. "Those can go with that stuff," she said, throwing the dress, skirt and top onto a pile of clothes on the floor.

Pauline tucked the poem into her pocket, opened another bag, and stuffed the clothes inside.

"These too." Shara dropped a pair of child's sandals and a rumpled shirt in the bag. "And these," she said, grabbing her knee-high moccasins. She paused and looked around the room. "I think that's it. Everything else is either Roxie's or . . ." She shrugged. "Who knows. Could be anybody's."

Pauline followed Shara back into the living room.

"I almost forgot." Shara went to the mantle and picked up a photograph. She passed it to Pauline.

Pauline studied the faces in the picture. "Why, that's Steven. But who is . . ."

"His friend Eric. That was taken at a temple in Viet Nam."

Pauline looked up. "I never even thought to ask him about what happened there. His friends . . . and . . ."

"Eric was killed in an ambush," Shara said, tossing her head to move a tendril that had fallen across her face. "It wouldn't do any good to ask. He won't talk about it."

69

STEVEN RESTED HIS head against the station wagon window and looked out at the outline of Alcatraz, receding into a fog bank. *Seems like I've been here a lifetime. Now that life is drifting away.*

Shara slid into the back seat beside him. "Vince and Vickie aren't up yet, so I stuck the key in their mailbox."

"Alright, is everybody ready?" Buck asked.

Donny curled into a ball with his head on Pauline's lap. "We're ready," she said.

Buck looked into the rearview mirror. "How 'bout you back there?"

Steven nodded as Shara slid down in the seat.

Buck turned on the ignition, gunned the engine, and pulled away from the curb. "Here we go."

Steven looked over at Shara. "D-on't w-orry, we can c-ome back," he whispered. "We w-on't be g-one for e-ver."

"Come back? For what?"

"To vi-sit."

"Visit who? Roxie was the closest thing I had to a family. Now she hates me." She slumped further in the seat. "In about two weeks nobody else will remember we ever existed."

Steven sighed and turned back to the window.

Buck drove north on College and west on Ashby. They passed a nice neighborhood with large homes and well-kept yards that merged into modest houses, apartments, and businesses. Then, into an industrial district of metal, brick, and asphalt, bordered by railroad tracks as the road descended toward the freeway.

Traffic slowed to a crawl.

Hitchhikers lined the side of the road and congregated at the on-ramp. Young men. Young women. Older people. Whole families. Some holding cardboard placards. Others holding out their thumbs. And a dog with sign around its neck, hitchhiking for its master.

Steven read the destinations -- LA. Chicago. Boston. Seattle. Anywhere but here. *Everyone going somewhere. The same tide that brought us here, washes us away.*

Buck sped onto the freeway. They passed a string of bayside cities. Albany. Richmond. San Pablo. Pinole. Hercules. Martinez. Benicia. Vallejo. "I remember when all the towns were separate," he said, steering with one wrist draped over the wheel. "Now it's one big city from Oakland all the way to Vacaville. Hey, speaking of Vacaville, want to stop and have lunch at The Nut Tree?"

"Uh, not now," Pauline replied.

"Why not? You love The Nut Tree."

"I do, but . . ." She clandestinely nodded toward the back seat. "Let's stop there next time."

Buck sighed. "Okay. Next time."

Miles passed.

Steven sank against the seat. He succumbed to the rhythm of the road, listening to his parents' voices fading in and out as the interstate turned east, undulating through the coastal range.

Low-hanging clouds broke into brilliant blue sky. Cattle dotted rolling hillsides carpeted in verdant green. Valley oaks replaced wind-bent cypress, and the highway blurred into a heat-wave as it descended onto the valley floor.

"Looks like it's gonna be a warm one," Buck said.

More than an hour passed. They went by a series of towns and mile upon mile of farmland. On the outskirts of

Sacramento, Buck pulled into a gas station. Rolling over a cable, a bell rang in a garage surrounded by immobile cars, trucks, and farm machinery.

A mechanic about his age looked out from under the hood of a pick-up. "Be with you in a minute," he called.

"If anybody needs to go, now's the time," Buck said, turning off the ignition.

Donny woke with a start.

Pauline slid out. "Come on, sleepy head, let's use the bathroom."

He yawned and scooted out after her. She took his hand, and they went around the side of the garage.

"I guess I might as well go too," Shara said, swinging her bare feet onto the pavement. "Crap! It's hot!" She danced on tiptoes a moment before bounding after them.

Buck shook his head. "That's why they invented shoes," he said under his breath.

The attendant looked up as Shara ran by with her red hair flying. He wiped his hands on an oily rag, straightened his grease-stained cap, and sauntered to the station wagon. Bending beside the window, the smell of sweat and gasoline radiated off him. "Don't serve that kind if I can help it," he said, pointing over his shoulder. "Damn hippies. Don't like 'em. But you two look okay," he added with a stiff nod. He glanced at Steven in the backseat. "Whuu-wee. That musta been one hell-of-a fight. Looks like you got the worst of it."

"Yeah, he did," Buck said. "I need some gas."

"Okay. Okay. I'll get your gas. What'll it be?"

"Ethyl. Fill it up."

"Check the oil?"

"No, it's fine."

"Radiator?"

"No, thanks."

"Tires?"

"They're okay."

The man frowned, went to the pump, pulled out the nozzle, and shoved it in the gas tank. As the pump rang out the gallons, he sloshed a dripping squeegee over the windshield, smearing dirt, grime and squashed insects over the glass. He dipped the squeegee a second time, sloshed the windshield again, then wiped it down with a wad of paper towels.

Buck drummed his fingers on the steering wheel, watching in the rearview mirror as the attendant went around to the back window. *Don't like that kind, huh . . . I'd like to punch your lights out.* He stared at the sun-baked furrows in a freshly tilled field. *But I think the same thing myself, every time I see her.*

The attendant yanked out the nozzle, hung it on the pump, and came back to the window. "That'll be $4.65," he said, holding out his hand.

"$4.65? That's robbery!"

"$4.65," he repeated. "Twenty-eight cents a gallon."

"Twenty-eight cents! It's only twenty-four in Placerville," Buck said, wrestling his wallet out of his back pocket.

"Well, this isn't Placerville," the mechanic grumbled.

Buck gave him a five-dollar bill. "Keep the change."

The attendant shook his head as he went back to the garage.

"That guy's an ass," Buck said to Steven's reflection. "Charging twenty-eight cents just because he's on the interstate."

Moments later, Pauline, Shara, and Donny returned.

"It's like a freakin' oven out there," she said, flopping onto the back seat. "It burned my feet."

Buck turned on the ignition. "It's called California for a reason. Caliente or Cali Fornay -- old Spanish for hot furnace or that's what they say anyway. Either your feet'll get used to it, or you'll start wearing shoes."

Rolling on the cable, the bell rang again. He glanced over his shoulder, then accelerated onto the freeway. Resting one elbow on the open window, he draped his wrist over the steering wheel again, and looked into the rearview mirror. "Shara, where are you from?"

"Iowa."

"Now that you're a Californian-by-marriage, you'll need to know the legends," Buck said.

"What legends?"

"Oh brother," Pauline said, shaking her head. "Here we go."

"For instance, did you know this highway used to be part of the Immigrant Trail?"

"What's that?" Shara asked.

"It was the trail the wagon trains used during the gold rush, when they came looking for gold. Have you heard of the mother lode?"

"Mother Load? Who's that?"

"It's not a who. It's a huge vein of gold up in the foothills. People say it's still there."

She crossed her arms. "If everyone knows about it, how come no one ever dug it up?"

He frowned. "How 'bout will-o'-the-wisp? Did you ever hear about him?"

"Honestly, Buck," Pauline said with a sharp exhale. "She's a captive audience. Are you going to pester her with every tall tale you know?"

"Well, remember will-o'-the-wisp when we drove through Copperopolis? They're not tall tales. They're legends. All the mossbacks know them."

Shara's eyes narrowed. "You're just making all that stuff up. I hate it when people do that. Like Santa. He's not real, but everyone acts like he is. And the Easter Bunny. And the tooth fairy. It's just a bunch of lies." She wrinkled her nose. "What's a mossback?"

"From the old saying, 'a rolling stone gathers no moss.'"

"Everyone's heard of the Rolling Stones, but I don't know what the heck that saying's supposed to mean."

"It means someone who's been around awhile. An old-timer, not a newcomer."

"It still doesn't make sense." She sat forward. "I hate it when people make up sayings that don't make sense. Like, 'you can't have your cake and eat it too.' What does that mean?" She raised her eyebrows. "Duh, if you eat your cake, then you still have it, because it's in your stomach."

Buck rolled his eyes. "Never mind."

Just beyond Sacramento, he looked over at Pauline. "Want to go the old way?"

"Fine with me," she replied.

He turned off the multi-lane tangle of freeway onto a two-lane road. The city and suburbs faded back into farmland and they came upon a row of run-down motels.

The Kokomo.
The El Dorado.
The Tahoe.
The Islander.
Decades past their prime, blinking neon and strobing arrows announced their amenities -- swimming pools, phones, TV, and air conditioning. And smaller signs, perpetually flashing:

VACANCY   VACANCY   VACANCY

"Steven, look," Pauline said. "The lady in the pink neon swimsuit is still diving into thin air. She was always your favorite."

He nodded and half-smiled.

Buck chuckled. "He's always had an eye for a well-built lady."

"Buck . . ." Pauline muttered.

"Well, he has. Nothin' wrong with that. Changing the subject -- " Buck pointed across the road to dark-green vines climbing hundreds of wire scaffolds running in rows like tall clotheslines across the landscape. "The hops are up early this year, so the summer'll be a scorcher."

"What are hops?" Shara asked.

"They make beer out of them. In the fall, after the harvest, they burn the vines, and the smoke chokes the valley for days."

Suddenly, Donny woke. He yawned and rubbed his eyes, then jumped up and stood on the seat. "Gwamma! Gwamma!" he cried, pointing to a roadside restaurant shaped like a giant hot dog, next to another shaped like an orange. "I wannu go to da hot dog!"

Buck looked over at Pauline. "Since we didn't stop in Vacaville, what do you say?" he asked, pulling off the highway.

As the old highway meandered through the foothills toward the Sierras, they passed Folsom, Shingle Springs, and Placerville. Tall pines joined the valley oaks, and cool air mingled with the heat. The road narrowed into the quaint, shop-lined main street of a tiny gold-rush town.

"Remember your speed," Pauline said as the road divided around a median planted with liquidambar and iris.

Buck down-shifted. "Once upon a time, I got a ticket here."

"More than once," she muttered as they rolled by the storefronts. Hardware. Bait. Bakery. Five and dime. And on the end of the block, a small grocery.

"The last leg of the journey," Buck announced as they went over a tall bridge, and the town disappeared in the rearview mirror.

Steven's heartbeat quickened. With his good hand, he rolled down the window. Crisp air flooded into the station wagon. He took a deep breath. *The last leg. Almost there.*

They crossed a river, surging white with the spring run-off. In the shadows along the bank, traces of snow still lingered. *The river.*

The road twisted and turned up into the hills where the terrain opened onto a flat grass plain. His heartbeat quickened again. *Alma's pasture.* Another turn, and the road narrowed into a steep descent. *The ravine.* They passed a huge sequoia. *Boaz -- the trapper's tree.* And a formidable granite boulder. *Richardson Rock.*

Moments later, Buck turned onto a gravel driveway. He stopped the car. "Here we are."

Pauline turned back. "Steven, dear, and Shara, welcome home."

Home. Steven took another long breath and closed his eyes. *Why did I think I had to leave? Every turn in the road. Every hill. Every valley. The trees. The towns. And the shops. I remember it all. But I never really noticed. Until now.*

70

THE PHONE RANG in Vickie's kitchen. "I'll get it . . ." she called. It rang again and she picked up the receiver. "Hel-lo," she said in a sing-song tone.

"Vickie? It's Roxie."

"Hey, hun . . . where are you?"

"I'm down in LA with Bob."

"Wow." Vickie sandwiched the receiver between her jaw and shoulder. "You must really like him."

"Yeah, but it's just casual for now. It's not like we're getting married or anything."

Vickie took the lid off a ceramic crock of kimchi. A spicy, slightly fetid smell filled the kitchen. "When are you coming back?"

"In a few days. Did Shara leave the key with you?"

"Uh, huh. We had a little reception for her after the wedding. For a small party, I had a really big hangover. Good news -- now Steven can talk. And you should see the rock her gave her. Wow, is it huge."

"Oh, yeah? Cool. Hey, here's a scoop. Bob's got invitations to a party. It's supposed be a real mystical, magical, mind-blowing event. If you want, I'll grab one for you and Vince."

"Where's it going to be?"

"The Orion Institute in Big Sur -- you know, that guru guy, Parker's place."

Vickie re-positioned the receiver. "When is it?" She took a serving spoon from a drawer, scooped a dripping wad of paprika-colored kimchi out of the crock, and glopped it into a bowl.

"June twenty-first, the night of the solstice."

"That does sound really mystical, magical and far-out, except Vince got approval for a sabbatical and we're going to a kibbutz in Israel for six months."

"Oh. Great that he got the sabbatical -- but, bummer. It would've been a blast to go to the party with you guys."

Vickie slid a spoonful of kimchi into her mouth.

"Hey, do you know Shara's new address?"

Vickie coughed and sputtered into the receiver.

"Vickie? Are you okay?"

She coughed again and dropped the spoon into the bowl. "Yeah. I just dug up a batch of kimchi from the back yard and it's blazing hot!" she said, wiping the perspiration off her forehead with the back of her hand.

"So, do you know how to get hold of Shara?"

"Uh huh." Vickie switched the receiver to the other ear and coughed again. "She gave me her new address up in the foothills. It's in my desk drawer in the other room. I thought you sort-of broke off the friendship since she decided to marry Steven. She thinks you hate her."

"Vickie, I don't hate her. I love her like she's my sister. I could never hate her. I just wanted her to, at least, think about what she was doing. You know how she is. She's always so -- leap before you look, and go whichever way the wind blows."

71

SHARA LOOKED OUT the station wagon window. The tall pines and valley oaks surrounding the Harpers' property seemed to close in around her. "This is in the middle of, freakin', nowhere."

Buck shook his head. "We prefer to think of it as peaceful and private -- our little slice of heaven." He got out, opened the mailbox, and retrieved a stack of mail and a newspaper. "Here," he said, passing them through the window to Pauline. As he unlatched the gate, Tailor came bounding to meet them. Buck scooped the dog into his arms, got in, and closed the door.

"Mommy, das Twailor!" Donny cried as the wiggling dog licked his face and scrambled over him to get to Pauline. "He's our dog! An we hab a horse!"

"A horse?" Shara repeated.

Buck put the car in gear, drove to the house, and came to a stop by the front door.

Pauline looked behind her. "Shara, honey, just bring in what you need for tonight. We can get the rest in the morning."

"I still think it's out in the middle of nowhere," Shara said under her breath as she picked up her purse and followed Pauline, Donny, and Tailor to the house.

Buck got out and stretched. "Okay, Steven, here we go." He opened the back of the station wagon and yanked out a folding wheelchair. "Hope I can remember everything the orderly told me when he loaded you in," he said, swinging the door open.

Steven looked up at him. "So-rry you ha-ve to do th-is."

"That's alright, son. Just do what you can and I'll do the rest."

After a deep breath, Steven swung his functional leg out. Buck reached in and hoisted him into the wheelchair. "That wasn't too bad," he said as he wheeled Steven toward a plywood ramp by the back door.

"You m-ade a r-amp f-or me?"

"Yeah. It's not pretty, but I figure it won't be around too long. I think you'll be walking again in no time."

Pauline swung the front door open.

"Man," Shara muttered, shaking her head. "Don't you even lock the door?"

"Why would we do that?"

"Burglars, criminals, and creeps. Aren't you afraid someone will break in when you're not home?"

Pauline shrugged. "If the door is unlocked, why would they need to break in?" She set the mail on the kitchen counter. "Since Steven is still . . . and he'll need Buck to help him at night . . . I wasn't sure where you'd want to stay, so I made up another room."

Shara stared at her. "If we're not sleeping together, then why'd we have to get married?"

"I just thought . . . well, stay wherever you like," Pauline said with a sigh. She ripped the rubber band off the newspaper, unfolded it, and caught her breath.

ROBERT KENNEDY SHOT

"Oh, dear God."

Shara leaned over. "What?"

"Bobby Kennedy. He's been shot."

Shara looked up at her. "Why would someone do that?"

"I can't imagine. It makes no sense. Even if you didn't agree with him . . ."

"How could anyone not agree with him? He was just trying to fix the country. It's not like it's perfect."

"Yes dear, I know. But people have different ideas about what needs to be fixed and how to fix it."

Shara grabbed her hair into a ponytail, then let it go. "It's like, they kill anyone who tries to make a difference. Bobby Kennedy. Martin Luther King. President Kennedy. Even Jesus." Tears filled her eyes. "Why, Pauline? Why do they always kill them?"

Pauline shook her head. "I don't know, honey. Ever since the president was assassinated, it's been one awful thing after another. I think people who hurt, want to hurt people."

Just then, Buck wheeled Steven into the kitchen. He looked from Pauline to Shara. "What's awful?"

Pauline held up the newspaper. "Bobby Kennedy, he's dead."

"Has everyone had enough?" Pauline asked, getting up from the dining room table.

"I had plenty." Buck reached over and took a toothpick from a small ceramic pot held by a wooden bear. "Chicken salad sandwiches and tomato soup -- perfect." He turned to Steven. "You did a good job eating by yourself, son."

Steven nodded.

"How about you?" Pauline said, looking over at Donny. "You didn't finish your dinner."

"Full," he replied. "Gwampa, you say we could put da tewescope outside an see da stars. You pwomise."

"You'll have to talk to your grandmother about that," Buck said.

Pauline crossed her arms. "You didn't finish your dinner so you could go outside?"

Donny stared down at the table a moment, then looked up at her. "Gwamma, Gwampa say we could put da tewescope outside an wook at da stars." Scrambling to stand on his chair, he knocked over a glass of apple juice.

"Donovaaan!" Shara snapped as the amber liquid ran across the table. She grabbed his arm. "Watch what you're doing!"

"I sowwy," Donny said with a pout.

"It's okay, honey." Pauline grabbed the glass, dropped her napkin over the spill, and went into the kitchen. Moments later, she came back, wiped up the puddle with a towel, and carried the dripping wad back to the kitchen.

"The telescope, huh?" Buck said.

Donny nodded, trying to stand on the chair again.

Buck caught his arm. "Careful, pardner. You better sit down before you fall off," he said as Donny slid down in the chair.

"I don't see why not. It'll be chilly, but if we bundle up, I think we can talk your gramma into it." He turned to Steven. "How 'bout you? Want to look at the Stars?"

"He's too li-ttle for the tele-scope," Steven said.

Donny frowned. "I am not too widdle."

"Maybe he can stand on the Gypsy table," Buck said.

"Gypsy table?" Shara repeated.

Buck twisted the toothpick in the corner of his mouth. "The furniture on the front porch. We got it down in the delta at the old Gypsy camp."

She looked suspiciously at him. "You mean real, actual Gypsies?"

"Yep."

She shook her head. "There aren't any Gypsies anymore. You're just making it up. Steven said you lie."

Buck's face reddened. "He said what?"

"Actually he said you make up stories. But, to me, that's the same as lying."

Buck pointed the toothpick at her. "I'm telling you, there was a Gypsy camp down in the delta. And we got the furniture on the front porch from them. If you don't believe me, ask Pauline."

Shara crossed her arms. "Okay, I will."

Just then, Pauline came to the table. "Ask me what?"

"Did real, actual, Gypsies live down in the delta?"

"As a matter of fact, they did. Why?"

Buck leaned back in his chair with a satisfied smile. "See, I told you." He looked up at Pauline. "I tried to tell her, but she wouldn't believe me."

"Well, I don't blame her -- the way you tell tall tales all the time." She turned to Shara. "I don't know what else he's been telling you, but you better take it with a grain of salt."

"What the heck does that mean?"

"Don't believe everything he tells you." Pauline picked up Shara's plate. "Honey, you hardly ate anything. Are you okay?"

"I'm not hungry."

"But you've barely eaten all day. If you don't like tomato soup or chicken salad, I'll make you something else."

Shara slumped in her chair. I just can't believe everyone is acting like everything's okay."

They all stared at her.

"Don't you get it?" She jumped up from the table and threw her hands into the air. "Bobby Kennedy is dead! The whole world is falling apart, and all you care about are Gypsies, telescopes, and tomato soup!"

72

WEARING A JACKET over his robe and pajamas, Donny fidgeted on the roughly-hewn Gypsy table while Buck stood behind him, holding the telescope. Steven sat in his wheelchair, wrapped in a coat and blanket, and Tailor curled up on the porch beside him.

"Isn't Shara coming out?" Buck asked.

Steven shrugged one shoulder. "She's get-ting her stuff sett-led in the bedroom."

Buck raised one eyebrow. "Won't it be kind of inconvenient helping you with her there?"

"She wa-nts to st-ay with me."

Buck shook his head. "Which constellations are out tonight?"

"I wannu do it, Gwampa. I wannu do it," Donny whined, grabbing for the instrument.

Buck spun him around. "No. Now, we already talked about that. The agreement was I find the stars and you look. If you keep whining, we're all going back inside. So, what's it gonna be?"

Donny dropped his hands. "Okay, Gwampa."

"Alright, Steven, what are we looking for?"

"Where do we look first?"

"To the n-orth, for Ursa Mi-nor, the L-ittle Dip-per. And Dra-co."

Buck stared into the eye-piece at the inky darkness, dotted with light and positioned the telescope. "Found it." He stepped back, still holding the instrument. "Okay Donny, look . . . now, don't move it. Can you see the stars?"

"Uh huh."

"Okay, what's next."

"L-ow in the sky is Le-o. And to the l-eft, the Big D-ipper."

Buck positioned the telescope again. "Found it." He stepped back. "Okay, Donny, take a look. Can you see it?"

"Yeah, Gwampa. I see da dipper."

"Now what?"

"Sou-thwest, the three st-ars in a row is the belt of Or-ion. An o-ver there, the Ple-iades, the Seven Sis-ters."

The clock in the living room struck ten. Tailor woke with a start and jumped up as Pauline came through the door. "Donny, honey, it's time for bed."

"I don wannu. Pweese, Gwamma. I don wannu," he cried.

"I know, baby, but it's way past your bedtime." Turning to Steven, she asked, "Didn't Shara come out?"

Steven shook his head.

"I hope she's okay. She was so upset. I'm surprised the assassination had such a big effect on her."

"It's n-ot that. I think it's ea-sier for her to freak-out about that th-an every-thing else."

"I hope we didn't upset her." Pauline picked Donny up off the table. "Okay, let's go," she said, carrying him into the house.

"Guess we're done with the telescope for tonight," Buck said. He turned and the porch light cast a harsh shadow across his face. "Speaking of Shara, how come you told her I lie?"

"I did-n't. I s-aid you m-ake st-uff up."

"That's a bunch of bull. Either I'm teasing, or I'm repeating well-known legends."

"D-ad, I know you're tea-sing. But Sha-ra has b-een lied to so m-uch, she doesn't be-lieve anyone. Ex-cept R-oxanne. F-or some reason it's l-ike every-thing R-oxie says comes st-raight out of the Bi-ble. Shara's so m-ixed up, s-he doesn't know if s-he's c-oming or go-ing. She'll pr-obably have to l-eave be-fore she knows she r-eally w-anted to st-ay."

Turning in his sleep, Steven felt his neck crack. He gasped and woke with a shudder. *God! What was that?* He looked over at the clock on the bedside table.

12:47

"Ahhhh," he gasped again, wincing at the sensation traveling through his paralyzed arm as his hand involuntarily flexed. *What's going on?*

He looked at the appendage, illuminated by pale moonlight coming in through the lace curtains. *Did it move? Or did I imagine it?* Another electric shock ran down his arm. His hand jerked again. Followed by a sharp tingling sensation that spread over his hand to his fingertips.

Maybe it's not real. Maybe I'm imagining it. He rubbed his hand. *No, I can feel it. I can feel it!*

Another jolt ran down his arm.

He looked over at Shara, lying with her back to him. The muscles in his arm trembling, he reached for her, then stopped. *Don't. Wait. Wait until you know for sure.*

73

PARKER PACED THE length of his new second story deck overlooking the rocky Big Sur coastline. Late morning sun coming up over the hill behind the Orion Institute cast a shadow on the freshly sawn redwood.

Seagulls soared overhead as a breeze gusting off the ocean caught his caftan and whipped the embroidered linen around the lean lines of his body. "But the door is completely off-center," he said, motioning to an entry sandwiched between two large windows. "It ruins the whole effect." He turned to Gregg. "Don't you agree?"

Gregg studied the door. "Oh, absolutely."

The deck shuddered slightly as a burly, long-haired carpenter came toward them. "But that's where you said you wanted it -- right there between the windows."

Parker squinted into the sun. "Yes, Monty, but I *assumed* you would be enlightened enough to know that I would also want the door centered. It throws off the spiritual circularity of the deck," he said, waving dramatically in the direction of the door. "Now it's leaning heavily into chaos."

Monty crossed his arms over his bare, tanned chest. "We talked about that. It has nothing to do with enlightenment. The door can't be centered because of the wiring. Besides, like you said in *Master of the Mind*, the chaos created by unexpected events can be strokes of fate or karma, and looking through the eyes of enlightenment it can become -- "

"Regardless of what I said in my book, I thought we came to an understanding."

"But the code . . ."

"Rules, and laws, and building codes are made to be broken," Parker said with a long sigh and another dramatic wave.

Monty took a faded bandana from the back pocket of his jeans and wiped the perspiration off his forehead. "It's not about rules, and laws, and codes. Your wiring runs right there," he said pointing to the space between the door and a window."

"But can't you move the wiring?" Gregg asked, staring at him.

Monty looked heavenward and rolled his eyes. "Even if I wanted to do it, I'm a carpenter, not an electrician."

Parker crossed his arms. "Monty, you chose to construct this deck for me as an offering on your path to enlightenment. And I must say, much of your work is utterly transcendent. Using limbs stripped of their bark to form the railing, and the branches made into balusters -- astrophysically brilliant. However, as it is now, you've also ruined the whole second story of the institute."

Monty dropped the bandana into his tool chest. "Like I said, I'm not an electrician. Wiring is nothing to fool around with. You don't want to burn the whole place to the ground, do you?"

Parker sighed. "It is a constant struggle not to become discouraged by the faithlessness of the supposed faithful."

Monty kicked the lid of his tool chest closed. "You know, the only reason I got involved with Orion -- I was tired of being fleeced by people representing a god that no matter what you do, you can't please him -- or them. I thought if I cut out the middleman it would be different. But this is just another crappy religion, with a stupid god who's never satisfied." He bent and closed the latches on the chest, then picked it up and headed for the door.

"But, you can't leave," Gregg said. "You haven't finished securing the deck -- it still shakes when you walk on it. And more importantly, you haven't fulfilled your promise to Parker."

Monty shook his head. "Oh, no, I'm finished. Finished with you and your stupid 'Master' and his ungrateful BS." He yanked the door open and stomped away.

Gregg looked up at Parker. "But Monty didn't finish . . ."

Parker glared at him. "Thanks to you. If you had given me a chance to appeal to his spirituality . . . but no, you had to rush in and rouse his brute masculinity."

"But maybe -- "

"No. I know Monty. He is only aware of the periphery of his spirituality. The bulk of his consciousness exists in his physical body. His journey to enlightenment has come to an end, and I doubt I will ever see him again."

"Parker, I'm sorry . . . I didn't understand."

Parker looked away. "Of course you didn't. How could you? You are only slightly more enlightened than he is." He turned back. "Monty is gone, but I no longer need him. The deck is almost finished. Someone will come along to fix it. Meanwhile, it's functional enough for the Cosmic Convergence."

74

WAVES OF SHEETS and towels fluttered on a clothesline behind the Harpers' house. Like a snowfall in spring, tufts from a cottonwood floated by on the breeze. A meadowlark sang in the distance. And a redwing blackbird clinging to a reed guarded his territory.

Pauline squinted into the morning sun as a lacy vapor trail from a plane dissipated in the sky. She looked over at Buck working in the garden, with Donny beside him. And Nahlah, shining like an opal in the pasture, raced through the tall grass as Tailor barked, trying to catch her.

She took a towel off the line, buried her face in the scratchy cotton, and took a deep breath. *Mmmm. Sunshine on fresh laundry.* She folded the towel and dropped it into a laundry basket. Through the space left on the line, she saw Shara wandering toward her in miniscule cut-offs and a gauzy peasant top.

Shara stopped on the other side of the clothesline.

"Well, how was your first night as a country girl?" Pauline said, smoothing her hair and brushing her hands over her housedress.

"It was okay. I couldn't sleep."

"Even after you went to the guestroom?"

Shara shrugged. "Not until almost morning."

"Oh, dear. Still upset about Bobby Kennedy?"

"No. It wasn't that."

"I've heard people from the city can't sleep if it's too quiet."

"It wasn't that either," Shara said. "It's like, I don't usually sleep by myself and I was kind of cold."

Pauline stared at her a moment. *Why would she be cold? She's always half-naked.* "Oh, honey, I wish I'd known. I have plenty of extra blankets up in the attic."

Pauline stopped at a linen closet in the upstairs hall. She put in a stack of towels and took out a feather duster. Yanking on the cord hanging from the ceiling, she opened the trapdoor and pulled down the stairs.

"A secret staircase?" Shara shook her head. "This place is like the Winchester Mystery House."

"Be careful, there's no rail," Pauline said. At the top, she flipped the switch, lighting the bare bulb, then coughed slightly in the dry, dusty air. "This is it," she announced. "It used to be a bedroom, but it gets really stuffy in the summertime. The blankets are in here." She went to a cedar chest near the steps, dusted off the top, opened it, and took out a quilt and several blankets.

"What's that?" Shara asked. "It looks like an ironing board."

Pauline looked up. "It is."

"But it's wood."

"That's how they used to make them."

Wandering among the bags, cartons and boxes, Shara came upon a stack of books on a console table. On top she found a faded photograph of a boy, an older woman, and a horse. "Is that Steven with the old lady?" she asked, holding up the picture.

"Oh, yes. Steven, his horse, Copper, and our neighbor, Alma Richardson."

Shara put the photo back on the table. "She looks mean."

"Alma's a crotchety old bird, and she thinks pretty highly of herself."

"How come?"

"Her family built one of the first roads over the Sierras. It was part of the Immigrant Trail that Buck was telling you about.

They had one of the original homesteads in the area, and they were very wealthy. So I guess she feels entitled to dislike just about everybody. Especially newcomers."

"Then I bet she'd hate me," Shara said with a frown.

"If it's any consolation, she doesn't like me either."

"Why not?"

"Beside the fact that I wasn't born and raised here, I think it's because Buck married me, instead of her."

"Really? She had the hots for Buck?"

Pauline laughed. "I guess you could say that. This property used to belong to Alma's family. It was the ranch foreman's house. When Buck's father, Senator Harper, bought it, Alma took a liking to Buck, even though he's ten years younger. A third-generation Californian and the son of a senator -- he was the kind of young man she wanted to get her hooks into."

"Buck's father was a Senator? Steven never told me that."

"Alma's always had a liking for Steven too."

"I'd be jealous if she wasn't so *old*." Shara stepped around a pair of antique wooden skis and picked up a large book with a tooled-leather cover. She wiped the dust on her cut-offs.

"Oh, honey, use this," Pauline said, holding up the duster. "That's the Harper family Bible. We'll take it downstairs and add you and Don -- I mean Donovan."

Shara looked up. "You're gonna put my name in a Bible?"

"Of course. You're part of the family now."

"My gram used to have a big Bible like that, but she didn't put my name in it. I guess she was mad at my mother for getting knocked-up. And she hated my dad. Actually, my mom ended up hating him too. He took off before I was born."

"Well, you'll be in ours. Like I said, you're part of the family now."

"Wow, thanks. You're kind of like my gram, only nicer." Shara leaned over and hugged Pauline, then her eyes shot open. "What're those?" she said, pointing to malevolent-looking jaws of rusting metal, hanging from a nail.

"Oh, those are Buck's old coyote traps. He used to be a bounty hunter -- the state paid him to hunt coyotes. He keeps the traps up here in the attic so they can't hurt anyone."

"What about the coyotes?" Shara asked with a horrified stare. "I bet the traps hurt them! Why would anyone trap coyotes, anyway? They're just furry little creatures that don't bother anybody."

"Actually, they're really quite a problem. They kill livestock, and carry rabies, and the population gets out of control. So the state pays people to trap them."

"So, he carried a bunch of dead coyotes around?"

Pauline shook her head. "No. He took an ear -- the right one I think, and turned them in for the bounty. He used to keep a burlap sack of ears in his Jeep."

"Eew! Yuck!" Shara scrunched her face into a grimace. "Rotting ears in a bag? That's totally gross! This place really is weird." She shook her head, then looked around again and pointed to the clarinet. "So, whose is that?"

"It's Buck's." Pauline set the bedding aside and closed the chest.

"He traps coyotes and plays clarinet? What about that?" Shara pointed to the saxophone. "Does he play that too?"

"No, that belonged to his brother." Pauline picked up the quilt and blankets. "I think this should do it," she said, starting toward the stairs. "Can you take the Bible?"

Shara picked up the thick book, then stopped at a half-open carton. She set down the Bible and moved a sheet of newspaper. Inside the box she found a dish decorated with a pheasant surrounded by a band of oak leaves and acorns. "It's beautiful . . ." she said, taking the plate out and holding it up to the light.

"The china? Yes, it's lovely. Wonder why the box was open? I thought I sealed it."

Shara put the plate on a nearby chair, then took a faceted goblet from another carton. "Wow. It's, like, shooting off rainbows. How come this stuff is up here in boxes?"

Pauline sighed. "It's a long story."

"I've got plenty of time," Shara replied, slumping onto a stool.

Pauline set the bedding down and picked up the duster. She brushed off the seat of a tattered easy chair and sat across from Shara. "Now that you're part of the family, you might as well know where all the skeletons are buried. The dishes and the crystal belonged to Buck's parents."

"So, how come they're in the attic?"

"You could say they're wrapped up in a lot of unhappy memories along with the clarinet, the saxophone, and a lot of other things."

"What about the clarinet?"

Pauline took a long breath. "Buck had a younger brother. Bernard Stephan Harper -- Bernie for short. He died in a car accident before we were married."

"How'd that happen?"

"Buck and Bernie were in a band and they played all around the area. The night of the accident they were both drunk. Bernie got a wild idea to drive up to Lake Tahoe. Buck was sleeping in the back seat, and Bernie wrapped the car around a telephone pole. It was awful. He went through the windshield."

"Wow," Shara said with a wide-eyed stare.

"Buck's mother, Nell, blamed Buck for the accident. That was her engagement ring," Pauline said, motioning to Shara's hand.

"Why would she do that?" Shara said, looking at the ring. "You're not your brother's keeper -- at least that's what people say."

"Buck was the oldest and Nell thought, somehow, he should have done something to stop it. But truthfully, she always preferred Bernie and she was heartbroken when he died. Maybe blaming Buck was her way of coping with the grief."

"But, what about his father? Couldn't he -- "

"He was so devastated by the accident and the scandal it caused, he died a short time later. Then Nell blamed Buck for that too. It all happened during Prohibition."

Shara looked blankly at Pauline.

"Do you know anything about that?"

She shook her head.

"Liquor used to be illegal. It was part of the platform Senator Harper was elected on -- keeping liquor illegal. Nell made a big show of being a supporter of the Prohibition Party. So, a Prohibition senator's son being drunk, not to mention having an accident, well, it was an outrage and a disgrace."

"His kids got smashed, so . . ."

"Exactly. After Nell died, Buck inherited the whole estate. But he didn't want the mansion in San Francisco. Or the furniture. None of it. Too many memories. He sold almost everything, except the ranch. It was his favorite place growing up. I managed to save the china, silverware and crystal. You should see the silver. It's in there," Pauline said, pointing to a wooden chest to one side of the china.

Shara stood and stretched. Her shorts rode up and her peasant top fell off her shoulders as she bent and lifted the lid on the chest. She took out a tarnished serving spoon. "Wow, it's so cool . . ." she said, tugging on the bottom of her cut-offs.

"I thought when Steven was older and had a family of his own, his wife might -- " Pauline froze. She looked at Shara and caught her breath. *Steven is older. He has a son. And he has a wife. All this time I've been saving the china, the silver, and crystal for her . . .*

75

SEVERAL DAYS LATER, Pauline repositioned a goblet and smoothed a brocade tablecloth over the dining room table. "There. That's how you set a formal table."

Shara studied the crystal, china, candlesticks, and silverware. "Wow, Pauline. The Harper family stuff is really super-beautiful." She looked up. "But it seems like a lot of work. If you cook, and clean, and set the table, that would take forever. At Roxie's we usually eat whatever, whenever, wherever. Mostly at the kitchen counter. Or if anybody has cash, we go out."

Pauline stared at her. "What did you think housewives do at home all day?"

Shara paused, chewing on a fingernail. "Um, I don't know." She slid into a chair at the table. "Most of the time my mom got drunk and laid around on the couch, watching TV. Or she went out with one of her boyfriends. She hardly ever cooked, and she never, ever cleaned."

Pauline sat down beside her. "Then who took care of you?"

Shara's pale eyes turned to ice. "Mostly my grandmother."

"And where is she, dear?"

"She died before we came out here."

"Oh. I'm sorry. Where did you live, uh, before?"

"Dubuque. We lived there until my mom and her stupid-jerk boyfriend moved out here so he could be a nightclub singer."

"Where's your mother now?"

Shara shrugged. "Who knows. When we first came out here, they had an apartment in San Jose. At night he sang at this dive bar around the corner, and my mom waitressed during the day. Everything was sort of okay until he took her to see that movie, *Lolita*. Then all of a sudden, he started hitting on me all the time." Shara picked up a salad fork from a place setting and traced it over the pattern on the tablecloth. "I had to lock myself in the bathroom half the time. Then he talked my mom into going down to Tijuana with him. They dropped me off in Golden Gate Park with twenty dollars, and they said they'd be back in a couple of days." She set down the fork and looked up at Pauline. "They left me alone in the park with twenty lousy bucks."

Pauline drew a sharp breath. "She left you? How could -- "

"I figured he was punishing me because I wouldn't let him, you know. But my mom . . ." She shook her head. "I still can't figure out what I did to deserve that. Roxie found me sitting in the park on the bench by the big windmill. She let me stay at her house in Berkeley. About a month later I met Steven and he moved in too." Shara's eyes filled with tears. "Now Roxie, the closest thing I had to a family, hates me, and Steven is . . . I thought he was going to die," she cried, dropping her face into her hands, sobbing.

"Oh dear." Pauline put her arms around her. "It's no wonder you get so upset about everything."

Buck came into the dining room and froze, staring at the table.

Pauline looked up. "Shara wanted to see how to set a formal table. I hope it's okay. I know you don't -- "

"It's . . ." His voice cracked. He cleared his throat, took off his glasses, and rubbed his eyes. "It's fine."

Just then, Steven wheeled into the dining room. Donny scooted past the wheelchair. "Wook! Daddy's hand got fixed," he squealed.

Steven held up his hand and flexed his fingers.

Shara caught her breath and dropped to her knees beside his wheelchair. "You can move your hand!"

"Oh, sweetheart, that's wonderful," Pauline gushed. "But how?"

"Last n-ight in bed, I m-oved my head, and my neck cr-acked, then my arm star-ted tingling. Like pins and nee-dles. So I tried m-oving it. My h-and is s-till stiff, but I can feel it!"

"I knew it," Buck said. "I knew you'd get better. Pretty soon, you'll be able to walk too."

Donny tugged on Buck's sleeve. "Gwampa, can we go get da mail now."

Buck shook his head. "You sure can shift gears. Is it time?"

Donny nodded.

"Then let's go."

Donny took Shara's hand. "Mommy, come wiff us so you could wide in da goff tart."

"Goff tart?" she repeated.

"He means golf cart," Pauline said. "Why don't you go, dear? You haven't been outside since this morning."

Shara stood. "Okay."

"Tailor! Time to get the mail!" Buck shouted.

The dog's back legs slid out from under him as he scrambled through the dining room. He ran to the back door and dove through the leather flap. Buck held the door for Shara and Donny. They followed him across the driveway. As he slid the barn door open, Donny and Tailor rushed to the cart parked inside.

"Shara, you hold Donny on your lap," he said.

She slid onto the bench seat and helped Donny up as Tailor jumped onto a small bench in back.

Buck got in and turned on the ignition. "Okay, here we go," he said as they rolled out of the barn, toward the front gate.

"You must really like golf to have your own cart," she said, her voice wavering with the bumps in the gravel driveway.

Buck smiled. "I won it in a card game."

Donny looked up at Shara. "He wond it in a tard dame."

"Then you must be really good at cards."

"Nope. I just got lucky."

"He dot wucky," Donny chimed.

"Then what are you good at?"

"Yeah, Gwampa what are you dood at?"

Buck thought a moment. "Guess you could say I'm pretty good at living an ordinary life." He stopped the cart, got out, and unlocked the gate. Tailor jumped off the back seat, followed him to the mailbox, and left a liquid greeting card on the post.

"Hmmm," Buck muttered, pulling out the mail. "Newspaper. The package from Ping. Some bills and . . . Shara, there's something for you," he said, passing a fat package wrapped in a paper bag.

"For me?"

"Wha's it, Mommy?"

"I don't know." Turning it over, her eyes widened.

Buck closed the mailbox. "Why don't you open it?"

"Um, no. It's taped. I'll open it when we get back to the house."

"Are you sure? I've got a pocket knife."

"He hab a tocket dife," Donny said.

"Um, I'll wait." She set the parcel on the seat beside her.

"Suit yourself."

"Yeah, soo you seff."

Shara hurried into the bedroom and shut the door. Setting the brown-paper package on the bed, she studied the return address. *Robert Morant. Pacific Palisades. Bob? Roxie?*

She pulled a small kitchen knife from the waistband of her cut-offs. *Hurry.* Jabbing the envelope with the tip of the knife, she sliced through the tape, pulled off the wrapping, and stared at the contents. *Wow.*

Hearing footsteps in the hall, she shoved everything under her pillow, smoothed her hair, and dropped onto the bed.

"Shara, honey, dinner's almost ready," Pauline called, tapping lightly on the door.

"I'll be there in a minute," Shara called back.

"Don't be too long."

"I won't."

Shara exhaled a long sigh. *Close call.* She moved her pillow and spread the contents of the parcel on the bed. Inside she found a letter tucked into a book, a handbill, and a baggie containing four joints. *Sweet Mary Jane, finally, some pot.*

She moved the book and handbill, and picked up the letter.

> Hey Shara,
> I figured you'd be going stir crazy by now. I thought you might want to expand your mind with some outrageous weed Bob calls Tahitian Mauve and a book by Parker. Also an invitation to a far out party at Parker's place in Big Sur. Bob says it'll probably be the best party of the summer. Maybe even the year. Maybe the century. Maybe ever!
> So, enjoy! xoxo I miss you.
> Roxie
> PS If you want to go to the party, let me know and I'll come get you. You can call me at Bob's.
> 213-456-2030

Shara picked up the book and studied Parker's picture. *He looks mean.* She flipped it open and read the chapter headings. *'The Circularity of Enlightenment. The Transcendent Journey to Orion. I Am and You Are I Am.'* She set the book down and shook her head. "That's at least a two-joint read."

She picked up the invitation.

COME CELEBRATE THE SUMMER SOLSTICE COSMIC CONVERGENCE AT THE ORION INSTITUTE
BIG SUR, CALIFORNIA – JUNE 21ST 1968

Shara gathered the contents of the package and shoved it on the top shelf of the closet. She went to the mirror above the dresser, pushed her hair into place and stared at her reflection. *Now, to go or not to go. That's the question.*

"Pauline, can I talk to you a second?" Shara asked, sitting at the dining room table.

"Would you like a cup of tea? We could sit in the kitchen."

"I like it better in here. The deer on the cuckoo clock gives me the creeps. It's like it's always watching me."

Pauline sat down beside her. "Then, what is it, honey?"

"Something you said's been bothering me."

Good gravy, what on earth did I say? "Oh? What's that?"

"When I was telling you about my mother and I started crying, you said, 'no wonder you're uptight all the time,' or something like that."

"Uptight?"

"I think you actually said, upset." Shara drew her knees to her chest. "Maybe the reason I'm so uptight is because I feel like I'm alone and I never know what I should do. Since Roxie's not around, I don't have anyone to help me figure things out."

"What about Steven?" Pauline asked. "Can't he help you? I'm sure you can trust him."

"He never did anything to make me not trust him. Except when he overdosed. It might seem mean, but now I'm not sure he knows what he's doing. Or, like, he's even going to be here. I mean, what if he would've died? It's sort of the same as my mom all over again. When I feel like I'm alone, it freaks me out."

"It doesn't seem mean at all. I can see why you'd feel that way." Pauline took a long breath. "I'm sure Steven has learned something from all this. I hope you'll give him a chance to prove you can trust him again."

"It's not only that. I always feel like I'm looking for something -- like some kind of answer. But I don't even know what the question is." Shara threw her hands into the air. "So, here's the real problem -- if I don't know what I'm looking for, how would I ever know if I found it?"

"Goodness, that certainly is a quandary."

"Yeah. Like, really." Shara shook her head. "I just want to, you know, find out who I am and figure out what I'm supposed to do with my life, or something . . . I guess. Sometimes I want to be a normal, ordinary person and have a normal, ordinary life. Then other times I want to be far-out, outta sight and outrageous. Know what I mean?"

"No, I'm afraid, I don't." Pauline thought a moment. "Sometimes people go to church to find those kind of answers. Maybe that would help. Have you ever been?"

"For my wedding."

"Well, yes, dear. Besides that."

"Once when I was real little I went to Sunday School with our neighbors in Dubuque. But now I'm pretty sure I'm Catholic."

"Why do you think that?"

"When Steven asked me to marry him, at first I thought he was breaking up with me. So I was crying by the elevators at the hospital. Then this little old lady came and told me, if I asked The Blessed Virgin to help me, she would. So I prayed, and The Virgin answered -- Steven asked me to marry him. That's why I think I might be Catholic."

Pauline forced a smile. *So I have the Blessed Virgin to thank for this?* "Shara, honey, if you were Catholic, you'd know."

"Everyone says that."

"Why don't you come to church with Donny and me? Maybe that will help you find the answers."

76

THE BABY BEN on Pauline's nightstand jangled out an alarm. She slapped the top of the clock. Buck stirred, then settled deeper under the covers. She looked into the pale sunlight filtering through a sheer curtain. *Wonder what this day will bring.*

Swinging her feet over the edge of the bed, she glanced at the immobile mound of Buck's body. *He always sleeps in on Sunday, just like his father. And I'm fighting a losing battle, just like his mother.* She sighed. *But someone in this family has to fight the good fight of faith.*

Pauline slipped into the simple, flowered dress she'd laid out the night before. Slid into a pair of flats, went into the bathroom, and switched on the light. Looking in the mirror, she wound her hair into the familiar French knot. "I'm in no mood to feed heathens. So breakfast will consist of cereal," she said under her breath, stabbing her hair with a hairpin.

She turned off the light and went into Donny's bedroom. Sprawling sideways on the bed, he was twisted in the covers, and Tailor was curled at his feet. She gently shook him. "Donny, honey, it's time to get up."

He moaned and flopped onto his back. Tailor yawned and stretched, then jumped off the bed.

Pauline shook him again. "Donny, it's time to get up."

He looked blearily up at her. "Gwamma?"

"Yes, baby. It's time to get up for Sunday School."

"Sunnay skoo?" he asked with a wide yawn.

"Uh huh. Put your robe on and we'll have breakfast." She slipped a robe over his cowboy-print pajamas. "Come on, sleepy head."

Tailor followed them downstairs, into the kitchen. Pauline set Donny on a chair at the table.

"I'll get you something, then I'll feed the heathens."

Sitting on his haunches, Tailor whined and pumped his forelegs.

"And you too," she said, pouring kibble into his dish.

Pauline set a bowl and box of corn flakes on the table. She put out a bottle of milk, a bowl of sugar, and clattered in a drawer for the spoons. "If they're too lazy to go to church, they're too lazy to eat anything but cereal," she said with a definitive nod, setting the utensils on the table.

Donny picked up a spoon. "Gwamma, wha's a heathwen?" he asked, sliding the handle into his nose.

"Someone who won't go to church." She looked up. "Don't do that. It might get stuck." She took the spoon, dropped it in the sink, and went to the drawer for a replacement. "Here's a clean one." She turned to the doorway and shouted, "Everyone! Come and eat!"

A short time later, Steven rolled into the kitchen and maneuvered his wheelchair next to the table.

"Is Shara having breakfast?" Pauline asked.

He shrugged. "I d-on't know. S-he's getting r-eady for ch-urch."

"Oh?" Pauline brightened. "She's coming with us?"

"I g-uess."

Just then, Buck lumbered in, rumpled and unshaven. He tightened a robe over his pajamas and slumped onto a chair.

Donny looked up at him. "Gwampa? Are you and Daddy heathwens?"

"Are we what?"

"Heathwens."

Buck looked over at Pauline and scowled. "Does he mean heathens?"

"No comment."

He picked up the cereal box. "Corn Flakes?"

"Uh huh."

"C'mon Pauline, you have time to make breakfast. How 'bout it?"

"If you're too tired for church, you're too tired to eat a big breakfast," she said, thumping him with a wooden spoon.

"Ow!" Buck rubbed his head and looked over at Steven. "Six days a week your mother is a wonderful woman. I don't know what gets into her on Sunday."

Pauline and Shara stopped at the double doors beneath the church's steeple.

"Well, here we are," Pauline said. "I'm glad you decided to come. But you might get a little warm," she added, staring at Shara's denim jacket, short skirt, and knee-hi moccasins.

"It took me forever to find this, since you said I should wear something not so, you know, *bare*." Shara glanced over her shoulder at the Sunday School building. "Are you sure Donovan will be okay in there?"

"Oh my, yes. He knows everyone and he already has a little girlfriend."

"A girlfriend?"

"He's quite a charmer."

"Was he scared the first time?"

"A little bit. How about you?"

"Heck, yeah. I feel like I'm going to choke, or faint, or barf, or something. Do all the new people feel like this?"

Pauline shrugged. "Goodness, I don't know. Most of our members are either born into the congregation, or they marry into it. There hasn't been a visitor since . . . well, I can't remember when."

"How long does it last?" Shara said, fidgeting with the fraying sleeve of her jacket.

"The sermon usually takes about forty minutes. But today it might go a little longer because we're collecting for pews. We'll know the pastor's done when the organist plays the Doxology."

"What's that?"

"It's a short hymn we sing at the end. When you hear the music, you know the sermon is over."

"How do you know how long he'll talk?"

"Oh, he almost always goes about forty minutes, except for Christmas and Easter. Then, it's longer because he gives an invitation. Or when we have a revival, he can go as long as an hour."

"An invitation? To what?"

"It's not an invitation *to* anything. That's when the pastor calls for souls and convicts the backsliders." Pauline swung the church doors open. "I always sit in the fourth row from the front."

Shara paused at the door. *Calling for souls? How the hell do you call a soul? And what the heck is a backslider?* She shook her head, and followed Pauline into the sanctuary, filled with rows of folding chairs, divided by a center aisle.

Pauline stopped at the fourth row, picked up a hymn book from the chair closest to the aisle and sat down.

Shara took the hymnal from the next chair and sat beside her. Squirming on the hard, metal seat, She glanced furtively around the congregation. Mostly female, white-haired and withered. *Everyone is staring. Why did I come?*

Pauline tapped Shara's arm. "The chair you're sitting in is usually vacant," she said under her breath. "Carolyn Cox and I put our purses on it. So she might get a little snippy."

"Should I move?"

"No, don't worry. She'll get over it."

Shara looked down. *Great. Now I'm sitting in the snippy person's purse-chair.*

Just then, Carolyn Cox came in with her daughter, Terrie -- Roy's wife. She maneuvered into the fourth row, took the hymnal from the chair next to Shara, and sat down. With an audible sigh, she put her purse on the floor as Terrie sat down beside her.

Shara caught her breath and quickly looked away. *Terrie? Oh no! What's she doing here?*

"Carolyn, this is Shara, my daughter-in-law," Pauline said. "Carolyn is Donny's Sunday School teacher."

Shara wound one leg around the other, looked up and nodded.

"Hello Shara," Mrs. Cox said with a manufactured smile, staring at Shara's clothes. "I believe my daughter, Terrie, went to your wedding. She said there was quite a party afterward. Roy had a terrible hangover. Terrie, say hello to Shara."

"Hello," Terrie replied with a cold stare.

"I'm glad to see you here, Shara," Carolyn added. "Church is important, even though most men don't think so, as you can see by how few are here."

"Is that why Pauline calls Buck and Steven heathens?" Shara asked.

Carolyn smiled and took her hand. "I'm sure it is. When it comes to church, regardless of how we feel about anything else, we women have to stick together. My husband, Tom, and Roy don't come much either. So, we're counting on you to start using your influence on Steven *and* Buck."

"How am I supposed to do that?"

Pauline leaned forward. "Nag them."

A middle-aged woman came in and went to the podium. "Everyone have a seat," she said, sitting down at an organ.

A dark-suited pastor came in and stood behind the pulpit. "All rise," he said in a tone suggesting he had said those words, without variation, thousands of times before. "Hymn 165."

Then, a moment of confusion as the congregation tried to sit, stand, and find the hymn at the same time. Amidst the soft rustling of pages, and the swell of the organ, the worshippers joined the song.

> Sow-ing in the morn-ing, sow-ing seeds of kind-ness . . . we shall come re-joi-cing, bring-ing in the sheaves . . .

Shara stared at the hymn book. *God must have terrible taste in music.* She looked around the congregation again. *And people.*

> Bring-ing in the sheaves . . . brin-ging in the sheaves . . . we will come re-joi-cing, bring-ing in the sheaves.

When the final chorus came to an end, as if on cue, the congregation took their seats. Shara leaned over and whispered, "Pauline, what's a sheave?"

"They're bundles of grain, gathered at harvest," she replied under her breath.

Shara looked around the sanctuary. "I don't see any sheaves."

"It's symbolic. Bringing in the sheaves represents bringing people to church."

"Oh." Shara sat back. She thought a moment, then her eyes got wide. *Oh my God! I'm a sheave!*

The pastor looked up. "It appears we have a visitor," he said, gracefully holding his hand toward Shara. "Please stand."

Shara dropped her gaze and sank in her chair.

Pauline patted her leg. "Stand up, dear. When the pastor announces a visitor, the visitor stands.

"No," she whispered, sinking further. "I don't want to be a sheave."

Pauline took a long breath, stood, and cleared her throat. "This is my daughter-in-law, Shara Harper."

"Wonderful," the minister said with a slight frown. "Let's welcome Shara to our fellowship."

77

SHARA HURRIED INTO the Harpers' kitchen. *Church. What a waste of time. And this house.* She looked around the room. *So quiet. No music. Nothing. Except stupid Lawrence Welk. Roxie might be a bitch, but living with her was way better than this.* She pulled Roxanne's letter and the invitation from a pocket in her skirt.

She picked up the receiver on the wall phone. In the background, she heard the muffled sound of a television. She rattled the hook several times.

"Who'th that?" a raspy female voice lisped.

"Who are you?" Shara asked. "I want to use the phone."

"Alma Richardthon. Who are you?"

"I'm trying to make a call."

"Well, who are you?"

"I'm Shara Brennan -- I mean Harper."

"Harper?" Alma repeated as if she was scowling.

"I'm Steven's wife. Pauline said you were mean and nosey. Do you always have to repeat everything everyone says?"

"What?" Alma snapped.

"Get off the phone!"

"Well!"

A sharp click and a dial-tone followed.

Crazy old woman. Shara spread Roxanne's letter on the table. "2-1-3-4-5-6-2-0-3-0," she repeated under her breath as she dialed the number.

Listening to the hollow ring, she stared up at the stag on top of the cuckoo clock, and at the maple leaf pendulum swinging with unnerving monotony between the pinecone weights. *I hate that stupid deer.*

After several rings a male voice answered. "Yep. What can I do for ya?"

"Is Roxanne there?"

"Who's callin'?"

"Um, Shara."

"Hold on, she's hangin' out by the pool. Hey . . . Roxie . . . phone!"

Shara drummed her fingers on the table. *The pool? I'm stuck here while she's hanging out by a pool?* She heard footsteps sloshing toward the phone.

"Hello."

"Roxie, it's Shara."

"Shara! You called!"

"I got your letter and the, uh . . ."

"Smoking materials? Bob's got the best weed in the world. That was him you talked to. What'd you think of the book?"

"Seems really heavy," Shara said with a shrug. "And that Parker guy looks mean."

"Yeah. It was too heavy for me too."

"If he's the one having the party, won't it be a drag?"

"Bob swears it'll be a blast. I hope you're coming. And not just to the party. I miss you, Shara. I want you to move back. It's not the same when you're not around."

"Then how come you told me to leave the key with Vickie? Not even goodbye, or good luck. Nothing."

"I was so upset that you were leaving, I just couldn't handle it. Maybe I was pretending it wasn't happening, or I don't know . . ." Roxanne paused a moment. "So, am I picking you up for the party?"

"Uh, I'm not sure. I -- "

"Not sure?"

"I mean . . ."

"*Sha-ra*, I'm not driving out to the middle of nowhere unless you're, definitely, for sure, coming. But I need to know pretty soon, because we're flying back to San Francisco in a few days."

"I want to go to the party, but I don't know about moving back because of Steven, and Donovan, and I took all my stuff. That's what I meant."

"Then let's just take it one day at a time. But, I'm coming to get you for the party, right?"

"How? You don't have a car."

"Bob's loaning me his van. It's parked at that guy Carl's house in San Francisco. Bob's going to a vineyard up by Napa with his ex for some reason, so I'm meeting him there. See, I can come get you, if you're for real about going."

"Okay, come get me. When are you picking me up?"

"The day of the party. As soon as I can get there."

Just then, Steven wheeled into the kitchen.

"See you," Shara said, then quickly hung up.

"Oh, y-ou're on the ph-one," he slurred.

"Not anymore."

Wheeling closer, he stopped and picked up the invitation. "S-ummer S-olstice C-osmic Con-vergence. Wh-ere did you get t-hat?" He looked at the signature on the note and set the invitation back on the table. "Oh, R-oxanne."

"Yeah," Shara replied.

"I th-ought she dis-owned you."

Shara shrugged. "Guess she forgave me."

"What's a C-osmic Con-vergence?"

"Some kind of spiritual gathering, I think."

Steven looked up at her. "Are y-ou go-ing?"

She stared back at him. "I don't know."

He paused, watching her a moment, then maneuvered the wheelchair out of the room.

Shara slumped against the table. *That was close. He'll find out sooner or later.* She took her crocheted handbag from the back of the chair and stuffed the handbill and the letter inside. *I need to think.*

She slipped out the back door and around the side of the house to the vegetable garden. Then through the garden to the pasture.

At the sound of the chain rattling on the galvanized gate, Nahlah looked up and wandered toward her through the verdant, waist-high grass.

"Go on," Shara said, waving the mare away. "I don't like horses."

With a toss of her head, Nahlah trotted off.

Shara looked up into the crisp blue of the sky, and at the tall pines bordering the pasture, gently swaying in the breeze. She followed a narrow path deep into center where deer had trampled the grass into a circular bed. Warmed by the sun, the grass gave off the scent of freshly cut hay.

She sank down in the clearing and pulled back a section of unstitched lining in her purse. She took out the baggie, containing the marijuana cigarettes and lit one. *Roxie's coming. And I'm going. For a day? A week? Forever?* "I wish all the voices in my head would shut up."

Pulling the smoke deep into her lungs, she both smelled and tasted the smoldering hemp. Holding her breath, she stretched out on the grass.

Closing her eyes, she waited.

As she exhaled, a humming sensation poured over her like hot, liquid sugar. Her heart beat faster. The cadence engulfed her, and the intoxicating scent of the pasture surrounded her. Opening her eyes, suddenly she was aware, brilliantly aware, of everything. *Colors like crayons. Sky -- blue. Grass -- green. Clouds -- white and cottony just like Donovan would draw them . . .*

She watched the clouds changing shape as two hawks circled overhead. Sound became distinct, the rustling of grass, the wind in the trees, and the hawks calling to each other. The crayon-blue sky reached down and touched her. Scent, sound, and color dissolved into one living, breathing vibration. The hum became deafening, and she melted into the rhythm.

"Mommy . . ."

Shara shuddered awake, with Tailor licking her face. *Donovan?*

Pauline and Donny stood at the gate, their voices drifting over the pasture like a breeze.

Shara sat up. The sun hung low in the sky. Nahlah had moved to the far side of the pasture, and the half-consumed joint had gone out in her hand. She quickly slid it in the baggie, and put the baggie in her purse.

"Mom-mie..."

Squinting into the light, Shara rubbed her eyes as Tailor waited expectantly beside her. *What time is it? How long have I been asleep?* Sitting cross-legged, she rested her head in her hands. "I'm not in the mood to be anybody's mommy, and I'm not in the mood to pet you," she said under her breath, pushing the dog away. "Now I'm even more depressed than before."

She peered over the grass.

"*Mom-meee!*" Donovan called, climbing on the bottom rung of the gate.

Should I get up? Or hide and hope they go away?

Tailor jumped on her as if they were playing a game.

"Go on! Get out of here!" she snapped.

The dog flipped onto his back and rolled happily in the grass.

"Your Mommy will be back in a little while," she heard Pauline say. "She probably just needed some time to herself."

"Why?" Donovan asked.

"Big people just need to be by themselves sometimes."

He rattled the gate. "But I wannu sow her my picture I colored."

"She'll be back in a little bit. We'll show her then. Tailor, come on," Pauline called. She took Donny's hand, and they turned toward the house.

As Tailor bounded after them, Shara sank down in the grass. *Will I go back?* She dropped her face into her hands. *Really, I just want to disappear.*

78

WEEKS PASSED.

The phone rang in Donatello's study. He picked up the receiver and balanced it between his shoulder and chin. "Sì," he muttered, pecking out a few more letters on the typewriter.

"Dona," a cheerful voice replied. "It's Lorenzo."

"Ah, Uncle," Donatello said.

"Are you okay? You sound like something's wrong."

"I think the banker is calling. I no want talk to him."

"Well, how've you been? Haven't heard from you for awhile."

Donatello sat back in his chair and ran his hand over his bare chest. "Bene, bene."

"And Slovika?"

"Bene."

Lorenzo cleared his throat. "You took the antibiotics..."

"Sì."

"All of them?"

Donatello sighed. "Sì. All."

"Good. Well, here's why I'm calling, Katrina wants you to come for dinner tonight. She misses Slovika and she wants to see her. She's beginning to think Slovika's a figment of her imagination."

A short silence.

"*Do-na*," Lorenzo whined. "You've cancelled the last two times. Now, don't say you're too busy. I'm a little miffed that you met the banker in San Francisco and you didn't make time to see me."

"But Lorenzo, I need finish screenplay. The banker, he always hound me. He no know *ispirazione*, it take time. He send someone to check the progress. And the die line, it comes."

"Die line?" Lorenzo paused. "Oh, deadline. The banker is hounding you. He's sending someone to check on your progress, and the deadline is coming."

"Sì. If I miss deadline there is una sanzion . . . uh, penalty."

"But you can't disappoint Katrina again. If you don't come, she won't let me hear the end of it."

"I must finish. San Francisco is so far, why you don't come here? I tell Lupe, make something special."

"Tonight?"

"Sì."

Lorenzo paused. "Okay. What time?"

"Come, seven. Dinner, eight."

"Good. Now that's settled, I'll let you get back to the screenplay."

"Ti amo, Lorenzo."

"I love you too, Dona."

Donatello hung up the receiver. He stood, adjusted the waistband of his rumpled gabardines, and wandered out of the study. "Lupe!" he shouted. Hearing a muffled sound, he followed it to the living room. He found her dusting a tall bookcase, standing on a step ladder. "Lupe . . ."

She caught herself on the bookcase. "Oh, Donatello. Goodness, you startled me. What is it?"

"I invite Lorenzo and Katrina for dinner. I tell them you make something special. They want see Slovika. They ask, uh . . . pacific to see her."

"Pacific?" Lupe thought a moment. "Oh, you mean specific," she said, smoothing her hair. "So there will be four of you tonight? What time?"

"I tell him, come seven. Dinner, eight."

"What about Slovika. You two aren't exactly . . ."

"Sì. I have only ora to perform miracolo."

350

Through the tall bay window behind his desk, Donatello looked up to see an unfamiliar car pull into the driveway. "Ave' Maria, why everyone won't leave me alone? Who is that?" His heart racing, he raked his fingers through his hair. *The butcher's virtuoso. Quick! Think!*

He swept the emaciated body of the screenplay into the top drawer of his desk. Then, slid down in his chair, scooted it toward the window, and peered over the sill.

A buxom blonde woman got out of the passenger side of a black Mustang Shelby GT350 with a gold racing stripe and stood in his driveway.

Looking heavenward, Donatello kissed his crucifix. *Ave' Maria! Thanks be to God, I am not doomed. Is only Deborah.* His eyes hardened. *But I never forgive her.*

Marching to a mirror above the stone fireplace, he pushed his hair back in place, yanked a wadded shirt off a nearby chair, and slipped it on. Without stopping to button it, he went to meet her.

Pushing the mansion's tall front doors open, he stepped out onto the stone portico and swaggered toward her.

Deborah took off her large, round sunglasses and waved. "You *must* be the butler," she called.

He stopped a short distance away.

"Don't they pay you enough to get your clothes pressed?" she said, motioning to his wrinkled shirt and gabardines.

He looked down at his clothes, then back up at her. "No, I am but a slave in the master's house," he said with a sullen stare.

"Well, that *is* a shame." She smoothed her sheer peasant top. "I hope I'm not interrupting . . ."

He glared at her.

"Donatello? What's the matter?" she said, fluffing her hair. "You don't seem very happy to see me."

He took her arm. "Deborah, when I am in LA you give to me a disease!" he said under his breath. "Why you do this?"

"Me?" she whispered with a petulant frown. "I thought I got it from *you*." She looked over her shoulder. "Actually, it was probably Bob. He'll sleep with anything that moves."

Donatello threw his hands in the air. "Who is this, Bob?"

"Shhhh!" she hissed, flapping her hands. "Robert Morant. My husband. You met him in LA, remember?"

"But how he gave it to you? You say he is just, tuo amico, uh, how you say, friend."

"Well, we are still married and, you know . . ."

"What you mean?" Donatello asked. From the corner of his eye he saw a man get out of the driver's seat of the Mustang.

Wearing a western shirt, fraying at the shoulders where the sleeves had been cut off, he shook his legs to straighten his threadbare jeans. "How's it goin', Mr. Bounty Killer?" he said with a broad grin, tipping his cowboy hat and pointing his forefinger like a gun.

Donatello frowned. *Bob.*

"Nice place," he said with a slow, rhythmic nod that undulated all the way down his torso. Squinting into the sun, he motioned to a weathered brass plaque to one side of the mansion's stone steps. "Mondscheinberg? That ain't your name. Is this place all y'alls? Or are you just rentin'?"

Donatello turned to Deborah. "What he say? Why you bring him here?"

"He wants to know if this whole place belongs to you. I brought him with me because you're his favorite actor."

Donatello turned to Bob and smiled. "All mine. The name is, uh, how you say, German for moonlight hill. It is the name before I buy it." He took Deborah's hand. "Come, I show you."

Bob slouched against the Mustang and pulled a pack of Lucky Strikes out of his shirt pocket. "Guess I'll stay here and have a smoke while I'm waitin'."

Lupe looked out the kitchen window as Donatello and Deborah passed. She dropped a nutcracker and a Dungeness crab onto the tiled counter. "Who is that slutty-looking woman? And that man waiting by the car?" She leaned over the sink, filled with broken crab shells and viscera. "Mary, Mother of God, where's he taking her? Can't see . . ."

She climbed onto the counter. Kneeling on the edge of the sink, she stretched over. "Still can't see . . ." Her hands slipped, she lost her balance, and splashed up to her elbows in the repugnant stew.

"Oh! Ick!" she gasped, scrambling back to the floor.

She brushed the wet, slimy bits of shellfish off her apron, washed her hands, and pushed the hairpins holding her chignon back into place. *He wouldn't dare invite them for . . .*

"Dinner!"

Lupe whisked the crab off the counter and held it over the sink. "Honestly, if that man doesn't drive me out of my mind. How can he be so charming and so horrible at the same time?"

She clamped down on the claw with the nutcracker. "It's his head I'd like to crack," she muttered as the rust-red crab shell splintered into the sink.

Donatello led Deborah past the driveway to a lichen-dappled rock wall separating the mansion and its meticulously tended grounds from the vineyard. A covey of quail darted into a wild oat thicket near the wall as he unlatched the ironwork gate and held it open for her.

Stepping through the gate, she put her hands on her hips and looked out over the sun-satiated hillside. "Very nice. I'm impressed, and it's not easy to impress me. You've done pretty well for yourself here in America, haven't you?"

He shrugged. "How you find me?"

"I read an article in 'The Reporter' that said you were living near Sonoma. There aren't that many Italian actor-directors who live around here, so it wasn't too hard. I also read that you're working on a musical. Weren't you even going to tell me about your new project?" She feigned a pout. "And all this time I thought we were friends."

"Deborah . . ."

She pressed herself against him. "It would be really great if we could work together, because as you already know, we have *fabulous* chemistry. Plus, I have a musical background, and I'm a leading lady."

He stared at her. "You come to ask for work?"

"No, silly. But I was just thinking -- "

"Deborah, I no control this film. The producer, he is butcher. It is . . . how you say, he that call the shot. I know nothing about musical, so he hire someone do the casting."

She shook her head as if to dislodge his words. "That's not what 'The Reporter' said. They said you -- "

Donatello grabbed her arm. "The story, it is for the publicity."

"But -- "

His grip tightened. "Deborah, the producer, he put in 'The Reporter.' But is not true. He want it to appaia . . . uh, to appear I control the film, but he hold all the cards."

Her face fell. "Oh."

He let go of her arm. "Because we are, um . . . friend, I speak to him. Maybe there is something . . ."

"Wow, that would be great." She smiled. "Now, show me the rest of your vineyard."

"Come." Donatello took her hand. "On other side of hill, the wine cave," he said, pointing as they walked. "The giardiniere cottage, and how you say . . ." He snapped his fingers. "Casa piante. The house where you grow the plants . . ."

"Oh, uh, greenhouse," she offered.

"Sì." He led her to a narrow footpath, bordered by brilliant wild mustard. "And grapevine," he said, motioning to the wire-topped scaffolds overgrown with verdant vines, traversing the hillside.

"Where *are* you taking me?" she asked, laughing as they followed the path through the grapevines. "Are we going all the way down to the ocean?"

"No. Just the end of vineyard."

At the bottom of the hill, they came to the moss-covered footbridge spanning the creek. Their footsteps echoed on the weathered-gray planks as they crossed.

Downstream from the bridge, the creek widened into a pond. Redwing blackbirds scolded from a stand of cattails, and a bullfrog ceased its mournful call as they followed the path along the edge. A short distance away, the creek narrowed again. Slipping under a loosely strung barbed-wire fence, it continued its meandering course through a grove of cottonwoods, across the valley floor to the ocean.

Donatello stopped near the fence. "This the end."

Deborah took off her sandals and stepped onto the soft grass beside the pond. She laughed and smiled. Her platinum hair turned to gold in the late afternoon light. Twirling with her arms outstretched, tiny bells on the drawstring of her blouse tinkled in the ocean-scented breeze. Then, a gust caught the sheer fabric and the sun created a gauzy silhouette of her figure.

He went to her and brushed the fingertips of his bandaged hand over her hair. *The sun itself dances on her. Perhaps I will forgive.* "You look, how you say . . . different. You have not so much make-up. And your hair, not so big. You more bella this way."

With a seductive smile she traced her fingernail in a tightening spiral over his bare chest. "I just don't feel like keeping up the 'America's Little Sweetheart' image anymore."

He stared into the blue-green abyss of her eyes. *I do not love her. But I want her.* "I am flatter you come all the distance to see me," he said, then pulled her close and kissed her.

Deborah sank against him. "Mmmm . . . Donatello, I've *really* missed you."

Lowering his eyes, he looked up at her and tugged lightly on the drawstring. "You want I should untie it?" he whispered. "No one will see."

"Well, yes and no," she said, smiling. "In all honesty -- yes, I came all the way to see you, and yes, you could untie it. But no, I'm also going to Big Sur to see Parker -- you remember, you met him that day on my show."

Donatello dropped the drawstring. He stepped back and fumbled to button his shirt with his splinted fingers.

"Donatello? What's wrong? Don't be like that."

He frowned. "Parker, Parker, why you always talk of this Parker?" He threw his hands into the air. "Why you . . . you so hang up on him."

"You mean hung up." She shrugged. "I don't know. I never actually thought about it before. Maybe it's because he's different from other men. They always look at me like all they want is to go to bed with me. Which is okay, I guess. But when Parker looks at me, it's like he's seeing *into* me, not staring *at* me."

Donatello turned away. Watching a school of tiny fish darting near the edge of the pond, he sighed. *If this is true, why does she work so hard to advertise what she does not wish to sell?*

"Oh, *Dona-tello*, don't get your feelings hurt. Parker's having a gathering to celebrate his birthday and the summer solstice -- you know, the longest day of the year. It's really cosmic. I was hoping you'd come with me. In fact, Parker himself asked me to invite you. It'll be absolutely *fa-bulous*." She put her arms around his neck and leaned against him. "Come on . . . don't be upset. You're not jealous, are you?"

He pulled her arms off and stared at her. "Why he invite me?"

She shrugged again. "Maybe because he likes you." Tilting her head to one side, she twisted the drawstring around her finger. "So, do you want to come, or not?"

He sighed. "I no know . . ."

"Well, if you don't know, then you might as well come with me, silly!"

79

DONATELLO MOTIONED FOR Bob and Deborah to follow him. He opened the front door of his mansion and went inside. He led them through the living room, down a hall past the formal dining room, to a smaller room next to the kitchen. Hanging low in the sky, the sun cast an elongated harlequin-patterned shadow onto the opposing wall.

"You stay for dinner?" he asked, pulling out a chair for Deborah at a long table.

"Actually," she said, sitting down. "Since Parker's gathering isn't until tomorrow, we were hoping we could stay the night. If it's not too much trouble..."

"Nope. Nope. Nope," Bob said, waving as if to erase what she said. He swung his leg over the back of a chair and sat across from her. "There's no *we* in any a' this. It's the first I heard of it. Since y'all didn't wanna stay in the city at Carl's, I thought we were staying at a motel."

"But we came all this way." She looked up at Donatello. "And your house and vineyard are so lovely, I just thought I'd ask..."

"Lupe, my house manager" Donatello said as she came into the room. "Deborah Donaldson, and Bob," he announced. "They will have dinner and stay the night."

Lupe glanced at a large clock above the kitchen door. *I should have at least another hour. They usually eat late, but nooo, not tonight.* "Why does he do this to me?" she muttered, dropping a spoonful of crab, cheese, and caramelized onions onto a tortilla. "He changes plans. Does he bother to tell me? No! He never tells me anything. Maybe Lorenzo isn't coming after all." She rolled the tortilla and nestled it in a baking dish next to several others. "Stretching dinner for two, four, or even six. I never know. Thank God I made extra."

Just then, the kitchen door swung open. Slovika stood in the doorway, her golden-brown eyes shimmering with tears.

They stared at each other a moment.

"Slovika . . ." Lupe motioned for her to come in. "Honey, what's wrong?"

Slovika looked away.

"Where have you been? Dinner is almost ready."

"I am no hungry."

"But you have to eat something . . . sometime."

Slovika fell onto Lupe's shoulder, sobbing. "I see them walking, Donatello and the LA devil woman. So I follow them. By the pond, he kiss her. Why he brought her here?"

Lupe put her arm around Slovika. "I'm sorry. I don't know."

"If it is her he want, why he won't let me go? Why he keep me in cage like animal?"

Lupe held her tighter. "I don't know that either. That's just the way men are sometimes. I don't know why they're here. Donatello didn't even tell me they were coming."

Slovika looked up. "They?"

"That woman and the man who came with her."

Slovika stepped back. "A man? What man?"

"They're in the small dining room. Maybe you can peek around the corner . . ."

They crept to the doorway. Slovika looked into the room, then motioned to Lupe and they went back to the kitchen. "He is her husband," she said, her lips quivering.

Lupe smiled. "You see, it's not so bad after all."

Slovika shook her head. "No, Lupe. You no understand. This man, he let Deborah stay the night with Donatello in LA."

Lupe's eyes widened. "He what?"

"He does not care if his wife sleep with another man."

Lupe shook her head. "Goodness, I've never heard of such a thing. Well, I *have* heard of it, but . . ."

80

LAWRENCE WELK AND the band were in full swing beneath the Geritol TV banner as Shara came into the living room. "Everyone in their assigned seats," she whispered.

Buck in his chair by the fireplace. Pauline on the sofa with her embroidery. Steven in his wheelchair reading a book. Donny sprawled on the floor playing with a new GI Joe. And Tailor stretched out on the floor beside him.

Shara wandered to the sofa and flopped down next to Pauline. Pauline looked up and smiled, then went back to her needlework.

A young baritone wearing a suit the color of lime sorbet with his hair combed flawlessly over his ears, took a microphone from its stand. Sweat began beading on his upper lip as he embarked on an emotive rendition of "I Wanna Hold Your Hand" by the Beatles.

Shara sighed. *How stupid can it get?* She looked over at Buck. *Any minute he'll say something.*

Buck shifted in his chair and frowned. "So, now they're playing Rock and Roll?"

Pauline glanced up over her glasses. "Mmmm hmmm."

"He looks nervous. The way he's sweating . . ."

"Well, who wouldn't with you watching?" Pauline replied with a frown. "They play too fast. They play too slow. The arrangements are terrible," she said, imitating his voice. "They play without feeling. They turn Big Band into baby food. Not to mention the dancers . . ."

Buck slouched in his chair. "Alright. Alright."

The TV camera moved from the young baritone to an organist, in matching lime-green.

Shara rolled her eyes. She got up and wandered to the loveseat and flopped down near Steven's wheelchair. "If your father thinks it's so terrible, why does he watch it all the time?" she whispered. "It's not like anyone's twisting his arm."

Steven looked up from his book. Steven shrugged. "I d-on't know. It's b-een the r-outine ever s-ince I can r-emember."

"Gwampa, wook," Donovan said, scrambling onto Buck's lap.

"What've ya got there, Donny?"

"A Dee Eye Doh. Wook." Donovan bent GI Joe's hands so he could hold his rifle.

"A Dee Eye Doh? Well I'll be. Where'd you get 'im?"

"GI Joe, honey," Pauline corrected.

"Gwamma got him for me at Pwasserville."

"Pwasserville?" Buck repeated, his eyes wide with enthusiasm.

"Stop that, Buck," Pauline scolded. "You should encourage him to pronounce correctly."

"Sorry, Don, old boy. Grandma's right. It's Placerville. You need to learn how to say the 'L'."

Shara rolled her eyes again and bit her lip.

After a swelling effusion from the organist, and another chorus, the song came to an end. The young baritone bowed and Lawrence encouraged the audience to give him "a big-a hand-a."

Shara jumped up and rushed out of the room.

Steven sighed and put down his book. Wheeling after her, he found her in the adjoining hallway. "What's wr-ong?" he whispered.

Her pale eyes flashed. "What's wrong? Your mother gave him a GI Joe!" she said in a hissing whisper.

Steven pushed himself up out of the wheelchair. Balancing against the wall, he stood and looked into her eyes. "So?"

"GI Joe is all about war. And we're not supposed to believe in war, remember?"

"Sh-ara, it's just a t-oy."

"Just a toy? Since we don't believe in anything anymore, she might as well buy him a real gun. No one asked me what I thought. No one ever asks me what I think about anything. It's like I'm not even here. Maybe I don't want him to play with guns."

"It's n-ot a g-un."

She crossed her arms. "Same thing. Don. Donny. Old boy! His name is Donovan! Why do they have to call him Don -- or worse yet, Donny all the time?"

"What's w-rong with th-at?"

"His name is Donovan."

"W-hy are you ma-king such a b-ig deal out of it? So they c-all him D-onny. So wh-at?"

"His name is Donovan. I'm his mother, and I named him."

"Ex-cuse me, but I'm his fa-ther, and we na-med him, remember? It's l-ike you're jea-lous or s-omething."

Her eyes flashed again. "I am not jealous! It's just they . . ." She threw her hands into the air. "It's like, Donovan doesn't even know I exist anymore. He totally ignores me. It's always, Gramma this. Grampa that. They're turning him into a plain, stupid, ordinary, boring kid just like all the other plain, stupid, ordinary kids in the world."

There was a short silence.

"Just like the p-lain, st-upid, or-dinary kid they t-urned me into?"

She looked away. "I never said that. I just want -- "

A sharp squeal and muffled laughter echoed in the hallway. Shara looked into the living room, then turned back. "Your father is tickling him until he's practically crying."

Steven put his hand on her shoulder. "D-onovan has a r-ight to be whatever will m-ake him ha-ppy. E-ven if it's pl-ain, st-upid, or-dinary, and b-oring. Would t-hat be so bad? He's h-appy now. He was n-ever h-appy before."

"What you really mean is, he was never happy with me." She pushed his hand away. "Roxie was right. She said it would turn out this way."

"R-oxie? W-hat's she got to do w-ith an-ything?"

"She said if I moved up here, you'd turn into a square, just like Roy and your parents. And you'd start siding with them all the time. Now you're just as plastic as they are."

"W-hat?" Steven paused. "Oh. Of c-ourse. N-ow I g-et it. How st-upid of me. This isn't a-bout you and me, and our s-on, p-utting our l-ives back together. This is a-bout R-oxanne t-rying to c-ontrol you and m-aybe get b-ack at Roy and me at the s-ame time. And if D-onny gets in the way, too d-amn b-ad."

Shara's eyes opened wide, then narrowed into slits. She swung back. With a sharp crack, she slapped Steven across the face. He lost his balance and fell back into the wheelchair as she stomped to the bedroom and slammed the door behind her.

81

LUPE PULLED A bubbling baking dish of enchiladas from the oven and let the oven door close with a crash. She slid a spatula into the dish, stomped into the dining room and set it on a trivet in the center of the table. The aroma of roasting chilies, cilantro, and melting cheese filled the room. "I'll bring the rice," she said, then went back to the kitchen.

Deborah grabbed the spatula and slid a heaping mound of enchiladas onto her plate. "I'm starved," she said, passing the spatula to Bob.

"Dang. Me too," he chimed. "Smells great. Let me at 'em."

Deborah cut a forkful off the enchilada. The melted cheese pulled into a long string as she slid it into her mouth. "Mmmm. This is so good."

"Damn good," Bob added as Lupe came back into the dining room.

"Finally, someone in this house is eating," she said, setting a bowl of spicy rice next to the enchiladas. She looked over at Donatello. "You should eat something, too."

"Sì. Lo farò. I will."

"Shall I get some wine from the cellar?"

"Sì. Sì." He nodded, then waved her away.

"Lupe is a wonderful cook. I can see why you hired her," Deborah said with a smile that wrinkled her nose. "It's actually none of my business . . . isn't she's kind of bossy for an employee?"

Donatello shrugged. "I no hire her. She come with the vineyard. She is here a long time before I buy it. Like she is everybody mother, she want everyone to eat, eat, always eat or she is, arrabbia . . ." He snapped his fingers. "How you say it -- upset?"

Just then, there was a knock on the front door. A moment later, Lupe came back to the table, bent beside Donatello's chair and whispered to him.

His eyebrows raised. "Lorenzo! I forget Uncle Lorenzo!" He jumped up, raked his fingers through his hair, and rushed down the hall to the foyer.

Lorenzo and his wife, Katrina waited in the entry.

Donatello gushed, "Lorenzo!" embracing him and feigning a kiss beside his cheek.

Lorenzo stepped back. "Dona, look at you. Wrinkled shirt. Wrinkled pants. No shoes. Did you forget you invited us?" he said with a frown.

Donatello glanced down at his clothes, then up at Lorenzo. "No. I have no time to change. Uh, other guest come I no expect."

"You have guests, dressed like that?"

"Sì."

Lorenzo exhaled a long sigh. "Well, that explains the Mustang in the driveway. Being the rental model, I didn't think you bought it. But then again, I never know." He glanced at Katrina. "We'll come some other -- "

"No, no," Donatello said, taking Katrina's arm and the sleeve of Lorenzo's silk jacket. "Come, we just start to eat. Lupe, she make enough for everyone," he added, dragging them toward the dining room.

Donatello cleared his throat as they came into the room. "My Uncle Lorenzo and wife, Katrina," he announced with a slight bow. "My friend Deborah and -- "

Before he could finish, Lorenzo stepped forward and took the empty seat next to Deborah.

"Deborah . . ." he said, deepening his voice. "I think we've met," he added, then took her hand, and kissed it.

Katrina rolled her eyes. "The only noticeable resemblance between Donatello and Lorenzo is how they behave around attractive women," she said, sitting beside Bob.

"I'm an actress," Deborah gushed. "You've probably seen me on the big screen."

Lorenzo looked over at Donatello and mouthed, "The actress?"

He lowered his eyes and nodded.

"I'm most famous for my starring role in *Beach Balls and Bongos*," Deborah said with a coquettish giggle.

"Beach Balls?" Lorenzo replied.

"And Bongos," she replied. "I was Julie."

"Julie. How could I forget Julie? But I bet that's not all you're famous for."

"Well, of course not, silly," she said, feigning a pout. "I've done tons of TV and movies. I got my start as a go-go dancer on 'Hullabaloo'."

Donatello motioned to Bob. "And this is Deborah's husband, Bob."

Bob looked up from his plate. "Howdy," he said with a mouthful of enchilada and a sideways wave.

Lorenzo nodded. "Ah, the husband of the *married* actress."

"That be me," Bob replied. "And you're 'The Bounty Killer's' uncle."

"His father's cousin, actually."

"Man, I love *The Bounty Killer*," Bob said. "The movie I mean. I saw it in Europe. But, ya know, when I met him I was kinda disappointed."

"Why's that?"

Bob pointed at Donatello with his thumb. "In the movies, he looks bigger'n hell. But in real life, danged if he ain't just a little bitty dude -- like a banty rooster."

Donatello turned to Deborah. "What he say?"

She scrunched up her nose. "He thinks you're great!"

Just then, Lupe came back with two more place settings and a dusty bottle from the wine cellar. After setting the dishes on the table, she wiped the bottle with a dishtowel and worked the cork out.

"He will taste," Donatello said, motioning to Lorenzo.

Lorenzo held out his glass and Lupe poured a small amount. He swirled the wine, then took a sip. "Not bad. Not bad at all," he said, smiling and smacking his lips as she filled the other glasses.

"To my guest," Donatello said, tipping his glass.

Katrina looked around the room. "Where's Slovika? Isn't she coming to dinner?"

"Who's Slovika?" Deborah asked.

"His wife," Lorenzo replied, with a flat stare.

Deborah's eyes widened. "Wife? You didn't tell me you were married."

"Slovika isn't hungry," Lupe said, glaring at Donatello. "She's having dinner upstairs in her room."

"She's not hungry, but she's having dinner in her room," Lorenzo repeated. "The lawyer in me says something's amiss. Trouble in paradise?"

"She's such a sweet girl, I wanted so much to see her, " Katrina said. "You'll tell her I missed her?"

"Yes, of course." Lupe folded her hands. "Anything else?"

Donatello shook his head.

After an awkward silence, she left the room.

"So, Dona, how's the screenplay coming?" Lorenzo asked, pulling the enchiladas toward his plate.

Deborah looked over at Donatello. "Dona . . . I like your nickname," she said with a wink, then turned to Lorenzo. "I usually know everything that's happening in the business. But I didn't hear anything about it through the grapevine -- no pun intended." She giggled. "He -- that bad boy over there kept it a secret. And you really have to work at it to keep a secret from me. I had to read about it in 'The Hollywood Reporter,' the same as everyone else," she added with a petulant frown.

"So, you're the married actress Dona met in LA," Lorenzo said, passing the enchiladas to Katrina.

"That's me -- unless he met someone else I don't know about. He was a guest on my talk show. We had a *fa-bulous* time together. My show's only in the local LA market right now, but we're going national in the fall."

"Dream on, baby," Bob said under his breath, then shoved a huge chunk of enchilada in his mouth.

"What does he mean?" Lorenzo asked.

"Oh, nothing." Deborah rolled her eyes. "He always makes snide little remarks like that."

"Just keepin' things intrestin'," Bob said with one side of his mouth bulging.

Lorenzo pointed his fork at the tattoo on Bob's bicep. "So, you're from Texas?"

Bob looked down at his arm. "Nope. Native son a' Oklahoma."

"Then why the Lone Star tattoo?"

"I got drunk at the Big Texan in Amarillo and woke up in Shamrock, branded."

Lorenzo raised one eyebrow. "Shamrock?"

"Shamrock, Texas. East a' Amarillo, west a' Oklahoma City."

"She's an actress. What do you do?"

"Me? I'm a drummer and run-a'-the-mill hellion."

Deborah wound a lock of platinum hair around her finger. "Bob is the least popular member of a pretty popular band," she said. "The Time Season Band. Have you heard of them?"

Lorenzo shook his head. "Can't say that I have."

"Remember 'Bargain With A Witch?' That's their song. It went gold. It was on the charts almost forever."

"Can't say that I do."

"Actually, oil's the family business," Bob said.

"Oh?" Lorenzo replied.

"My grandfather's a wildcat driller. My father -- same thing, only wilder and richer. He pretty much wrote the book on raisin' hell, so to get any respect, I really had to rebel."

"Had to?"

Bob slouched in his chair and hooked his thumb through a belt loop on his jeans. "Sure. Rebellin's practically a Morant family tradition. They're all expectin' me to go into the family business. So, to have a rat's-ass chance of bein' my own man, I had to rebel. At least long enough that they'll think twice about tryin' to railroad me. Anyway, I was a pretty good drummer, The Time Season Band came along, and the rest is -- "

"History?" Lorenzo offered.

"Yep."

"But everything's okay now? With your family, I mean."

"Nope. Currently, I'm disinherited. I supposedly trashed my new stepmother's spotty reputation -- my dad married a carhop from Arkansas, who's younger'n I am. She trashed her reputation all by herself. I just made the mistake of noticin'. But eventually my ol' man'll go on a bender, find God again and forgive me. That's what usually happens."

"Usually?"

"Sure. The ol' man backslides, then gets saved, or I should say, re-saved every so often. You know how it goes."

"But you and Deborah *are* married."

"Yeah. Well, sort of. That's a long story too. It'd take from now 'til Jesus comes back to tell ya."

"Try me."

"I can guaran-damn-tee-ya I didn't marry her for money, if that's what you're thinkin'. More like the other way 'round. But you gotta admit she's got other obvious assets."

"Bob!" Deborah snapped.

"Your words, darlin', not mine -- and you say it all the time."

Lorenzo rubbed his forehead. "I don't want to pry, but you said sort of."

"All that's holdin' us together now's the piece a' paper."

"Then what brings you here?"

Deborah leaned forward. "I . . . I mean we," she said motioning between Bob and herself. "We came to see Donatello. And also another friend of mine."

"But not a friend of mine," Bob muttered.

Deborah scowled at him. "Anyway, as I was trying to say, my friend in Big Sur is having a fantastic event to celebrate the summer solstice. And this friend . . ." She turned to Bob and glared at him.

He looked puzzled.

"Aren't you going to say it?"

"Say what?"

"Something stupid.'"

"Why would I wanna do that?"

"Because you always say something ridiculous when I'm trying to make a point." Deborah shook her head. "Anyway, as I was saying, my friend is having a big event to celebrate the summer solstice. It's a very cosmic day, and he invited me -- I mean us, to spend a few days with him. And he invited Donatello to come too."

She turned to Donatello. "You know, maybe Parker could help you and your wife find your true internal, eternal selves. Then you'll both be free like Bob and me."

82

DONATELLO SET HIS fork aside and pushed his plate away. "Lupe," he called.

A short time later, she came into the room.

"We will have sambuca and empanadas on the patio," he announced.

"Another wonderful dinner," Lorenzo said, looking at Lupe.

"Yes, superb," Katrina added.

Lupe smiled and nodded, "gracias," and went back to the kitchen.

Donatello stood. "Come," he said, motioning for the others to follow. He took them down a hallway, opened a wide French door, and stepped out onto a flagstone patio. "We sit here," he said, waving to a group of carved wooden seats surrounding a burlwood table. He brushed a scattering of leaves off a chair and sat down.

Waning daylight filtered through grapevines draped over a slatted pergola, and chirping crickets punctuated the distant whisper of waves wafting on a cool evening breeze.

"So, Deborah, who is this friend of yours who's having the cosmic event?" Lorenzo asked, settling himself next to Katrina.

"Parker," Deborah replied.

"Parker who?"

She giggled. "That sounds like a knock-knock joke. It's just Parker. He wrote the bestseller, *Master of the Mind*. And he's the founder of The Orion Institute in Big Sur. It's kind of like a retreat, or a, you know, commune. Have you heard of him?"

Lorenzo took a long breath. "Maybe. But, if I remember, what I heard wasn't good."

"I bet you read a nasty article by one of those government-controlled reporters, like that Cal what's-his-name."

Lupe came in carrying a tray of glasses filled with iced, milky-white liqueur, and plates with half-moon shaped pastries. She set the tray on the burlwood table.

"Wait a minute," Lorenzo said.

She froze, looking at him.

"Oh, not you. It was rhetorical." Lorenzo turned back to Deborah. "Orion . . . Orion. Now I remember. It used to belong to the Campenella family. Rancho Campenella something," he said, snapping his fingers. "It had cabins and everything. The old man . . . I forgot his name. He died a few years back and left the property to his kid -- he was a lounge singer in Vegas. But how that Parker person got hold of it . . ."

"I'll tell ya'," Bob interjected. "The kid -- Anthony Campenella, was hangin' around Parker, before he conveniently disappeared. Nobody knows what happened, but there's plenty of rumors."

"That's not true," Deborah said, her eyes darting from Bob to Lorenzo. She leaned forward, winding the drawstring on her blouse around her finger. "He works for the government, you know."

Lorenzo stared at her. "Who? Campenella?"

"No. That horrible Cal what's-his-name. The columnist who writes all those terrible articles about Parker. I can't stand him. He's supposed to be an expert on philosophy and religion. But I don't think he has a spiritual bone in his entire body. Harry, the producer of my show, insists we have him on all the time. He says we need to have some balance."

"Sounds fair," Lorenzo said.

Deborah frowned. "The government would love to destroy Parker and Orion."

"Why? Seems like they have better things to do than go around destroying people for no reason."

"Parker is like god and Jesus put together. I don't know why anyone would be against him, except the government."

"Or anybody with a brain," Bob muttered.

Lorenzo rhythmically tapped his fork on his plate. "So, this Parker person is god, and the government has it in for him?"

"Parker is who he says he is. He always tells the truth."

Lorenzo looked at Katrina, then Donatello, then Bob, and back at Deborah. "Always?"

"Always. Whenever I need advice, I ask Parker. He's like my savior. Everything I am is Parker."

Bob leaned forward. "Let me tell ya, it's been great havin' him as the third party in our two-some."

"Parker advises you, personally?" Katrina asked.

"He doesn't personally advise everyone. He has to sense that you're especially spiritual."

Bob took a long swallow of sambuca and sat back in his chair. "It's funny he decided you were so dad-burn spiritual, once he found out you're an actress."

"So he bases how spiritual you are, on -- " Lorenzo began.

"How much you can pay," Bob replied.

Deborah shook her head. "That's what those stupid, lying government reporters say."

"But is it true?" Lorenzo asked.

"No! It's because they can't control Parker. The government is always afraid of what it can't control."

Lorenzo stared at her. He pushed his plate away and motioned to Katrina. Katrina dabbed her mouth with her napkin, picked up her purse, and rested it in her lap.

"And what about you?" Lorenzo asked, looking at Bob. "What do you think about all this? I get the impression you don't buy into it."

"I think Parker is as useless as a twenty-two shell in a twelve-gauge shot gun. It's like he lives in a Lava Lamp. But somewhere in his sick, acid-soaked brain he probably thinks he's actually helping people."

"Bob!" Deborah snapped. "You don't mean that."

"I absa-freakin'-lutely do too." As far as I'm concerned, he's responsible for breaking up our marriage. It was never great, but since you've been takin' that butt-head's advice . . ."

"The only thing Parker is responsible for is setting me free."

"Free from what?"

"Free from the disappointment of being married to -- "

Bob shook his head. "Well, I'm real damn sorry you're so damn disappointed. I never claimed to be anybody but who I am. You should've thought that through before you married me." He looked over at Lorenzo. "I hear this kinda' crap all the time. Her only problem -- Parker hasn't been able to pull out of the cosmos how she can keep givin' him dough all the time without me. But now? I don't give a rat's-ass what happens between her and me."

Lorenzo's expression darkened. "Then why are you going to this solstice-thing?"

"For the party, man. You could say, I'm just along for the ride."

Lorenzo motioned to Katrina. "I think we better be going," he said, standing and helping her up. "We've got a long drive."

"Uncle, you go too soon," Donatello said, jumping to his feet.

"Dona, you know how far it is." Lorenzo nodded at Deborah and Bob. "Nice to meet you."

Donatello took Lorenzo's arm and walked them to the door.

Lorenzo stopped in the doorway. "I need to talk to Dona," he said, handing the car keys to Katrina. "I'll be there in a minute."

She smiled wistfully at Donatello, then patted his face and kissed the air beside his cheek. "Tell Slovika I missed her, and I hope to see her soon?"

He nodded.

The crickets stopped as she walked across the driveway and got into the car.

"Katrina's still got great legs," Lorenzo said, staring after her. He turned and rested his hands on Donatello's shoulders. "Dona, I know I'm not your father, but I swear on a stack of Bibles, I love you like you're my own son. You know I do." He took a long breath. "I think Deborah's trouble."

The crickets began chirping again. `Donatello's jaw stiffened.

"I can see what you like about her. Hell, you'd have to be blind not to. If I was younger, I'd, well . . ." Lorenzo scuffed at the stone step. "You know I'm no angel, but for Bob to let Deborah . . ." He shook his head. "That I don't understand. In my Catholic eyes, a man might be able to justify committing adultery, or even keeping a mistress. But only in secret and only if he goes to confession. But his wife? Letting her be with another man? I can't even imagine . . ."

Lorenzo shook his head again. "And that retreat place -- I don't think you should go. If it's anything like I've heard, they're into all kinds of weird stuff down there. With *The Bounty Killer* about to come out, you can't afford the bad press. Plus, you've got the banker's deadline is coming up. Besides, what would your father and your brother think?"

Donatello's eyes narrowed. "Lorenzo, I know what I do."

"Sure you do, Dona. I'm not suggesting you don't. I'm just saying be careful. This isn't Italy. You could be in over your head before you know it." Holding Donatello at arm's length, Lorenzo looked into his eyes. "Do you understand?"

Donatello looked back at him with a resolute stare.

"Just don't get into anything you can't get out of. Okay?"

No response.

"Well then, I guess I'll see you later." Lorenzo pressed his cheek against one side of Donatello's face, then the other. "Give me a call when you come to San Francisco."

Donatello nodded. "Sì."

"Promise?"

He nodded again.

The crickets stopped again as Lorenzo walked across the driveway. He got into his car and gunned the engine.

"Uncle, I know what I do," Donatello said under his breath as the crickets resumed, and the tail lights disappeared down the driveway.

83

SLOVIKA HURRIED UP the stairs and down a long hall. *I am Gypsy. Roma. Nomad. My blood cries to be free.*

Stopping at a door at the end of the hall, she opened it and went inside. *Will I ever share this room with him again?* She sighed and shook her head. "Always lies. Always excuses. Never the truth."

She went around the bed, past the master bathroom and opened the door to Donatello's closet. Switching on the light, she went in. She took a long breath and the heady scent of his cologne captivated her. "So many clothes," she whispered, drawing her hand over a row of shirts, the sleeves pressed sharp as knives. "And shoes . . ." tracing her fingertips over the calf skin, snake skin, ostrich, and alligator. She paused in front of a full length mirror and smoothed the slick fabric of her short silk robe. "I would forgive him, if only he loved me." *Though he says the words, he is an actor. How can I believe him?*

Putting her hands on her hips, she looked around the closet. "He is smart, but I am smarter." *Where would 'The Bounty Killer' keep it?*

She went to a dresser to one side of the mirror and opened the top drawer. Velvet-lined partitions separated cufflinks, watches, tie clips and bracelets. She picked up a ring -- a large garnet flanked by diamonds. *His wedding ring. Red like blood. But he never wears it.* She set the ring back in the drawer and searched the other drawers. *Nothing.*

Resting her hand on the dresser, she felt a slight movement. She pushed on the chest, and it rolled back, revealing a small door. "What is this? A secret hiding place?" She wiggled the handle. *Locked. Where would he keep the key?* She glanced around the closet. *Maybe the dresser.* She slid the top drawer open and rummaged through the contents. Then the other drawers. *Nothing. Think.* She opened the top drawer again. In front, her fingertips found a small ledge, and she felt the key. *So simple.* "I am smarter," she whispered, taking the key from the ledge.

She slid it into the lock, opened the door, and slumped against the dresser. "Maybe not so simple after all," she said, staring at a polished black safe.

Slovika looked frantically around the closet. *The combination? Would he memorize it? Or write it down?* She paused. *Maybe his birthday.* She rolled the tumbler. "The day and month."

Two, right.
Eight, left.
Zero, right.
Seven, left.
She jerked on the handle. *Nothing.*
Think! "The month and year."
Zero, right.
Seven, left.
Three, right.
Five, left.

She yanked on the lever. Three inches of steel swung open. "Ahhh, I am much smarter after all."

On the safe's top shelf she found an inlaid wooden jewelry box. She lifted the lid. *Maybe here.* Inside, a ring with a large emerald, a gold watch with diamonds around the face, and a woman's picture. *His nonna's ring. But the watch . . .* She took it out and read the inscription on the back. "Amore Mieka." Then she looked at the picture. *Caggiano's mistress. She gave it to him.*

Slovika dropped the watch back in the box and closed the lid. *Always the same.* She rifled through the other shelves. *Only papers.*

Moving the documents, she found a yellowed envelope leaning vertically against the back of the safe. She glanced over her shoulder -- the scent of Donatello's cologne seemed to close in around her. *Please, Saint Sarah e Kali. Please . . .*

She picked up the envelope and pulled out three small booklets. "His passport," she said under her breath, dropping the passport and envelope. *Banque Suisse?* "A secret bank account?" she whispered, opening the book. *Thousands upon thousands of francs . . .* She flipped to the back. "Zero balance. But he spends as if he has all the money in the world." She dropped it beside the envelope.

Tears filled her eyes as she ran her fingers over the Yugoslav seal on the cover of the last booklet. Opening it, she stared at her own picture. *Thanks be to God, I am free!* She kissed her passport and slipped it into the pocket of her robe. *He must not know.*

With shaking hands, she grabbed the envelope, shoved his passport and the bankbook inside, and set the envelope back in the safe. She closed the safe and spun the tumblers. Shut the small door and locked it. Put the key on the ledge in the dresser and pushed the dresser back in place.

Taking a deep breath, she tightened the sash of her robe. *I am Gypsy. And I am free.*

"Slovika?"

Gasping, she spun around.

"Why you in my closet?" Donatello said with an odd expression. "You find what you are looking for?"

She stared at him. "I . . . I think I might find you here."

"I know." He looked deeply into her eyes.

She put her hand over her pocket. "You know?" she said, her voice trembling.

"Sì." He gripped her arm. "Of course I know. Is evident, you wish as much as I, to be, how you say it? Riuniti . . . together."

She blinked several times. "Uh, yes," she stammered. "Yes, is true. I wish to be together."

He lowered his eyes and smiled. "I know you no can be angry forever," he said, then kissed her neck and ran his fingers through her hair.

"You wish me to forgive?"

"Sì, Slovika, of course. Amore mio. I love you."

"Me?"

"Why you say as if it is sorpresa, uh, surprise? I love you since the day first I see you."

"If you love me, why . . ."

He put his fingertips to her lips. "No question," he said, leading her out of the closet, into the bedroom. Stopping beside the bed, he pulled her close and stared into her eyes. "That we are apart, is not right. As the scripture say, 'Come into my garden, my sister, my bride.'" He ran his fingers through her hair again, then slipped the robe off her shoulders. "'And we drink our fill of love until morning light.'"

84

STEVEN STIRRED INTO half-consciousness. The last recollections of a dream slipped into the ether, replaced by the sounds of his mother in the kitchen, starting the day. Turning, he brushed his face on the pillow. "Ow," he whispered, putting his hand to the sore spot on his cheek. *Shara sure nailed me.*

He reached for her.

"Don't," she muttered, pushing his hand away.

It might be summer outside, but it's winter in here. He sighed. *And it doesn't seem like it'll thaw out anytime soon.*

Pauline sat on the front porch, sipping a cup of tea while looking past the garden to the rugged peaks of the Sierras. She took a deep breath of morning air. *Mmmm, the smell of summer.*

Wayward spray from a lazy sprinkler hitting the driveway gave off the scent of cool water on hot gravel. A riot of red, peach, and pink blooms on a Joseph's Coat rose climbing over a trellis, added a fragrance redolent of cloves.

Shara came out. The screen door creaked as it closed behind her.

"You're up early," Pauline said.

Shara jumped. "I didn't know you were out here."

Pauline set her cup on a nearby table. "Come, sit down," she said, motioning to a chair.

"I don't want to," Shara said with a frown.

"Honey, what's wrong?"

"Everything. I'm sick of everything." Tears spilled down her cheeks. She wiped them away with the back of her hand, then slumped into the chair.

Pauline pulled a tissue from a pocket in her house dress and passed it to her.

Shara blew her nose and another flood came. "My life is such a drag. I wish I could die."

"You can't mean that. You have so much to live for. You're young and beautiful. And you have a husband and son who love you."

"Husband." Shara shook her head. "I don't know why we got married. We're not even close to being in the same head space anymore."

"What?"

"It's just a saying. It means, like, not having anything in common. I feel like I'm going crazy, and if I stay here much longer I'll drive everyone else crazy too."

"But Steven and Donny need you."

"No, Pauline, they don't. Steven is home, and he has you, and he has Buck."

"What about Donny?"

"His name is not Donny. I keep telling everyone that. It's Donovan. Don-o-van." She rubbed her temples. "He needs you. He always needed someone like you. I told Steven when I was pregnant, I didn't know how to be a mother."

"But Shara . . ."

"No, Pauline. I'm the one who wasn't there, who left him alone while his father was passed out on the floor. I'm the one who let him run around in dirty diapers. And I'm the one who never even noticed he had lice in his hair! Donovan doesn't need me for anything."

"Shara, as much as I hate to admit this about my own son, Steven is equally responsible. For all of it."

Shara shook her head and twisted the tissue into a knot. "I'm Donovan's mother and that makes me more responsible."

"In whose eyes?"

"In the eyes of The Blessed Virgin, or God, or somebody." Shara looked away. "Or maybe just my own eyes . . ." Her voice trailed off to a whisper.

"But you can't leave." Pauline put her hand on Shara's shoulder. "Think how Steven and Donovan will feel. Think how you'll feel."

Shara brushed her hand away. "I'll feel fine. Steven will feel fine. And Donovan will feel like I did when my mother left me. He'll feel like he's better off." She stared blankly at Pauline a moment, then looked away. "I don't want to talk about it anymore."

Pauline sighed. "Well, I should go start breakfast." She stood and watched Shara a moment, then picked up her cup and went inside.

Shara drew her knees to her chest. Hearing the crunch of gravel on the driveway, she looked up. Buck stopped at a faucet near the porch and washed his hands, then wiped them on his overalls. His boots echoed on the porch as he sauntered up the steps. "Something wrong?"

Shara shook her head.

"Mind if I sit down?"

"They're your chairs."

"Yeah, well, just being polite." He sat down, then leaned forward and rested his elbows on his knees. "Is there something you want to talk about? Steven says I need to learn how to listen."

Shara looked up at him. "I don't know what to say."

"Quite a pair. You don't know what to say, and I don't know how to listen." He sat back. "Let me guess. Nothing turned out the way you hoped it would. You're stuck out in the middle of nowhere with a kid you didn't plan on, a husband who could be crippled for life, and his parents who are old as the hills. Does that about cover it?"

She shrugged, then wadded what was left of the tissue into a ball. "I'm not sure I can handle being married to someone in a wheelchair."

"But, you didn't mind being the girlfriend of a drug addict."

Shara looked up at him. "You said you wanted to listen, and now you're laying a guilt-trip on me." She stared out over the garden. "I think Steven and Donovan will be better off without me."

"Why do you say that?"

"I'm sure Steven told you about me. What kind of a person I am."

"He's told me some."

"Well?"

Buck paused. "Doesn't seem like you did anything wrong. You couldn't help what happened to you."

Shara's lips trembled. A single tear fell onto her hand. She wiped it away, then dabbed at her eyes with the wadded tissue. "Most of the time I feel like . . ."

"Like what?"

"Garbage. A throw-away. A piece of trash. Like a stray cat that's always getting picked up by strangers."

Buck sighed. "Shara, now you have people in your life who love you. You can walk away from the past. Just let it go. People do it all the time."

"Some people call that running away."

"I don't care what they call it. You don't have to live chained to the past. Unless you want to."

"Is that what you did?"

His eyes narrowed. "In some ways, yes."

She slumped further in the chair. "I don't know what I want."

Buck paused. "Well, then, like Steven said, maybe you'll have to leave to find out you really wanted to stay."

Shara stared at him. "What? Why would he say that? It's like he wants me to go."

"He married you and brought you here because he wanted to. I don't think he's changed his mind."

"What if I changed mine?"

"Then, like he said, maybe you won't know that until after you've gone. But on the other hand, sometimes when you leave something behind, there is no going back." Buck stood and patted her shoulder. "Just something to think about."

85

DONATELLO STARED AT his reflection in a mirror above the marble sink in the master bathroom. *Perhaps I am wrong about this man, Parker.* He looked at his crucifix. *I want to be free. Free from popes, bishops and cardinals. And saints who stare down from stained glass windows. And from the Blessed Virgin, and Jesus dying, always dying, from his broken, bleeding heart.* He switched off the light and went into the bedroom where Slovika was sleeping.

A cool morning breeze came in through the open window as he sat on the edge of the bed. "Slovika," he whispered. "You are awake?"

No answer.

He rested his hand lightly on her shoulder. "Slovika..."

She stirred in her sleep and looked blearily up at him.

"Buongiorno, amore mio." He brushed her hair from her face. "The morning, it is beautiful, no?"

She rubbed her eyes and looked out the window. "Yes. You wake me to tell me this?"

Donatello cleared his throat. "I want you go with me..."

Her eyes narrowed. "Where?"

"To Big Sur."

She pulled the sheet tight around her. "Who is this, Bick Sir?"

"A town by the ocean. A little way south."

"Why we go there?"

"Deborah -- "

Slovika sat upright. "Deborah! I no want go anywhere with the LA devil woman."

"No, no, no," he said, waving as if to erase her words. "We all go. Deborah, her husband . . . me . . . you. She invite us to party where we will find free . . . uh, freedom."

Slovika's expression softened. "Freedom?"

"Sì. At grande, uh, big party."

She sat up. "At this party, there will be dancing?"

He shrugged. "I no know for sure, but maybe. So, you come with me?"

"For how long do we go?"

"One night. Maybe two."

She paused. "Yes, I will go."

"Then, hurry. We must pack."

Leaning on the Mustang, Bob took a long drag off a Lucky Strike. "'The Bounty Killer's' got a real great place," he said, looking around. "Nice room -- even though we had to stay together. And Lupe made a damn good breakfast. You should learn to cook like that."

"Oh, sure. Just call me June Cleaver." She drummed her fingers on the hood of the car. "Where are they? They're taking *for-ever*. The whole Convergence will be over before we even get going." She turned and stared at Bob. "Do you always have to smoke? It's like, no matter what's happening, you have to smoke. The whole world could be ending, and you'd make everyone wait for you to light a cigarette before they blew it up."

Bob took another drag, and held up the butt. "Spoken like a true ex-smoker."

"You could be an ex-smoker too, if you would listen to Parker. But no . . . you had to insult him."

"Deb, I wouldn't listen to anything that beef-brain said, no matter what it was, just on principle." He stubbed the cigarette out on the sole of his boot, then flicked the butt into the grass alongside driveway.

She frowned. "That's how forest fires start."

"Don't worry, I put it out," he muttered, blowing a plume of smoke out his nose. "And we ain't in a forest, are we?"

Deborah shook her head. "I swear, you could get a job with a ventriloquist."

"Quoting Parker... practice patience, patience practice," Bob said in a sing-song tone, wiggling his fingers as if conjuring a ghost.

She threw her hands into the air. "Why is there always this annoying voice-over following me around all the time? Why didn't you go with your groupie girlfriend to San Francisco?"

"Because you always expect the annoying voice-over to pay for everything. Besides, that was the deal -- I pay your way to the party and I tag along. And I rent the car and drive it up to 'The Bounty Killer's' vineyard."

"But I didn't know you were going to rent a Mustang. I thought you'd rent a dumb sedan. I want to drive too," she said, sliding into the driver's seat and pretending to spin the steering wheel. "Come on, Bob. Don't be a creep..."

"Oh alright. Quit bitchin'."

Just then, Slovika came out of the mansion. Wearing a short gathered skirt with a blouse slung below her bare olive shoulders, she carried a purse and small overnight bag.

Bob whistled and tipped his battered cowboy hat. "Mornin' Miss," he said as she came toward the car. "I think we met in LA."

"Don't lay it on so thick, Bob. Haven't you heard, chivalry is dead?"

"Not in my neck of the woods, and not when a gal's as easy on the eyes as she is. I'll put that in for ya," he said, taking Slovika's bag and swinging it into the trunk. "Guess you an me are in the same fix -- ridin' in the back like kids goin' on vacation with the folks," he added, pulling the seat forward. "It'll be tight, but we'll fit."

"We sit in back?" she asked.

"Yep."

"We will find freedom?"

"Well, uh, I don't know about that," he said as she climbed into the back seat.

Deborah glanced at her in the rearview mirror. "You'll love Parker."

Slovika looked up. "Who? Who is this, Parker?"
Deborah glared at Bob.
"Don't worry. I ain't sayin' nothin'," he muttered.
Just then, Donatello came out, wearing tight velvet pants, snakeskin boots, and a pale silk shirt. He lugged a suitcase stuffed so full it strained the latches.
"What the . . ." Bob muttered, pushing back his hat and rubbing his forehead.
Donatello dropped the suitcase near the trunk.
"What on earth?" Deborah got out. "What are you wearing? We're not going to The Oscars. And why are you bringing all that?" she said, motioning to the suitcase.
"You say it is party. We stay one day, maybe two," he replied. "You never know. La fortuna favorisce il preparato."
Deborah and Bob looked blankly at him.
"Uh, fortune, it favor the prepared."
Deborah frowned. "How are we going to get *that* in the trunk?"
"It'll take some wrestlin', but it'll fit," Bob replied.
"Then wrestle it so we can get going."
Bob re-arranged the luggage, slammed the trunk closed, and climbed in back beside Slovika.
Donatello got in on the passenger side, and Deborah dropped onto the driver's seat. She turned on the ignition, shoved the Mustang in gear, and gunned the engine. Switching on the radio, Jefferson Airplane's 'White Rabbit' flared from the speakers. "Finally! We're off to the 'Summer Solstice Cosmic Convergence.'"
Bob laughed. "Get ready for blast-off, daddy-o!"

86

AS STEVEN PAGED through Parker's book, Donny repeatedly smashed GI Joe headfirst into a cushion on one end of the couch, and Tailor slept belly-up on the other.

"Don-ny, if you k-eep d-oing that his head w-ill c-ome off," Steven said. He turned a few more pages, then set the book on a nearby table. "B-unch of BS," he muttered.

He looked up as a battered Volkswagen van pulled into the driveway. Painted flaming orange, swirling magenta, metallic silver, and day-glo green, it sputtered, coughed, and backfired before the engine died. Tailor woke. He fell off the couch and scrambled to the front door, barking.

"W-ho the . . ."

A woman got out. She tugged on the bottom of her excruciatingly short cut-offs and tightened her halter-top. Strutting in a pair of multi-colored cowboy boots, she looked around.

Steven sighed. *Roxanne.*

The back door slammed. Shara ran across the driveway wearing her lace tunic and carrying a duffle bag. Her eyes were outlined in black, and her neck dripped with jewelry.

His throat tightened into a knot. *She's leaving.* "C-ome on, Don-ny, let's go p-lay in the b-edroom."

Donny looked up. "Why?"

Steven turned the wheelchair toward the hallway. "L-et's t-ake GI J-oe and go p-lay," he said, then rolled down the hall with Donny following along. Donny flopped onto the bed as Steven maneuvered the wheelchair into the room. Turning to close the door he saw the open closet. He sank in his chair. *Empty hangers where her clothes used to be.*

He wheeled alongside the bed. Shara's wedding ring sat on a bedside table. Tears pooled in his eyes.

Donny bent GI Joe's arms and legs backwards, and with a whistling sound, dropped him like a bomb off the side of the bed. He looked up. "Wha's da matter, Daddy?"

Steven wiped his eyes with the back of his hand. "N-othing. You s-tay here and p-lay. I'll be b-ack in a min-ute."

"Why, that's Roxanne," Pauline said, drying her hands on a dishtowel as she looked out the kitchen window.

Buck dropped the newspaper on the table, got up, and stood beside her. "That's Roxanne alright."

"Then Shara-is leaving."

"Looks like it."

"I can't believe it," Pauline said. "I don't understand how she can just leave. I think this is going to break my heart."

"I'll tell you what I'd like to break -- both her legs. Or, plant my fist on her jaw hard enough that, hopefully, it'd dislodge several of her teeth."

"Honestly, Buck. Sometimes you say the most awful things."

"Well, I would." He sighed. "Oh hell. What I'd really like to do is turn her over my knee and blister her backside."

"I don't think it would do any good. She's so mixed up, she barely knows what day it is."

"Might make me feel better, though. I bet Roxanne's behind all of it. I think I'm going out there and give her a piece of my mind."

"Buck! Don't you dare. Steven doesn't want us to interfere."

"I'm not doing it for Steven. I'm doing it for me. Criminy sakes. I'm not gonna sit by and watch Roxanne wreck havoc in my family without her hearing my two cents."

"But what if -- "

"Don't worry, I'm not gonna lose my temper."

"Oh, I'm not worried you'll lose it. I'm pretty sure you're gonna find it."

Buck tromped to the door, flung it open and stomped out.

Oh dear," Pauline muttered as as the screen slammed behind him.

"Oh, oh," Roxanne said. "Don't look now, but there's an awkward situation approaching."

Shara's eyes widened. "Roxieee . . ."

"Don't worry. I'll handle it," Roxanne said crossing her arms.

"That's what I'm afraid of."

Buck stopped in front of them. "Who said you could come onto my property?"

Roxanne cocked her head and glared at him, then rolled her eyes, and turned away.

"Hey! I'm talking to you." He clamped his hand on her arm and spun her around. "Look here, missy. You're not gonna ignore me on my property and get away with it."

She jerked her arm out of his grasp. "Touch me again and I'll call the cops. Shara saw how you practically tried to rape me."

Shara's jaw dropped. "Roxie!"

"What!" Buck snapped.

"Besides that, you don't really own this property, you pig."

He rolled his hands into fists. "What do you mean I don't own this land? I most certainly do. When the cops get here and haul you off, that'll prove it. And I wouldn't rape you if you were the last woman on earth!"

Roxanne planted her hands on her hips. "You can't really own land because it's part of the earth, and the earth is part of the universe. And you don't own the universe. Besides, I could care less about you and your stupid property. I'm only here to get Shara."

"Yeah well, she's Steven's wife now."

"Just because he talked her into getting married, it doesn't mean he owns her. She can leave if she wants to."

"I'm pretty sure she wouldn't want to, without a lot of coaxing from you."

Roxanne stepped forward.

Shara's eyes grew wider. "Roxeee..."

Roxanne pointed at Buck. "Listen here, geezer, Shara wants to go with me. She called and asked me to rescue her from this dump. You can keep your pathetic cripple, Steven, and your snotty-brat grandkid, but Shara belongs with me," she said, pointing at her chest with her thumb. "You can't hold her prisoner."

Buck crossed his arms. "You know, that's pretty funny," he replied with a slight laugh. "According to you, I don't own this property, and Shara doesn't belong with her husband, but she belongs with you. I've got to hand it to you, that's an original load of bull."

"I wouldn't expect a dinosaur like you to understand."

"Well then, I wish you'd take her and get the hell outta here," Buck said, jerking his head in the direction of the road.

Just then, the gravel crunched behind him.

Steven wheeled toward them. He stopped beside Buck and looked up at Shara. "W-eren't you e-ven go-ing to say g-ood-bye?"

She looked away.

Steven watched her a moment. "F-orget it D-ad. Sh-ara's old e-nough to m-ake up her own m-ind. W-e've al-ready said all that n-eeds to be said."

Just then, Donny came running from behind. "Mommy! Woxie!" he called with a wide grin.

"C-ome h-ere." Steven grabbed his arm. "I t-old you to s-tay in the bed-room."

"But Mommy, and Woxie..." Donny said, glancing from Shara, to Roxanne, then back at Steven.

"C-ome on," Steven said.

"But, Mommy..."

"I said c-ome on."

Donny looked at Shara again, then scrambled onto Steven's lap. Steven turned the chair around and wheeled back toward the house.

    Buck crossed his arms. "I'm sure you two'll be real happy together, living in your own private universe, where there are no pathetic cripples or snotty-brat kids. You're perfect for each other." He picked up Shara's duffle bag and threw it at her feet. "Don't forget your crap."

87

ROXANNE PULLED THE Volkswagen van out of the Harpers driveway, onto the road. "Wow, what a trip!"

Shara propped her feet on the dashboard, and nervously tapped her fingers on the armrest to Steppenwolf's 'Born to be Wild' crackling from the radio. She watched the sun dancing on a collection of rosaries hanging from the rearview mirror.

Roxanne rose off the seat and tugged on her cut-offs. "I thought Steven's dad was gonna punch me out. Didn't seem like he was real sad you were going. And Steven didn't either. What a pair of jerks. It's like they were actually hoping you'd go."

Shara shrugged, then turned to the window.

Roxanne looked over at her. "Hey, don't get all bummed-out after I came way out in the middle of nowhere to rescue you. We're going to a party, remember? So, where'd you get the lace outfit?"

Shara sighed. "Vickie. I wore it to my wedding."

"Oh," Roxanne replied. "So, you dig the van?"

"It's alright, but it's kind of beat up. Not to mention the Flower Power daisies," Shara said, pointing to faded stickers attempting to hide cracks in the dash board.

"Bob's band used to tour in it before they were famous. It's got a mattress in back and everything. Hey, check out the posters. I might buy it, but he'd probably give it to me if I asked him."

"Buy it?" Shara asked with a skeptical stare. She turned in her seat and parted the strands of beads acting as a curtain. The roof in back was papered with psychedelic handbills and posters from the Fillmore and Avalon, and the mattress spread with yards of batik fabric. "Where would you get the money?"

"First and last, plus deposit."

"What?"

"I leased my mom's house to a friend of Vince and Vickie's -- a visiting professor. She gave me the first month's rent, last month's rent, and a deposit. Vince and Vickie took care of the details. Check it out." Roxanne pulled a brown and white cowhide shoulder bag from behind her seat. "Like it?"

Shara frowned. "Cow fur? Where did you get a cow fur purse?" she asked, opening the bag and staring at a thick roll of bills.

"That's cowhide. Bob bought it for his soon-to-be ex, but she didn't want it. So he gave it to me."

"So, now what are we gonna do? We won't have anywhere to stay."

Roxanne grinned. "Bum around and see where life takes us."

"For how long?"

"Six months to start -- that's how long the lease is -- then just see what happens."

"See what happens?"

"*Sha-ra*, you know we'll have places to stay. Heck, I just got back from staying at Bob's place in LA. Maybe we'll go back down there, or . . . who knows, but whatever, it'll be fun."

"Vickie said I could stay with her if I ever need a place to crash," Shara added. "Maybe she'll let you stay there too."

"Speaking of Vickie, let me see your ring. She told me Steven gave you a honkin' rock."

"I left it there," Shara said.

Roxanne turned. "So, does that mean you're not going back?"

"No . . . I don't know. Maybe I can't go back, after what just happened."

"Hey, did you hear? They're going on a sabbatical to a kibbutz in Israel."

"Who?"

"Vince and Vickie. They're leasing out their house for six months too. That's where I got the idea."

"What's a sabbatical?"

"Sorta like a long working vacation."

"Oh. What's a kib-butch?"

"That's *kib-butz*. It's like a commune, only Jewish."

"Just like that? They're going to Israel for six months? Good thing I didn't believe her," Shara said, bouncing her head to the music.

"Who? Vickie?"

"Yeah. She said she wanted to be the mom I never had. And anytime I needed anything, she'd be there for me. Actually, she's more like the mom I *did* have." Shara paused. "Hey, Roxie, do you ever miss your mom?"

"Sure. Lots. How 'bout you?"

"She was such a loser, I try not to. I keep telling myself I'm better off, but I still miss her. Guess I can't help it."

"What made you think of that?"

"Um, I don't know. Talking about Vickie, I guess. So, is Bob meeting us at the party?"

"Yeah. He said he'll find us."

"He's turning you into a real cowgirl," Shara said, staring at her boots.

"Yep. He's even naming his motorcycle after me. He said he's gonna have my name painted on the gas tank."

Shara's eyes widened. "Wow, Roxie. That's far-out. It sounds like you're getting really super-serious."

"Yeah, I guess we kinda are."

"That's great. I'm practically breaking up with Steven, and now you're practically shacking up with Bob."

"Don't worry. Whatever happens, you and I will still be tight. We'll always be best friends." Roxanne reached over to switch the radio station.

"Don't change it," Shara said. "I like that song."

"*Walk Away Rene*? You can't be serious. It's so, bubble-gummy."

"I don't care. I like it."

Roxanne shook her head. "Just be glad I rescued you when I did. If you would've stayed there any longer, no one would recognize you. You would've turned into a complete cube. Speaking of being square, do you still think you're Catholic?"

"Everybody says if I was, I'd know. So, I guess I'm not. How about Bob -- all those rosaries," Shara said, motioning to the rearview mirror.

"Who knows what that's all about. Anyway, I'm glad you're not Catholic 'cause it's the summer after the summer of love. That means it's the summer of . . . well, I don't know. But it's like everyone is playing a huge game of musical chairs, and now you're free to play along!"

Shara sank in the seat and turned back to the window. She watched rows of crops passing by a stretch of farmland and tapped her fingers in time with the radio, *Don't walk away Renee . . .*

I can still see the hurt in their eyes . . . She bit her lip to stop the trembling.

The summer after the summer of love and I'm finally free.
Free.
Free.
Free.
Why don't I feel free?

88

DONATELLO STARED OUT the car window, watching the city of San Francisco and the neighboring towns passing by. He tapped his splinted fingertips on the armrest to the surf music blaring from the radio. *Talking, talking, always talking. And always about Parker.* He looked over at Deborah. "How far it is? We drive, drive, drive, and never get there."

She shook her head. "We haven't been on the road *that* long. What's your problem?"

"Correction," Bob chimed from the back seat. "We've been on this cattle drive for close to two hours and we just got off the Golden Gate Bridge."

Deborah sighed. "That's just not true Bob, relax. We're practically to Redwood City. Besides, it's a beautiful day."

Donatello squirmed in his seat. "The suitcase, it have more room than this. And you drive like una lumaca . . . uh, like escargot," he said with an irritable wave.

"Oh, hold on to your shorts."

"What is this shorts?"

"She means underwear, hoss," Bob replied.

Donatello squinted his eyes. "Why she want me to hold my underwear? And what means hoss?"

Bob furrowed his brow. "Figure of speech. You can thank your lucky stars, you're in front. If you think it's like a suitcase up there, it's like a freakin' wallet back here." He bumped the back of Deborah's seat. "C'mon Deb, give it some gas. I feel like a tuna that's been shoved into a can a' sardines."

Deborah frowned into the rearview mirror. "I'm going the speed limit."

Bob bumped her seat again. "Pull over at Woodside."

"But, you said I could drive . . ."

"You drove. The deal was -- I pay for everything and you do what I say. Now, get off at Woodside so we can use the can, get a gnosh and somethin' ta drink at the Peanut Farm."

"The Peanut Farm?" She said, scrunching up her nose.

"Sure. It's a bitchin', old-timey beat-nik waterin' hole Carl turned me on to. Then we can go over Skyline Boulevard and hit Highway 1 after La Honda. Carl says it's a real cool drive. And if we wanted we could go to that nude beach at San Gregorio "

Deborah frowned into the rearview mirror. "Oh, alright but I'm not going to the beach." She pulled off the highway at the next exit, onto a rural road to a cross street, and turned into the parking lot of a low building that resembled a house. Except for the neon beer signs hanging in the windows and the billboard on the roof reading, "The Peanut Farm."

She turned off the ignition. "I *guess* we're here."

"Yep. This's it," Bob said as Donatello, Deborah, and Slovika piled out of the Mustang. "Y'all 're gonna love this place," he added, bounding ahead and opening the door.

A strata of smoke floated above the dimly-lit bar. The plank flooring bounced slightly as they went inside. Patrons turned and stared. A man wearing a black beret and a striped boat-neck t-shirt sat beside two weathered men in dirty jeans and overalls, while others slouched around tables. The man in the beret tossed a peanut shell over his shoulder, then all the patrons went back to cracking peanuts and drinking.

"Well, whadda ya think, Mr. Bounty Killer?" Bob asked with a wide smile. "Pretty cool, huh?"

Donatello's boots crunched on the spent shells. "This place, it is like barn. They act like animali," he said with a scowl, looking around the dark panelled space.

Bob put his hands on his hips. "Whadda ya mean?"

"Why they throw the peanut on the floor?"

"Ya mean the shells? Hell, that's part a' the charm. Don't ya get it? Peanut shells? Peanut Farm? Where else are ya gonna find bohemian beatniks drinkin' with buckaroo wranglers?" He shook his head. "Man, I thought, bein' 'The Bounty Killer,' y'all would be cooler than this."

A fresh salt breeze poured in through the open car window. Donatello stared at the steep, rocky coastline and azure waves below. He looked over at Bob behind the wheel. "The road, it curves, and curves, and nothing on either side. And, my stomach, it rolls from the Peanut Ranch."

"That's Peanut Farm. Whadda ya mean nothin' on either side? You got the whole dang Pacific Ocean out there," Bob said with a broad wave.

"For hours I see ocean, ocean, ocean. How much longer? You say it is quattro ore drive."

"That's if somebody woulda had their foot on the gas pedal," Bob said, nodding in Deborah's direction.

She crossed her arms. "Or, if we stayed on the freeway. Besides, we're practically there."

A short time later, Bob turned off the highway, onto a steep driveway, winding up a manzanita dotted hillside. Partway, they came to a parking lot. Rusting posts strung with heavy chain separated the parking area from a steep precipice that dropped off toward the ocean. Another chain blocked the driveway as it continued through a grove of wind-bent pines to a lodge surrounded by several cottages.

"Finally! We're here," Deborah gushed.

Slovika yawned and rubbed her eyes. "Where?"

"Orion, silly."

Donatello looked around. "No valet? No garage? Nothing?"

Deborah laughed. "This is where you park. Orion is on top of that hill."

He stared up at the bluff. "This ridicolo. Why we stop here? Why we don't go there?"

"Because Parker doesn't like cars."

"Too many spooky, materialistic vibes on cars," Bob said with another ghost-like finger wiggle. "Everything in his pain-in-the-ass life has a vibe attached to it."

Deborah rolled her eyes. "Bob, would you please shut up."

"What is this material vibe?" Donatello asked.

"It's like, you know . . . things. Worshipping things keeps you bound to the material world. So Parker doesn't like having a lot of things laying around."

"Why we don't drive the car up there, but don't worship it?"

"Boy's got a point." Bob got out and went to the rear of the car. He opened the trunk and pulled out his duffle bag.

Deborah got out and stretched. "It's not that far. You're not afraid of a little hike, are you? I'm soooo excited! This is going to be just *fa-bulous!*" She went to the trunk, took out her overnight case and hurried up the hill, leaving Donatello and Slovika sitting in the Mustang.

Who this Parker think he is?" he muttered.

"I no care who he think he is," Slovika said, sliding across the back seat, and squeezing out the driver's side. "And I no care who, the devil woman, she think he is. We drive forever and all she do is talk. And all she talk is Parker! Thanks be to God, finally I fall asleep!"

Slovika wound her hair into a knot and secured it with a barrette, then tied on a bright, flowered scarf. Stomping to the rear of the car, she pulled her bag from the trunk, and trudged up the hill after Bob and Deborah.

Donatello got out and watched as she disappeared into the grove of pines. The salt breeze clashed with motionless air heavy with the smell of roasting evergreens and arid earth.

He looked up the hill. *The driveway goes all the way to the sky.*

An engulfing silence surrounded him, and a sinking sensation came over him. Followed by a shimmering kaleidoscopic aura, and an electric buzzing. Chaos enveloped his mind, and the taste of metal flooded his mouth. He gripped the car door.

God help me, a seizure . . .

Several moments passed.

After a soaking flush of perspiration and a single crashing jolt in his head, the symptoms subsided.

Strange, there was no explosion.

He wiped the perspiration from his hands on his velvet pants. With a deep groan, he hoisted his bag out of the trunk. The oxblood leather banged against his thigh as he lugged the suitcase in the afternoon heat. *Lorenzo was right. Maybe I should not have come.* He stepped over the chain blocking the driveway and let the bag slide into the parched weeds beside the cracked asphalt. "Parker . . ." he said under his breath, rubbing his temples. "I am certain that I hate him."

89

FROM HIGH ATOP his new deck, Parker looked through the eyepiece of a brass telescope, and adjusted the lens, sharpening the focus. He watched a group of sea lions basking on the cliffs surrounding a narrow, craggy beach, and sea birds gliding, single file above the waves.

Gregg came from behind and cleared his throat. "Guests are arriving," he said, running his hands over the stubble of his hair. "Deborah, the gilded bird, brought two extra. Her husband and a young woman."

Parker frowned. "She brought that moronic cowboy who had the audacity to insult me to my face? My perception was that the night would be perfect. Exactly ninety-nine enlightened guests. The perfect number for such a cosmic event."

"Yes," Gregg said. "That was the perception."

"Now, the night is falling into chaos."

Gregg cleared his throat again.

Parker sighed. "What, Gregg? What is it you are trying so very hard not to tell me?"

"I'm told the invited guests have invited guests. And the uninvited guests have invited guests. People are wandering all over the grounds. The invitations were made into handbills and they are posted up and down the coast. Now there is no way to know how many are coming."

Parker slumped down on the deck. "Then my perception was wrong and the night will not be as I planned. How could this have happened?"

Gregg sat beside him. "Maybe the number was supposed to change, and the change was hidden within the circularity of fate."

"Maybe. But being god, why didn't I perceive it?"

"As you say in your book -- your most famous statement, 'The chaos created by unexpected events can be strokes of fate, leading to a transcendent outcome.'"

Parker sighed. "Why must everyone quote my book to me?"

"Well, your book is brilliant."

Parker nodded. "Yes. Of course, you're right. The change must have always been there, but hidden from me for some unknown purpose."

90

AT THE TOP of the hill, the cracked asphalt driveway leading to the Orion Institute turned to a crumbling cement walkway. It meandered past several stucco cottages, and the three-story timber-framed main house, to a courtyard paved with broken terracotta tile. In the center of the courtyard a circle of cinderblocks formed a planter filled with parched plants, dried weeds, and an ancient valley oak.

Deborah stood in the middle of the walkway, squinting into the sun, watching the rise. Bob stepped over the blocks, set his bag on a patch of weeds, and sat cross-legged in the arid shade of the oak.

Slovika came up the walk, dropped her bag, and sat on the edge of a cinderblock. "Is like oven," she said.

"I wonder what's keeping Donatello," Deborah said with a frown.

"Maybe he got cooked on his way up," Bob replied.

A few minutes later, Donatello trudged up the hill, lugging the suitcase as if he had a bad limp. Rivulets of sweat ran down his back, soaking his silk shirt. Pale and perspiring, he dropped the suitcase and slumped onto a cinderblock beside Slovika.

"It's about time," Deborah said, crossing her arms. "I thought we might have to go get you."

"Now, Mr. Bounty Killer, you're gettin' a taste a' what I been puttin' up with," Bob grumbled. "Hey, are you okay? You don't look so good."

Donatello wiped glistening beads of perspiration off his forehead with the back of his hand. "Sì. Fine."

Deborah picked up her bag. "Well then, come on." She started toward the house, then turned to Bob. "Are you coming?"

"Y'all go ahead. I don't wanna mess up Parker's vibes."

Cloaked in heavy drapes, the sightless ground-floor windows of the main house were stenciled with the symbols of the Orion Institute -- a hieroglyphic eye surrounded by a circle. And painted on the front door in psychedelic color, the surreal love-child of Vishnu and Lakshmi with two swirling eyes, and a third one painted around the knocker.

Deborah dropped the heavy knocker twice in rapid succession. She was about to drop it a third time when a gaunt young man with a shaved head opened the door. Bowing slightly, he stepped aside and motioned for them to enter.

Deborah traipsed in, Donatello swaggered after her, and Slovika hesitantly followed.

"Will you tell Parker we're here?" Deborah asked as the man closed the door behind them.

"He knows," the young man replied over the intricate droning of a sitar, played by a dark-skinned man in a white turban, sitting in a corner. He bowed, then disappeared through a doorway beneath the staircase at the far end of the room.

Donatello dropped his suitcase. The hollow sound echoed through the cavernous space, intruding on the hum of the sitar. He looked around the room. "It is, how you say, vacante. Like no one live here. You say this is party?"

"Shhhh!" she hissed. "Quit saying that. I keep telling you it's not a party. It's a gathering to celebrate the solstice. It's very spiritual, and very cosmic."

Donatello crossed his arms. "Why this, Parker, he is so comic?"

"Not comic. *Cos-mic.*"

Just then, a silhouette appeared in the doorway beneath the stairs.

Deborah looked up. "Parker!" she gushed, rushing to meet him.

The rustling of his pale Nehru-collared caftan accompanied the drone of the sitar as he appeared to glide into the room. "Don't touch me as I have not yet ascended," he said in an odd monotone. Then, as if he could not help himself, he laughed.

They stared blankly at him.

He raised an eyebrow. "I'm quoting scripture. Even god must *act* like god at times." He stopped in front of Donatello. "I am *that* I Am," he said, holding out his hand in a strangely affected pose, as if he expected Donatello to kiss it. "And, I am very glad you came." He paused, then, with a petulant sigh, dropped his hand. "You are mesmeric, yet so arrogant and unenlightened, it is almost unconscionable. I see the war between utter brilliance and stagnant mediocrity still rages within you."

Donatello turned to Deborah. "What he says?"

Shaking her head. "Oh, nothing."

"Now, what I say is nothing?" Parker said with a rancorous stare.

"No, it's just, he wouldn't understand," she replied.

Donatello waved around the room. "No other guest?"

Parker waved the comment away. "Why my guests are a concern to you, I can't imagine. The others I invited, have not yet arrived." He turned and stared at Slovika. "You were not invited. Yet here you are," he said in a poetic timbre, almost like a whisper. "Perhaps the change hidden from my perception is for you. Why have you come?"

She looked blankly back at him.

Parker brushed his fingertips over her cheek. "I see aged eyes staring out of a young face. Youth swallowed by sorrow. Yes. I recognize what it is that I see in your eyes. Pain. Too much pain for one so young. Caused by those who have used you like a pawn."

Donatello stepped forward. "She is my wife," he announced, with an arrogant wave.

"Oh?" Parker looked piteously at him a moment. He turned back to Slovika, his eyes seeming to bleed with sincerity. "Well, I am sorry. Because, though he is brilliant as the sun, he is also pathetically unenlightened. But, you already know this." He took her hand. "You will all stay here, in the main house with me tonight. Someone will take your things to your rooms. Rooms chosen to enhance your experience of enlightenment. Come, I have something to show you," he said, taking Donatello's arm.

Donatello pushed his hand away.

"Suit yourself," Parker said with a sharp exhale, his eyes flashing like polished daggers.

Two skeletal men with shaved heads, wearing caftans similar to Parker's, came up the the path. They stopped and stared at Bob sitting in the planter, smoking.

"I'm surprised Parker would invite tobacco-consuming riff-raff," one man said with a smirk.

"Apparently fresh from Texas," the other said, pointing to Bob's tattoo. "Tell me, *pardner*, are you a real cowboy?"

Bob pushed his cowboy hat back. "Yeah," he replied with a guttural growl. "I'm into ropes."

The men looked at each other, then back at Bob.

"Ooooo," the first man said. "Sounds intriguing."

"Yeah, well, maybe some other time." Bob stood and brushed off the back of his jeans. "Now, if ya'll hyper-educated, pseudo-intellectuals will excuse me, it's gettin' kinda stuffy out here. I need some fresh air." He picked up his duffle bag, stepped out of the planter and wandered toward the main house. "Couple a' tweaked dweebs," he muttered under his breath.

He noticed an over-grown path near a rusty propane tank a short distance from the main house. *Wonder where that goes . . .* He went over and shoved his bag behind the tank, and followed the path down the hill into the scrub brush. The papery vibrato of grasshopper wings punctuated the hot afternoon stillness as they scuttled out of his way.

Music . . .

Stalking the faint chords of an acoustic guitar, he came to a clearing surrounded by Manzanita bushes, poison oak, and wind-bent pines. Sitting among a group of ragged transients, a young musician wearing black sunglasses strummed a mournful folk song. Some sang along, others sunbathed in the buff on a blanket spread over a weathered picnic table and the benches, and still others set up camp among the trees.

Bob hooked his thumbs in the pockets of his jeans. *There's gotta be more than the cosmic ninety-nine wanderin' around already.*

The guitarist looked up. "Hey, you're . . ." He motioned to the others. "Hey, everybody, he's the drummer for The Time Season Band! He's, like, the best drummer ever!"

Bob smiled. "That be me."

The young musician put down his guitar, got up, and bounded toward him. "They call me Davey Shades 'cause I wear 'em all the time," he said, lowering his sunglasses and shaking Bob's hand. "Far-out! I didn't know you guys are playing tonight." He gathered his long, tangled hair into a ponytail, then let it go.

"We're not -- playin' I mean," Bob said with a shrug.

The guitarist's shoulders drooped. "Oh. Too bad. Would've been cool to play with you guys."

Bob looked around the clearing. "Hey, Davey, how come y'all are hangin' out down here like a bunch a' refugees?"

"We're crashing the party. Up at the Institute, they said you had to have an invite." The young musician pulled a crumpled handbill from a pocket in his threadbare jeans. He smoothed it over his thigh, then passed it to Bob. "I got this in a headshop in The Haight, but they said it doesn't count. Should be interesting though, because these handbills are plastered all up and down the coast. I heard they're way up by Crescent City, down past LA, and over by Sacramento."

Wonder how many extras ol' Walrus printed up. "No kiddin'," Bob said, passing it back to him. "Guaran-damn-teed, tonight's gonna be a whistlin' good trip."

"Yeah. No kidding. Everybody I talked to is coming." The guitarist shoved the handbill back in his pocket. "Sounded like the coolest gig of the summer, so I hitched on down." He motioned to the people lounging in the shade and sunbathing around the picnic table. "Some of them were crashing up in the hills and they heard about it through the grapevine. And some hitchhiked from wherever, like me. Anyway, the real party's gonna be down here in the gulch, man. That's what we're calling it -- the gulch."

Bob nodded. "Prob'ly so. There's a bunch a' hyper-spiritual jerks up at the main house. They're nuttier 'n squirrel turds. Which in my opinion, don't bode well for a good time."

"We got plenty of weed and we panhandled enough for a kegger. Wanna join us?" Davey asked. "It'll be a blast."

Bob looked around the clearing. "Maybe. I'm waitin' on a lady."

The young guitarist sighed and shook his head. "Who isn't?"

"Speaking of ladies, better go see if she showed up yet." Bob tipped his hat and turned back to the trail.

91

DONATELLO FOLLOWED PARKER, Deborah, and Slovika up a staircase to a second floor landing, then up another flight of stairs to a narrow hallway. Halfway down the hall, Parker stopped at a doorway crudely cut between two windows, opened the door, and led them out onto his new deck. The structure rocked slightly with their footsteps.

He stalked to the center and turned with his arms outstretched across a view that extended from the treetops, over the ocean, to the horizon. "My new balcony," he announced as a gust of wind caught the sleeves of his caftan and whipped them like flags.

"Oh, wow! It's beautiful!" Deborah gushed, mirroring his actions.

"It was finished just in time for the solstice. Here, on this most cosmic of nights, we will watch the sun go down together."

Donatello went to the perimeter of the deck. Leaning against the rail, he stared at the striking color of the freshly sawn redwood, then down at the waves breaking on the rocks below. *So strange. Many of the things he does, she does also. Where does she end and he begins? Is it me she wants? Or is it Parker?*

Slovika stood to one side of the doorway, pressed against the wall as if she was nailed there. *How does this god-man know my thoughts? And how does he see inside Donatello?*

Parker came and took her hand. "Don't be afraid." He slipped her purse off her shoulder and set it on the deck. Lifting her chin with his fingertip, he looked into her eyes and bound them with the intensity of his stare.

Helpless to look away, tears spilled down her cheeks.

"I see memories . . . painful memories," he said slowly and hypnotically, as if he had drifted into a trance. "Yes. So very, very painful. The universe within can be such an empty, tragic place. Like fire, it burns and tortures, yet it can also purify. But by allowing the watcher . . ." He touched his chest to indicate that he was the watcher. "By allowing the heart of the watcher, the one who knows your pain to come into that bitter, lonely agony you can survive the fire."

A look of concern clouded her eyes.

He smiled. "Don't worry, your pain won't harm me. It will only magnify the heart of the watcher within me."

Just then, footsteps echoed behind them.

Deborah tapped his shoulder. "Parker?"

His stare wavered. Slovika looked away and rushed past him.

Parker took a long breath, then turned. His pale eyes glistened. "What, Deborah. What was so very, very important, that in all the vastness of eternity, it could not have waited one more moment? I needed just one more moment to begin the resurrection of her tortured, dying soul."

Standing at the far end of the deck near the telescope, Slovika gripped the rail. He came and stood beside her. Her peasant top slipped off her shoulder. He slid it back in place, then rested his hand over hers. "You have nothing to fear. I won't hurt you."

She turned to him. He looked at her a moment and smiled, then slid her scarf off and unclipped the barrette. Holding the scarf up in the wind, he let it go.

"My scarf!" she cried, grasping for the fluttering square of fabric as it whirled away. She stared in disbelief. "Why you do this?"

He ran his hand through her hair. "You are so much more beautiful without it," he said as a gust whipped her hair like a banner. "Now it is free. As free as you can be."

She looked up at him, her lips trembling.

"It was only a piece of cloth," he said with a disbelieving stare.

"No, my mother, she gave to me when I am a child. It is all I have left of her."

"But don't you have her in your heart?"

Slovika shook her head. "No. Now it is gone."

"It was fabric. It had no soul. It could not love you or hold you or set you free." Parker waved across the expansive view. Light passing through the diamond on his little finger fractured into tiny, glinting rainbows. "Like this ring. I would give it to you if you asked at the right space in time."

"You would give it to me?"

"Of course. It's only an object. Like your scarf, it has no soul." He stared intently at her. "Hmmm. Your eyes, a most unusual color, almost like gold. They are more beautiful than any ring." He rested his hand lightly over hers again. "And your name? What is it?"

"Slovika," she replied, her voice shaking.

"Slovika," he repeated. "Your name tells me you come from far, far away. Where?"

"Serbia."

"Serbia. Behind the iron curtain." He looked out over the ocean. "A barrier designed to separate people and from their lives, from themselves, from enlightenment." He turned back. "Yet here you are. How did you come to be here?"

"Donatello. He bought me."

"You mean he *brought* you," Parker corrected.

"No." She lowered her eyes. "My father, he sell me. And Donatello's father bought me as a gift. The match was made by a fortuneteller. It is our custom."

Incredulity and disgust flashed in Parker's eyes. "Oh. I see. And whose anachronistic custom is it to sell a woman like merchandise?"

"We are Gypsy. Sem Roma sam."

"What does that mean?"

Slovika looked up at him. "Sem Roma sam? Many people made into one. No matter our tribe. We are Roma after all." She looked away. "All over Europe, we are, how do I say it? Despise? Sometime I think this is why Donatello's father bought me." Her voice trailed off to a whisper. "So Donatello would have someone to despise."

She stared out over the ocean, and she was there again, waiting with her father near the walled city of Dubrovnik, high on a bluff overlooking the rocky coast of the Adriatic. The sky was gray, and the salt air so crisp it stung her face.

> *My wedding day. And I am given away for a price.* She turned to her father. "But I have not met the man."
>
> "He is from Italia. His father buys him a Gypsy bride to bring him luck."
>
> Tears filled her eyes. "But . . ."
>
> Her father rested his hands on her shoulders. "You don't understand," he said over the gusting of the wind. "He will take you to the west. And there, Slovika, my daughter, you can find your freedom."
>
> "But . . ."
>
> He smoothed her hair. "Slovika, you must trust me. It is better this way. Here there is only hatred and oppression. You will never be free."
>
> Stiffening her jaw, she willed the tears not to fall. "I have no choice?"
>
> Her father shook his head.
>
> "Then, my only hope -- " Her lips trembled. "He will not be old. Or poor. Or horrible. Or ugly."

Slovika shuddered. "On the day I am married, when first I see Donatello coming with a priest, I think I wander into a dream. But so quickly, the dream turned to a nightmare."

Parker took her hand. "A fortuneteller told Donatello's father to buy you?"

"Yes."

"Why? For what purpose?"
"To bring Donatello luck."
"Luck?" Parker said as if he couldn't comprehend the word.
"That is what the fortuneteller tell him. But I cannot even think of the real reason." She turned away. "Because the fortuneteller . . . she was my mother."
"Your mother?"
"I bring a good price. To my family, it was fortune. To Donatello's father? Next to nothing. And from the first, Donatello make it clear, this what I am worth to him. Next to nothing."
Parker took a long breath. "So that is the pain I saw in your eyes. And all the light within you has been shrouded by darkness. How old are you?"
"Twenty."
"And Donatello?"
"Thirty-three."
"How long have you been married?"
"Two year."
Parker ran his fingers through her hair again, then tucked a strand behind her ear. "Does he love you?"
Slovika shrugged.
"Do you love him?"
She shrugged again. "I want to."
"A starving woman will eat almost anything."
"I do not understand all the words, but I know they are true."
"Then why do you stay?" he asked.
"I don't know yet how I will leave, or where I will go." She stared down at the waves washing over the rocks. "Without him, I am alone in this country."
"If you like, you can stay here with me. I would never buy you, sell you, hurt you, or despise you." He took her hand. "Is there anyone you love?"
"I think my father and mother. But when they sell me, now I think maybe I love no one."
"Then, is there anything you love?"

"Dancing, I love. And freedom, I want."

Parker smiled. "Dancing. I don't know how to dance, but if I did, I would dance with you. Freedom. That I have in abundance. And I will share it with you." He turned to the ocean. "Look, it's fishing," he said, pointing to a pelican diving into the water. "Quick, look in the telescope."

She grabbed the instrument and peered into the eye-piece.

"It has a fish. Do you see it?"

She nodded. "Yes."

"And over there -- " he said, pointing to an otter rolling itself in seaweed. "Can you find it?"

She nodded again. "So many creatures," she said, smiling.

"Yes, so many creatures." He put his arm around her.

She let go of the telescope and sank into his embrace. *Fear... it all drifts away...*

Several minutes passed.

"Would you like an appetizer? Aperitif? Or antipasto before the party?" he asked with a smile.

She looked quizzically at him.

"Come, sit." Parker sat cross-legged on the deck and turned his back to the wind. He pulled a small brass box from a pocket in his caftan. Then took out a twig of marijuana wrapped with a silk thread.

She sat down beside him.

"Soon, all your pain will sink into the sea." He untied the thread and pulled off the tightly curled leaves. Taking a pack of rolling papers from the box, he wrapped the leaves in a paper, then ran his tongue over it. Striking a match on the deck, he lit the joint, took a long drag, then offered it to her. "Have some."

Slovika looked suspiciously at him. "I no know what this is."

"Go ahead. It will be like a dream, I promise," he said as wisps of smoke escaped from the sides of his mouth.

Slovika hesitated a moment, then took the joint and pulled the pungent smoke into her lungs.

"Now, hold your breath."

After a moment, she exhaled. He motioned for her to take another hit. Then another. She passed it back to him.

Several minutes passed. A strange humming sensation spread over her. *Indeed. It is true, I am caught in a dream...*

After taking another drag, he stubbed the joint out on the deck, put what was left in the brass box, and slipped the box back into his pocket. "The universe within you can be as free as you want it to be. Everything within you belongs to everyone and to no one at the same time."

Her eyelids sank. "I no understand," she said with a bleary smile.

Parker ran his fingers through her hair again. "No one can own you no matter what they say. Do you want freedom, or do you want Donatello?"

She shrugged. "I no know." Then laughed. "Maybe both?"

Parker stood, took her hand and helped her up. "Sometimes a man must see something slip away before he knows that he wants it," he said with a faraway stare.

"What does this mean?"

"Come, and I will show you."

Donatello looked up as Parker led Slovika back inside. "Deborah, where Parker takes her?"

She slipped her arm around his waist. "Who?"

"Parker. Where he takes Slovika?"

"How should I know? What difference does it make?"

Donatello stared at her. "Deborah, she is my wife."

"So?"

He whirled to face her. "Why you brought me here? Why you don't just be with Parker yourself? If it is as you say, he is love, and he is not like other men?"

"Well, he is love." She laughed. "And I do love him, but I also love you. He's not the only one who wanted you to come."

"What this means?" he asked, looking in the direction Parker and Slovika had gone.

"You and Parker feed different parts of me. He feeds my spirit and you feed -- " She followed the trajectory of his stare. "Hey, you're not even listening. *Do-na* . . . if you want to be free, then you have to let her go. You can't be free and hung up at the same time."

He searched her eyes. "Deborah, I bring Slovika to this country. Like a child, she know nothing of the world."

Deborah shook her head. "I bet she's not as innocent as you think. Besides, you don't own her."

Donatello threw his hands in the air. "What does this mean?"

"She needs love."

"Why you say this? She has me."

"Oh, Dona, don't be so . . ." Deborah sighed. "Parker is god and he is love. She needs love *and* she needs god."

"She already has god. An icon in a wood box. A painting of the Madonna e Bambino circondata da oro . . ." He snapped his fingers. "Uh, how you say, the Madonna and Child, a painting surround by gold. And another, Sara e Kali, the patron saint of her people, also a painting in a box. It is their custom."

Deborah crossed her arms. "Dona, it's not the same. No one can love a god in a wood box. She needs a god she can love. And, like I said, Parker is love."

"I know you no want believe this, Deborah, but Parker is not god. He is just man."

She leaned against the rail. "Maybe not actually god. But he is a form of god. Anyone who has any enlightenment at all can see it. Can't you?"

Donatello locked his gaze on Deborah, then made the sign of the cross over his chest. "No Deborah. Is like, how you say, like the new clothes of the emperor -- I no see it."

92

PARKER LED SLOVIKA down a hall to the far side of the house, up another flight of stairs, through a darkened bedroom, into a dressing room.

"Sit here," he said, motioning to a small bench upholstered in dark green velvet in front of a dressing table made of beveled mirrors. "I will be back in a minute."

Slovika sat down on the bench. As he closed the door, she stared into a tarnished mirror, hanging above the dressing table. *My head spins. I understand nothing of what this god-man says. Why did he bring me here?*

Moments later Parker returned. He closed the door, then stood behind her. "One of my disciples will bring refreshments," he said, resting his hands on her shoulders, looking at her in the mirror. "I often sit where you are sitting. Here, I entertain demons and speak into the mirror of god," he said, placing his hand on his chest to indicate he was speaking of himself as the mirror. "And I am changed into that image."

There was a light knock on the door.

"Come," Parker said.

Gregg entered, carrying a tray with a bottle of vodka and two small glasses. Parker motioned to the dressing table. Gregg set the tray down, bowed, and backed away, closing the door behind him.

"A private party," Parker said, smiling. "I assumed you might like vodka. Is that true?"

Slovika laughed. The buzzing in her head became a din as her reflection bounced from one mirrored surface to another in dizzying duplication. "Yes. But Donatello must not know. Because he is the only man I have been with, he think that in all things I am like the Virgin Mary." She put her finger to her lips. "Shhhh. You cannot tell him I am not. I even steal my passport so if I want, I can leave him."

Parker smiled and stepped from behind her, opened the bottle and poured the shimmering liquid over the ice. He passed a glass to her.

"Parker, I feel..."

"Enlightenment?" He drank the vodka in one swallow. "As if you are in a dream?" Standing behind her again, he looked intently into the eyes of her reflection. "You are here, in a place where many, many people would give anything to be. A place where they can be changed into the image that is found within the mirror of god. They cannot attain it. Yet here you are." He motioned to her glass. "Drink it."

I feel myself smiling. It is as Deborah said. He is like God, embracing me with his attention. She picked up her glass took a sip, then choked down the rest. Its effects washed over her like a warm rain.

"You are striking, yet, I sense there is a universe of ethereal, brilliant beauty within you that has yet to be revealed," he said slowly and hypnotically, combing his fingers through her hair. "The eternal, internal you. Do you see the beauty within me?"

Slovika shrugged. *I do not know. His words have no meaning.*

"You are naïve, it is true..." he said. "But will you, can you, give something to god in exchange for the pain that torments you? To release the beauty within?"

"Yes," she replied with a hazy stare. *I would give him anything.*

Parker took a pair of scissors from a drawer in the dressing table. He paused a moment. Then separated out a long chestnut lock and snipped it off. He set the scissors and the strand of hair on the table, and bent to embrace her. "It is that simple." He picked up the bottle and filled their glasses again. "Drink."

She took her glass and drank it.

He stared at her reflection. "Will you give me all that I need to set you free?"

"I will give you anything," she said, then emptied her glass in one swallow.

"Anything . . . everything . . . nothing. In the end it is all the same." A vacant, trance-like stare clouded his eyes. He gathered all the loose strands of her hair, picked up the scissors and violently sawed through them, leaving a jagged, lopsided mop no longer than her chin. "I call you into being, into the freedom of your new identity and your new name, Golden Light Dancing. Perhaps, the most exquisite entity I have ever created."

Slovika gasped as he let the hair fall from his hand.

"What's wrong?" he asked with a puzzled expression. "Your new name -- like you, it's simple, yet utterly brilliant. Golden, for the color of your eyes. Light, for your new enlightenment. And Dancing, because you love to dance."

"Why you do this to me?" she cried, grasping what was left of her hair.

"It's so elementary, I'm surprised that even you don't understand," he replied in an odd scolding tone. "If you choose to, you can leave all the pain that belonged to Slovika there," he added, pointing to the chestnut mound on the floor. "And stay here with me, embracing the freedom in your new eternally transcendent self . . . Golden Light Dancing."

93

BOB SAT ON a flat, sun-baked boulder overlooking the parking area, the driveway, and the highway below. Cars, vans, and pickups filled the parking lot, and both sides of the driveway were flanked with vehicles. He pushed back his cowboy hat and rubbed his forehead. *If Roxie don't hurry up, she'll have ta park in San Francisco.*

A scruffy couple walking with a load of camping gear and two young children, turned off the highway and started the uphill hike. Behind them, what appeared to be the migration of a tribe of hunter-gatherers. And in the distance, the faint rumble of engines.

"Bikers." Bob shook his head. "Now, for sure, tonight's gonna be hairy."

Minutes later, the procession of hikers scrambled to get out of the way as a motorcycle gang roared up the hill. The hikers resumed their uphill march as the bikers sandwiched their motorcycles into the few remaining spaces in the parking lot. A ramshackle school bus rambled up the hill, followed by a VW bug. The bus sputtered, then backfired, and the engine died.

What resembled a troupe of mimes and circus performers in day-glo costume piled out and started up the hill, leaving the bus partially blocking the driveway. The occupants of the bug and several cars behind did the same, leaving the driveway jammed with abandoned vehicles.

"Nobody's gettin' outta here 'til it's all over," Bob muttered, picking at the crumbling granite. "Roxie should'a been here by now. I'll give her five more minutes."

A group of giggling teenagers traipsed past. Followed by four blonde, windblown surf bums. Then, through the trees, Bob saw a brunette and a lanky young woman with wild red hair walking along the highway. "They made it."

"Hey! Roxie!" Bob called, standing on top of the rock waving as Roxanne and Shara came up the hill.

They ambled toward him, and dropped onto the boulder. "That was like climbing Mount Everest," Roxanne sputtered as another group of hikers passed.

Bob turned to Shara and tipped his hat. "Howdy, Miss. We met at that birthday bash in Berkeley. But you prob'ly don't remember. You were loaded as a mule headin' out on a ten-day haul."

She smiled. "Yeah, and I had the hangover to prove it."

"I was startin' to think ya'll weren't comin'. Where'd you park?"

"Down on the highway," Roxanne said, pointing over her shoulder with her thumb. "It was a five-hour drive, and I nearly got the crap beat outta me by a geezer."

"Huh?"

"It's a long story. So, where's the party?"

"You got your choice," Bob replied. "The get-down, get-funky kegger party in the gulch. Or the hyper-spiritual Cosmic Convergence up at the main house."

Roxanne turned to Shara. "How 'bout both?"

"Sure, Cosmic-Funk!"

94

ROXANNE AND SHARA followed Bob down into the gulch. "Looks like there's already been plenty of get-down, get-funky going on," Roxanne said as they came to the clearing.

Unconscious bodies were strewn alongside a group dancing to acoustic guitars and bongo drums. The motorcycle gang had commandeered the keg. A burly biker, wearing a studded black leather vest and black chaps over his jeans, filled paper cups for a queue of partiers. Still sporting his sunglasses, Davey Shades set down his guitar, got up, and stumbled to the front of the line.

"Get to the back," the biker ordered.

"Hey man, tha's our beer. We bought it, an you're drinkin' it all," Davey loudly complained.

The biker stepped forward. "Yeah? Well, I'm making sure there's no bogarting. Everybody gets some. And you already had more than your fair share. You can't hardly stand up."

"Who appoin-ned you, anyway?"

The biker crossed his massive tattooed arms over his chest. "Nobody. I appointed myself. You got a problem with that?"

Another biker, even larger than the first, came from behind. "Hey, Crossbone, don't make a big deal out of it. Give 'im what he wants."

The first biker shook his head, then handed the musician a dripping paper cup. "Don't worry. We won't leave you hangin'. Someone'll go on another beer run before this kegger's gone."

Turning, Davey saw Bob and with a wide grin, sloshed toward him. "Welcome to the parry!" he slurred. "Onesh we tapped the keg, the parry started." Stepping back, he blearily sized up Shara and Roxanne. "Whish one is your old lady?" He looked at Roxanne. "Are you?"

"You bet she is," Bob replied, draping his arm over her shoulder.

"How 'bout the skinny red-hair one," Davey said, rolling his head toward Shara.

"Her too," Bob said, slipping his arm around her waist.

"Damn. Where'sh the love, man? You got two schicks. And I got none." Davey slid to the ground beside the path, spilling the beer in his lap. "Guess you gotta be flamous."

"It don't hurt," Bob replied. He shook his head. "The longest day of the year is just about over for him, he looks as lost as a ball in tall grass and it ain't even dark yet."

95

ON THE EDGE of nightfall, palpable anticipation electrified the Orion Institute. As if drawn by an irresistible force, the partiers stared toward the horizon. Some on the rim of the bluff overlooking the ocean, some on rock outcroppings high in the hills. Some to the west-facing windows on the upper floors of Orion's main house, and some onto the roofs of the surrounding cottages.

Donatello, Deborah, and the other invited guests crowded onto the deck, waiting to watch the sunset with Parker. The structure vibrated with the movements of the crowd.

As the sun sank in the sky, it seemed to stand still, hovering over the ocean. Touching the horizon, the water appeared to boil. Cheers, shouts and whistles rose from the deck, and a muffled tumult from the woods and cottages. Shots and firecrackers rang in the distance as the golden orb sank into the sea.

"I wonder where Parker is?" Deborah said in the gathering darkness as some of the guests began leaving the deck. "I guess we might as well go too."

They jostled their way downstairs, through the crowd, to the greatroom. Into a sea of jeans, cut-offs, dashikis, and tunics; beads, bracelets, and headbands; and sandals, boots, and bare feet. Tabla drums, bongos, acoustic guitars, and a zither joined the droning sitar. Some celebrants milled and mingled, and others danced chaotically in the center of the candlelit space. A gathering with shaved heads sat on the floor watching the mismatched dancers and musicians.

"Hey, that's Debbie Donaldson," someone shouted as Donatello and Deborah reached the bottom of the stairs.

Pushing through the crowd, a thin, withered man with a cow's horn strapped to his forehead came toward them and bumped into Donatello.

"Why you no watch where you go?" he snapped.

The man laughed manically, bugged out his eyes and lunged as if he intended to gore him.

Donatello flicked his splinted fingers from under his chin.

The man thrust up a middle finger. "Same to you, jerk," he said, dancing away to a beat completely different than that of the music.

Deborah frowned. "What did you do that for?"

"He is lunatic," Donatello replied, throwing his hands into the air. "Like a bull, he try to kill me. You want I should do nothing?"

She shook her head and took his arm. "Come on. You're so high-strung and hot-tempered. You need to relax." She led him to a vacant loveseat near the staircase. He dropped onto the torn cushion, and she sat down beside him. The sofa sank under their weight and they found themselves sitting uncomfortably close to each other as the convergence closed in around them.

"Where Parker went? And Slovika? We wait, but they never come," Donatello said over the noise of the celebration.

Deborah sighed. "I know. Parker. Bob. Slovika." She shook her head. "Where is everybody? The sunset is over, and I'm supposed to transcend to the next sphere of enlightenment."

Donatello clutched his stomach and sank further into the loveseat. "There is nothing. No food. No wine. Nothing since the Peanut Ranch. Never have I been to party like this," he muttered.

"I keep telling you, it's not a party. It's a cosmic awakening."

He threw his hands into the air again. "Why we can't awaken with something to eat? We are too spiritual for food?"

Just then, a young man who looked like a fraternity brother after a hard weekend came by with a boxy camera hanging by a strap around his neck. "Hey! You're Debbie Donaldson!" He smiled and held up the camera. "Can I take your picture?"

"That's *Deborah* Donaldson," she replied. "No. No photos," she said, putting her hand over her face.

"Oh, come on Debbie -- I mean, Deborah, I know you want to. 'America's Little Sweetheart' . . . you're the biggest star here. You'll be helping support the future of journalism."

"Actually, he's probably the biggest star here," she said pointing to Donatello.

The frat-boy reporter's eyes widened. "Really? Who are you?"

"Donatello Dragghi," he said with an arrogant stare. "I make *The Bounty Killer*. You know of it?"

"Outta site, man. You're an Italian actor? Hey, you got a great name. Haven't seen the movie yet, but I heard about it, and yeah, like-wow, I want to see it."

Donatello smiled.

"So, can I?" the photographer asked, lifting the camera. "It's for the *San Francisco Oracle*."

"Deborah, what he say?" Donatello asked. "You know of an Oracle?"

"It's not a person, it's an underground newspaper," she said, rolling her eyes.

"How a newspaper is underground? What this means?"

Deborah shook her head. "I keep forgetting you don't know anything. It's . . . uh . . ." She looked helplessly at the photographer.

"It's a counter-culture newspaper. Come on, Deborah . . . America's Little Sweetheart' goes counter-culture. It'll be great."

Deborah sighed. "Oh, alright. But you promise. It's only for the *San Francisco Oracle*."

The frat-boy nodded. "Yeah, sure. Of course."

Donatello nudged Deborah. "He can take the picture, no?"

Just then, a pair of enthusiastic dancers ran into the photographer. He laughed and re-positioned his camera. "Now, Donatello, put your arm around her and make it look, you know, real sexy."

They struck a provocative pose.

"Smile. Say pleeease . . ." The flashbulb went off with a hot ozone flare. "Couple more?" He popped the bulb off and caught it.

They smiled again, and again, and again, bulbs flashing as they seduced the camera.

"Thanks, man. That was really cool," he said, then turned and joined the celebration.

A striking, pubescent girl with a shaved head came by the loveseat, carrying a basket. Wearing a sheer caftan, similar to Parker's, but with long flowing sleeves, she fluttered toward them like a mystic butterfly. She turned and watched the photographer go.

"That's my friend Quinton. I really like him," she said with a seductive grin. "He doesn't have an Orion name yet. My Orion name is DoPenny Ahhh. Would you like a party favor?" she blithely offered, her eyelids sinking like lazy, waning moons. She tipped the basket for them to look inside. "Michoacán cannabis, Blond Leb hashish, mushrooms, peyote buttons, or blotter acid?"

Donatello looked up at her. "Why you have this name? DoPenny . . ." he questioned with a wave of his bandaged hand. "What that means? And why you have no hair?"

The young hostess stepped closer. "It's my Orion name. I'm one of Parker's favorites. He named me that because I will 'Do' anything he asks. 'Penny' -- that's the first name my parents gave me. Parker likes it, so he let me keep it. And 'Ahhh'. I added that part. It's what people say after." Her voice softened to a sigh as she stared seductively into Donatello's eyes.

Deborah shook her head. "You don't seem like all that."

"But you haven't been with me, have you?" the young woman countered, holding out the basket. "Take something."

Deborah tapped her chin with a frosted fingernail. "We don't have a pipe, but, um, some Michoacán for starters."

The hostess pulled out several dried greenish red buds of marijuana flowers. Spreading them into the cedar tray pulling out the seeds.

"Don't you have any already rolled?"

"I'll roll some for you." The hostess smiled at Donatello. "Take something. Or if you want I can come back when I finish passing out the party favors."

He shook his head.

She put her hand on his knee. "Are you sure you don't want . . . anything? Your pleasure would be my pleasure," she purred.

"Not now," he replied.

DoPenny shrugged, then went back the way she came.

Donatello watched her go. "Why this girl, she has no hair? And why Parker give her that name? Is ridicolo, how you say, ridicule."

"You mean ridiculous? It's part of the Orion process. Once you're immersed into Orion, Parker cuts off your hair, and he gives you a new name to match your new self."

"What is this . . . immerse?"

"You know, sort of like, absorbed."

"How you do this?"

"There's more to it, but in essence, Parker is immersed in you and you are immersed in him."

Donatello stared at her. "Then you have not -- "

"Of course, I've been with him, silly. And I've given him lots of offerings."

He sat back. "Then why Parker no give you ridicule name? And why you no have hair like that girl?" he said, waving in the direction the hostess had gone.

"I'm not . . . I still need to work out the details. For instance, how can I host 'The Deborah Donaldson Show' if I don't have any hair and I'm not Deborah Donaldson anymore? I could wear a wig and use my old name, but then, what's the point? I'll have to, pretty much, get a whole new career. Or not have a career at all. Then what am I supposed to do? Depend on Bob? Or live here? Like I said, I haven't figured it out yet."

"Why, if Parker is god, he no tell you what you should do?"

"Parker teaches people how to think. Then they *know*."

"So, why you no know?"

Deborah shook her head. "So many questions."

"There is one more. I wonder, if you are with Parker, maybe he give to you the disease you give to me?"

Her eyes shot open and she caught her breath. "Parker? You must be kidding. God doesn't have diseases. Besides, I might not be the one who gave it to you. Maybe it was someone else. Maybe Slovika . . ."

"No." Donatello grabbed Deborah's wrist. "I am the only man to be with her."

Deborah yanked her arm away. "Don't get all freaked-out. I said maybe. You never know."

"I know. She no do that. I want find her."

Deborah rolled her eyes. "If *you* want to be free, you have to let *her* go."

Looking around the greatroom, Donatello felt his jaw weaken.

A cloud of smoke hung in the air. The flare of flashbulbs punctuated the candlelit twilight. Electric guitars, an organ, and a drum set joined the bongos, tabla drums, and sitar. The convergence took on a frenetic energy. People laughing. People dancing. People stripping off their clothes. Couples coming together. Couples joining couples.

He caught his breath. *So many women -- even men . . . they have no hair.* He looked over at Deborah, then glanced around the room again. *Somewhere, Slovika is with him . . .*

96

THE YOUNG HOSTESS returned with three slim joints and pressed them into Deborah's hand. "Enjoy. Both of you," she said, winking at Donatello. "Are you sure you don't want *anything*?" she asked, staring into his eyes.

He shook his head, and she fluttered away again.

Deborah rifled through her purse. "I guess she's got a crush on you. She's not shy about it either." Pulling out a rumpled matchbook, she opened it, and yanked out a match. Then struck it several times on the worn emery before it caught fire. Lighting the joint, she took a long hit, then held it out to Donatello.

He waved it away. "I want, uh, trovare . . . find Slovika."

"Oh, Dona, come on," Deborah moaned. "Are you still hung up on that? If I recall, you weren't all that married to her when you called me over to your table at the Villa Nova. And you didn't seem married at all that night in my dressing room. Or on my show. Or at your vineyard, down by the creek. Anyway, if Parker is with her -- believe me, she's more than fine."

"Where he take her?"

"How should I know?" Feigning a pout, Deborah exhaled the smoke in his face. "Quit being such a drag. If you're going to act like this, why did you come?"

Donatello threw his hands into the air. "Why you invite me? You know, sometime you molto bella, and other time you are bitch. Do duo Deborah share your body?"

"Actually, Parker invited you because you're so up-tight and he's trying to help you," she replied in a screeching voice. She took another long drag, then licked her fingers and pressed them over the end of the joint. "Why don't you just leave, since it's obvious you don't want to be here?"

"Sì. Lo farò, I will."

Just as Donatello started to get up, Gregg came by carrying a brass tray and two glasses filled with shimmering liquid the color of black coffee. He passed one glass to Deborah. "For you."

"Thank you, Gregg," she said, forcing smile.

He held the other out to Donatello. "And for you. A Black Russian. Parker's favorite drink. He sensed you are uncomfortable. He learned from your wife that you like vodka."

Donatello sat forward and took the glass. "She is with him?"

"It is Parker's wish that you enjoy this most cosmic of nights," Gregg said. He bowed slightly, then stepped back, and seemed to disappear into the celebration.

Deborah tipped her glass toward Donatello, then took a sip. "Mmmm. It's really good. You see, Dona. I told you." Even with all these people here, Parker is thinking of you."

He stared into the glass, then looked around the room again. *Deborah, beside me . . . but I am alone inside myself.* Sinking back against the loveseat, he wound the chain of his crucifix around his finger. *All the freedom I ever dreamed of -- even more than I wished for . . .* He let the chain fall.

"What's the matter?" Deborah said. "Why don't you drink it?"

Perhaps . . . Donatello put the glass to his lips. The syrupy coffee taste filled his mouth, and slid down his throat. He drank the rest and set the glass on the floor beside the sofa.

Several minutes passed.

Deborah leaned over. "Let's dance. That bass-line they're jamming is sooo sexy."

Her voice rang strangely hollow like the sound of a stone toppling into a canyon. The words echoed inside his head as if she was speaking to him from far away. Their meaning vanished into a river of thought, drowning in the waterfall sound of the crowd.

"Come on, let's dance . . . ance . . . ance . . ."

Donatello wiped his palms, on his pants. *My heart, it never feels like this before.* His hands began to shake. His heartbeat quickened. Panic gripped him.

Then, like an explosion, suddenly he tasted words, heard color as thought, and felt the vibration of light as they all swirled into one. *In my head, I hear my heart louder than I see the music.* "Deborah, I no understand . . ."

"What?" she asked, her voice sounding rasping and hawkish.

"Qualcosa . . . wrong . . . I see . . . che sento . . . my hands . . . my heart . . ." The room blurred as a hallucinogenic wave washed over him. He gripped her hand.

"Dona, just relax . . . ax . . . ax . . . ax . . ."

Roxanne and Shara followed Bob up the path from the gulch to the main house. Illuminated by a full moon, the darkened landscape glowed like tarnished silver. Throbbing drums and the wail of the electric guitar grew louder as they approached. The gathering spilled out of the house, into the courtyard. With the women on either arm, Bob plunged into the sea of people.

"This party is huge," Shara said, giggling and staggering slightly as they jostled their way into the greatroom.

"Yep, it's huge alright," Bob replied over the din.

Just then, a large woman danced by without any clothes.

"Whuu-wee!" he said. "How come it's always the chunky ones who go runnin' around without any britches?"

Roxanne and Shara looked at each other and broke out laughing.

"C'mon, let's go find 'The Bounty Killer.' Ya'll 're gonna love him."

Raising her voice Shara said, "Are you and him good pals or something?"

He shook his head. "Nope. Just a fan. He only made the most outrageous movie, ever."

Just then, a young man in renaissance costume bounded toward Shara. "Wow! You're like a spaced-out Celtic godess all dressed up in lace! Wanna dance?" he asked with a toothy grin. "Come on!" He took her hand and pulled her away from Bob and Roxanne, into the pulsing throng of dancers.

Roxanne waved. "Bye, Shara. Meet me at the van in the morning."

Donatello looked up to see a man and woman with whirling, melting smiles pass by over and over, like dominoes falling in a line.

"Hey, Mr. Bounty Killer, this's Roxanne," Bob announced.

Roxanne looked at Donatello, then Bob. "That's him?" she asked under her breath. "He doesn't look too good."

Just then, Quinton came back. Bulb flashing, he snapped a picture. "How about another one?" he said, holding up the camera.

Bob dropped Roxanne's hand. "Who're you?"

"He's with the *San Francisco Oracle*," Deborah said.

"*The Oracle*?" Bob frowned. "There ain't no more *Oracle*. It was closed down in February."

"Uh, I mean *The Barb*," Quinton stammered. "I work for *The Berkeley Barb*." He bent and grabbed Donatello's glass, then rushed into the crowd.

"Hey! I oughta' break your camera!" Bob called after him.

A spasm ran the length of Donatello's body. "Colore... infiammante..."

"What's with him?" Bob asked. "He looks terrible."

Deborah's eyes darted to Donatello and back again. "I think he took something."

A flush of perspiration beaded on Donatello's upper lip. He exhaled sharply, and his head dropped back on the couch. "No, I take nothing," he said, gripping Deborah's hand.

"Ow," she snapped, pulling her hand away. "If you don't panic, you'll be okay."

Bob knelt beside the sofa. "Hey, what's goin' on, man?" he asked, feigning a chuckle.

Donatello looked up. "I see over and over... and thought... before I think, it fade away. Niente... tutto... niente..." his voice trailed into a whisper.

Bob patted his knee. "No big deal. There's nothin' to be scared of. You're just seein' trails." He stood and motioned to Deborah.

She got up from the sofa.

"Somebody musta dosed 'im."

"Who would do that?"

"Your ol' buddy, Parker, comes to mind."

"Parker doesn't do things like that."

"Yeah, right. Ya'll better tighten your saddle straps, 'cause he's in for a bumpy ride."

"And just what do you mean by that?"

"Damn it, Deb, he's on the verge of freakin' out. His eyes 're wild. His pupils are dilated. He's got that panicky stare, and he's breathin' like bull gettin' ready to charge."

She crossed her arms. "So."

Bob threw his hands into the air. "Why'd ya bring him here if you're gonna act like that? This is kinda heavy for a greenhorn. You better get him outta here before he freaks-the-hell-out."

"And just how am I supposed to do that?"

Roxanne stepped forward. "You're a big girl."

Deborah spun around. "Roxanne, one thing you'll notice about Bob, if he stays with you past tomorrow morning, that is. He's always sticking his nose in other people's business. Just like you!"

"At least I'm not a sell-out."

"Sell out?" Deborah planted her fists on her hips. "That's rich coming from a groupie."

Roxanne laughed. "Bob says you're just a cheap pair of boobs to dress up some 'B' movie."

Deborah glared at Bob. "So, I'm a cheap pair of boobs? When you get back to LA, get your junk out of my house!" She shoved him out of the way and vanished into the celebration.

"Voci..." Donatello put his hands over his ears. "No capisco..." Exploding into fear and rage, he shot up from the sofa.

Bob caught his arm. "Hey, man... come on... sit down..."

"Lascilo andare!" Donatello shouted. Wrenching free from Bob's grasp, he swung back. The blow folded Bob in two.

Nearby partiers turned and stared.

Donatello swung again.

A sharp hook split Bob's lip and sent him sprawling backward onto the floor.

"Oh my god!" Roxanne shrieked. She dropped to her knees beside him as Donatello rushed into the crowd.

"We have ta go after 'im," Bob wheezed.

"What? He just about murdered you!"

Bob scrambled to his feet and wiped the trickle of blood oozing from his lip with the back of his hand. "Dog, girl. We gotta find him. He's 'The Bounty Killer!'"

97

BOB AND ROXANNE found Donatello cowering behind a potted palm in a corner on the second floor landing. Cradling his bandaged hand against his chest, he shuddered, followed by incoherent babble.

Bob knelt beside him. "Hey, why're you hangin' around here?"
No answer.
Bob looked over at Roxanne. "He's really messed up."
She hooked her thumbs in the pockets of her cut-offs. "What are we gonna do?"
"I dunno. Find somewhere he can ride it out, I guess." He looked around. "Maybe in there," he said, nodding in the direction of a nearby room. "Take a look."
Roxanne went and opened the door, and peered inside. She came back a moment later. "It's not very big. There's a mattress and a bunch of books and boxes all over the place."
"That'll work. Help me get him up."
Bob pulled Donatello's arm over his shoulder, and Roxanne got on the other side. They led him, stumbling, into the room and lowered him onto the mattress. Curling his knees to his chest, he rambled in an unintelligible mix of English and Italian, as his body trembled.

Moonlight spilled in through a window, and muffled sound from the party vibrated the floor.

Bob leaned back. "We prob'ly better stay with 'im awhile."

"But . . ." Roxanne said with a pout. "This was supposed to be the best gig of the summer. Now we're babysitting a bad trip."

"The night's not over yet. Got any weed?"

"A little. I thought you'd bring some."

"I did," he said. "But it's in my duffle bag, stashed out back behind a propane tank."

She produced a small baggie from her cowhide purse.

"Papers?" he said.

She pulled out a crushed packet of Zig-Zags.

"See, Roxie, we got our own party," he said with a broad grin. "I got me a woman, and somethin' to smoke, so I'm doin' alright." He sat up and fumbled with the papers. "Turn on the light for a second, will ya?"

Roxanne got up and flicked the light switch. She flicked it again, then looked up into the empty fixture. "There's no bulb."

"Hey, there's a candle over on the windowsill," he said.

She picked up the fat, slumping candle and sat down beside him again. He lit the wick and set the candle on the floor. The flickering light faintly illuminated a garish, free-flowing mural on one wall, and a large hole in the cracked plaster on another. A scattering of empty wine and beer bottles had been abandoned in one corner, and a partially crushed carton filled with copies of Parker's book occupied another.

Bob sprinkled a pile of dried leaves onto the rolling paper. "Looks like we ain't the first to party here," he said, nodding toward the empty bottles. He put the joint to his mouth. "Ow!" he moaned. "My lip feels like a mini-inner tube."

"Let me see," Roxanne said. "Boy, he really let you have it."

He passed her the joint. "You light it."

She lit the fat reefer, took a drag, and passed it back. "Since Deborah flipped out, how are we getting back to LA? And where are we gonna stay"

"At my house, of course. But bein' as she's on the rag, I damn-sure don't wanna be on the same plane with her. I'll prob'ly cash in the tickets and drive the van back down. How 'bout goin' with me?"

"Okay, but she's not gonna like it."

"Who cares. She'll be lucky I don't throw her butt out."

"Um, my friend Shara was gonna stay with me for awhile. Can she come too?"

"Yeah, sure. It'll piss Deb off, so the more, the merrier." Bob settled back on the mattress, drew in a long drag, held it a moment, then passed the joint back to Roxanne. Just then, a sound from behind startled him. "Whew. Mr. Bounty Killer, you scared me."

Donatello's voice trembled. "Bisogno una sigaretta . . ."

"Huh?" Bob looked over at Roxanne. She shrugged.

"Cigarette," Donatello said.

"Oh, okay, I'll get ya a smoke," Bob replied. He pulled a pack out of his shirt pocket, took one out, lit it and passed it to him.

The glow of the cigarette joined that of the joint, the moon, and the flickering candlelight.

"Seems like he's doing better," Roxanne said.

"Yeah. Let's find someplace and finish our party," Bob whispered.

"How are we gonna do that if you can't even kiss me?"

He thought a moment. "I ain't from Texas, but I'll remember the Alamo."

"What the heck does that mean?"

"Never mind."

"How long, I am here?" Donatello asked.

"You're outside the time-space continuum, man, so time'll be pretty much meaningless -- 'til ya come down, that is." Bob took Roxanne's hand. "Come on. We got a party ta finish." Choking back laughter, they got up, and staggered out of the room.

Donatello watched Bob and Roxanne leave several times before the aura faded from his mind. Lying motionless, except for the vibrating of his hands, he set the cigarette down beside the bed.

Space is big as the sky and close as my own skin. How long have I been alone in this universe?

Just then, a gaunt male face appeared in the doorway.

A shudder ran the length of Donatello's body. The man's face, the flickering candlelight, and the sprawling, florescent mural swirled into an expansive sea of stars circling in a night-sky hallucination above him.

It is true. Time is meaningless . . .

98

SLOVIKA WOKE FROM a fitful sleep with her head resting on Parker's bare chest. She heard a distant clock faintly chime three. *My head aches. The sunset is over.* Parker stirred in his sleep. Sliding his arm off her shoulder, he moaned, and rolled onto his side. She touched the warm, damp place where he had been sleeping. *What do I feel for him? Love? Attraction? Anything?* She ran her fingers over the course, shaved stubble of her hair. *Maybe I will have to stay with him.* Tears pooled in her eyes. *But am I free?*

Either by instinct or intuition, she looked out a window beside the bed, into the charcoal darkness. Thick low-hanging clouds with an odd gray-gold glow sped past the glass.

"Parker?" She gently shook him. "Wake up."

"Anthony, I didn't . . ." he said under his breath, then opened his eyes. "What? What is it?"

Slovika pointed to the window. "The clouds . . ."

Throwing off a thin cotton sheet, Parker went to the window and stared at the sky. His eyes popped open. He grabbed a linen caftan and slid it on. "Those aren't clouds! It's smoke! Get up!"

She stared blankly at him.

"Get up!" He threw a short tunic at her. "Put it on!"
She grabbed the shirt and struggled to pull it over her head.
"Run!" Throwing the door open, Parker rushed out into the hall.

The horizon stretched, dark, flat, endless, and black as a skillet over a dancing flame. Stars, rolling like sparks of garnet, citrine and amber rose as quickly as they fell against the night sky.

Staring into the fire, a Cherokee in ceremonial dress appeared among the embers. His face was covered with white ashes, and the creases in his skin deep as if they had been carved by a river. His gray eyes bore witness of what had to be done.

"It is time for you, my friend," he said, rising and standing in the blaze. He pointed to the sparks mounting in the sky, then to the coals flaming at his feet. "You must run through your own fire."

Bob fell to his knees before the crackling blaze. The heat singeing the inside of his nostrils seemed to sear his face. "I can't do this."

"There is no way to get out, but to go through the fire," the man said, dancing to the beat of a distant drum through the flames licking around his legs. "You must go in to get out."

"I will not run."

"Run! You must run!" The Cherokee's voice boomed like a thunderstorm over an open prairie. "Run! Run and get out!"

"Fire! Run!" Voices, varied in pitch and volume, echoed with the beat of footsteps on the landing.

Bob opened his eyes from the dream. Drenched in sweat, he bolted awake with a choking inhale as if he had been holding his breath. His gaze darted to Roxanne, sleeping on a bare mattress beside him. Then around the darkened room, veiled in a hazy golden glow. *Fog? Clouds? Smoke!*

"Fire! Run! Run to the highway!" voices on the landing shouted.

"Roxie! Get up! Fire!" Bob said, stumbling to his feet.

Struggling to throw on their clothes, they rushed half-dressed out of the room, into the cloud of smoke hanging over the landing. Instantly, a crush of bodies, pushing and shoving, pulled them toward the stairs.

"I need to find Shara!" Roxanne shrieked. "What if she's -- " Coughing and sputtering, she wiped her eyes. "God! The smoke . . . I can't breathe!"

Bob grabbed her hand. "She'll be okay. We gotta get Donatello!"

Heat and muffled crackling emanated from the room where they left him, and smoke escaped from under the door. "God! He's in there!" His heart pounding, Bob lurched for the knob.

"Don't open it!" someone yelled. "That's where it started!"

"Holy shit, Roxie! We left him there!"

Roxanne dug her nails into his arm. "He's probably -- "

"Don't even say it." Looking frantically around the smoke-hazed landing, Bob glimpsed a mound huddled in a corner. "Roxie, look! He's over there!" Taking her hand, he pushed through the throng. He shoved a panicked woman out of the way. "Give him some room!" he shouted.

Donatello looked up. His eyes glazed, a bloody froth stained his mouth, and sweat glistened on his pallid skin.

Bob knelt beside him. "Hey! Talk to me!" he said, shaking him.

"Colore' . . . ovunque . . ." Donatello moaned, then his head fell forward onto his chest.

Roxanne crouched next to them. "I've never seen anybody trip like that before."

"Y'ain't whistlin' Dixie, girl. We gotta get him outta here." Yanking Donatello's arm around his neck, Bob lifted him to his feet. "Watch his broken hand. Go on the other side and we'll get him down the stairs."

As they stepped out of the corner, the crowd instantly swallowed them.

"They keep pushing! I can't hold him!" Roxanne shrieked as Donatello's arm slid off her shoulder. "Bob!"

Just then, glass shattered overhead. Screams erupted and the shoving intensified.

"Roxanne!" Bob reached for her, but she disappeared in the melee. He gripped Donatello in a bear-hug, and the throng drove them toward the stairs. "God! Help!" he gasped, as he felt his footing slip. Pushed by bodies behind. Falling onto bodies ahead.

Then, for a moment, another step. Lurching forward. Falling with the crowd. Another step. Elbow stabbing his side. Shoulder jabbing his back. Feet stomping his feet. Stumbling. Reeling. Falling again. And again. And again. Then, tumbling into a flailing mass at the foot of the stairs.

Donatello let out a cry.

Pushing and shoving, Bob yanked him out of the pile of bodies and pulled him alongside the wall.

"Bob! Help!" Roxanne screamed.

Won't this nightmare ever end? Looking up into the haze, he saw her trapped on the stairs. Smoke billowed through the wall behind the landing. Waves of flame danced on the ceiling. Glass shattered. Panic crashed in like a wave.

Gotta get them out! "Roxie! Climb over!" he shouted. "I'll catch you!"

She slid her leg over the rail. The crush of the crowd pushed her off, and she tumbled down beside Donatello.

Bob pulled her to her feet. "Are you okay?"

"I'm so scared!" she cried as tears streamed down her cheeks.

Gotta go in to get out. "Help me stand him up," he said over the din. Wiping the sweat off his face, he scanned the room. "Through there," he shouted, pointing to a doorway.

"The way out's the other way!" she shrieked.

"It's not burning yet. And no one's going that way. Come on!"

Hoisting Donatello between them, they staggered against the flow of the crowd, into a deserted kitchen.

Then, over the commotion -- a loud crack, a thunderous thud, and more screams.

Shara pulled away from a long, wet kiss. "Brodie, what was that?" she breathlessly said to the young Renaissance man, slouching beside her on a redwood bench outside the Institute.

Brodie ran his hand over his mouth. "I'll go see." He stood and climbed through the scrub brush and dry grass a short way up the darkened hillside. Shock crossed his amber glowing face. "Hey, Shara, Orion's on fire!" he shouted.

"What?" She scrambled up the hill and stood beside him, looking down on the main house. "Oh my god!"

Just then, a burning timber broke from the second story and toppled onto the propane tank beside the house. Sparks scattered as the falling beam dented the tank and snapped off the pressure gauge. Instantly, a pillar of flame bolted from the broken gauge.

"Man, we gotta split, and I mean quick!" Brodie flailed his arm in the direction of the house. "The grass is dry as tinder. This whole hillside could catch fire!"

"But my friend, Roxanne..." Shara cried. "She's probably still in there!"

"Too late now. Come on!" Brodie grabbed Shara's hand. Clambering through the brush, he pulled her down the hill toward the highway.

Roxanne sank under Donatello's weight. "I can't hold him. I need to catch my breath."

Run and get out! Bob shook his head. "We can't. Didn't you hear that? The whole place could collapse any minute! Come on!"

They stumbled through a narrow doorway, onto a small service porch cantilevered over a darkened hillside. Coughing and wheezing, Bob propped Donatello against the wall. The rumbling of the fire, muffled shouts of the crowd, and the wail of distant sirens echoed around them.

"Now what?" Roxanne asked.

"Stay with him while I look around." Bob went to a split-rail fence surrounding the porch. Supported on stilts, the porch extended out over a brush-covered hillside that dropped off into a steep ravine. His heart racing, he sank against the railing. *No way out.*

A violent convulsion seized Donatello. His knees buckled. Thrashing out of Roxanne's grasp, he slid down the wall, into unconsciousness.

"Bob!" she shrieked.

The propane tank ruptured, a deafening blast, a shockwave. The air peeled away. Bob and Roxanne were flattened to the porch. Like falling stars, a shower of sparks, splinters, shrapnel, and debris rained down around them.

Bob looked over at her. "I'm waaaay too stoned for this."

99

STEVEN ROLLED HIS wheelchair into the darkened living room, silent except the rhythmic ticking of the mantle clock. The clock struck four. Through the picture window, the moon faintly illuminated the night sky. *Hate when I can't sleep. And tonight of all nights, I want to be asleep.* With a thump, one wheel went over a plastic toy soldier. "D-amn it, D-onny," he said under his breath. "Why d-on't you p-ick up your t-oys?"

Tailor wandered in and looked quizzically at him.

Rolling back and forth, he freed the wheel, then knocked over a toy cow-in-a-can. It let out a long, lonely, "Moooo-oooo." He shook his head and sank in his chair. Tailor stretched out on the floor beside him.

He turned on a lamp beside the couch. Bright yellow on the lower shelf of the end table caught his eye. *National Geographic.* He reached for it. *Already read that one.* He set the magazine aside. Cocking his head, he noticed a large book with a tooled leather cover.

The family Bible.

He reached down and wrestled the aged book onto his lap and carefully opened it. Inside, a fragile page in Old English type.

Births

He scanned names and dates written in scrolling script with fluid ink. *Most of them, I never heard of.* At the bottom of the yellowed page he found his father's name. *Buckley Arlington Harper Jr. born March 30, 1900.* Then the uncle he was named for. *Bernard Stephen Harper, born April 9, 1902.* And his own name, written without embellishment in blue ballpoint pen. *Steven Bernard Harper, born July 28, 1943.*

He turned the page.

Deaths

He found his uncle. *Bernard Stephen Harper, died June 6, 1925.* And his grandfather. *Buckley Arlington Harper Sr. died October 12, 1926.* "All of th-em gone be-fore I was b-orn."

Tailor flopped over onto his back and began softly snoring. He turned another page.

Marriages

Bet mine isn't in here. He glanced at the bottom of the page. "S-ure en-ough." *At least they won't have to mess up a perfect record by crossing it out. Bet there isn't even a place for divorces.*

Divorce. He sat motionless, listening to the clock.

God, if you exist, where are you? Randomly flipping a whole section of the brittle book, he happened to glance at a text by the ancient prophet, Hosea.

> ... she burned her incense, she offered her sacrifices, and adorned herself with earrings and jewelry. Then she followed after her lovers, and she remembered me no more ...

Steven sank under the weight of a sigh. *Shara.* Tears filled his eyes. "Hunger always gets what it wants." Through the haze he read the text again, now spotted with his tears. Then he heard the soft patter of footsteps.

"Daddy?"

He quickly wiped his eyes.

Donny stood barefoot in the doorway, his shoulders sagging, and his face a picture of sadness. Tailor woke, got up, and licked his hand.

"D-onny?" Steven motioned for him to come closer. "What's w-rong?"

"I hear da cow moo. I can't sweep."

"You can't sl-eep? How c-ome?" Steven set the Bible on the table.

Donny rested his head in Steven's lap. "Why did Mommy go away wiff Woxie?"

Steven ran his fingers over Donny's hair. "I d-on't kn-ow."

Donny looked up at him. "Will she come back?"

"I don't kn-ow that either."

"Doesn't she wuv us?"

Steven sighed. "I kn-ow that I l-ove you," he said with a weak smile.

Donny's lips trembled.

Steven lightly touched his chin. "You w-ant to look at the st-ars?"

"Okay, Daddy," Donny said with a sniff.

"If you o-pen the door, m-aybe I can g-et out w-ithout w-aking everybody up."

Donny went to the door and held it open. Steven wheeled outside with Tailor following along. The crickets stopped chirping as he positioned the chair on the porch, and Donny closed the door.

The cool night air gave off the scent of damp earth. Crickets resumed their chirping, joining the mournful drone of a bullfrog. Thin clouds hovered like ghosts around the moon, and an owl streaked past on silent wings. The lonely voice of a train called in the distance. Calling to someone far away.

Donny came and stood beside the wheelchair. "I wannu see Owion. Where Mommy and Woxie went."

"W-hat?"

"You said Mommy went to Owion."

"They're not at that O-rion. We w-on't see the con-stellation O-rion a-gain until fall."

"Daddy, I wannu sit on you lap."

"Okay, cl-imb aboard."

As Donny scrambled up and settled against Steven's chest, Tailor jumped onto a nearby chair and curled into a ball.

"Tell me da stars, Daddy," Donny said, sucking his thumb.

"O-kay, let's see w-hat we can f-ind," he said, scanning the sky. "S-ee? In the mi-ddle, there's Le-o. Then up high-er is the big bear, Ur-sa Ma-jor."

He turned the wheelchair. "And in the east, w-ay up th-ere is Draco, the d-ragon. P-retty soon Her-cules will come up. Her-cules al-ways ch-ases the d-ragon."

Steven caught his breath. He sat motionless, holding Donny. *Chasing the dragon. That's how it all started.*

Several minutes passed. A shooting star flashed across the sky.

Steven glanced down. Donny had fallen asleep with his thumb still in his mouth. Stroking his hair, Steven watched him sleeping. "We w-ill be o-kay," he whispered.

"Her-cules will con-quer the d-ragon. And m-aybe, in au-tumn, O-rion will b-ring her back a-gain."

Continued in Volume 2 of 2
A FAR STRANGE COUNTRY:
Feast of Consequences

ISBN: 978-0-9834442-7-5 (eBook/ePub)
ISBN: 978-0-9834442-9-9 (Paperback)
ISBN: 978-0-9834442-4-4 (Audiobook)

A Sample of Volume 2 is on page 453

Acknowledgements

First, thank you to my mother and my husband for their unwavering belief in me and my ability as a writer. Sadly, my mother never had a chance to read the book as she passed away before it was finished. To my husband and best friend Robert, my deepest gratitude for all you've done to make this possible, as well as for a beautiful cover, contributions and countless hours spent polishing the final version of the first book.

Secondly, thank you to Anne McCoy for the pep talks and encouragement during the fragile, early days of this journey, and for wading through a very rough first draft.

Thanks to Ruth Danner the exceedingly supportive moderator of the critique group I attend. And to the regular members who have become friends, and who held my hand through the process. In no particular order: Mark Golden, who has an arcane sense of humor and is always appreciative of an interesting font; Sharon Riedenbacher and Carol Krebs, who are discerning readers and intuitive editors; James Vasquez, for his vast knowledge and poetic use of the English language; Paul Lecoq, my go-to guy for all matters logistical and esoteric; Deborah Crum, for always providing a unique perspective, and pardoning me for giving an aging starlet the same first name; Sally Peters, whose scenic descriptions continue to inspire me; Robin West, for her humor, insight and infinite ability to mercilessly cut extraneous words and for the first edit of both books; Tracie Taylor for her support and eagle eye on little glitches in the books; and Judith Palpant and Donna Schweiger for the beautiful spirituality of their writing.

Finally, a special thank again to Ruth Danner for proof-reading and editing while combing through the nine hundred plus combined pages of Volume I and II. We're so grateful to you.

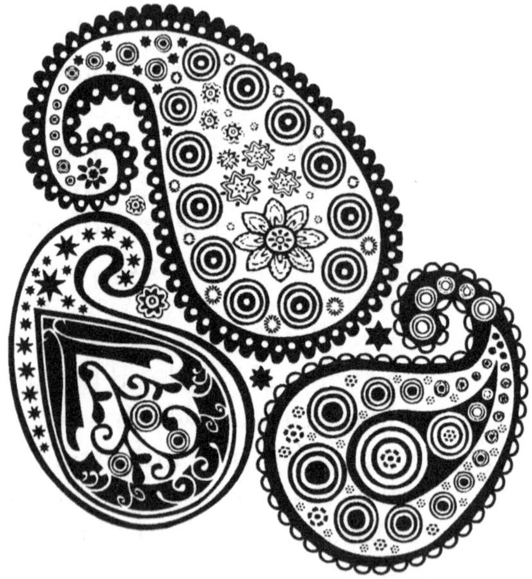

VOLUME 2 SAMPLE
CHAPTER 1 - PAGE 1

A BLINDING FLASH.
   A deafening blast.
   A shockwave.
   And a pillar of fire shot into the night sky.
   Inside the Orion Institute, the great room shuddered as the propane tank ruptured. Flames ravaged the ceiling. Smoke choked the air. Screaming. Shoving. Trampling. Panic raged.
   Pinned against the rail on a second-floor landing, a large man and a young woman struggled to free themselves. The railing cracked and they fell headlong into the bedlam. The crowd broke his fall, but with a sharp crack, she hit the floor.
   "Oh, my god!" an onlooker screamed as blood oozed from her head.
   Two others fell from the landing. The floor joists splintered, and the whole structure gave way, crashing into the chaos below.
   Those outside the Institute were thrown to the ground like matchsticks by the explosion. The second story deck collapsed, sending the people trapped there into free-fall over the darkened hillside. A shirtless young man scrambled to his feet. The fringe on his suede pants fluttered in the heat as he started toward the flaming propane tank. "Out-rage-ous, man . . . " he said with a hypnotic stare, brushing his hair off his face.
   "Like Hendrix said, the golden ship is passing this way . . . "
   A young woman reached to grab his arm. "Don't! It's not real!"
   "Hey, man, yes it is. It's so real I can taste it . . . " He pushed her away and staggered toward the fire, a silhouette outlined against the blaze.

Made in the USA
Middletown, DE
19 October 2024